Breathless

Celeste Bradley and Susan Donovan

St. Martin's Griffin
New York

BREATHLESS. Copyright © 2018 by Celeste Bradley and Susan Donovan. All rights reserved. Printed in the United States of America. For information, address St. Martin's Press, 175 Fifth Avenue, New York, N.Y. 10010.

www.stmartins.com

The Library of Congress Cataloging-in-Publication Data is available upon request.

ISBN 978-1-250-00806-0 (trade paperback)
ISBN 978-1-250-15981-6 (ebook)

Our books may be purchased in bulk for promotional, educational, or business use. Please contact your local bookseller or the Macmillan Corporate and Premium Sales Department at 1-800-221-7945, extension 5442, or by email at MacmillanSpecialMarkets@macmillan.com.

First Edition: June 2018

10 9 8 7 6 5 4 3 2 1

Breathless

A biography is considered complete if it merely accounts for six or seven selves, whereas a person may well have as many as a thousand.

—Virginia Woolf

THE PAST

Prologue

1827

I am The Swan.

Another wave crashed overhead; her lungs were desperate for air but finding only water.

With such an alias, shouldn't I be a more accomplished swimmer? And shouldn't a lifeboat mean life, not certain death?

But the small wooden dinghy had been no match for the wild tide and the rocky arms of the cove. She felt its planks splinter about her in the storm, her sodden gown sucking her down into the swirling void of the sea.

Only hours ago she had been grateful for the little boat—and for the ship captain who had saved her life during a mutiny. He had forced her into the vessel and lowered her into the water, sure her chances were better set adrift than caught in a bloody uprising.

But fear had choked her. Terror strangled her as she watched the clipper raise sail and disappear into the gloaming, its buxom white sails fading into blackness.

The storm hit soon after, pitching her in the waves like a bit of worthless rubbish until she'd hit against a shoreline. To think . . . all those hours she remained adrift, aching for the safety of land. Now it was clear the land was just as cruel, poised to inflict the final blow.

The tide hurled her forward once again, slamming her body into the stones, yanking her fingers from the slimy, barnacle-encrusted rock. The roiling seawater tumbled her until she lost any sense of up or down. The waves tangled her skirts about her legs, filled her mouth with froth instead of air, only to hoist her weakening body high . . . then slam it down upon the rocks again.

I am The Swan.

Her mind protested one last time, alive through the slicing pain, craving survival even as the world began to die away into nothingness.

I *was* The Swan.

THE PRESENT

Chapter One

Paris

Door hinges groaned with age and disuse as Fitch Wilder got his first peek of history.

"*Un capsule temporal* . . ." His employer had whispered those words only moments before, as they'd climbed the narrow stairs of the vintage Paris apartment building and waited for the flat's door to be unlocked. Yet even as Fitch's eyes adjusted to the murky light, he could tell these rooms were more than a time capsule—he was about to step into a fine art wormhole.

"*Oh, mon Dieu!*" Jean-Louis Rasmussen gestured madly, pointing as if Fitch couldn't see the eerie sight for himself—a richly appointed tomb, still as death, undisturbed for seventy-five years.

Until right at that instant.

The indirect light of the hallway began to illuminate the details. Fitch saw heavy velvet drapes and Persian carpets, a gilt bronze writing desk, ornately carved tables covered in figurines, clocks, and blown glass. Paintings in gilded frames were stacked six-deep against Louis XV chairs. Sculptures hid in shadowy corners. Vases lined the fireplace mantel like soldiers from mismatched armies. It looked as if someone had planned a seriously badass rummage sale and then decided against it.

Perhaps not so far from the truth.

As he had recently learned, a young woman inherited this apartment from her grandmother on June 11, 1940. Talk about rotten timing. The very next day, Paris braced itself for the Nazi invasion, and the young mademoiselle locked down her grandmother's residence in the ninth arrondissement and fled to the south of France, never to return. Through the following decades, the woman's solicitor paid the taxes and insurance on the apartment until his client passed away just weeks ago at the age of ninety-three. In her will, the never-married woman carried out the wishes of her long-gone grandmother and bequeathed the apartment's contents to a variety of foundations, universities, and museums.

That was where Fitch came in. One of his occasional employers, the private Musee de Michel-Blanc, was among the beneficiaries, and he'd been hired to advise them during acquisition. In addition to tracing the provenance and rightful ownership of each work, Fitch would also oversee laboratory testing to verify age and authorship. He was the museum's insurance policy against the worst offense within the world of art: display of a forgery or a stolen work.

"*Allez!* What are you waiting for?" Jean-Louis jabbed his bony fingers into Fitch's side, nudging him onward.

Pressing a firm hand on the curator's shoulder, Fitch turned his attention to the attorney who had unlocked the door. "May we proceed, *monsieur?*"

The lawyer gestured listlessly, as if opening a crypt was just another day at the office. "*Apres vous.*"

Jean-Louis shoved past Fitch and into the apartment. "We are the first!"

Fitch stepped inside, resting the heel of his cowboy boot on the decades-dusted parquet floor. He wanted to savor the moment, since this was the kind of once-in-a-lifetime treasure hunt every art investigator dreamed of. More than that, he wanted to honor it. Fitch knew he was about to take a breath of history itself.

And he wondered . . . whose lungs last pulled oxygen from the air of these rooms? Whose fingertips had last brushed across these chairs or drawn closed the draperies? He'd been told that the solicitors had never entered the apartment, as requested in the will, and it was unknown whether the granddaughter ever had a chance to examine her inheritance before she escaped the city. All things considered, Fitch knew it was possible that the grandmother—a woman born during Napoleon III's reign—had been the last human being to walk these floors.

Astounding.

Fitch drew in the stale air, and blew it out.

With an excited outburst of French, Jean-Louis flung open the drapes. And just like that, a beam of morning light split the dim room, illuminating every corner. Millions of dust particles twirled in the sudden air current.

In his agitated state, the curator stumbled, then gasped in horror. Fitch tried not to laugh, but the sight of Jean-Louis cowering under a seven-foot-tall taxidermied ostrich wasn't an everyday occurrence.

Fitch tossed his employer a pair of white cotton gloves, then shoved his own hands into an identical set. "Let's keep moving. We don't have much time."

A random lottery had given the Michel-Blanc first access to the apartment. Like each of the sixteen beneficiaries, they were allotted four hours to locate the items bequeathed to them, conclusively match each item to the inventory within the grandmother's original 1940 will, crate the works, and exit the premises.

Fitch knew why Jean-Louis was so twitchy. Among the items earmarked for the little museum was a signed Rembrandt in black and red chalk, dated 1631, and given the decidedly generic title of "Mother and Child." From the moment Fitch arrived at baggage claim at de Gaulle yesterday, Jean-Louis had spoken of little else, going on about how the drawing would be a major coup for the small museum. He was right, of course, but only if he found it to be authentic, and Fitch knew signed-and-dated Rembrandts from that period were exceedingly rare. He told his employer to keep the celebratory champagne corked until he'd finished with the X-rays.

Though Fitch was looking forward to examining the Rembrandt, he was more intrigued by the less conspicuous items on the list, and, though he'd kept the thought to himself, he had a hunch one of the institutions might walk away from this Paris flat with an explosive find. Fate had smiled on this private collection. The closed-up apartment had served as a kind of a safe house during the Third Reich's invasion of Paris, allowing the artworks to slip beneath the notice of Nazi raiders determined to plunder the city's cultural treasures.

Only God knew what could be in this place.

Fitch set up his camera and reminded Jean-Louis not to move anything until he had documented its location.

"*Oui, Oui!*" Jean-Louis headed into the dining room. He threw open those drapes as well, flooding the area with sunlight and exposing an even larger jumble of tapestries, oil paintings, figurines, and what looked like a carved frieze from the Middle Ages.

Jean-Louis sent his hands fluttering over his head. "Do you have your copy of the list?"

Fitch nodded, snatching it from his jacket pocket and holding it up for his employer's reassurance.

Within the first hour, Fitch found three of their items: a Fabergé egg dated 1902, a still life of lilacs in crystal signed with Manet's telltale scrawl, and a Guangzhou period vase much like one he'd seen auctioned off for a quarter-million dollars the year prior. As Fitch was matching the vase to the solicitor's inventory, his employer began screaming in French that he'd found the Rembrandt. He could barely compose himself enough to hand the drawing to the solicitor for verification.

"It is the real thing, *oui*?" Jean-Louis looked up at Fitch with a pleading expression. Since the poor man was overwrought, Fitch didn't mention that he'd already asked that question six times in as many minutes.

"Like I said, no red flags are jumping out at me. Everything looks right—the correct chalk pigment for the date, the appropriate type of laid paper, and an authentic-looking mark—but I won't be sure until I've done research and run some tests. If I could've phoned in this job from Santa Fe, I would have. You know that, right?"

The curator nodded, wiping tears from his eyes. He patted Fitch on the arm. "*Bien sur.* You are the best and I will be patient."

Once the crating process had begun and Jean-Louis was overseeing a team of museum workers, Fitch wandered off to continue his search. According to the list, four items had yet to be located—a series of original French political cartoons from 1899 through 1901, a female nude oil on canvas of unknown age and origin, a Japanese kimono that had allegedly belonged to an eighteenth-century geisha, and a 1929 signed and inscribed first edition of Hemingway's *A Farewell to Arms*.

Ole Granny was probably one hell of an interesting dinner guest.

Fitch wandered into a breakfast nook off the vintage kitchen and winced at what he saw—a jumble of unframed canvases leaned against a window seat, a particularly unkind way to store paintings. Luckily, the apartment had been nearly airtight all these years, and the drapes had been drawn, which cut down on light damage, moisture, and dust accumulation, though Fitch knew unframed canvases were vulnerable to warping in the best of environments. He lowered himself to one knee for a closer look.

Carefully, Fitch slipped a gloved finger between two canvases, separating them. He began to divide each canvas from its neighbor, one after the next, making quick mental evaluations of each work. There were watery French country fields, seascapes, and studies of Paris street life through various decades. Though they were important and worth further study, Fitch was on the clock, and so far there had been no sign of any cartoons, kimonos, or mysterious female nudes.

The very last canvas was larger than all the others, perhaps forty-by-forty inches. It was draped with an old embroidered bedsheet, and when he gently pulled at the linen he found the painting was faced away. Its back was covered by a layer of coarse muslin, frayed and tearing along the tacked-down edges. Fitch leaned closer, frowning, his brain suddenly humming with alarm. One touch of the muslin and his heart skipped a beat.

Okay—this was nuts. He had only seen the back. He had to be fucking crazy to be thinking what he was thinking.

He set all the other canvases off to the side, stood to open the window's shutters, and returned to the floor, where he balanced on both knees. With the benefit of better light, Fitch confirmed that his sanity was intact—there were, in fact, similarities. Was it unlikely? Hell, yes. Was it impossible? Not in his line of work.

First, he took a few photos to document exactly where the canvas had been found and in what position. Then, with a gloved finger, he pushed back a corner of the ragged muslin and turned on the flashlight app from his phone. Peering underneath, he saw how the canvas was supported by strainers of ancient olivewood and held together mortise and tenon joints—an exact match to the others.

"Holy God," he whispered to no one. "You've got to be kidding me."

His hands trembled slightly as he turned the canvas to face him. It was upside down. He set it upright. The shock of what he saw sent him back on his heels, his breath coming fast. In the bottom right corner was the familiar mark of an *L* and an *A* done in a bold cursive hand.

Fitch grabbed the list and double-checked the wording . . . *"female nude oil on canvas of unknown age and origin."* Of course it had been unknown back in 1940! The Siren Series hadn't been assembled as a collection of five paintings until after the war and even then . . . well, hell, that was all that had ever been "known" about anything. Even today, the artist, muse, setting, and date were a mystery.

He shoved the printed list back into his pocket and tried to get his brain and his breath to slow down.

Fitch heard himself laugh out loud.

He couldn't deny it. Everything was there. This painting had the lively brushstroke, the familiar play of light and shadow, and the golden touch of sunshine on the model's warm skin. Fitch recognized the boudoir, too, with its wide windowsill framing the sea, the rugged stone walls, and the unvarnished oak of the simple bureau.

But it was the subject he knew best of all—her tumble of sun-streaked blond hair, her smoldering, powder-blue eyes, the sleek curve of her shoulder. And there was the fantail birthmark on the side of her right breast, exactly where it should be. That mermaid-shaped mark had inspired the only name by which this outrageously sensual muse had ever been known.

The Siren.

But Fitch had never seen her like this. No one had.

She was pregnant. The Siren leaned back on her hands at the edge of an unmade bed, as if the painter had caught her in the process of pushing herself to stand after a long and luxurious rest. Her full breasts and slightly rounded belly were gilded by the sun. Her lean legs stretched out before her as she gazed directly into the soul of the artist.

Any shred of doubt Fitch might have been harboring was gone. The Siren's bold eye contact with the painter—and the intense sexual connection it revealed—was what set these paintings apart from nearly everything else in the art world. That heated connection was the trademark of this unknown painter's work. And of his muse.

Fitch didn't call for Jean-Louis right away, but instead allowed himself a few moments of quiet study. This painting was as technically brilliant as the other five, to be sure. The colors were as luminous and rich. The wash of light and hint of movement were the same. And yet . . . this painting was *more* than the others. The sum of all its elements had created something tangibly alive. It was as if the woman's gaze had burned through the artist himself, onto the canvas, and through time to reach Fitch.

The Siren wasn't daring him, exactly. It was more of an invitation.

I have a story to tell. Are you prepared to listen?

The sound of approaching footsteps jolted Fitch from his trance.

"Where *are* you? We need to—" The curator stopped behind him. "*Qu'este-ce?* No! It cannot be! Is this—?"

"Without question, my friend."

"But . . ." He leaned over Fitch's shoulder and pointed at the canvas. "She is with child here. This is . . . this has never been seen before!"

Fitch nodded.

His instincts had always told him there were more than just the five paintings—and he'd been right. So if this canvas had been hiding for seventy years in an abandoned Paris apartment, how many more were hidden away and forgotten? And where on earth could they be?

"We've just found the sixth in The Siren Series." Fitch turned and smiled up at his employer. "And it is now the property of the Michel-Blanc. That is, unless or until—"

"*Mon Dieu!*" Jean-Louis slapped a hand over his mouth. His eyes flashed in comprehension as he did the math in his head. Like everyone else in the art world, he knew this single oil painting could be worth more than several small Rembrandts, simply because of one man's obsession. Billionaire London art collector H. Winston Guilford was unabashedly fixated on The Siren, and had spent the last twenty years acquiring all five paintings in the series. He would surely offer an obscene amount of money to get his hands on the sixth.

From the twinkle in his employer's eye, Fitch suspected the Michel-Blanc would be only too happy to enable Guilford's addiction.

Fitch popped to his feet, the thrill of the chase already rushing through his veins, a plan already forming in his mind. He would run tests on this painting while it was still the property of the Michel-Blanc. And if he got extremely lucky, he would find something he could use as leverage with Guilford, something that might convince that crusty old bastard to let him take the rest of the series into the lab—and perhaps even to public display.

And after that . . . ? As always, he would wait and see where the hunt took him.

Fitch carried the painting to the solicitor, making a mental note to cancel his return flight to the States. It could be a while before his boots once again roamed the blue-skied streets of Santa Fe.

Chapter Two

Cambridge, Massachusetts, Three Months Later

Professor of Sociology Dr. Brenna Anderson clicked the remote control, bringing the next image to the huge screen at the front of the lecture hall.

"Erotic art not only reflects contemporary society's sexual norms, it can actually expedite a culture's acceptance of less typical facets of human sexuality."

A student in the third row raised his hand.

"Yes?"

"What about bondage and sadomasochism? You know, BDSM?"

A few snickers and snorts echoed through the large Harvard lecture hall. And to think . . . Brenna had almost forgotten she was teaching an undergraduate introductory course. She smiled at Justin Langley, well aware that the young man had been primarily seeking laughs this semester, not an understanding of the history of eroticism in art.

"Hmm." She tapped her lips with her index finger in mock contemplation. "I believe I may have heard of this—what did you call it, Mr. Langley? BD of the SM?"

Full-out laughter rang through the main floor and balcony. Justin became red-faced as he shifted in his seat.

Brenna returned to the center of the stage, her heels clacking on the highly polished wood. She smoothed down the seams of her wool and cashmere pencil skirt before she continued, "Mr. Langley, I would think that after sitting in this classroom for fourteen weeks you might have some understanding of how atypical sexual behaviors have been depicted in art through the ages. However, to be on the safe side, would anyone care to enlighten Mr. Langley?"

A hand shot up toward the back of the room and Brenna nodded. "Yes, Miss Powell."

A woman with short, spiky dreadlocks stood. "Well, even the earliest human civilizations found ways to depict what they considered 'deviant' sexual behaviors, though that definition has changed as often as human culture has changed."

Brenna smiled. "Can you provide examples for Mr. Langley?"

The girl shrugged. "Sure. Twelve thousand years ago, Paleolithic peoples were painting on cave walls a variety of sex acts, and many ancient cultures—especially in Asia—attached spiritual or religious significance to human eroticism as depicted in art. And when archaeologists unearthed the ruins of Pompeii, they found all kinds of kinky frescoes—threesomes, spanking, and even bestiality."

Brenna smiled, pleased to find that at least one student had been paying attention. "Anything else?"

"Oh, yeah. Thousands of years later, medieval monks copying manuscripts doodled all kinds of freaky stuff in the margins. Of course, later, in the eighteenth century, our boy the Marquis de Sade illustrated his bondage and torture stories with some really explicit engravings, women hanging from the rafters and stuff like that."

"Thank you." While the student had been speaking, Brenna

had returned to her laptop. She decided to pull up examples that weren't necessarily part of the day's lesson plan, but would help provide badly needed context to the subject at hand.

She again clicked the remote control, and five images began a slow rotation across the screen. "As some of you may know, these paintings belong to what is called The Siren Series, considered among the most intensely erotic oil-on-canvas portraits in pre-Victorian Western art. As it happens, the paintings were the subject of my doctoral thesis in sociology."

Brenna stopped on the first painting, which had always been her favorite. The model was tying the laces of her chemise. She sat framed before an open window that faced out to the morning sea, her blond hair spilling from its pins, luminous in the golden light. The painting captured her just as she glanced up at the artist. Brenna had always believed the painter caught the half-dressed woman by surprise. And yet . . . there was a bold curiosity in that cool blue gaze of hers, a sensual knowledge that led Brenna to develop a theory as to the social status of The Siren. Certainly, she was no innocent peasant girl, and yet she wasn't a prostitute. She was no tradition-bound wife. But clearly she was more than just a model.

Brenna believed she was the painter's beloved—his woman—and each painting in the series was a love letter intended for her eyes alone. Brenna's scholarly instincts led her to propose that these paintings were never intended for public view.

Of course it was just a theory, one she had never been able to verify, to her great frustration.

She continued with the lecture, "Modern laboratory analysis has never been allowed on these paintings, due to the eccentricities of the man who now owns them. However, they feature methods and materials used in European oil paintings of the first half of the nineteenth century. The setting lends itself to a Mediterranean village, possibly in France as two of the paintings were discovered in a falling-down barn near the city of Marseille."

She clicked to the second painting in the series, in which The Siren lay on her back in a messy bed, the rumpled sheet covering her lower body as she made dreamy eye contact with the painter. "Everything else about the series is unknown, including the artist. He—and I'm certain the artist is a man, based on his lusty appreciation of the female form and spirit—used only the initials *L* and *A* to sign the works. When the first two canvases were found in 1910, French scholars began referring to him as 'Le Artiste.' The French can be a no-nonsense people."

Brenna clicked on the third painting. The Siren stood with her back to the painter, framed in the familiar sea-facing window. Her chemise had fallen down her bare back, and the transparent fabric clung low on her hips, dangling from her fingertips. The Siren had twisted just enough to look over her shoulder and into the eyes of the artist.

"Note the birthmark on the underside of her right breast. It is present in every painting." She zoomed in. "Since many believe they see a mermaid shape in that mark, that's how she got her name. Her true identity is a mystery."

Brenna clicked on the fourth in the series—a partially draped Siren bathing in the sea—and the last, in which she lay on her belly, nude, every curve and dip and swell of her body awash in Mediterranean light. A knowing smile played on her lips.

"If you could use only one word to describe these paintings, what would that word be?"

A hand shot up from a student in the balcony. "Intense."

"Hot," said another student.

"Sexy."

"Personal."

"Erotic."

"Isn't that interesting?" Brenna brought all five paintings to the screen simultaneously. "Do you see any bestiality here? Or spanking, torture, rafter-hanging, or any of Mr. Langley's BD of the SM?"

A low rumble of giggles went through the classroom.

"An intense eroticism was achieved through brilliant technique and without explicit sexuality. How do you suppose that's possible?"

"There's some serious heat between the painter and the model."

Brenna smiled at the answer from none other than Mr. Langley. "You are absolutely correct. These paintings are erotic not because they are explicit renderings of carnal acts or shocking images of taboo activity, but because of the sensual force generated between artist and muse. It crackles with invisible electricity produced by their emotional investment in each other. In essence, the subject of these paintings is not the female nude herself, nor is it sex. The subject is the power of erotic love."

Brenna paused, searching the faces of her students. "This kind of evocative eye contact and intense sensual energy does not exist in other oil paintings from that period, and it would have been considered revolutionary. Though these paintings are clearly hundreds of years old, there is no record of any of these works anywhere before 1910—no documentation of sale, exhibit, ownership, or origin."

She clicked on a series of images showing a variety of nineteenth-century sculpture, painting, and drawings for comparison, wandering about the stage as she spoke. "In my thesis I proposed that The Siren Series not only tells the story of a subject and an artist, but actually documents the deepening intimacy between the individuals as time went on. I believe these paintings are nothing less than their love story."

A student near the exit sign waved her hand.

"Yes?"

"You're talking about five paintings, but I saw online that an art historian found another one in an old apartment in Paris. The article called the place a time capsule."

"The painting he found was really hot," offered another student. "But not as smokin' as the historian himself."

Brenna froze, fighting to maintain a pleasant expression. There were many things she could say in response to those comments, but nothing appropriate for a classroom of undergraduates.

"Fitch Wilder is not an accredited academic." Brenna heard her voice sharpen but was unable to hide it. "Wilder is a con man who sells his alleged treasure-hunting skills to gullible collectors."

An uncomfortable silence filled the lecture hall. Brenna turned her back to the class and returned to her laptop.

Idiots. Both of them.

H. Winston Guilford was a wealthy industrialist who hid The Siren Series away from the world just because he could. And Wilder was nothing but Guilford's errand boy. And both men had shut her out of what could have been the crowning glory of her academic career.

She detested them for that.

No matter how many times she had petitioned Guilford, he had never allowed her to view the series in person, let alone conduct any tests to learn more about their origins. Each time Brenna approached him during her thesis research, he only laughed. "The Siren is a woman of intrigue, and that's a large part of her value. Why in the world would I want to put my substantial investment at risk?"

And Wilder? Just last month, the slow-talking cowboy refused the offer of her expertise during the authentication process of the latest find—then had the nerve to basically recite from her dissertation during a TV interview! Without attribution! How could he swat away her input, as if she were nothing but an annoyance, and then steal her research?

No wonder he didn't welcome her input—her expertise would show him up in front of his sugar daddy.

She remembered Wilder's last statement like she'd heard it moments before. She would always remember it.

"If we needed your advice, we would have contacted you. We don't. So we didn't."

What an ass-hat.

Brenna turned back to the class. "It is correct that the painting was found in a Paris apartment. And, yes, it is believed to be the sixth in the series. Here it is." She tapped a few keys on her laptop and brought the image of the latest painting to the screen.

"Holy crap," muttered one student.

Brenna raised her gaze to the giant screen, and though she'd studied this painting a hundred times, her reaction was unexpected. The floor seemed to give way beneath her feet and for an instant she lost her bearings. The sensation passed but left an empty ache in her chest.

At thirty-five, Brenna had achieved everything she had ever desired. She'd escaped from a small town in Minnesota and the shame of her father's name. She'd earned a tenured position at Harvard. She owned a lovely condo and enjoyed a low-impact lover who respected her need for personal space. She had all the freedom necessary to paint the picture of her own life, on her own terms, as an academic and as a woman.

So why, then, did this portrait leave her feeling empty?

Brenna swept her gaze across the achingly beautiful vision of the newest painting. The pregnant Siren was incandescent, the side of her cheek touched by gilded sunlight as she turned her attention to the painter. Her eyes were open and vulnerable,

welcoming the man behind the canvas into her most private being, the way she had most assuredly allowed him into her body.
The beauty of it was staggering.

It suddenly occurred to Brenna that she and The Siren could
not be more different. The two-dimensional Siren was the em-
bodiment of lush sensuality, a living, breathing tribute to erotic
love and emotional connection. Dr. Brenna Anderson studied
the human sociosexual experience as an academic concept, not
necessarily applicable to her own life.

How could a painting be more alive than she was? She
pushed the ridiculous thought aside and ended class early.

The knock on Brenna's office door was so soft she thought she'd
imagined it. Hearing it a second time, she looked up from her
desk. "Come in."

Sociology Department Chairman Lowell Snowden poked his
white head inside the door. "Got a minute? I know your office
hours just ended."

She smiled at her mentor. "Of course, Lowell. Please have a
seat."

As her boss got situated in a worn chair usually occupied by
students, Brenna took a moment to tidy her desk, which was
stacked with a dozen first drafts of honors theses. She glanced
up in time to see Lowell's eyes nervously scan the artwork lining her office walls. When his glance stopped at an illustration
of proper sexual technique from the ancient Chinese love manual *The Golden Lotus,* he looked away, agitated.

And just like that, Brenna got a bad feeling about this visit.
She closed her eyes. *Not again . . .*

"Brenna, I am sorry to have to bring this up. But the parents
of one of your undergraduate students—"

"No, Lowell. No more of this absurdity. This is Harvard!

My course is part of the diverse liberal arts curriculum for which our university is known, not pornography—"

"I know that." He cleared his throat. "However, this particular parent is a state legislator and a major donor to the Faculty of Arts and Sciences. He is threatening to withdraw much of his recent gift if . . ."

Brenna propped her elbow on her desk and let her forehead fall into her palm. This would make the third time this semester that a parent had complained to the Sociology Department about the subject matter of her introductory class.

". . . in particular his concern is the focus on unorthodox sexual behavior."

Brenna looked up, blinking in disbelief. "This is the twenty-first century, Lowell, a time when there are smartphone apps for every sexual fetish imaginable, when you can't watch the evening news without being bombarded with commercials for erectile dysfunction and vaginal dryness! You cannot be serious."

Lowell looked at her sadly. "We both know that universities have been challenged in this economy, Brenna—"

"How have I become the target of parental outrage when they're showing a Hollywood BDSM blockbuster down at the student union this very weekend? Please explain this double standard to me."

Lowell stared down at his entwined fingers before he spoke again. "Brenna, all I ask is that you attend a meeting I've set up for next week with the academic dean, the director of The Harvard Fund, the parent, and myself."

She frowned at him, finally seeing the exhaustion in his dear old face. She felt just as tired. "I am a tenured professor, Lowell. My curriculum was approved and my position is protected. What are they going to do to me for being such a naughty girl? Will I have to write a letter of apology to the concerned politician?

Will I have to sign a pledge to not talk dirty to his kid? Who is his kid, anyway?"

"His name is Justin Langley. His family has a hundred-year relationship with Harvard—the student's great-grandfather was a respected member of our biology faculty."

Brenna leaned forward, forcing Lowell to meet her gaze. "What about me, Lowell? Am I not a present-day faculty member deserving of respect?".

"You know I have always supported you, Brenna."

She sighed. "And I've always appreciated that support, but I can't help thinking that if I were a man the administration would not be so quick to throw me under the campus shuttle bus." She stood. "I've got to get going. Is there anything else?"

Lowell rose from the chair but made no move to leave. "Uh, yes, Brenna. I'm afraid the recent social media incident with that art investigator has not helped the situation. There are those who believe your conduct was not worthy of a tenured professor."

Oh, *that*. After Wilder quoted her work on Twitter without crediting her, she'd given him his own hashtag: #thisguycould-ntfindhisasswithbothhands. She'd since taken it down, but the damage had been done.

"Not one of my better moments, but I've already apologized. Anything else?"

Lowell shook his head. Brenna followed him out, locked up, and found him waiting for her in the hallway.

"You do have options, Brenna," he said.

"Really?"

"Yes. You can choose to attend the meeting and hear everyone's concerns. Or, you could take a paid leave of absence until the fall, or perhaps even a research sabbatical."

"*What?*"

"It's not a bad idea, Brenna. Justin Langley will move on to another class next semester, and his father's indignation will surely find a new home. And I . . ." He stopped and rubbed a hand over his face.

Brenna stilled. "Lowell? Are you all right?"

He shook his head and produced a weary smile. "I'm just a bit worn down, I'm afraid. The politics of academia—"

"Wait. Is there something more going on?"

He sighed heavily. "I suppose you'll hear about this sooner or later. I'm being asked to consider emeritus status. With me gone, well, the department could pursue a more . . . *conventional* agenda."

Despite his careful words, she understood what he meant, and it was unfathomable.

"That's horrible, Lowell. You're the most inclusive soul in all of Harvard's Faculty of Arts and Sciences. Diversity would be set back fifty years!"

He looked away. "Brenna, I'm tired. Sick and tired of the constant battle. I don't want to leave all my protégés to fend for themselves, but—"

She reached for his hand. "Just hang in there, Lowell. I'll think about stepping back—" Brenna did not want to give into the bastards, but the college couldn't afford to lose a man like Lowell Snowden. "I'll . . . I'll think of something. I promise."

Why wasn't he picking up?

Brenna had called Galen three times in the last fifteen minutes, and if she had to sit in traffic for another second without venting her frustration to someone, she was going to explode.

God, how she missed Piper. Not that Brenna wasn't thrilled for her best friend's happy and adventurous life—because she was. If anyone deserved the undying devotion of a handsome and brilliant man it was Piper, and if anyone deserved to have a beautiful, healthy baby girl, it was Piper and Mick Malloy. But with them on the road for the next season of their cable TV archaeology show, she'd felt a little lost. Video chats via unreliable Internet connections were better than nothing, but not the same.

She needed Piper tonight. She needed her perspective on this whole mess. Brenna wished she could laugh with her best friend over a glass of wine. Or two. With some Belgian chocolate on hand in case of emergency. In fact, she would have given anything to have Piper in town tonight.

It wasn't an option.

So she dialed Galen's number once more. This time he picked up.

"*What is it?*" he hissed.

Brenna's head snapped back in surprise. She'd been dating Galen Fairchild for nearly ten months, and it had been a serviceable arrangement for both of them. He was an incredibly hot investment banker who shared Brenna's level of interest in long-term committed relationships, which was none at all. He was smart and articulate and impressive at academic functions. The sex had been nothing less than outstanding. And he'd been good company for weekend ski trips, the theater, and the Boston Symphony season.

But the way he'd just spoken felt like a slap across the face.

"Hello to you, too."

"Sorry."

Since Brenna heard muffled talking in the background, it was unclear to whom he'd just apologized.

Galen cleared his throat. "Look, I'll have to call you back."

She glanced at the clock on her dashboard. It was after six thirty. They had a seven o'clock reservation at Union Oyster House, yet he sounded as if he were in the middle of something. "Are we still on for dinner tonight? Can you wrap up in time?"

She heard more muffled voices and the sound of a closing

door. "For fuck's sake, Brenna! I'm in a meeting. What's with the nonstop calling, anyway? You know I can't stand clingy women!"

Brenna glanced through the windshield at the churning mountain of gray clouds headed her way, a strange emptiness seeping into her bones along with the damp. A spring storm was about to hit.

Brenna made certain her response was calm. "I've had a very bad day, Galen. Thank you for your concern."

"Oh, please. Don't—" A voice in the background cut him off in midsentence. Brenna clearly heard the word "baby" delivered in a high-pitched whine.

"I'll let you get back to the business at hand, Galen." Brenna's finger rested on the disconnect button of her headset. "I hope she turns out to be a wise investment for you."

Click.

The rain began hitting the windshield of Brenna's Acura, big fat drops exploding on impact with the glass. She touched her cheek to find it was wet as well, and immediately checked to see if the roof was leaking. It wasn't.

She couldn't remember the last time she'd shed a tear. She hadn't cried at Piper and Mick's wedding, or at the birth of beautiful black-haired, blue-eyed Ophelia Malloy. She hadn't cried at her father's sentencing or her mother's funeral.

Her phone rang. She really didn't want to draw out the unpleasantness, but she had always preferred closure.

"It's not a catastrophe, Galen." Brenna decided to make this brief but on-point. "I told you I didn't want a serious relationship, but you agreed to be exclusive as long as we were together. *No double-dipping*—that was my only rule. And you blew it."

Her statement was met with silence. Had the call been dropped?

"Galen?"

"Fascinating." It was a woman's voice. "As much as I appreciate the insight into modern romance, I'm afraid I wasn't your intended audience. This is Claudia Harrington-Howell."

"Oh."

Oh, God! Could this day get any worse? Brenna rolled her eyes at her own ridiculousness—she'd just lectured a member of Harvard's Board of Overseers on the finer points of double-dipping!

"Hello, Claudia. What an unexpected pleasure."

The older woman chuckled. "Clearly."

"How are you?"

"I'm fine, but I hear the neo-Puritans are up in arms again."

"News travels fast."

"Lowell just called me and . . . oh, for the love of God, this whole thing is ridiculous. Poor man! He's embarrassed about this whole situation, Brenna. He's stuck in the middle."

Brenna said nothing, because saying nothing was the smart thing to do in this situation.

"Anyway, my dear, if you're not busy this evening, you should stop by the house. We're overdue for a nice visit. I'll have Charles whip up something for dinner."

Brenna smiled wryly to herself. It was a good thing her plans with Galen had fallen through, because this was not a casual invitation. It was a summons.

Claudia Harrington-Howell was one of the most influential—and unconventional—philanthropists in Boston society. She was notorious for dangling huge sums of money in front of institutions while insisting they make their assets more available to the public. In the last two years, Claudia had become a fairy godmother of sorts to Piper, Mick, little Ophelia, and by extension, Brenna.

Claudia had entered their lives entirely by chance. When Piper was still a senior curator at the Boston Museum of Culture and Society, she sought out Claudia's assistance in preparing an exhibit on early women's rights proponent Ophelia Harrington, Claudia's famous ancestor. When Piper accidentally discovered secret diaries detailing the young Ophelia's years as a courtesan in Regency London, the exhibit blew the lid off Boston history. Piper expected to lose her job and make a lifetime enemy out of Claudia, but the older woman surprised everyone by praising Piper's courage and dedication to the truth. Since then, the wealthy widow had treated the whole lot of them like family.

"I'm only about fifteen minutes from Beacon Hill," Brenna said. "Is that too soon? I don't want to barge in on you."

Claudia laughed. "No one barges in on Claudia Harrington-Howell, my dear."

Chapter Three

Rome

Fitch always appreciated a good view. This was a great one.

The Italian headquarters for Blackpool Mining was located on the top floor of a commercial building on the Piazza Navona, a site known more for its romantic fountains and baroque architecture than for business. And yet it made sense that H. Winston Guilford would choose this as his office.

His family's billions might have come from the multinational sale of gold, copper, and molybdenum, but Winston's passion was art. Fitch had brokered several deals for the industrialist in the last few years, and had even helped him acquire entire private collections from estate sales. Fitch was there today to negotiate Winston's purchase of the sixth Siren painting.

"Wilder!" Winston swung open an ornate door and held out his hand for a shake. "Please, come in. You know you could have waited until I got back to London. I'll be home in a few days."

Fitch followed his gesture and sat in one of two luxurious leather club chairs. "The Michel-Blanc wishes to have this matter settled in a timely fashion."

"I see." Winston folded his hands in his lap and nodded. "There are other buyers waiting in the wings, I assume?"

Fitch smiled. "Oh, no. I assured them there was only one buyer for The Siren, and that was you."

The corner of Winston's mouth twitched. "And you're certain it's authentic?"

"No doubt whatsoever. Not only is it authentic, it is spectacular. The digital images I sent you do not do it justice."

"Have they determined an asking price?"

Fitch pulled a large white envelope from the inside pocket of his jacket. He placed it on the walnut table between them. "You should know that there are conditions that could affect the price."

"Oh, I would expect nothing less." Without giving the envelope another thought, Winston rose from the chair and made his way across the room to gaze out the windows to the Fountain of the Four Rivers below, as if Fitch weren't in the room. The industrialist was well over seventy now, fit and healthy with a thick head of light gray hair. He wore an expensive Italian suit with no tie that day, but Fitch knew he was the kind of British aristocrat just as likely to be wearing an ascot—and not ironically.

Fitch was used to Winston's . . . *eccentricities*. He'd met plenty of the ultra-rich in his line of work, and he'd learned that they viewed the world much differently than the rest of humanity. It was as if everything and everyone were there for their use and had value only in relation to them. But Fitch always had a soft spot in his heart for H. Winston Guilford and the loneliness that lived just below his surface.

Fitch had been a teenager when he first met Winston. The billionaire had traveled to Santa Fe to visit Fitch's father, Robert, a gallery owner and art appraiser. That was the day Fitch's dad had told him the story of how these two men from very different worlds had become friends.

Before his career in Santa Fe, Fitch's father had been a talented New York painter who turned to forgery to make ends meet—and got caught. Robert avoided prosecution by agreeing to serve as a forgery consultant for the FBI, and when his efforts led to the prosecution of a crooked dealer who'd profited from Winston's trust, a bond was forged. Winston later hired Robert to do what no one else had been able to—acquire the other three Siren paintings. When Robert died and left the business to Fitch, Winston's loyalty extended to the son.

Fitch had a theory about his client's obsession with The Siren Series: the paintings were a substitute for his late wife. It was as if Winston had chosen to focus all his adoration on a set of canvases that he could possess, secure, insure, and never, ever lose.

Winston kept his eyes on the piazza below as he resumed his conversation. "I suppose you're going to try to convince me to let you poke and prod and point your laser beams at her before I whisk her off to safety."

Her—it was always how Winston referred to any, or all, of The Siren paintings. "No, sir. I've already done that."

Winston spun around, his eyes wide.

"The painting is currently the property of the Michel-Blanc, of course." Fitch smiled politely. "They requested I oversee a series of tests, which I have done. We've learned quite a lot about our lovely and mysterious Siren."

Without a word in response, Winston returned with two shot glasses of single-malt scotch, handing one to Fitch. He sat again and raised his glass. "Bold move, Wilder."

Fitch laughed, clinked his shot glass to Winston's, and then downed the whiskey—smooth as butterscotch. "Lucky move, more like. As you know, I've been waiting for an opportunity like this for years and I finally got it. The results were worth waiting for."

Winston crossed his legs at the knee and stared at Fitch. "And?"

"And what?"

"Oh, for fuck's sake, Wilder. Is this some sort of game?"

"Not at all." Fitch set his shot glass on the table. "You have made it clear that you have no interest in the provenance of The Siren paintings. 'Mystery over history' is what you always say. I assumed you would not want to know about the underpainting we found behind the sixth portrait."

Winston's back straightened. One eye squinted. "There is another image on the canvas?"

"Image? No—but there are *words*. Beneath the portrait is a short love poem from the artist to The Siren." Fitch paused for dramatic effect. "And oddly enough, it is written in *English*."

Winston's eyes flashed with surprise before he scowled. He leaned forward, elbows on knees. "You do not have my permission to make that poem public."

Fitch was prepared for this. "I do not need your permission, Winston. The X-rays were taken at the request of the Michel-Blanc, and the information is theirs to do with as they choose. But they are willing to abide by your request, should you purchase the portrait."

He waved his hand in dismissal. "I have no desire to know what the poem says."

"As you wish."

"And I would prefer those words are never picked over and analyzed and scrutinized by academics and wannabe collectors."

"I understand."

Winston snatched the envelope from the table and opened it

without delay. One eyebrow immediately arched high on his forehead. "*This* is their condition? Ha!" He held up the document, quickly reading over it. "If I agree to loan out all six paintings for a temporary exhibit at the Michel-Blanc the price is sixteen million euros? But if I refuse it goes up to twenty-two?"

"Those are the terms."

Winston shook his head, tossing the agreement to the table. "Good God, man—it's worth every cent to keep her from prying eyes! Where do I sign this bloody piece of extortion?"

Winston tapped the speakerphone on the table and began patting the inner pockets of his jacket until he located a fountain pen.

"Get Miles in here," he said into the intercom.

"Of course, Mr. Guilford."

Before Winston had finished initialing and signing where indicated, a winded young man appeared at the open door.

"Yes, sir?"

"I need to make an electronic funds transfer. Immediately."

The sale was complete within the hour. Fitch made arrangements to personally deliver the painting to Winston in London the following week, once Winston had wrapped up his mining business in Rome. They shook hands cordially and Fitch was shown the door.

By the time Fitch had exited the building and stepped out onto the sunny piazza, he was laughing. Talk about a deal where everyone walked away happy!

Winston would be able to retreat to his London manor, where he could sit for hours in a gallery dedicated to the private display of The Siren paintings. There he could wallow in the satisfaction of having "her" all to himself, never having to share "her" with another soul.

Jean-Louis and the board of directors of the Michel-Blanc would be thrilled with their sudden infusion of cash. They could finally repair and renovate the museum's home, a crumbling neoclassical behemoth on the edge of the Parc Monceau.

And Fitch would be nicely compensated for his trouble. His commission of 2.5 percent of the sale price plus Winston's finder's fee would make Fitch more money than he'd managed to scrape together in the last five years.

And this was only the beginning. When Fitch delivered the painting, possessive Winston would not be able to resist viewing the underpainting—and the game would be on. The moment Winston learned from the poem that there might be many other paintings out there, he would move heaven and earth to get his hands on them all, bankrolling Fitch's treasure hunt in the process.

He shoved his hands in his pockets as he strolled through the busy square and he realized he was starving. He was in the mood for some spectacular pasta carbonara and a few glasses of Pino Bianco, and he knew just the place to find it. And to think—the underpainted poem might next take him to the Catalan coast of Spain. Within days, he could be in Barcelona, digging into a platter of paclla heavy with mussels, scallops, and prawns, washing it down with a cold, sparkling bottle of Cava.

Goddamn, he loved his job.

As he walked, Fitch's thoughts wandered to the artist's hidden poem, and he was struck by a twinge of guilt. He'd used modern technology to expose an ancient secret, all in the name of profit. He'd known there was a chance the infrared scans would reveal a rough sketch or a first draft of the painting—if he was lucky. But a poem? Never would he have expected to see those ghostly words rise out of the past as they did.

Fitch frowned. It was a love poem set in Catalonia and written mostly in English. What was that all about?

And who was he to dredge up something never meant to be shared?

Thirteen paintings
And three seasons
Since you came to me,
Broken bird in a Catalan storm

This soldat dement shall fail
To capture the radiance
Of his bellesa de la cala,
Brighter now than ever before

Chapter Four

Boston

Claudia's ever-present caretaker, Charles, welcomed Brenna inside the historic Edwardian mansion and offered her a cup of tea.

Before Brenna could respond, Claudia swooped in.

"Thank you, Charles, but I believe it's a cocktail kind of evening." Claudia held out her arms, a pastel silk duster flowing behind her. "Brenna! Lovely as always." She kissed her cheek and, in a breeze of Hermès eau de toilette, led her into the parlor.

"As I recall, you enjoy a vodka martini with lemon. Is that correct?"

"On all counts, Claudia."

"I hope you don't mind that I made a fire." She gestured for Brenna to sit on a velvet settee near the hearth. "What a blustery New England day it is out there!"

Brenna smiled sadly. "I could use a little warmth right about now."

Claudia tossed back her silver bob and laughed. As Brenna got comfortable on the sofa, she eyed her hostess with the usual combination of fascination and bemusement. Claudia was one of a kind, certainly, and Brenna admired her independent nature. But more than that, she appreciated Claudia's rare ability to locate the needle of honesty in a hayloft of bullshit.

"My ancestor was a courtesan before she was a human rights crusader—so what?" she'd once told a crowd of wealthy museum donors. "If you're offended that a young woman decided to fully explore her sexuality and escape a repressive society, that's your issue, not hers."

Much of Claudia's lifestyle seemed exotic to Brenna. As a childless widow whose husband left her more money than she knew what to do with, Claudia spent half the year traveling to holy sites across the globe to study under any number of gurus and priests. Last year it had been Buddhist monks in Nepal and shamans in the American Southwest. But there was one aspect of Claudia's personality Brenna understood all too well—the older woman's fondness for revealing only a hint of her thoughts and feelings. Since that was Brenna's modus operandi as well, she recognized a kindred spirit in Claudia.

The two enjoyed their drinks and chitchat before the fire. Afterward, they relocated to the room's small dining table to further discuss the finer points of academic subterfuge, all while enjoying lovely grilled salmon with spring vegetables. When they finished the meal, Claudia dabbed at her lips with the corner of a linen napkin and draped an arm over the back of the dining chair.

"Tenure might protect you from being fired without due process, Brenna, but it will never shield you from criticism or backroom politics."

Brenna produced a weary smile and nodded.

"If this is truly an attempt to force you out—they can make the environment so untenable that you walk away."

Brenna shook her head. "I've worked too hard for my position. My job is my life. They can't have it."

Claudia sighed. "Then you have a fight on your hands, Dr. Anderson."

"I suppose I do."

After a pause, Claudia rose from her seat, her nearly six-foot frame towering over Brenna. "Well! Then I say *screw the needle-dicked bastards!*"

Brenna burst out laughing. When Claudia exploded with her trademark booming guffaws, Brenna couldn't help but wonder . . .

How would she have turned out if her own mother had possessed even a fraction of Claudia's chutzpah? How would it have felt like to see her mother stand up to a narcissistic husband instead of cowering before him? Would Brenna have turned out more trusting? Less guarded? Would she have become a woman open to love?

Claudia walked past her and patted her shoulder. "I will support you however I can. In the meantime, how about I have Charles rustle us up some coffee?"

Brenna excused herself and made her way down the hall to the first-floor powder room. She flipped on the light and saw her reflection in the ornate mirror. She was still smiling to herself. Claudia had her back. Aside from Piper, Brenna couldn't imagine anyone she'd rather have in her corner when the unpleasantness hit the fan. Brenna glanced around the room, and her smile widened.

If ever there were a human being with perfect taste, it was Claudia. This room—like the rest of the vintage structure—had undergone multiple remodels over the centuries, and like all the rooms it featured the underpinnings of classic design with an unexpected touch of whimsy. The walls were covered in traditional white-on-cream brocade wallpaper, and the floors were beautiful black and cream onyx inlaid tile. Ah, but then there was an antique red lacquer Chinese bureau Claudia had converted into a vanity, like a sparkling maraschino cherry on top of an ice cream sundae.

Brenna closed the door behind her, turned, and saw her reflection in the mirror from a slightly different angle. Her lips parted in shock.

What . . . the actual . . . *fuck?*

She blinked . . . once, twice, realizing that what she'd seen was real, not the product of two vodka martinis with a chaser of job stress. On the opposite wall hung a small oil portrait. It was surrounded by faded matting and framed in damaged giltwood. And though her brain was buzzing with wonder and doubt, she was certain of two things: the picture had not been there the last time she'd visited, and, for some ungodly reason, a lost portrait of The Siren now hung in Claudia's guest bathroom.

Brenna reached up to trace her fingertip along the jagged edge of the battered frame. Then she lifted it from the wall.

She stood under the powder room light, holding the painting up for inspection as she held her breath. There was no signature, but she pressed on, trying her best to remain objective while examining all the nuances visible beneath the glare of old glass.

It took many minutes before her mind calmed and her thoughts became rational.

The image differed markedly from any of the other Siren paintings, including the one discovered just months ago in Paris. This small portrait was a bust only, and the muse squarely faced the painter, her shoulders exposed by a loosened peasant top, freckles scattered across her nose. There was no seductive tilt of cheek or curve of neck here, no sight of the telltale birthmark or view of the ocean. It was a simple face-to-face reckoning, an up-close standoff between subject and artist. *This is me,* the Siren's eyes seemed to say. *This is who I truly am.*

The vulnerability in those light blue eyes took Brenna's breath away.

She fought to regain focus. She had to figure this out. She had to make sense of what was completely nonsensical.

She would begin with the things she knew were true. Yes, this was the same woman brought to life by the same hand in the same setting. No doubt about it. She saw the familiar iridescent light. She saw the sun-streaked curls, the bronzed cheeks dotted with delicate freckles, and the exposed gaze of those cool blue eyes. And all of this came alive with the brushstrokes, color palette, and sense of movement that were the calling cards of Le Artiste.

Brenna gazed up at the bathroom ceiling and laughed out loud at the absurdity of the situation. After a decade of begging and pleading, she finally had been given the opportunity to see a Siren painting with her own eyes, to hold one in her own two hands—and all she had to do was need to pee!

Which begged many questions. How did it get here? How did it end up in the United States, in Boston, and in Claudia's freaking *bathroom*?

With the portrait clutched to her chest, Brenna rushed back to the parlor, nearly crashing into Charles on his way out. Claudia glanced up from her spot near the hearth, where she stood over the coffee set. Her eyebrows rose in surprise and her fingers loosened around a set of silver-plated tongs. A sugar cube plopped into her cup and spewed liquid into her saucer.

Claudia blinked softly at Brenna. "I know you've had a trying day, my dear, but there's no need to make off with my art collection." She returned to the coffee. "You take cream but no sugar, correct?"

Brenna's head was spinning. Inside she might be losing her shit, but on the outside she needed to remain calm. "So, Claudia. Did you happen to purchase this on your travels?"

Claudia seemed puzzled.

Brenna sat politely on the settee, propped the painting against the armrest, and gestured toward it. "This was in your bathroom."

Claudia sat across from Brenna and casually sipped from her china cup. "Yes, dear, I know. I put it there. I found that portrait many years ago in one of Ophelia Harrington's trunks."

Brenna's mouth fell open.

"Yes, I do mean one of *those* trunks, the ones with the secret compartments that held her courtesan diaries. I've always thought the girl was lovely. The thought has even crossed my mind that perhaps this is a painting of the Swan. And since it had such a nice seaside vibe to it, I've kept it at my beach house on the cape for forty years."

Brenna nearly choked.

"You remember The Swan, don't you? Ophelia's mentor—the one who trained her to become the courtesan known as The Blackbird?"

Brenna found her voice. "I know who she is."

"Lovely. So I recently gave my beach house to my grandniece and her two very rowdy boys and brought my things back to Boston. The boys broke the frame while throwing a football indoors, if you can believe it. I keep reminding myself to get it redone."

Brenna nodded, trying to order her thoughts into something other than the panicked tangle of questions now crashing through her mind. Why would Ophelia have one of The Siren paintings? Had she traveled to the South of France before immigrating to America? Where did she purchase it? From whom? What year? And why would she store it inside the trunk that held her intensely private story, the secrets of her heart and soul?

Or could it really be that simple? Were The Swan and The Siren one and the same?

Brenna decided that as soon as she got home, she would Skype Piper. She didn't give a damn what time it was in Herzegovina—this was an emergency.

"Did you want your coffee, Brenna?"

She stared absently at Claudia for a moment and shook her head. "No, thank you. But could you please tell me why you think this is a painting of The Swan?"

"Certainly. I had to ask myself why Ophelia would have squirreled away this little painting with her most treasured items, wrapped inside the baptismal gown her children wore, no less. Most of the artwork she and Malcolm had owned was still displayed in my grandmother's house at the time, and anything that wasn't had been crated in a separate section of the attic."

She took a sip of coffee.

"Even stranger yet, the first time I laid eyes on you—the night of the museum opening—I was struck by how closely you resembled my little portrait in the beach house. I've always thought you looked like her."

Brenna looked up, heat spreading across her face. "That's . . . that's not true." She adjusted the painting in her hand—and the bottom right corner of the frame separated, falling apart in her hands.

"Oh, no! Claudia, I'm so sorry!"

Claudia craned her neck over the coffee things, then waved away Brenna's concern. "Like I said, I've been planning to get it reframed. The frame means nothing. It's the portrait I love."

Claudia rose and situated herself next to Brenna on the settee.

"Here. I don't want to do any more damage." As Brenna transferred the portrait to Claudia's hands, the entire frame fell apart, exposing the right edge of the canvas and glass. Brenna gasped.

Right there, in the lower right-hand corner—in a spot that

had been hidden by the frame—a small segment of writing came into view. Brenna leaned in for a better look.

"What does it say?" Claudia squinted. "I'm blind as a bat without my reading glasses."

"It says L. A. *Le Artiste*." As Brenna uttered those words her heart began to race. "May I check the back, Claudia?"

When Brenna held the painting once more, she gently turned it over to examine the back for identifying marks. Linen had been unevenly tacked down around the edges, and at the center of the bottom was writing in a familiar hand.

It said: *"Catalonia, 1828."*

Brenna's head popped up. She stared into Claudia's wide eyes for a moment, her thoughts racing. "That's Ophelia's handwriting."

Claudia nodded. "I think you're right. Does that mean anything to you?"

Brenna's thoughts continued to race. Catalonia? As in *Spain*? Not France? What else about The Siren paintings had she—and everyone else—gotten wrong? Could there really be a connection between the elegant London courtesan and the freckled seaside muse? If so, how? Why? What was The Swan doing in the middle of nowhere?

Suddenly, Brenna realized the entire landscape of her career had changed. For the first time, she had a shot at original-source research, groundbreaking scholarship! She now had a location, a date, and a possible connection to a figure already part of the historical record. Research of this magnitude could save her position as well as Lowell's. With this new discovery, there was no telling how far this little painting could take her.

Brenna looked up and smiled at Claudia. "Now that I've given it some thought . . . a sabbatical sounds perfect."

* * *

"Is there anything else I can get you?"

Brenna looked away from the spread of endless ocean and smiled at the flight attendant's gentle inquiry. Though only halfway to London, Brenna decided that Claudia had been correct about traveling business class—it was worth every penny. She might even arrive at Heathrow well rested and clearheaded. "Another herbal tea, when you have a chance, please."

"Of course."

Brenna relaxed into the reclining leather seat and returned her gaze to the Atlantic Ocean, stretched out forever in the waning daylight. She regarded the horizon, the dividing line between heaven and earth, and smiled to herself. It did not escape her that she might one day look back on this trip as a dividing line in her own life, the end of one phase and the beginning of another.

Brenna had decided to do whatever she wanted and to hell with everyone and everything else, including the objectives of her five-year plan. This was a first for her. She had always seen major life decisions as a delicate balancing act. Her goals were important, of course, but were always tempered by what others expected of her, what would benefit her academic career in the long run, and what was the wisest use of resources.

Well, fuck that.

Brenna had just made a spontaneous decision to chase an outrageous theory without the slightest concern for what it looked like, how much it cost, or how it would affect her career. And it felt *fabulous*.

There was nothing holding her to Boston. She loved her job but hadn't been allowed to do it without restraint. Her most recent lover had left the taste of disenchantment on her tongue. And her best friend was married and off traveling the world. So why not?

Goodbye, Galen. Goodbye, Justin Langley.

The process had been surprisingly easy. She informed Lowell

that she would accept the sabbatical offer, effective immediately. She emailed her teaching assistants, giving them a detailed lesson plan for the rest of the semester and a copy of the final exam. It took just one afternoon to clean out six years of accumulated books and papers from her faculty office—while Lowell stood in the doorway, frowning at her.

"The office is still yours, Brenna. There's no need to do this."

"I would be more comfortable taking everything home."

Lowell had lowered his voice to a whisper. "Should you decide not to return for fall semester, please let the college know by July."

"I'll let you know."

"No. I . . . I might not be here."

Brenna stopped what she was doing. He really was about to quit. The thought began to fill her with equal parts anger and panic, but then she realized something. By July she would break open The Siren's story, and Harvard would beg her to return— and on whatever terms she chose. And the terms would include Lowell.

She'd placed both hands on her mentor's shoulders. "Promise me you won't make any decisions about your position until you hear from me in July."

Lowell had promised.

It took just a few days to dismantle the rest of her world. There was no lover who demanded an explanation. She had no parents to reassure. No cat. Her hypochondriac neighbor, Mr. Chekowski, offered to care for her houseplants and pick up her mail. When Brenna admitted she had no idea how long she'd be away, Mr. Chekowski frowned. "I'm almost eighty and my triglycerides are off the charts. Don't dawdle."

Piper was thrilled out of her mind to hear that Brenna was off to find a possible connection between The Swan and The Siren Series. Her best friend's enthusiasm made sense, of course, since The Swan was Piper's discovery. The London courtesan would have been forever lost to history if Piper hadn't found Ophelia's detailed diaries, created the museum exhibit, and written the abolitionist's biography.

As Piper had discovered, The Swan began as Ophelia's aka The Blackbird's—mentor but became her best friend. The diaries described The Swan as a no-nonsense entrepreneur and a woman with an outrageous disregard for Regency England's strict gender roles. Physically, she had been tall and slim, with pale blond hair and icy blue eyes, a woman Ophelia said was always refined in appearance and pragmatic in mind-set. She was invited to all the best balls and private gatherings, where she was whispered about by the same wives and daughters who admired her fashionable beauty and calm demeanor.

But other than these tidbits, Ophelia's diaries had offered almost no insight into The Swan herself—her family, her personal history, or even her name—leaving Brenna to wonder how well Ophelia truly knew her friend.

Or was it that The Swan did not wish to be known?

The flight attendant returned with Brenna's tea, bringing her back to the present. She powered on her laptop and reviewed her schedule for the next several days.

She would begin in London, where she would search for details of The Swan's life. She had a string of appointments with archivists and librarians at the British Library, the National Archives, and the British Newspaper Library—just to start. She sought to find the infamous courtesan's real name, a record of her passage to Spain, tax documents, and the specific location of The Swan's London home, a Mayfair residence Ophelia had described as "a few blocks and a million degrees from Society."

Once Brenna was armed with this information, she would pay a little surprise visit to the residence of H. Winston Guilford. Perhaps, finally, she would have the leverage she needed to gain admission to view The Siren Series. She would trade information for access.

After that, Brenna had no agenda, no idea where she would go or what she would be searching for. She sipped from her teacup, attempting to calm the anxious flip of her belly. *No idea? No agenda?* She let go with a nervous laugh, staring out at the ocean once more.

She was only hours from Boston and she barely recognized herself. Who was this daredevil, and what had she done with the safe and controlled Dr. Brenna Anderson?

THE PAST

Chapter Five

At Sea

I, The Swan, celebrated seductress of noblemen, lay upon a simple bed in the sea captain's cabin, listening to the creaks and pings of a ship under full sail. Had it been only a day since I prepared for one last evening at the London opera? The intricately beaded blue silk gown I had donned the prior evening had now been stripped from me, along with my home and my freedom. I was no longer The Swan, London's paramount courtesan. I was simply a penniless prisoner on a merchant ship bound for parts unknown.

Though difficult to believe, this state was actually an improvement over my position the night prior. At least I was alive and unhurt at the moment, and most importantly, there was no longer a knife pressed to my throat.

I stared at the arched timbers of the ceiling above me, asking myself a host of questions. What had I done wrong? How had I managed to get myself into such a predicament? How would I survive?

I was certain of one thing. Becoming a bound captive gave me plenty of time to ponder the details of my past.

This was not a particularly welcome development.

* * *

The Swan had been in top form only a few short months ago. All of London society had fawned at my feet—at least the male population!

Yet I found myself in an odd state of mind. For the first time, I felt detached from it all. It did not seem to matter to me whom I chose to be my companion, as men seemed so much the same. Previously, the prospect of a fresh start had invigorated me, caused me to feel a renewed sense of adventure and possibilities. This time, all I felt was a heavy dullness of spirit.

Eventually, I chose someone new, if only to halt the ceaseless pestering from a parade of suitors. My selection was Lord H—, a man powerful in the government, married with a family. Yes, I broke my own unbreakable rule. I "took up" with a married man. His family was old and wealthy, but he was devoted to his work in politics. That was why I chose him.

I rather liked the idea of a busy man, a man who would leave me to my own devices a great deal of the time.

He also assured me that his wife had her own "pursuits," just as he had. I took that to mean that she had her own lovers. I certainly did not suspect that she was, in fact, a devoted mother and respectable pillar of her community. As I later discovered, her devotion to her husband would prove to be heated and possessive.

Hence my rule against married men. Oh, how I wished I had heeded my own counsel!

About a month into my affair with Lord H—, I spent a vigorous morning in my lover's arms.

He grabbed my hips in his large hands and drove into me from behind. I yelped my gratified response into my pillow as I ground my bottom back against him. "Oh, be careful, my darling! Please remember, you're too big for me!"

It wasn't a complete lie. He was nicely endowed.

Another powerful thrust. I panted into the downy feathers. "Oh, yes! I feel every inch of you!"

Every man enjoys a little reassurance.

Then the slippery friction began to propel me to my own orgasm. I stopped talking and started moaning instead. I liked his big hands on my skin. I focused on that as I shut my eyes and found my own satisfaction. I knew how to attain an orgasm, yet remained quite aware of my surroundings. I never forgot where I was or who I was with, or what he expected of me.

My lover liked short animal yelps and long breathless whimpers. I delivered, and he found his satisfaction shortly afterward, holding tight to my hips as he groaned in his orgasm.

Afterward, we fell upon my bed and caught our breath. He rather charmingly pulled me into the curve of his body and kissed the back of my neck.

"You are delicious. I should have you served up to be my breakfast, lunch, and dinner."

These were hardly the most romantic words I'd ever heard from a man, but that suited me just fine. For me, love was an art form, not an emotional indulgence.

I put on a satisfied smile and rolled over to face him. He looked very good naked. He was tall and handsome in a self-satisfied way, with black hair and brilliant blue eyes. He had excellent taste in diamond jewelry and his bed performance was enthusiastic, if not refined. I found his political conversations more interesting than his pillow talk.

I ran a polished fingernail down the center of his chest. "I have kept you long enough. The Prime Minister depends upon you. It is my duty to England to send you back to your office in Whitehall."

That was all that was required to remind him of his duties. Within minutes, he had dressed himself once more. I tied his cravat like the devoted wife I wasn't, then kissed him goodbye like a lascivious whore, although I was not that either.

Thus bemused by my contradictions, precisely as I had planned, he wandered off back to the Prime Minister and left me to my own devices.

If only I had known what was coming, I would have sent him away forever.

That very afternoon, Lord H—'s wife accosted me as I was leaving the shop of the famed dress designer Lementeur.

"She dares venture out in the light of day!"

I turned to see who addressed me in such an angry tone, only to discover that I was being pursued by an elegantly dressed—yet disheveled—woman. Her gown was fine, but her pelisse was misbuttoned and her bonnet was slightly askew. On her face was a fury that had not been directed toward me since my unfortunate childhood in Newgate prison. I drew away from her obvious madness, alarmed by what seemed to me an entirely unprovoked attack.

Then I recognized her from the miniature that Lord H— kept upon his watch chain. This disturbed woman was my lover's wife.

Lady H— was an attractive woman. She looked no older than my own thirty-two years and possessed a figure that was generous but still shapely, remarkable considering she had borne Lord H— four children. The gown she wore did little to accentuate her assets, but it was modest and well made, which indicated her priorities. Her facial features were roundish and pretty, neither lovely nor plain, but her complexion was good. Her hazel eyes were smallish but her hair peeking from her disarrayed bonnet looked to be a nice chestnut color. I imagined she would cut a pretty picture in a nightdress. The many offspring gave proof that Lord H— did not find her distasteful.

However, he spoke rarely of his wife, and usually in reference to their children. I had the feeling that he cared for his family, but in a distant way. Pleased with his children's progress, displeased with their faults, gratified that others seemed to admire his fine family. Not a loving father. Not an adoring husband.

Not my dilemma . . . until that moment.

Lady H— advanced upon me. "You are a parasite!" Her tone was a hiss of disgust. "You creep into the beds of honest men and lure them away from righteousness! You take their money and their time and feed them your sick fantasies of love!"

I nearly laughed at that. I knew she had been wed for more than a decade. I had to wonder what an experienced wife would see as "sick fantasies." Oral stimulation, perhaps? A bit of play with blindfold and riding crop? Poor little goodwife. Did she long to experience some of Lord H—'s "fantasies" at home?

Did she even know what they were?

She saw my amusement. How could she not, with her nose scarcely fourteen inches from my own? Her face reddened further as her teeth clenched so tightly she could barely speak.

"I hate you," she hissed. "I hate him, too. I cannot look at him, knowing what he—" Her voice cracked. "What he did with you!"

I might have flinched from her slip into simple human agony had I not been so tensed for battle. I realized that my selfishness had led to this woman's pain.

Yet I could not bow to her fury. I had worked too hard to win the adoration and respect of the town. My own pride would not allow me to appease my incidental victim.

"If your husband prefers my company to yours," I said in arch tones, "that is not my responsibility. See to your own house, my lady, before you presume to clean mine."

As I look back on this encounter, I can see my cruelty clearly.

I know what such a woman's lot is in this life. A rich husband, yes, but likely not one of her own choosing. And I knew Lord H— to be an obstinate, somewhat thoughtless man, a man used to being obeyed, and quickly at that.

To me, he came as a lover, wooing and prepared to exert himself to win me. As for Lady H—, he doubtless treated her as a piece of functional but expensive furniture, securely looked after but largely ignored until needed. Certainly never treasured or coddled.

In the heat of my pride and insult, and yes, with a flash of guilty shame, I did not take her poor opinion in my usual nonchalant stride. Did she not know who I was? I was The Swan, whom every man wanted and every woman wanted to be! To me, she was a peasant shepherdess in a pastoral painting, pretty to look at, but bland and without impact. Her life was as alien to mine as a milkmaid's. I did not eat, sleep, or breathe the same way she did. We were not the same kind.

I advanced upon her. She took a step back from my greater height and cold expression, her surprise etched upon her plump features. No doubt she had expected me to flee in shame, cowed by her righteousness.

Unfortunately for her, I had long ago lost any care for puritanical opinions. The viewpoint of the wealthy was unearned, in my opinion. It was far too easy for those who had everything to judge those who struggled to survive. It was effortless to be "moral" when it cost you nothing. The woman before me would never, for example, rescue a child sentenced to an undeserved prison sentence simply for being born within the walls of Newgate. Such unfortunates were invisible to her. Her motherly instincts did not extend toward children sold into brothels so foul that she would vomit from the mere knowledge of what happened therein. She was of no use to anyone but her own little circle, and therefore her picture-perfect righteousness rang hollow and sour in my heart.

"He is your husband, not mine, and husbands are worthless creatures," I told her. " 'Tis why I have never burdened myself with one. Everything that I have, everything that I am, I have given to myself. No one owns me, and most certainly no one buys me."

I leaned closer to her. She gazed at me in dread fascination, as if I were a serpent advancing upon a mouse. "Take a lesson from my freedom, my lady." Oh, the devilish need to plant dissent among the righteous ranks! I was a temptress indeed, but I could not pass up the opportunity to disturb her self-secured awareness! "If your existence is one of powerlessness and resentment, I suggest that you go home to your worthless husband and take back your pride by standing with your own strength! Do not ask me to fix your problems for you!"

Then I turned and stalked away from the distaste I suddenly felt for the encounter, the wife, and myself. To be ruthlessly honest, I had lost interest in Lord H— soon after I had attached him. I think I had only smiled my way through the ensuing months so that I would not be tasked with the wearisome process of choosing yet another lover.

Apathy, thoughtlessness, and pride were my crimes. Those, and being an unprotected woman on the fringes of society, a creature belonging to the twilight realm of the demi-monde.

To my horror, my eventual punishment would be far worse than the scorn of the righteous. The rendered verdict would be a death sentence.

The dowdy Lady H— took my advice too well. Not only were her husband's wandering shoes placed neatly back beside her bed, but he gave up his position with the Prime Minister and moved quite permanently to their country manor in Sussex.

For my pains, I received a bluntly worded note. "*S, I must hereby withdraw my attentions. H.*"

I admit I was somewhat peeved to have been rejected, when I was the one accustomed to call the final moments of my games. However, I gave a careless laugh and tossed the note into the grate without another thought. Good riddance, I told myself. I had been bored from the start. I had mostly appreciated Lord H—'s talent for being elsewhere.

Then the whispers began. It had happened before, when my rageful former lover, the Duke of Mark, tried to shame me with my whorehouse beginnings. This latest assault was more finessed, perfumed with the kind of half-truths and bent suspicions that could only come from a woman scorned.

At first, the scandal sheets declared I was older than I looked, much older. There were reports that claimed the truth became apparent when I was undressed. How so, I could not imagine, when it is always our faces that age first.

Next, it was said that I was unclean. Poxy rumor followed me, until one day a shoemaker refused to touch my foot to measure its length.

Finally, and most ludicrously, in my astonished opinion, I was rumored to be entirely poverty stricken. This, after all, is the foulest sin one can commit in society—empty pockets! The rumor was widely believed, it seemed. Salespersons began demanding coin in advance of custom, and even the butcher would not drop the latch on his cart until my housekeeper laid four pennies into his hand.

How these rumormongers explained my fine house and my exquisite horses drawing my signature white-enameled carriage, I did not know.

I turned to my friend Lementeur for explanation, but he was as astonished as I.

"I tell everyone that I know that there is no truth in these tales, but I fear there is too much delight in your downfall. Someone keeps feeding the town stories of your depravity," he added sadly. "I fear that there is much you do not even know."

I insisted that he tell me, and he did so, most reluctantly. It was far, far worse than I realized. At those rumors of debt I had laughed. When I heard hints of my alleged disease, I had thrown an ugly porcelain duck (a gift from Lord H—) at the wall and took pleasure in its destruction.

But I wept in horror when Lementeur told me that many in society truly believed I was capable of the abuse of children. I knew this vicious lie was a stain that time could not wash away. No amount of wealthy extravagance or continued good health could prove this foul lie untrue. It would forever linger in the hearts and minds of society.

It was time to leave London behind me.

I returned home immediately. First, I summoned my solicitor, who would need to arrange for my travel the withdrawal of my accounts. While I awaited his arrival, I wrote to my dearest friend, Ophelia, informing her I would soon join her and Malcolm in America.

Once the solicitor departed, I hurried to my bedchamber and began to ransack my jewel chest. I had earned every ruby and every sapphire in those drawers, but I did not want them. I did not want to look at them for the rest of my life and remember where and when—and from whom—I had received them.

The jewels I had received from the Duke of Mark brought nothing to my mind but the memory of physical pain and anguish.

The rest meant nothing to me. But they were of great value and I knew I could put them to good use. So I made up my mind to exchange this tainted treasure for an innocent's freedom. I did not seek to combat any kind of vicious rumor.

I did it for my own soul.

The only items I wished to save were a beautiful choker and matching bracelet, twining ropes of tiny pearls braided flat around aquamarine ovals. I had purchased the set myself on impulse because they had made me think of my mother. I had no real memory of our life before we were tossed into Newgate for my father's crimes, but in my imagination, I could picture her wearing such lovely and delicate jewelry.

I set them aside. The rest of the collection I poured into a satchel and stared down at the tangle of cold diamonds, ornate and gaudy jewels, necklaces, bracelets, and rings. Then I called for my carriage and left the chamber, casting the empty jewel case onto the floor.

I ordered my driver to take me to a certain house. I had never been there, but I had known of its existence since I was about ten years of age, when I had gone to live with Valentine and her girls.

My driver was a capable and always respectful man named Westen. I had already warned him of my approaching departure from London, and he had seemed genuinely sad to learn of it. Now, he looked at me with some worry. "Miss, that place—"

I shook my head to cut him off. "I know what it is. Drive on, if you please."

When I arrived at the house in question, it looked entirely ordinary. It was very fine, of course, with a great, carved entry and a polished wood door.

However, I knew its elegant and sedate exterior did not reflect the foul purpose of its interior. When I alighted from my carriage with the aid of one of the house's footmen, there was nothing remarkable about the steps or the door before me. I carefully looked into the face of the nearest footman. He was, of course, beautiful. I expected that. Yet, his expression was entirely blank and the light behind his eyes barely flickered. I don't think I had ever seen such dead eyes on a man since the turnkeys of Newgate.

I shivered and withdrew my hand, realizing that despite the double layer of gloves I could feel the chill of his inhumanity. He stepped back and bowed, still silent. I raced up the steps, lifting my skirts with one hand and gripping my satchel in the other. As I approached the door, it swung open for me. Within stood another beautiful, soulless young footman.

He gazed at me with distant inquiry. "I need to see him," I said simply. "Tell him I am the—"

But he had already delivered a sharp bow and was gone. I waited, and though the place made me feel as if slime covered my skin I knew I had very good reason for remaining.

Then I saw the face that had haunted my nightmares for many years. I had not seen him up close since our first encounter. Elden—the monster I had once thought of as "the clean man"— approached me with a smile like a shard of ice.

"The Swan herself! Whatever could possibly bring such an esteemed lady of the bedchamber to our humble little house?"

He extended his hand to take mine. I thrust the bag of jewels into it instead. "I want to buy as many as possible. Forever."

He lifted a brow and made a little moue of mock disappointment. "Really? How tiresome. And here I thought you had come to discuss business with a competitor."

The thought of being classified so by him, at being anywhere near him, forced me to swallow the bile rising in my throat. But when he turned and walked away with a little come-along gesture, I quickly followed.

I attempted to make quick work of the negotiations. "How many?"

Elden poured the satchel out upon his leather blotter and tossed the bag aside. The jewels gleamed in their gold settings. Diamonds glittered; pearls shimmered. He poked through them with a finger and an assessing gaze.

Then he looked up at me. "One."

I shook my head quickly. "There is enough here for at least three or four!"

He shrugged, then pulled out the best piece. It was a large, well-cut diamond set in a cluster of sapphires. We both knew its value was more than a gem in a setting—the necklace itself was a work of art.

It was also a gift from the Duke of Mark. I still shuddered every time I saw it. If not for its incredible value, I would have tossed it into the rubbish long ago.

Lifting the necklace into the light, he twisted his lips in cold appreciation. Then he laid it back down on the blotter, treating it with rather more respect than I had done. He turned his dead gaze back upon me.

"Two," he said. Then he raised his hands and gave a single clap. The door opened and a silent footman stepped smartly into the room. "Take her to the attic." Elden's tone was more amused than anything. "And . . . give her five minutes to choose. No more."

I didn't wait for the footman, but picked up my skirts and ran for the great winding staircase. He was right behind me of course, but I continued up until I had reached the top. He led me down a hall to another, plainer stair secreted behind a hidden door. I ran up it as well. I dared not waste a single second on decorum!

In the attic at last, I started to run ahead, but the footman held up a commanding hand for me to halt. He walked to a door and opened it. I peered in at the room of older children. I nearly keened. I was too late, too late for them! I turned my back, although it tore at me to leave them to their fate. I pressed both hands to my breaking heart and found my voice. "Younger," I told the footman.

He took me to another room. This one was filled with girls. They too sat in abnormal silence. They too had gazes poured from bottomless wells of darkness.

I turned quickly and slapped the footman across the face with all my might. "You waste my time intentionally! Younger!"

The next room held what I was looking for. As he opened the door, I heard the telltale scuffling of small feet scurrying back to their beds. I pushed past the footman and entered the room.

I knew I had a single moment to decide. If my time lapsed, I had no doubt I would be thrown out, without my jewels, and I would never have another chance.

Tick-tock.

I wanted every one of them.

Then, at the end of the long room, I saw two small children. They seemed to be no more than five or six years of age, a boy and a girl. They stood together, with their hands clasped tightly. They were dark-haired, pink-cheeked cherubs with matching green eyes. Siblings, possibly twins.

Tick-tock.

I lifted my hand to point. "Those two."

The footman lifted a child into each arm, carrying them easily. They remained relaxed in his hold, so I knew that they were new arrivals and that I had come in time for them.

Then I turned my eyes down and fled from the room, leaving a dozen others to their fates. I felt as though my heart was ripping from my body. I did not even realize that I wept until I could no longer see the stairs beneath my feet.

I brushed my hands over my eyes, grateful that the footman walked ahead of me. But the children gazed curiously back over his shoulders at me. The little boy had his thumb in his mouth. His eyes had grown wider and a little worried. He was right to worry. We were not yet out of danger. I dared not allow Elden to detect any signs of weakness. I dried my eyes and lifted my chin. Then I smiled at the children and put one finger to my lips. They smiled back, the girl widely and the boy tentatively.

"Put them down," I commanded Elden's footman once we had reached the front door.

He lowered the children to stand on their own little feet. I took a tiny hand in each of my own and turned to walk them from this house of horror.

"Oh . . . Swan?"

It was Elden's voice. I did not dare stop. I continued down the stairs, to the carriage and our freedom, so close . . .

I did not turn around and kept the children aimed at the carriage.

"I just want to tell you how proud I am of you." The evil in his voice caused me to shiver. I began to run. He raised his voice to call out after me. "I find it difficult to believe you were once that unattractive boy I met straight from Newgate . . . *Jinx*!"

I ran, hard, like the boy Jinx I had once pretended to be, not like the lady I had been for fifteen years! I pushed the children through the carriage's lacquered white door and to safety.

I lifted myself to the step and stood on the running board. "Go!" I shouted at Westen.

He drove. I hung on to the side handles of the carriage and gazed behind us. Elden now stood on the walk with his minions and watched me drive away.

I had intentionally not given my driver a destination while near that house. Even now, I called for him to stop a block from the simmering evil behind us.

After drawing him down from his seat for a hushed conversation, he walked away from the carriage with enough silver in his hand to complete my request. I climbed back into the compartment with the children to wait. Although the doors on either side had pretty little latches, I did not think they would hold should Elden chase me down to take back his property.

At that moment, I wished I had spent my money on less fashionable and more secure transportation. Alas, I was to have that thought again, later that very night.

Westen came back in only a few minutes, hopped back up to his seat without a word, and the carriage jolted to a running start.

The children looked at me. I looked at them. I had not been near a child since I myself was one.

"Hello," I said carefully. I did not introduce myself, for that association would do them no good in the future. "What are your names?"

"'M Tess," the little girl said promptly. "'E's Tim."

Her accent was common. I wondered where they had come from. I hoped they had not been stolen from their parents, for I had no intention of putting them back into the situation that had led them into the hands of that fiend. So I did not ask them about their home, or their mother. Instead, I found a few lemon drops in my reticule and unwrapped them for the children while I told them a nonsense story about a dog with too many bones.

It did not take long for another vehicle to join me. It was a little pony cart, a dashing little sport carriage drawn by a pony of such gleaming whiteness that he looked as though he'd been bathed in milk.

The children climbed up on their knees to look out the window. "Oh, pretty!" Tess caroled.

She no doubt meant the pony, for the man driving it was an appealing little fellow, but no one could call him pretty.

A light tap sounded on the carriage door and then it opened to reveal my dear friend Button, known to all of London as the dressmaker Lementeur.

"Hello!" His tone was cheerful and entirely without distress. "What a lovely day for a trip to the park!"

His smile infected us all. I relaxed for the first moment since I had made my decision. He was a slight and frail sort of savior, this funny little man, but at that moment he was more beautiful than any man I'd ever known.

His gaze flicked to mine for a second.

"They were Elden's," I murmured in briefest explanation. "Purchased by me. They deserve the best people you can find, Button."

His brow arched in what might have been admiration, judging by the gentle pat he gave my hand. Then he turned his attention back to the children.

"My pony is named Copernicus," he told them confidentially. "Would you care to meet him?"

They both clamored yes, then looked to me as if for maternal permission. Heavens, when had that ever happened? I shooed them on with a smile. "Go, have a lovely drive."

Have a lovely life.

Lementeur lifted the children down, chattering cheerfully all the while about Copernicus and his stall-companion, a small white cat named Contrary. I think the children almost thought of him as another child, for they were at ease with him in a way they had not been with me.

I did not leave the carriage. I did not want to expose the children to my very recognizable face any more than was necessary. When Lementeur turned back to me with a nod, I caught at his hand.

"Thank you. Thank you for everything, my friend!"

He covered my hand with his own. "Only the very best

family," he assured me, struggling to maintain his composure. "I shall miss you terribly." Then he drove away in his pony cart, with Copernicus prancing as if he knew to put on a show and silly stories rattling from his driver's lips. The children were so distracted that they drove away from me without looking back even once.

I never saw Tess and Tim again, but I have always held on to the belief that their lives would be magical and full of love. I know my own heart longed to go with them. To start over. To leave my world behind.

Hours later, I did leave my world, but not in the manner I had planned. Instead of a passage to America, I would be taken from my carriage as I left the opera. Abducted.

I had forced myself to attend the performance that evening despite my melancholy, as I wished for one last triumphant appearance before The Swan disappeared forever. I knew I would sustain dagger gazes from all of society for my audacity, and that I could expect nothing in the way of support from the people I had once counted as friends, but I could not allow them to think they had gotten the better of me.

I stepped out that night simply to prove that my enemies could not prevent me from doing so. My dearest Ophelia, now living happily with her husband, Malcolm, in Boston, had taught me not to cower from the cowardly. It had been one of many gifts she had given to me in our time together. Oh how I looked forward to reuniting with her, the truest friend of my life!

I cannot recall the evening's music, or even the faces that swam beyond the railing of my private box. It took my every nerve to lift my chin high, as if I cared nothing for anyone's opinion, as if I had actually come only to hear the singers.

Finally, exhausted from the effort of rising above the pettiness,

I made my way from the hall in a sedate fashion. I did not linger, nor did I hurry. I kept a mildly mysterious smile upon my lips the entire time, as if I had a delicious secret, and I floated my gaze just above the eyes of everyone I saw—as if I had suddenly decided to take an interest in hats!

It was with these little skills, mostly advice given to me long ago by the genius Lementeur, that I kept my dignity and persona intact against the bitter whispers and scathing glares prompted by my appearance.

However, once I had languidly ascended into my carriage and shut the door upon the still-simmering crowd outside the hall, I fell back upon my seat in exhaustion. My limbs trembled and my head ached abominably. My eyes burned with impotent outrage and my throat remained far too tight to speak, let alone cry.

I had never been a weeping sort, anyway. Tears would indicate leaks through the cracks of my shell—cracks I could not afford as I prepared to journey into my new life on the morrow.

How silly my concerns seemed to me now. How ridiculous I was to worry that I might cry before people whose good opinion would soon become so meaningless! My pride, my place in society, and my petty concerns would become naught but absurdities.

Because in the next instant, everything would be taken from me!

The carriage lurched to a sudden halt, throwing me hard into the frame, then sideways down upon the seat. I was still blinking away the startling blow to my temple when the door opened and hard hands fell upon me. I fought them, of course, but I have ever been frail and offered only laughable resistance. Never have I felt so helpless! I was bound as easily as a child. The coarse ropes around my wrists and ankles stole the feeling from my hands and feet. The rough sack that was tossed over my head robbed me of my sight and very nearly my breath as well, especially when I was lifted from my carriage and thrown forcefully onto a wooden surface. It swayed beneath the impact and I realized I lay in the bed of a wagon. I still writhed and called for help as loudly as I could, but my voice was lost beneath the clatter of hooves and wagon wheels as my captors drove onward.

It had happened so quickly. The whole matter was over in seconds. Even if anyone had witnessed the abduction, I doubt they would have had time to act.

On the other hand, the ride in the jolting wagon seemed endless. It stopped at last and I was pulled from it. I was tossed over a thick male shoulder in such a way that took my breath, then lugged for some distance before being put down. My captors pushed me low into something unstable and damp. I felt an inch of water in the bottom where I lay. That and the nauseating sway of it told me that I was in some sort of small boat, like a skiff. I felt as it was pushed away and was aware of the rhythm of someone rowing.

After that wet and chilling ride, I was carried once more like a sack of flour, then finally set upon my numbed feet. When the hood was finally pulled from my head, I found myself standing on the deck of a ship.

It seemed terribly important to commit to my memory every sound and impression at the time, though I cannot imagine why I thought so. Perhaps it was merely my rational mind occupying itself so that panicking animal instinct would not overrun me.

I truly don't think it would have mattered either way, for in the end, there I stood, on the deck of a ship already far out into the Channel, bound and captured, held in the grip of a pirate!

Chapter Six

At Sea

"I ain't a pirate," the captain told me. His tone sounded rather stung. "Thief, maybe. Smuggler, that's for certain." His men laughed as they stood back from where we stood. One grunt from him and they turned away en masse, slipping off into the murky darkness of the deck.

His rough hand was wrapped in my hair, holding me entirely immobile. The tip of a knife was pressed to my throat, and my mind fixed upon the fact that the knife was warm. Perhaps it had been stored in the pirate's—er, smuggler captain's—boot sheath and his body had heated the metal. I'd always imagined that a blade would feel icy cold as it punctured my skin.

My mistake. Merely the latest in a series of so many.

His breath was hot on the exposed skin of my neck. Such a warm death. I considered that it wasn't the worst way to go. A slicing pain, the hot rush of blood, then it would be over in seconds. A short voyage indeed. I had seen much worse ways to leave life during my childhood at Newgate and later in my time of employ in the bordello.

However, that did not mean that I intended to go easily.

My mind raced with thoughts of buying my life—only to

realize that my jewels were gone. Then I prepared to beg, to throw myself upon this rough brigand's mercy. But I truly doubted he had any.

Through the chaos of my panicked last thoughts, I felt his chest expand against my back.

Ah. I had not been pursued by dukes and princes alike to mistake when a man is inhaling my scent! Under the pretense of going weak in the knees from fear—perhaps not pretense at all—I managed to press my bottom against his groin.

Even through my evening gown and his rough trousers, I could feel the thick rigidity of his erection.

At last, something I could work with.

"Captain, I—"

His grip tightened. "Beggin' will do ye no good, woman! The buyer wants ye dead. I keep me bargains!"

I cleared my throat gently. "I see. You have your own honor." I kept my tone even, with no attempt to be sultry . . . yet. "However, might I inquire—"

"The buyer's name be no concern of yers. Secrets be part of the deal."

"I would not ask you to break your word. I only want to know, before I die at your hands—" His fist tightened in my hair. I was careful not to flinch. "Did I fetch a good price? I should be ashamed to be assassinated for anything less than fifty pounds."

"Then ye've no worries 't all." He grunted in amusement. "I don't lift me hand for any less, meself."

"Thank you. I feel quite validated." I felt his hand loosen in my hair. He changed his grip. I fancied he enjoyed the silky feel of it. How nice to know that my years of rainwater rinsing hadn't been for naught.

I tried to ignore the sharp touch of the blade as it settled into a fresh position on my neck. "That is very painful," I mentioned mildly. "Was the cutting of my throat a specific request?"

"Does it matter?"

I could not shake my head and toss my hair. I could not face him to drop my eyelids half closed in a sultry manner. I could not reach behind me to seduce him with my touch, for my hands were bound before me. I did not think it wise to throw a sensual purr into my voice, although I spoke softly, as warmly as I dared. This man was no side-alley thug. He could not command this ship full of bandits without equal measure of brain and brawn.

Besides, painting myself too much of a piece of sexual meat could backfire, badly.

"I only wonder why the desired end would be so quick," I said with a hint of confusion in my tone. "If I am so hated by someone, I would expect they would request that I suffer terribly."

A grunt of dark amusement stirred the hairs on the back of my neck. "Aye, that ye might. Fair foamin' at the mouth, the buyer was. But if a soul is too squeamish to broker clear terms, I takes me own way. Quick and done. I got nothin' against whores, meself."

I am not a whore. I am a courtesan. I am an artist of love.

However, it didn't seem the right moment for that nuanced lecture. Perhaps another time.

If I had any more time.

"So your employer did not specify my end? How curious. If I should go to such trouble to rid myself of someone, I would be very particular."

More to the point, if I ever felt it necessary, I would do it myself. I had a wide knowledge of herbs and their uses. A bit of dried, ground foxglove in brandy would do the trick, and leave none the wiser.

My murderer was a fool. A rich fool, apparently.

Which didn't help much in identifying the particular enemy. I was a wicked creature who kept company with the highest stratum of London society. The list of rich fools who might hate me was rather depressingly long.

"No employer. I'm me own man, captain of the *Bodicea*! The buyer is just a buyer."

"I stand corrected. The buyer."

My pirate captor seemed to agree with me. "S'cowardly, 'tis. Too fancy to say the words, even." His tone went nasal and mocking. " 'Dispose of the harlot.' "

His ridicule of a highborn accent was rather good. Another time I might have smiled, or even laughed. At the moment, I had too many worries.

Did he say *dispose*?

"So your, uh, buyer did not actually mention killing? I am disappointed that I shall be taken down by someone so hypocritical." They all were, really. Every single person I knew in London, now that Ophelia and Malcolm had left.

My glittering existence in that grand city was merely gilt over dross, wasn't it? Especially if it were to end here, on the gently rocking deck of this dark ship, as my blood flowed overboard to be followed shortly by my lifeless body.

The night air was cold. My hands were icy and my feet were numb.

How could it be that the knife was so warm?

Steady. You have a chance, a tiny thread of hope. Pull upon it.

I gathered my despairing thoughts. "I suppose, if you wished it, you could 'dispose' of me in many ways."

"Aye," he replied. "Slittin' yer throat will hurt, I suppose, for a wee bit. I could toss ye into the sea. It'd be a near thing, whether ye'd drown first or be eaten by sharks. It's not so much a question of which one," he explained, "but in what order, if ye take me meanin'."

The horror his words invoked in my mind made my pulse throb loudly in my ears and my vision darken in panic. I couldn't faint. I knew that if I did, it would make it too easy for him. I would never awaken.

I heard the icy waves slap forcefully against the hull. The sea and sky were nothing but blackness outside the meager circle of light provided by the swinging lanterns. The never-ending wind was cold and salty against my face.

I forced my mind to return to the problem at hand. The monsters beneath the waves would have to wait just a moment longer to taste of me. "If your instructions are to dispose of me," I repeated, "then can you simply not take me somewhere else and toss me ashore? Would that not fulfill his lordship's request?" For I surmised that it must have been Lord H— who had hired out my demise. If his wife had dealt him the kind of prolonged torment she had so busily inflicted upon me, I could almost sympathize with the desperation of his motive.

The captain snorted. "I suppose it does no harm to tell you t'weren't no 'lord.' "

Ah. Her ladyship herself. I had not given her credit for the nerve to hire thugs on her own accord. I realized then that no amount of pain Lord H— went through would be too much. The lying bastard had ruined my life and did not possess the bollocks to temper his wife! I could only hope his life would be a long and hellish one in return!

My curiosity satisfied and my curses silently cast, I slowly lifted my bound hands before me until my cold fingers encountered his warm ones at my neck. "I could make the voyage most enjoyable for us both," I murmured so that his men could not overhear. "As for my disposal, any port will do, will it not?"

He did not speak, but I felt his grip loosen slightly. The roots of my hair tingled painfully, but I remained calm. "Where is your ship bound? Is there nowhere a woman like myself might find safe harbor?"

I don't know precisely what I said that convinced him. He

wasn't a talking man, either then or later in our acquaintance. Suddenly, I was standing quite alone. He stepped away, then slashed his knife down between my wrists. I was far too numb and slow to flinch, thank goodness. The ropes fell away from my wrists. He freed my feet as well.

I staggered and reached out, for I did not wish to fall at his feet. He caught my upper arm in a rough grip and began to haul me across the deck.

Had I ruined my last chance? Was he about to toss me into the black waves?

Then I saw the worn wood peak of a gangway before me, its door secured by a rusting latch. I was too chilled and dizzy to make my own way down the steep stair behind it, so I was once again tossed upon a thick male shoulder for my journey into the dark bowels of the ship.

A dark narrow hall. My side and shoulder dragged against the plain plank wall. Then, another doorway and a chilly, dark place. I could not suppress a yelp as I was tossed through the air. I landed sprawled onto a surface most familiar to me—a stuffed mattress.

Then a candle flame entered and I saw the captain take it from one of his crew. He used it to light a heavy iron–and-glass lantern. The dull glow filled the room and I saw we were in a bedchamber. The captain's cabin.

He shut the narrow door and locked it, then turned toward me. I braced myself on my cold hands and sat up warily.

"I have made promises and I shall keep them, Captain, but I do not wish to be forced."

"And I have no wish to force ye." The captain gave me a crooked smile. "Every day is a fight on this ship, so I'll be lookin' to you for a bit of comfort."

I realized that although he was unkempt and unshaven, he was not a foul-looking fellow. Not handsome either, but I hadn't found pretty men attractive. Not since the Duke of Mark.

"I'm an ugly sod. I know it." He grinned down at me. "Yer a right mess, yerself, milady."

I sat up and raised an eyebrow at him. "And whose fault is that?"

His grin widened. "But yer a sharp thing, nonetheless. Good. I like me cats with claws."

Stinking and disheveled on a stranger's bed, I drew myself up into the most dignified pose possible. "Perhaps you ought to outline your expectations of me, Captain."

He threw back his head and bellowed a deep laugh. I nearly smiled along with its infectiousness. When he looked back down at me, his eyes were twinkling.

"Pleasure, that's what ye promised, didn't ye?"

I nodded carefully. "I am quite skilled in it."

His gaze roamed over me. "Ye must be, I vow. For yer a skinny bird, with hardly an arse to fill the palm of me hand."

I could not be affronted by his assessment. Skinny I had always been. It seemed that no matter how I ate or drank, I could barely keep myself endowed with any bosom or bottom at all.

"Pretty eyes, though . . . like a misty morning."

"Thank you," I said seriously. "I feel quite fortunate in them. They also work very well."

His grin twisted. "More's the pity for ye tender sensibilities, then, for I'm no prancing lord."

I narrowed my eyes and tilted my head, plainly assessing him. "I like big men," I said. "And I suspect you'll clean up quite well, once you've had your bath."

He grunted in surprise. "What bath?"

"The bath you will take after I have had mine. The bath you will take before you come to my bed."

His gaze riveted on me for a long moment. I wondered if I had gone too far. He said he liked my sharpness. I hoped he'd not been lying.

Then a grin tugged at the corner of his mouth. "Aye, 'tis bout time I had a washing day at that, and ye look more mangy than some of me crew." Then his grin disappeared. He moved in close, until he loomed over me. With one callused finger beneath my chin, he lifted my gaze to meet his. "But it be my bed, little bird, and don't ye be forgettin' that."

I replied seriously. "Yes, Captain."

He nodded once, as if satisfied with my awareness of my place. "I've things to see to on deck," he said, turning to go. Then he turned back. "I'm glad I decided not to kill ye yet."

Yet. I fought the urge to swallow hard.

Still he must have seen me flinch, for he grinned again, toothily, like one of those aforementioned sharks.

"Like I said, I got nothin' against whores. I'll fetch ye a bucket of seawater." He left before I could say another word, shutting and locking the door behind him.

I decided that I would not make a point of correcting him. After all, I had just traded my body for my life. What did that make me?

Alive, I reminded my pride. *I am alive*.

The captain came to me with his hair still dripping from his seawater bath. I smiled at his capitulation.

His chest was bare beneath his open greatcoat. A drop of water fell from his curling hair and ran down between his pectorals. He was a well-built bandit, with well-defined muscles in his wide chest and abdomen. A mat of dark hair covered that chest and ran in an arrow of masculinity down to the waistband of his rough breeches.

The erection I had noticed on the deck was back. As he gazed at me, sitting on his bed clad only in my chemise and my own damp hair, it enthusiastically grew even more. I bit my lip in anticipation of the size of his attraction for me. I will not rank my lovers by such a superficial criteria, but suffice it to say that such length and breadth was always an intriguing surprise.

"I found your brandy." I raised my glass to him as I toyed with a lock of hair that hung between my breasts. "I may have started without you."

The white grin flashed once more, this time revealing one gold tooth. "I see that. Have no fear, darlin', I will be catching up to you before long. I'll just be takin' a moment to enjoy the view."

I took another slow sip, then licked my bottom lip while I considered him. I had thought he might lunge quickly upon me, finding me thus. I certainly had not expected easy banter and warm appreciation of my . . . er, wit.

Perhaps this was to be a somewhat tolerable journey after all.

It came as no surprise to me that the captain wanted to be on the bottom. I had found in my adventures that the more powerful a man was in life, the more powerless he wished to be in bed. Weak men wished to dominate me, and strong men wanted me to do all the work. Not that I minded, for the captain was a marvelously rough change from the procession of manicured men I had known.

The days passed. Though the captain remained passably clean, at least when he wished to come to my bed, he rarely shaved or combed his unruly mane. Though his voice was rough and his accent common, his big hands were gentle and skilled on a woman's flesh. Well, mostly gentle.

Perhaps at this juncture I should mention that the captain liked to spank.

The first time I discovered this, I was crawling over his naked body kissing my way up from the rigid erection that had just been deeply down my throat. I kissed his navel, licked his nipples, and then nibbled on his neck. I suppose I bit a little too hard. The next thing I knew, his hard hands had wrapped around my waist. I let out a yelp when I found myself being lifted easily off him and then deposited across his lap.

Slap, slap slap!

The first three smacks came fast and hard. I was so surprised that I failed to play along, as I might have with a little warning. Instead, I cursed him roundly and tried vainly to push off of him.

One wide palm pressed down across the small of my back and held me in place.

"Milady cusses like a guttersnipe," he accused me with laughter in his voice.

Slap, slap, slap, slap! I received a spank for each foul word that had slipped from my lips. The captain was not playing at punishment. Each hard slap echoed through the chamber. I imagine that the seamen in the next three cabins could hear perfectly well. The pain was startling and intense, but I was surprised how quickly the burn faded to a hot, radiating sensitivity.

I wasn't sure how to react. Anything I might say or do could be cause for more of the same. I wasn't afraid, exactly. After all, this man could kill me anytime he wished. So far he had preferred to bed me. If this was a bed game, then I simply needed to learn the rules.

His callused hand slid across my red-hot bottom, caressing and gently squeezing. My skin was wide-awake, alert to every touch. I shivered, and realized it was not from fear or pain.

Well, a little bit of pain.

Then with one hand still firmly pinning me down on his lap,

his other slid between my thighs. Two thick fingers found my slit and to my surprise, I was wet and more than ready. His fingertips found my clitoris and quickly coaxed me into an orgasm.

When I had panted my last moan into the coverlet, I raised my head to peer at him through my tangled hair. "I didn't . . . You shouldn't . . . ."

He grinned at me warmly, his gold tooth glinting. "Ye'll not be tellin' me what to do." His hand returned to my bottom and squeezed each buttock firmly. "Methinks you need another lesson."

I opened my lips to protest that I did not need another lesson, that I was well instructed in the art of pleasing a man, that there was no need to—

Slap. Slap. Slap!

I gave up on self-restraint at some point during this, and yelped freely. Tears began to gather in my eyes.

When it was over, I lay across his lap limply, weeping quietly. His big hand roamed across my hot, sensitized bottom with evident appreciation.

"Now there is a pretty sight," he murmured. "All rose and white, like a field of flowers." His hand slid down to test my readiness.

I was more than ready. I gasped and twitched at his single light touch.

In a deft maneuver, he moved me from his lap and then knelt between my sprawling legs where I lay facedown on the bed. With his big hands around my hips, he lifted me up to impale me upon his thick cock.

He made me come again before he roared like a jungle beast and thrust deep into me one last time.

He let me fall to the cot and then sprawled half on top of me as his cock throbbed inside me.

"Aye," he gasped. "It's like me papa always said. A hard hand brings a thorough job."

I laughed at him then, a low chuckle rasping from my spent throat. He rumbled a deep laugh back and then he casually fisted his hand in my hair and lifted my head from the bed to face him. He gazed fondly into my eyes.

"Ye liked it. I can tell t'weren't no playact. Ye'll not be bitin' me again, d'ye hear me?"

I met his gaze. "Yes, Captain."

Lesson learned.

Chapter Seven

At Sea

The captain kept me comfortable over the next several days, although I was without a doubt his captive. One afternoon, after the ship had been tossed by a storm, I watched from the cabin's porthole as the sun reappeared.

I glanced behind me to see the captain seated at his massive desk, the top spread with nautical charts. I dared to ask the question burning my lips. "Am I being held prisoner in your cabin?"

"Naught!" he declared cheerfully. He did not even look up from his charts. "The crew shouldn't bother ye none if you go topside, but be sure to keep yer pretty feet on the deck. No climbin' the riggin'."

I assured him that ascending the mast posed no temptation for me. He snorted at my double entendre, but his attention was then lost entirely as he focused on the charts before him.

My evening gown had been stained and torn in the shoulder and waist during my abduction. I wrapped the bed's coverlet about me to hide the exposed skin and opened the door to the captain's cabin for the first time since I had entered it six days before.

There was a long, dark hallway, so narrow that were I a voluptuous sort, I might have had to turn sideways. The captain had assured me that I had nothing to fear from his men and I ventured on. I had never been a timid sort, for my various personas over the years had not allowed it.

I smiled to think of Jinx. He would have liked this adventure. I briefly considered asking the captain for a suit of male clothing, so I could don Jinx's mask of nonchalance for the journey, but everyone on board already knew that I was a woman. In fact, I was certain they all believed me to be a whore, not a lady, despite my once-fine attire.

Would that work in my favor or not?

At the end of the hall ran a set of stairs that were nearly steep enough to be considered a ladder. I gathered my silk skirts in my hand and awkwardly managed to climb it. Ah, what I would not have given for Jinx's knee breeches!

I'll not pretend to have become any sort of expert on ships during my journey. There was a flat wooden deck above, which I recalled from my midnight near-murder. The creaking that I had since heard above my head was the result of the wind toying with the complicated arrangement of canvas, rope, metal, and wood that rose like a monument from the deck.

The stairs I had just ascended were framed in an angled roof, likely to keep the rain out of the stairwell. When I emerged from this little structure, with one hand up to shield my eyes from the daylight, I had assumed there would be some sort of reaction from the men on the deck.

There was none at all that I could see. A few glanced my way, then turned back to their work. It was clear that I did not exist in their world—or at least they knew better than to behave thusly. I wondered what sort of master the captain was, to inspire such profound obedience. Recalling the steel at my throat, I supposed that insubordination to such a man would have bloody and permanent consequences, especially out on the sea.

The deck was full of activity, but it proceeded at a measured pace. There was efficiency without urgency. Holding the coverlet tightly against the wind, I strolled the deck, carefully staying out of the way of the busy sailors. They ignored me for the most part.

I found my unfamiliar invisibility refreshing.

Then I noticed one fellow leering. I realized the wind had blown my cape from my ragged gown, revealing more of me than I intended. His open appreciation seemed harmless, but I did not welcome the captain's probable response to it. I tried to ignore him, turning my back to him although the wind whipped my hair into my face from that direction.

One of his fellows spoke sharply to him. I heard a hard smack, and then a thud. I stiffened at the obvious sound of violence, but did not turn. Instead, I began to make my way back to the stairway. My enjoyment of the fresh air had chilled along with my body. I no longer wanted to be on the deck.

Loud shouts ensued. Some of the men near me raised their attention from their tasks. A few even started toward the ruckus, running past me, leaving mops and tools and ropes to fend for themselves. I hurried to the small housing of the stairway. Only then did my curiosity outweigh my caution.

I looked over my shoulder to see a brawl in the making. Several of the sailors were fighting each other in earnest, while others encircled them. Some chided the antagonists. Some urged them to further violence. In the center of them all was the large, bold fellow who had dared to look openly upon the captain's woman.

I scampered down the steps with no regard to modesty, then ran as quickly as I could down the hall to the door of the captain's cabin. Opening it, I slipped inside and gently shut the door behind me.

The captain remained at his desk, the charts still spread before him, but this time his attention was arrested. I realized with a sinking heart that the sound of the brawl could be clearly sensed through the ship's wooden skeleton. I could practically feel the thud of bodies through the vibration in the walls, beams, and floor.

I folded my hands before me. "It did not go well on deck." I thought it would be best to inform him immediately. I was certainly capable of lying, and doing it well, but this was not the sort of man by whom I would care to be caught in a lie!

"Hmm." He glared at me, his heavy brows drawn together. I swallowed. He could be a very frightening person, my seagoing lover.

"I did not speak to anyone," I said, hating the way my voice shook. "I tried to stay out of the way, so no one would notice me."

He drew back at that. "How could a man not notice ye?"

I had heard pretty words with similar sentiment before—but he did not mean to flatter me. Besides, as the only woman on a ship with forty men, I could resemble a barrel and still be an object of attraction.

He tapped his fingertips on the maps for a moment. I was surprised at his hesitation, for he did not seem the indecisive sort. Then, when there came a rap at his door, I realized he'd been waiting to see if his first mate could address the issue without him.

The first mate entered the cabin. He shot me a single sour glance. There was fresh blood on his sleeve near his wrist, and a bruise forming along his cheek.

"Aye, O'Neill?" The captain's tone was deceptively mild.

The first mate nodded shortly. "T'was Niles, cap'n." He

inclined his head in my direction without looking directly at me. "She didn't speak to no one, nor smile even."

For a moment, I was grateful for his validation of my behavior, but then his lips twisted in anger. "Didn't have to, now did she?"

I found out later that my short visit to the deck had cost the man Niles his life, and the ship its strongest crewman.

I did not leave the captain's cabin again. This was not a pleasure cruise, and I was not among gentlemen. The captain's previously amiable treatment of me remained civil, but had lost some of its congenial nature. There was no more easy teasing, and certainly no more freedom. It was very clear that a woman did not belong on the ship, and that I was held responsible for the death of a man whose name I'd not heard until he died violently on the deck, the same deck where I could yet meet my end.

Locked into the captain's cabin as I now was, I often had little idea of what happened elsewhere unless the captain saw fit to inform me. In the days following Niles's death, my seagoing lover became even more surly and withdrawn.

Even as tightly wound as the captain was, he still wanted me. If anything, he wanted me more. I found myself appeasing him with lovemaking out of some sort of survival instinct. I had always been good with difficult men. My childhood in the warrens of Newgate no doubt had something to do with my alertness to any hint of anger directed my way.

However, the captain's battened-down rage seemed to have little to do with me. Indeed, his former swaggering seductions and rough playfulness became something altogether more tender. He silenced his bluster and kept his swearing tongue taughtly to himself, as if he feared to speak something into existence in superstitious fear. As he relished the feeling of my skin against his palm, or buried his face in my hair to breathe deeply of me, I had the strangest feeling that he was memorizing me.

This struck me as simultaneously poignant and utterly terrifying. If he already mourned my loss, what did that mean for my precarious future? What danger loomed to make such a fearless ruffian hold me so close in the darkness?

His increased hunger for me was almost more than I could appease. He came to me at night, of course, and also pulled me to him early in the morning. A few times, he even ducked into his cabin in the middle of the day, sweeping me from my little fabricated occupations to carry me to his bed, where he would take me with fierce and aching attention.

It was on one such early evening that he entered the low door, ducking through in such a rush he barely bothered to slow down. I expected him to reach for me. Instead he stood in the middle of the room, drenched in seawater, breathing heavily. He looked as though he'd been in a terrific brawl. The captain's surcoat was torn at the shoulder, exposing the lining. It swung open and my gaze fixed upon the twining, exposed threads where the proud gold buttons had once hung.

I shook off my stunned puzzlement and met his black gaze with wide eyes.

"Are we being boarded?" He had often told tales of the dangers of the smuggler's life, of losing the goods to pirates and even the military, which looted under the guise of apprehending miscreants.

He shook his head and spat one word. "Mutiny."

I swallowed hard against the fear that lodged in my throat like a stone. If the crew took over—if he lost authority over that brutal mob . . .

"They'll kill ye," he growled. "After they rape ye, to a man. Use ye up and toss ye to the sharks."

Later, I would piece together the small things he had told me in confidence, of the payloads they had lost to raiders or that had to be thrown overboard when the military was in pursuit.

One too many losses might have created an air of dissatisfaction among the crew and led to Niles's disobedience. The captain did not say as much, but I knew things had changed after the day his best sailor lost his life. Perhaps the death of one of their own would not have unduly disturbed the crew on a more profitable voyage. Or one with fewer storms and sickness. Or one without the presence of a woman to stir discontent.

In that moment, however, I could only rise and dress quickly with shaking hands. I made a silent vow that I would throw myself overboard before allowing myself to be meat for the ravenous hounds. Yet I also knew my bravado might fail when the moment came. Ever the survivor, I might hang on to the last, fully aware of the horrible assault that was to come.

The captain was pulling me toward the door I had not passed through since my doomed trip to the deck. His hard grasp kept me on my feet, though my fear made me clumsy on the steep stairs at the end of the passageway.

Then the cold air of the deck struck my face and I saw that it was only just sunset, the last rays still streaming through the low, heavy clouds above us, glazing the choppy waves with diamond points of light.

That sea, that sun, and that lowering sky would linger in my memory as a singular moment of spectacular beauty, an instant of calm before the blood and madness that followed.

He towed me along the deck. I lifted the skirts of my ruined opera gown with my free hand, careless now of any that might see my ankles or calves. I ran hard, fleeing the fight that rampaged bloodily at the foredeck. I could hear the grunts and howls and even screams of pain. I could hear the thuds and slashing ringing of steel on steel and horrible, wet noises where steel murdered flesh—but I did not look back.

I quickly realized he was taking me to the aft starboard

where the jolly boats hung from their pulleys, always ready to launch should the smugglers need to abandon ship.

The captain shoved me low with a single barked order, "Down!" I dropped to my knees beside the rope-wound crank. Only then did I risk that single glance behind.

I immediately wished I hadn't. The last man standing was the faithful first mate, O'Neill. The giant fellow loomed like a wall between the mutineers and his captain—and by association, myself. Just ahead of O'Neill was an advancing horde.

With a roar of triumph, the mutineers sprang at the outnumbered first mate, and the human wall fell. Our last hope crumbled beneath the vengeful hacking blades of the murderous crew.

Perhaps not our last hope? The captain untied the jolly boat and the small vessel began to swing out over the side of the ship. Only a single rope held it in place.

The captain knelt and wrapped his thick arm around my waist. He tossed me into the dinghy and I fell to my knees. I landed upon something made of iron that tore into my leg with hot ferocity. I could not help but cry out.

It was not a loud sound, but it was enough to attract the attention of the marauders. I saw their menacing figures near the ship's starboard side, their faces mere pale ovals in the twilight.

"Captain!" I cried out to him and held out my hand. "Come!"

He risked a look over his shoulder. As if that was all that was needed to loose the hounds, they sprang into motion.

"Come!" I ordered again, but his instincts could not be so easily abolished. The captain turned to face his crew, holding out one hand. "Stand down!" he called out, his voice commanding and deep.

For an instant, I hoped they might actually heed him. But

the bloodlust was too far gone. I had never before seen a murdering mob, but I saw one then. The captain must have realized it as well, for he turned toward me.

I held out my hand, pleading him to come into the boat with me. It was too late, and he knew it. He pulled his sword, but instead of turning to defend himself, he swung one mighty arc—and severed the rope keeping the jolly boat attached.

The little wooden boat swung in a violent outward arc, nearly flinging me over the side. If not for the heavy iron contraption tangled in my skirts, I might have been lost then and there, his sacrifice for naught.

Then I heard the pulleys running freely and I began to fall. The boat struck the water with a mighty smack that sent me hard to the wooden bottom. My head struck oak and my vision swam. I might have blacked out if not for a clear shout coming from one of the men. "She's still hitched! Pull her up, lads!"

I scrambled, dizzy and shaken, to the side of the jolly boat, where one rope still twined about the iron pulley bolted there.

Even as the rope began to raise the boat above the water once more, bashing it into the side of the ship, I frantically dug at the soaked hemp with useless fingers. Then something snapped, and I felt the rope slither out of my hands with a force that burned the skin of my palms. I released it and fell back against the side of the boat. The small craft hit the water once again.

There were lanterns on the deck now, globes of light held high and searching, but I had already drifted outside of that weak circle.

I bowed my forehead to the splintery seat of the skiff and closed my eyes against the sight of those searching lanterns, as if hiding my face could hide an entire dinghy.

I lifted my gaze, suddenly afraid one of the men had jumped overboard to retrieve me.

It was then that I saw, by the hellish glare of the mutineers' lanterns, the captain go down beneath the flailing blows of the angry crew. I rose to my knees but caught no more glimpse of him in the melee.

I drifted farther away from the ship. Once the darkness closed about me completely, I leaned over the side of the boat to vomit violently into the sea. My shaking body slid down into the bottom of the tiny craft and I let unconsciousness overwhelm me, if only to block out my dark imaginings of the captain's fate.

I do not remember how long I lay unconscious, but I recall waking to a great *crack!* and flash of light. Another storm, and instead of being dry and sheltered in the captain's cabin, I was tossed helplessly on the waves, beaten by rain, and powerless to do aught but cling to a battered boat now taking on water.

Through the slashing downpour and pounding waves, I looked up. I blinked against the storm, attempting to discern whether I was dreaming. Was that a row of lamplights upon higher ground? Could those be dwellings on a coast? The thought that I was so near to safety gave me hope.

I shouted and screamed until my throat was raw, though I knew one woman's cry would be lost in the thunder, white-capped waves, and rain.

Suddenly, the tiny boat was heaved upward and slammed down again. I tumbled half out and became lost in the water, clinging to the boat's bench with my hands. The skirts of my gown twisted about my legs as I struggled to find air. Then the small wooden boat crashed against something hard and slick, breaking apart beneath me.

I heard the wood splinter—or was that my own bone? My fingers clawed. Pain wracked my body.

The Swan was no more.

THE PRESENT

Chapter Eight

London

The woman flashed like a gilded beacon in a sea of gray. She was faced away from Fitch, stuck in a crowded UK customs queue, a pair of dark sunglasses perched on a sleek head of pale blond hair. Her legs were long and lean, covered in tight denim and tucked into a pricey pair of high-heeled, knee-high leather boots with fancy silver buckles at the ankles. She held an expensive bag in the crook of her arm and struck a pose—one leg slightly extended, slim hip cocked. She looked like an impatient supermodel. He was acquainted with the type.

The attitude gave her away as American, somewhere in her early thirties, and arriving at Heathrow for something other than tourism. She held herself like a gal with important places to go and notable people to meet.

"Step lively, Wilder. Keep your focus on one stunning blonde at a time, please." Winston's assistant, Miles, patted the rolling shipping crate with reverence as he pushed it through the airport.

Fitch took one last peek. The woman had turned just enough for him to see the soft curve of her cheek in profile, the angular line of her chin. Certainly beautiful—and oddly familiar. He pushed down a strange twinge of recognition, telling himself that his problem was that it had been too long since he'd enjoyed the company of a beautiful woman. Under different circumstances, he would have waited for this particular woman to clear customs and then suggest they recover from jet lag together.

It was not to be.

"You cramp my damn style, Miles."

His travel companion rolled his eyes.

Winston had dispatched his personal assistant Miles Bancroft to babysit *The Siren* on its trip from Paris to London. If there hadn't been a gigantic finder's fee waiting for Fitch at journey's end, the arrangement would have been intolerable. Miles had insisted on maintaining physical contact with the crated canvas at all times, patting it on the short, private jet ride, and now wheeling it around like a newborn in a stroller.

Fitch made a mental note to push for a "no assistant" clause when he negotiated his next assignment with Winston. Hunting down the fate of at least eight missing portraits was going to be detective work, pure and simple. It was work he preferred to do alone.

The instant the two men stepped through Heathrow's automatic doors and onto the curb, a shiny, black SUV appeared. Miles and the driver exchanged pleasantries, wasting no time before they gingerly placed the crate inside a custom foam-lined trunk and buckled it in place. H. Winston Guilford might have more issues than a magazine rack, but he did treat his art collection with respect, which was fine by Fitch.

He took a seat in the back while Miles rode shotgun. It was a forty-five-minute drive through London traffic to Kensington Square, and since no one seemed to be in a chatty mood, Fitch decided to check his voicemails and email. It didn't take long before he realized he couldn't concentrate.

All he could think about was *that woman*. She reminded him of someone, someone who elicited in him a strange mix of attraction and anger. It felt as if he'd observed her out of context in the customs queue. Was she an actress he'd seen in an otherwise forgettable movie? Had he bought her a drink in New York, Rome, or Paris? Her identity—and why she looked so familiar to him—was a mystery.

And mysteries bugged the hell out of him.

Winston must have been waiting at the door. He bolted from his elegant row house as soon as the SUV pulled into the semicircular drive. He made a beeline for the trunk, refusing all offers to assist him with the crate. He struggled with the large container as he made his way up the front marble stairs and through the foyer. He and the painting disappeared into his private elevator without a word.

As the elevator door closed, Fitch glanced at Miles. "I guess he wants us to take the stairs."

When they reached the third floor, Winston was already in The Siren Gallery, on his hands and knees on the gleaming parquet floor, frantically using a hammer and screwdriver to disassemble the packaging. Miles and Fitch knew to keep their distance, and remained a good ten feet away as he ripped open the crate like a sugar-buzzed kid on Christmas morning. Eventually, Winston stretched out his arms to support the large canvas in front of him. Tears rolled down his cheeks.

Miles cleared his throat. "Mr. Guilford—"

"Out! Both of you!"

"The framer is on his way, Mr. Guilford. Perhaps you shouldn't handle the canvas until it is safely—"

"Out!" Winston then turned his glare on Fitch. "And you— I know what you're up to. I'll contact you should I decide we have anything further to discuss."

Fitch nodded and backed out. "I'll be in London for the rest of the week. You know where to find me."

Once downstairs, Miles assured Fitch that his bags were on

their way to his B and B and offered him a lift in another vehicle. Fitch turned him down. "A walk will do me good."

He made his way out through the electronic gate, then headed up Derry Road, across Kensington High Street, and past Kensington Palace. Being early May in London, the weather was far from postcard perfect and certainly not ideal for a stroll through the park. That was fine with him since it would thin the tourist herd. Fitch pulled up the collar on his suit jacket and shoved his hands in his trouser pockets, continuing with his walk.

There was no question that he missed the clear blue sky and intense sunshine of home, but he knew in his gut that he had other places to go first. Winston would take the bait. He would call Fitch and insist on knowing about the poem and any other test results. No question.

The question was where, exactly, Fitch would begin his search for the rest of The Siren paintings, and his only real clue had him leaning toward Spain.

The artist had called *The Siren* a "gift from a Catalan storm," and referred to himself as a "poor *soldat dement*," which meant "crazy soldier" in the language of Catalonia, a region along the Mediterranean in northeast Spain.

As far as clues went, Fitch realized these were just a place to start. The good news was that these clues did not contradict the scientific analysis of the most recent Siren painting. Data obtained from the testing of pigments, cracking patterns, and the olivewood canvas stretcher were compatible with the geographic region of Catalonia during or after the Peninsular War.

As he continued to walk, Fitch felt that familiar rush go through him, the electric buzz that told him he was closing in on something big. It occurred to him that he was now closer to uncovering the history of The Siren than anyone had ever been.

His leisurely stroll had left him damp. Fitch decided to duck into the pub for a pint and a hot bite to eat.

"Fitch! Good to see you, old chap." Davy the bartender reached out his hand for a firm shake. "How long will you be gracin' us with your presence?"

Fitch laughed. Whenever he had business in London he stayed at the same Russell Square B and B just a few doors down from Davy's Pub, home of a killer shepherd's pie and a wide variety of India pale ales on tap. He had known Davy for almost a decade.

"Just a few days."

"Bad news for London's lovelies, but you'll make the most of it, right? So what'll you have?"

As the shepherd's pie and ale warmed his bones, Davy updated Fitch on his wife, kids, business, and British politics. The familiar bell over the door tinkled every so often, causing Davy to interrupt his narration to greet each new customer with a friendly shout. Most, if not all of them, were regulars.

But then the bell rang and Davy looked up in silence, his eyes widening and his mouth going slack. Fitch turned to check out the unexpected customer.

Golden hair sparkling with drizzle. Knee-high boots fit for a musketeer. Such a stern expression on such a pretty face.

Dark shades. In the rain.

With precision, the new arrival snatched the sunglasses off her head and looked around. "Do I seat myself?" She looked Davy's way.

"Please. Anywhere you like."

"Thank you."

And suddenly it clicked. That woman in the airport—the woman who was now striding across the old wood floors just three feet in front of him—was none other than Dr. Brenna Anderson, his favorite ball-busting Harvard sociology professor. No wonder he hadn't been able to place her! He'd only talked to her on the phone and seen her in photos and videos.

So what the hell was she doing in London?

Oh, shiiiit.

Fitch spun around on his bar stool and propped his chin in his palm. Her timing was no coincidence, of course. The only reason she would be here, now, was *The Siren*. Damn, but that woman would *just not give up*! She was here on a fool's errand if she thought she could force Winston to let her see the newest—or any—painting. Fitch already knew how that matchup would end. Still, it might be fun to watch.

The professor chose a corner booth near the window. Fitch observed her out of the corner of his eye. There was no need to rush things, he decided. This was an unexpected encounter, but it didn't have to be an unpleasant one, despite their history. He just had to figure out the best way to approach her.

In a husky voice, Dr. Anderson ordered a pot of tea and a Cornish pasty. Fitch tried to remember the last time he'd spoken with her on the phone—well over a month ago now, when she was still trying to wedge herself into the authentication process. He'd thanked her for her interest but declined her help, assuring her he'd already determined the painting was legitimate.

And *whoa*—she'd launched into what felt like an interrogation. Which lab was running the tests? Had he done microscopic analysis of the pigment and binder? Had anything interesting come up on the infrared reflectology, like an underpainting? How deep and extensive was the craquelure? Any sign of restoration work? At that point, Fitch simply wanted the torture to end. He told her he had no idea what the Michel-Blanc planned to do about testing. Then he hung up.

And now she sat just a few feet away, a woman who had never tried to hide her disdain for Fitch. She was a puzzle to him. How did she get those sharp edges? She couldn't have reached her level of achievement without some redeeming qualities, but seriously—he'd known plenty of nerdy academics who possessed at least some sense of humor. Why didn't she?

He wondered if he'd ever get a chance to see what she'd look like with a smile on her lovely face.

Fitch sipped his IPA, deciding to give the professor a chance to enjoy her meal. She might be more open to conversation afterward.

"So you know her?"

Fitch frowned at Davy and put a finger to his lips. The last thing he wanted was for Brenna Anderson to think he was gossiping about her. "Not exactly," he whispered. "We know *of* each other. She's an American academic and we have common interests."

Davy leaned his elbows on the bar and peeked around Fitch to get a look at the corner booth. "If you ask me, you'd be daft not to go talk to her."

"I didn't ask you." Fitch finished off his ale. "Besides, that woman is hard-core. She can be a complete—"

"Excuse me!"

Davy perked up and went over to her table. He came back and spoke out of the side of his mouth. "She's askin' for the bill. You best make your move."

Fitch placed cash on the bar. He donned a mask of friendly surprise and approached Dr. Brenna Anderson's booth.

His mask melted.

She sat in the glow of a wall sconce, framed by a large window overlooking the rainy evening street. Her head was bowed as she hurriedly buttoned her trench coat, causing her hair to fall like a curtain of gold satin around her face.

Fitch stared. Then he stared some more. He knew he was being rude but he was powerless to do anything about it. His feet had morphed into concrete blocks and screwed themselves into the floor joists. She looked tired, and even a little vulnerable. He could not take his eyes off her.

The professor's fingers suddenly stopped moving. Her shoulders stiffened. Slowly, she raised her head, blinking in disbelief.

Nothing existed but her. There was no noisy pub, no pulse in Fitch's veins, no sense of time or place. The only reality was her gorgeous face now lifted toward him in the light. He felt heat slowly spread across his chest.

What did he see in those stunning pastel-blue eyes? Was she embarrassed to be caught by surprise like this? Something else?

The vision began to speak.

"What . . . the actual . . . *fuck*?" The professor stared. "*You*? Seriously?"

This was bad. Very, very bad. Brenna kept telling herself that she despised this man. She kept trying to reach inside herself to locate that hard ball of righteous anger she felt for him, but all she found were butterflies.

Fitch Wilder had seated himself across from her under the pub light, making it easy for her to detect a few narrow strands of silver in his light brown curls. His early crow's-feet were highlighted too, along with the stubble along his jaw and two identical deep lines at the corners of his lips. She had no idea how old he was. Late thirties probably, unless the New Mexico sun had aged him prematurely.

Those were spectacular man-lips, by the way. What had her student called him? *Smokin'*?

It had to be the jet lag.

Brenna pulled herself together and addressed him in a calm tone of voice. "How lovely that you've added stalking to your repertoire of skeezy professional services."

Wilder's chuckle was warm and rich. Flat-out sexy. And she certainly didn't want to associate warmth, richness, or sex with this man. What a disaster.

"It's a pleasure to finally meet you, Dr. Anderson." His eyes twinkled as he flashed a wide, white smile. "So what brings you to London?"

She leaned back into the booth and crossed her arms tight across her buttoned coat. "I'm on sabbatical, if you must know."

He nodded, glancing casually out the window to the busy London street. "So you're doin' one of those eat-pray-love kinda things?"

She ignored his snarky commentary, feeling giddy with relief as the bitterness finally rose to the surface. "And you, Wilder? London is awfully far away from your home on the range."

As he stared at her, Brenna saw nothing but a friendly curiosity in his eyes. She stared back at him with what she hoped was the same benign politeness. But wait . . . what color were his irises, exactly? Green? Gray? Did she see flecks of gold in there, too? And why were his eyelashes so long?

"I'm here on business."

She had to get out of there. Brenna gathered her bag and began to scoot out of the booth. "This has been fun, fun, fun, but I need to go."

"Will you try to see Guilford while you're here?"

She stilled, raising an eyebrow. "I am here for academic research, Wilder, and I have a very full schedule starting early in the morning. Mr. Guilford is not on that schedule."

That was a true statement. She wouldn't insist on seeing him until she had definitive proof of a connection between The Swan and The Siren, which wouldn't be for a few days yet.

"Huh." Fitch glanced down at his hands and looped his fingers together. He had beautiful hands—wide and masculine. She wondered how they would feel caressing her hip, her thigh . . .

"Guilford's got the sixth painting. I just delivered it to him."

Brenna stood up, her heart racing. She tried not to think of it—that six of the seven existing Siren paintings were within walking distance and in a few days she'd have enough information to gain access to them. The idea was thrilling—but not as thrilling as the secret knowledge that there was one more portrait, in Boston, and she and Claudia were the only human beings on earth who had any inkling of The Siren's real identity.

She smiled at him. He looked startled. Then a little alarmed. *Good.*

Wilder stood, too. He became a barricade of manly flesh, a head taller than herself and built like an athlete. He had chosen to wear a dark blue button-down shirt and gray tweed jacket with jeans and, not surprisingly, a pair of scuffed-up Western boots.

Brenna looked away, but in doing so inadvertently caught the scent of him—a mix of rain and clean male skin that sent a shiver of awareness up her spine. And though he wasn't exactly blocking her exit, she felt confined nonetheless.

"Excuse me." Brenna took a wide step around him.

"She's really something, you know."

His words caused Brenna to spin on her heels. She looked up into his eyes. There was more to this man than she'd assumed. He was rather sharp. And he wanted to go toe-to-toe with her in regards to The Siren Series.

The poor fellow was out of his league.

She was Dr. Brenna Anderson, the youngest sociology faculty member to earn tenure in the history of Harvard. And she knew something he did not. She held the key he didn't even know existed.

"She's fascinating, all right." Brenna smiled, batted her eyelashes, and headed toward the pub door.

"See you around."

"Not likely."

Only after Brenna's feet reached the wet pavement of Montague Street was she able to breathe.

Dear God! She had never been blindsided by a man like that! She'd known plenty of shockingly attractive men in her life, and she'd always maintained the upper hand, and proudly so. She had taught Piper how to handle Mick Malloy, with complete success. So why had she felt so unsure of herself? Was it because he'd caught her unaware? Was it, in fact, due to jetlag? Or was it because while rehearsing this meeting in her mind over the years she had always envisioned Fitch Wilder to be a dolt devoid of charm and wit?

She began her short walk to The Montague on the Gardens Hotel. *One of those eat-pray-love things?* That was actually quite funny.

She did her best not to smile.

"She's getting so big, Piper!" Brenna threw one last kiss to her best friend's dark-haired angel, now being whisked away by her daddy.

"Say bye-bye to Auntie Brenna."

Little Ophelia reached out with an open palm and squeezed her chubby fingers open and closed. This baby version of a wave never failed to make Brenna laugh.

Piper waited for her husband, Mick, to leave the room and returned her attention to the video chat. "So what have you found out?"

"I hardly know where to begin, Pipes. This has been an immensely productive visit. The first thing I've got to tell you is I found her house! It's still there! It's a real estate office now, but the Georgian-era building is still lovely."

"Are you kidding? Did you find her legal name?"

Brenna shook her head. "Not yet, but everything started to come together once I tracked down the scandal sheets' coverage of The Swan's downfall. Those things were brutal, almost like a Regency England version of revenge porn. They printed her address and her daily routine and encouraged the 'respectable' members of society to commit acts of vandalism and violence. It was unbelievable."

"Sounds like terrific stuff. Since it's related to Ophelia's world, I'd love to get copies."

"Absolutely. I've got a whole stack of stuff to send you, but in the meantime you've got to let me read this one thing to you."

"I can't wait."

Brenna grabbed a copy of the document she'd uncovered at the British Newspaper Museum. "This is dated April 13, 1827— and keep that in mind because it's important later. This is from something called *Fannie's Follies*, which was filled with unflattering cartoons of public figures and gossip about balls and country houses and who did what to whom, kind of like TMZ but without a pesky legal department."

Piper laughed.

"So the article is accompanied by a horrific drawing of The Swan." Brenna held up a printout of the shot she'd taken with her phone in which The Swan had been drawn with big webbed feet sticking out from The hem of her dress, a long and crooked white neck, and a huge orange beak. She was portrayed as thin as a skeleton. "So here's what the article says. 'The diseased fowl known as The Swan still paddles her way through the muck of the lowest engagements, her gaudy attire unable to hide her moral depravity and near-constant inebriation, her jewels in contrast to the greenish tint of her social distemper.'"

"Damn," Piper whispered.

"There's more. 'Take heed good wives to protect your husbands from the reach of her foul evil, and remember that only chaste conduct can combat the hideousness of fornicative consequences.' "

"They didn't mess around."

"Right? So once I got her address I found her home was in a solicitor's name, and with that I discovered records of bank deposits, accounts, and household staff records. But by late April of 1827—nothing. She completely disappeared. The house was sold five years later in what was referred to as a 'decrepit and un-used state.' There was no mention of her again in any context."

"So they ran her out of town."

"Seems so. But the question is where did she go? I found that her solicitor purchased ship passage to the states for April 23, 1827, but the newspapers reported he was in court trying a case three days later. He might have bought it for her."

"Did she go?"

"I have no idea, but records show the ship arrived safely in New York as scheduled, no wrecks or mishaps. And you know better than I that Ophelia never made any mention of seeing The Swan again. And if we're to believe the handwriting on the back of Claudia's portrait—"

"She went to Catalonia. So that's where you need to follow her trail."

"I plan on it, but first I have to make my pitch to Guilford. I need to pique his interest and get him to talk to me. Then I'll promise to share my future research in exchange for access to the paintings. Piper, this is my chance and I won't let it slip through my fingers no matter who is here to stop me."

Piper tipped her head and frowned. "Why would someone try to stop you?"

"Oh." Brenna cleared her throat and tidied the copied documents. "I forgot to mention—because it's really not that important—but Fitch Wilder is here."

Chapter Nine

London

"Spain? Are you certain?"

Winston was holding court with Fitch in his private Siren Gallery. They were seated in front of Fitch's laptop at a small library table. Behind Winston was the pregnant muse, gloriously framed in gilt on the south-facing wall, claiming the place set aside just for her.

The painting was centered beneath a recessed fiber-optic lighting system designed to maximize visibility while limiting ultraviolet and infrared light damage. Along with the other paintings, it was secured by an alarm system and protected by a climate maintained at a constant eighteen degrees Celsius and 50 percent relative humidity.

The *Mona Lisa* wished she had it so good.

It had taken Winston four days to summon Fitch to his Kensington Square home, which had given Fitch enough time to prepare a detailed proposal. Winston now glared at the large screen of Fitch's laptop, repeating his question.

"Are you absolutely sure?"

"Of course not, Winston. The only thing I'm sure about is

test data, because data never lie. The poem goes beyond data. It's a glimpse."

"A glimpse of what?"

"The heart of the painter. The poem tells us that the day the artist put his paintbrush to this particular canvas, he had already painted The Siren *thirteen* times. That means your latest acquisition is, in sequential order, the fourteenth portrait."

Winston's eyes widened.

"You have only six, which means there could be at least eight additional paintings out there in the world somewhere, in barns and attics and thrift shops and closed-up apartments, anywhere on the planet! I'd like to find them for you."

Winston rested his chin on a fist, gazing at the flowing cursive writing displayed on Fitch's laptop. "He hid the poem on purpose?"

"It was no accident. The artist allowed the poem to dry completely before he painted over it."

"And what's this 'crazy soldier' nonsense in Catalan?" Winston pointed to the first line of the second stanza.

Fitch shrugged. "I really have no clue what that's about or why the painter would call himself that. It might even be a kind of inside joke."

Winston looked away from the laptop and surveyed all six paintings in his gallery. "Are there poems beneath all of them, do you think?"

"We will never know unless—"

"Absolutely not." Winston closed his eyes and shook his head. "I can't allow beauty to be reduced to digitized data. I couldn't live with myself."

"Would you at least hear me out?"

He opened one eyelid.

"How about we make a deal? You finance my search and

give me permission to test whatever portraits I find *before* I deliver them to their rightful home."

"Why would I do that?"

Fitch grinned. "Because I'm that good and you know it. If the paintings are out there, I'll find them."

"Hmmph."

"You could always hire someone else, of course, someone who wouldn't ask for such a concession. But they'll come back empty-handed, and the rest of The Siren Series will be lost forever. Could you live with that?"

Winston narrowed his eyes at Fitch. "You think I'm so mad and so wealthy that I'd pay for your open-ended treasure hunt-slash-holiday to Spain's Costa Brava?"

Fitch laughed. "Well, you're the richest and craziest bastard I've ever met."

Winston laughed, too. His guffaw bounced off the gallery walls. He was obviously giddy with the idea of possessing every Siren painting ever made. Suddenly, Winston stopped laughing, sighed deeply, and looked once more at the laptop screen. "Why, Fitch?"

"Why what?"

"The testing. Why is it so bloody important to you?"

Fitch figured there was no risk in answering him truthfully. Winston couldn't exactly accuse him of being eccentric. "I believe I owe it to the paintings, to my father, even, to put all the puzzle pieces together. He didn't have access to the technology available today. If he had, I know he would have used it. He would have wanted to know."

Winston shook his head. "Lovely. Now tell me the real reason."

Fitch chuckled. "Hell, Winston. You know I can't tolerate a mystery. To you, the enigmatic origins of The Siren make her more desirable, more valuable, larger than life. All I see is a treasure map, a riddle that's taunting me, daring me to solve it. I can't walk away."

A knock on the door interrupted their conversation. Miles stuck his head inside. "Mr. Guilford, sir, there is someone here to see you. She says it's urgent."

"Well, who is it?"

"It's that Harvard professor, Dr. Anderson. She insisted I give you this note."

Winston wiggled his fingers for Miles to enter, snatching the piece of cheap stationery from his hand as soon as it was at arm's length. He quickly unfolded it with a look of annoyance on his face.

Fitch could plainly see the raised block print at the top of the paper. Apparently, Dr. Anderson was staying at a hotel just a few blocks from his B and B.

"Dear God!" Winston shoved the letterhead toward Fitch. "Is there a sign on my door? Does it bid welcome to 'all ye who claim to have groundbreaking evidence on the origins of The Siren Series'?"

Fitch wasn't laughing.

In a fine script, Dr. Anderson had written just two sentences.

My new research indicates that The Siren was an infamous London courtesan who disappeared in 1827. I know a good portion of her story, and I think you should wish to know it, too.

Fitch stared at the note. What in the hell was this? Why was she suddenly confident enough to make such a strange claim?

Fitch glanced up at Miles, then Winston. "Aren't you going to let her in?"

"Bloody hell, no!" Winston stood. "You're hired, Wilder, and that woman is now your problem. Find out what this drivel is all about and go find me my *bloody paintings*!" Winston lowered his very English chin and smiled down at Fitch. "And one other thing."

Fitch stood, tucking the folded stationery into his jacket pocket and dreading the other thing.

"Two weeks," Winston said. "That's all I'm paying for. And I expect a daily progress report." He gestured for Fitch to see himself out. "Perhaps I'm not so mad after all, eh, Wilder?"

The shiny brass doors of H. Winston Guilford's elevator opened and Fitch Wilder came strolling out. Brenna groaned inwardly, her mind racing to the fact that he must have read her note! *Dammit!* She should have known he'd be territorial about Winston.

With a few long strides, a still-smiling Wilder was at her side. "Hello, Dr. Anderson." Without her permission, he slipped his hand through the crook of her arm and pivoted her toward the door.

"Take your hand off me!"

A shiny black SUV pulled up to the house.

"Are you kidnapping me?"

There it was again—that husky, warm laugh. She really wished he wouldn't do that. It was distracting.

"Kidnapping isn't as lucrative as one might think, Professor. I'll just stick to murder for hire." He leaned down and rapped his knuckles on the front passenger door. The driver opened it. "Yes, sir?"

"Montague on the Gardens, please."

Dammit! Not only did he know what she was working on, he knew where she was staying! Thank God for small victories—she'd been wise to leave out any detail in Guilford's note. If she had mentioned The Swan by name she would have jeopardized any chance she had to publish original research. She wouldn't put it past Wilder to make another round of TV talk shows for the sole purpose of pirating her latest work. Just for the fun of it.

"Shall we?" He opened the door for her.

"We shan't." Brenna planted her feet on the sidewalk and crossed her arms over her chest. There was no point in discussing the note he'd just read. She would be in Barcelona the next morning, seven hundred miles away from Fitch Wilder. She could forget all about this series of distasteful coincidences.

"Have you had a chance to enjoy your hotel's traditional afternoon tea? It's something worth doing while you're here."

She ignored him.

Fitch let go with a rich and leisurely chuckle and leaned against the car. With him all stretched out and relaxed like that, it was obvious to see the appeal Fitch Wilder might have to some women. He was long and lean. His wrists had an elegant turn to them, the muscle and bone etched in his tanned skin. His shoulders were exceptionally broad, and his waist slim and solid. And those complicated eyes . . .

It was difficult not to stare. But she managed.

"No? Then we should have tea together. That way I can tell you all about the underpainting I found beneath the sixth Siren portrait."

Brenna's spine stiffened in alarm. "The *what*?"

"Here's my proposition, Professor—I'll show you mine if you show me yours." The look on Wilder's face was pure amusement. He was enjoying this!

She was not.

"I have no interest in 'yours,' Wilder."

"Don't kid yourself. You know you do."

"Mine is far more significant than an underpainting."

"You don't know that for certain—mine could be a pretty big deal, too."

She narrowed her eyes at him. "What I have changes art history."

Fitch's smile widened, revealing a set of white, straight teeth. He raised up from the car. "Yeah? What I have is a love poem from the artist to The Siren. Mine doesn't change history, it *is* history." He wiggled an eyebrow as he gestured for her to take a seat in the SUV. "How about that cup of tea?"

A few minutes later, the driver had turned into London traffic. The two of them sat quietly in the backseat, their eyes locked in a dare. Brenna's muscle and tendons were pulled so tight she heard her cells strumming. She had to remind herself that this guy was no more than an arrogant con man. She couldn't believe a word he said. And yet . . . the notion that Fitch Wilder knew anything more about the artist and his muse than she did made her see stars.

He didn't intimidate her. Not in the least. But a love poem? She had to know what it said. The only way to deal with Wilder would be to offer him a crumb in exchange for the poem, and then walk away and never look back.

She nearly hissed at him. "Game on, Wilder."

"You got it."

"Tell me about the poem. Now."

"At tea—much more civilized."

It wasn't long before they sat at a dining table overlooking the rainy, early May English garden. The linen-covered table had been set with a small bouquet of fresh flowers, bone china, heavy silver, and crystal. A three-tiered silver tray had just been placed between them, laden with a colorful tea-for-two. An assortment of finger sandwiches and delicate sweets was displayed on white doilies.

Sharing high tea with a cowboy swindler seemed surreal, to say the least.

Frankly, Brenna was surprised the maître d' had let Wilder

into the dining room in the first place. He was still wearing those jeans and battered cowboy boots. No tie. Not even a collar this time—just a generic charcoal-gray T-shirt. And it didn't appear he'd taken the time to shave since she'd seen him four days before. When he took a dainty sip and set the fragile teacup back in its saucer, it appeared as small as a child's toy in his large hand.

And yet . . . she'd had to stifle a laugh when Wilder ordered a pot of passion fruit Darjeeling as easily as she imagined he'd order beer in a saloon. Then he peered over the tray with wide eyes and said, "Yes! I love clotted cream!"

She sat back against her chair now and studied him. It occurred to her that she had no idea who this man really was. Half of what had transpired between them had obviously been pure farce.

"Who the hell are you, Wilder? Really?"

Fitch had just shoved a scone into his mouth. His large green-gray-gold eyes went wide with surprise as he swallowed. "Mmm?" He dabbed at the corners of his mouth with a linen napkin. "I was just being the man you expected me to be."

Brenna eyed him skeptically. "You're a con artist."

"And you're so freakin' easy to mess with, Professor, that I couldn't resist. Besides, you deserve it."

She squirmed in her seat, her breath shallow and fast. She kept staring at his lips. A smile quivered at their corners like an actor waiting for his cue. And those eyes . . . so intelligent and playful that she had to look away.

If Fitch Wilder were anyone else—*absolutely any other man on earth*—she'd drag his chiseled ass to her bed and make him her plaything.

Women likely lined up for blocks to give themselves to Fitch

Wilder. Not Brenna. She was an expert on the human psycho-sexual experience. Every one of her lovers, to a man, would insist that they won Brenna through skill and dogged determination, but only because Brenna wished them to think so. In truth, she was always the seducer and never the seduced. Without exception.

But she had standards. She never seduced a man she did not respect.

"You haven't even tasted your oolong," Wilder said, gesturing with a half-eaten scone. "Why not loosen up, Professor? Let your hair down. Get your tea on."

She laughed in disbelief. "You think you're the best thing to happen to women since sitting on the dryer, don't you?"

Wilder coughed. He covered his mouth with his napkin in an effort to stifle the hacking sound now echoing off the dining room walls.

Brenna sipped her oolong and tossed her hair. She was proficient in the Heimlich maneuver, and if absolutely necessary she would save him from death by scone. She wasn't a horrible person. In the meantime she selected a pretty little smoked salmon sandwich and took a nibble.

Fitch eventually stopped coughing. The appalled dining room guests returned to their refreshments and conversations, and Brenna sat across from him, clearly pleased with herself. He poured himself a fresh cup of tea, envisioning the lovely Brenna Anderson riding a front-loaded Kenmore, her head thrown back in permanent-press rapture.

Not a chance. A woman that gorgeous would never have to turn to household appliances for a good time. Despite her frosty disposition, plenty of men would risk hypothermia for just one taste of her.

"I got another proposition for you, Professor."

She concentrated on spreading a thin layer of cream on her scone. "We haven't dealt with the last one. I'm still waiting to see the poem."

Fitch relaxed into his chair and threw an arm over the back, appraising her. Brenna had elegant hands. Though she could benefit from a few minutes of sunshine, she had nice skin. Her hair looked especially bright in the warm tearoom light, and he wondered how silky the long strands would feel between his fingertips. She wore a tight gray skirt and a floaty top that shimmered like mother-of-pearl. The skirt would have shown off her legs were it not for the D'Artagnan-meets-Madonna leather boots.

Fitch wondered if he'd ever get to see the porcelain knees, calves, and ankles she kept tucked away in there.

He stifled a smile. Yeah, he had to be nuts to admit it, but he liked Dr. Brenna Anderson. She was growing on him. Fitch was intrigued by her complexity and her intelligence, and planned to find out what existed beneath that prickly-pear exterior of hers.

"Professor," he said. "How about we clear the air between us before we trade Siren secrets. I'll sit here all proper and silent while you open a can o' Ivory Tower whoop-ass on me. Go on. Tell me every single thing—big or little—that you despise about me, no matter how long it takes."

Brenna checked her watch. That made him chuckle.

"Fine." She set her knife down on her plate and met his gaze with calm, cool blue eyes. "You claim to be an art expert yet you have no degree."

"That's correct. What I have instead is a lifetime of experience working with my father in art appraisal, investigation, and sales, and I apprenticed with the country's foremost authority in technological applications in fine art."

"Oh really? And who was that?"

"Edna Abrams at Carnegie Mellon. Ring any bells?"

A look of surprise flashed across her face.

"Don't hold back on me." He raised his teacup. "Continue with the whooping."

Brenna lowered her chin and steeled her gaze before she spoke. "All right, Wilder. Your father was a notorious New York art forger and convicted felon."

"You're correct." He returned his cup to the saucer and leaned forward. "He took a plea and agreed to become a consultant to the FBI's Art Crime Team, a job he held until he died. He also moved to Santa Fe to become a highly respected businessman. I happen to be very proud of the man my father was."

Her laugh was dismissive. "Santa Fe?"

"Yes, Santa Fe, a world-class center for art collection and home to one of the highest concentrations of artists anywhere on earth."

Her eyes narrowed, a sign that she was about to get to the nitty-gritty. "You plagiarized my dissertation during that TV interview. Maybe you're more like your father than you'd like to admit."

Fitch leaned even closer, careful to keep his voice low. He moved his plate to the side so he could fold his hands on the tabletop. "You know what, Professor? I did credit your work during that interview, but they edited it out to shorten the segment. I was about to call them and insist they do a correction when I saw your tweet. And then I thought, *Well, to hell with that.*"

The delicate skin of her left eyelid began to twitch. Otherwise, she remained unflappable, even in the face of the uncomfortable truth. He had to admire her resolve.

"And just so you know, I can find my ass with both hands just fine. In fact, sometimes it only takes one."

Her mouth pulled tight. "I apologize."

"Apology accepted."

"Great. So now that we're BFFs, how about you show me the poem?"

Fitch nodded. He wanted the details of her courtesan theory, and this was the only way he'd get them. He reached into his pocket.

Just then, Brenna's phone rang, and she began digging in her bag like she expected to find pirate treasure. Her eyes flashed in surprise at the caller ID and she looked up at him. "I need to take this." She turned away in her seat.

Of course he listened. How could he not? It couldn't be classified as eavesdropping if she stayed right there at their table.

"*Claudia?* Wait. Slow down. I can't understand—"

She took a furtive glance Fitch's way, but he pretended to be reading a pamphlet on the history of the hotel's afternoon tea. She went back to her call.

"Letters? Really? But what kind of . . . ? *What?* Oh, my God! I don't believe this. Hold on."

Brenna turned all the way around in her chair so that her back faced Fitch. She shielded one side of her face with an open hand and lowered her voice to a whisper. "You faxed one *here?* Why only one? All right, all right. I understand. I'll check with the front desk but . . ." She stood up, grabbed her bag off the chair. "Just a second, Claudia."

Brenna turned toward him, her resting-professor face back in working order. "I have to go. Excuse me." She began walking away.

He called after her. "We haven't finished our game of show-and-tell!"

"Hold on, Claudia." Brenna spun around on her musketeer high heels, her eyes narrowed. "I've changed my mind. I don't want to play anymore. Goodbye, Wilder."

He watched her swish her fabulous ass across the dining room, letting the finality in her dismissal sink in. Whatever the subject of that call had been—and whoever this Claudia person was—Dr. Anderson had just accelerated to overdrive. Fitch watched her make a beeline for the lobby, no doubt on her way to the front desk to pick up her fax. *Damn.* He still had no idea what she was up to.

There were always ways to find out.

When Fitch got the check a few moments later, he engaged the waiter in a friendly chat, all the while conspicuously counting out cash. "I find myself needing a little special assistance with something here at the hotel."

"And what would that be, sir?"

He continued stacking the euros on the table, one after the other. "Something off the books, so to speak."

The waiter nodded in the affirmative, his face contorted in alarm at the pile of money. The young man then glanced around the dining room making sure no one was watching.

Fitch handed him the check—along with the ginormous tip. "That's just to start," he said.

He stayed behind to finish his pot of Darjeeling, mulling over his next move. Brenna claimed she didn't want to play anymore, but he didn't believe that for a second. He raised the teacup to his lips.

"Game on, Professor," he whispered.

"Yes, of course. So I took the painting to my framer and told him I wanted to duplicate the original mat and frame as much as possible. He began to remove the old linen tacked to the back, where Ophelia had written. And I couldn't believe it, but two envelopes fell out onto his worktable."

"Can you describe them?"

"Well, they were clearly very old, made of some type of burnished paper with a faint silvery blue cast—the same as the stationery. It must have been very beautiful at the time, obviously feminine, and probably expensive. On the back of each envelope was a wax seal with the letter *S* that had been broken upon opening, and inside each envelope were several sheets of paper. The letters were addressed to Mrs. Ophelia Harrington at the house she shared here in Boston with Malcolm. The pages I faxed to you were in the best condition, by far."

Brenna's heart dropped. "How bad are the others?"

"I blame myself, dear. If I'd had any idea of the importance of that little painting or what was hiding inside I never would have hung it over the Victor Victrola in the front room of our beach house! All that humidity and salty air over all those years! I could just smack myself."

"You didn't know."

Claudia sighed. "All I can do now is try to repair the damage. I've already sent them to a document restoration and conservation specialist here in Boston, and I've asked them to do whatever they can—as fast as they can—to stabilize the paper enough that it can be copied. I'll fax pages to you as soon as they become available."

"No more faxes, Claudia. Send them as email attachments." Brenna didn't want to sound paranoid, but the last thing she wanted was to make it easy for others to get a peek at the contents. Besides, though these new letters would keep her in London for a

Chapter Ten

London

"I click on this little button at the top of the computer screen, right?"

"I don't know where you're pointing, Claudia. All I can see is your face, remember?"

"Wait! I've got it!" Claudia raised her chin so she could focus through her trifocals, giving Brenna an outstanding view of the interior of her patrician nose. "I've figured it—"

Beep, beep, beep. Claudia Harrington-Howell had just disconnected herself from their video chat for the third time in the last fifteen minutes.

Brenna grabbed the bottle of white wine off the nightstand in her charming Victorian hotel room and poured herself another glass. She was dimly horrified to see she'd drained nearly the entire bottle, but really, who could blame her? The letter now spread upon the duvet in front of her was a bombshell. And attempting to extract details from Claudia with the use of modern technology was like banging her head against a steel door.

Brenna's phone rang. "Screw that," Claudia said. "Let's just have a phone conversation like God intended. So where were we?"

"You were telling me about how the letters were found."

few more days of research, traveling to Spain was still on her agenda.

"I will, but you need to know the paper eroded completely in some places—just dissolved—especially at the edges and where the letters were folded. There are fourteen pages in all, and I would say about a quarter of the writing has disintegrated."

"Oh, no." Brenna took a gulp from her wineglass. She had to keep this in perspective—even if she learned only three-quarters of The Swan's story, that was 100 percent more than she'd known just weeks ago.

"And I'm sorry about Guilford. That man has always been a pill."

Brenna perked up. "Wait—you *know* him?"

"Not well, but we've met. Back when Terry was alive, we crossed paths at a few gallery openings and benefit balls and the like. I did enjoy his wife, however—such a lovely and engaging woman—French, as I recall, and quite a bit younger than him. But truly, the last time I saw Guilford had to be thirty-five years ago."

Brenna drained her wineglass for courage. "Is there any chance you—"

"I doubt he remembers me, dear, but I can try. You know, one dinosaur to another . . ."

Brenna thanked Claudia again and they said their goodbyes. She closed her laptop and gathered her phone and the faxed pages, putting everything on the small desk by the window. She was starving. She'd barely eaten anything at tea and now all she could think of was the little pizza place she'd seen around the corner. She grabbed her bag and on the way out, her eyes darted into the adjoining bathroom and its huge claw-foot tub. It hadn't even occurred to her to take advantage of the amenity, but at that moment she realized her shoulders were tight and her neck ached.

The lingering effect of spending time with Fitch Wilder, no doubt.

Nothing that a thin-crust pepperoni and a hot soak couldn't cure.

The maid's name was Miriam, and she waited for him inside the supply closet at the end of the hallway.

"She left ten minutes ago." Miriam held out her palm and Fitch filled it with another wad of euros. He'd have to take out a loan if he didn't change his tipping practices.

"Did you see the faxes?"

"They're on the desk by the window, underneath her laptop." Miriam shoved the bills in her apron pocket and slipped him the key card. "I don't know where she's gone or how long she'll be out, but I will tell you this—if you're not back here in five minutes I'm leaving and reporting my passkey stolen."

"Got it." Fitch took a step toward Brenna's room.

"Oh." Miriam touched his arm. "If you get caught I don't know who the blazes you are."

Fitch winked at the maid. "Thanks for the heads-up."

Seconds later he was at the door. After a quick check to make sure no guests were in the vicinity, he slipped the key card into the slot and turned the door handle. To him, the mechanism sounded like a shotgun blast. He hoped to God no one took notice.

He slowly pushed the door open, his eyes making a quick scan of the room—not to his tastes, that was for sure. The place looked like *Downton Abbey* on steroids. There was a huge tufted headboard in pale purple velvet, surrounded by girlie tables and chairs. The bedspread matched the wallpaper. He needed to get out of there before she discovered him or he passed out from the paisley overload, whichever came first.

He moved quickly toward the desk, his feet silent on the

thick carpet. He pulled the sheets of fax paper from beneath the laptop. He spread them on the bed directly underneath the lamp and clicked several photos of each page. He immediately gathered the papers, put them back in the same order he'd found them, and shoved them under the laptop.

That was when he heard the click of the key card in the door. *Oh, shit.*

Fitch had no time to make a better decision, so he slipped behind the velvet floor-length drapes near the desk. He tried not to breathe. The toes of his boots were sticking out from the fabric but he couldn't risk moving his feet. *How the hell am I going to get out of this one?*

He heard the door close. A few seconds later he detected the unmistakable scent of pizza, and he nearly groaned in dread. He would have to stand there, not breathing and not moving, while she enjoyed a pizza? This would not end well.

But he heard her feet cross the room. Next came the sound of the bath running. This was his chance. Fitch peeked through the drapes to be sure he could leave undetected, and what he saw left him immobile, frozen in place.

Brenna was faced away from him. The pizza box and a bottle of wine sat on a side table as she began to strip off her clothes. She was humming something familiar, but he had no time to name that tune because she slipped the frothy blouse over her head and unhooked a slinky lace bra. When it dropped to the floor before her, Fitch felt his eyes pop out of his head. All that satiny, perfect skin on such a beautiful back. He could see the poke of her shoulder blades, the faintest outline of her spine, the swell of her hips.

Her hands reached for the zipper of her skirt. She tossed her hair down her back. It was an outrageously sensual kind of movement, languid and seductive. A lump formed in his throat.

Time to go.

He pushed the velvet drapes aside and made his move.

The room was hot with the essence of flowery bath salts, pizza, and half-naked woman. He told himself to keep moving.

He was a lot of things, but a peeping Tom was not one of them.

He heard a faint singsong voice echoing in the tiled bathroom. "*What's love got to do . . . got to do with it?*"

He stifled a chuckle at the professor's song choice and opened the door.

That woman cracked him up.

He made his way down the hallway, and all the while the inside of his head was filled with a deafening buzz. Because the truth was, all he wanted to do was go back, put hands on that perfect pink skin, and kiss her the way a woman like Dr. Brenna Anderson should be kissed.

Where the hell had that come from?

Fitch reached the supply closet.

"You're a lucky bastard. I was just about to leave."

He handed the maid the key card and muttered a quick thank-you. He decided to skip the elevator and raced down six flights of back stairs to the lobby. He was out on the street in a flash, headed toward his B and B, his head swimming with everything having to do with the professor.

On the surface she was brilliant, determined, and a general pain in the ass. She was also one hundred percent drop-dead gorgeous from head to toe, someone who could chill enough to eat pizza in the bathtub. He liked that in a woman.

Maybe it was wishful thinking, but Fitch believed there was more hiding under her facade, parts to her that were authentic and caring.

God, how he wished he'd never seen her slipping out of her clothes. More than that, he already had a sinking feeling about the whole situation. He never should have snuck into her room. It would bite him in the ass one day—he was sure of it.

Back in the B and B, Fitch headed directly for the small business center off the lobby. He emailed himself the images and logged onto the hotel computer so he could print off the attachments. Within minutes he was in his room, where he kicked off his boots, plopped down on the bed, and stretched out his legs.

He'd been damn smart to take several shots of each page, because the lack of flash made the images faint. He selected the clearest version of each and leaned back against his pillows to read. Read what, he had no idea.

London, April 16, 1827

My dearest O,
Since you left England, its shores have been much dimmed by your absence. How I long to confide in you, old friend! How I miss the manner in which you laugh at me. Do not try to deny it! You know you take great joy in making me forget myself!

I am sorry to have let so much time pass since my last letter. I have much to tell you, but I find myself most unwilling to confess my foibles.

I fear I have made a grave mistake. You know my practice regarding married men. I drilled it into your mind often enough, as it was drilled into mine. A courtesan will never win out over a wife in the end, nor should she wish to try. A man with a wife is a man already owned, and therefore may only be borrowed, and then only most discreetly. I have never cared to walk that delicate line, and so therefore I warned you never to bend that rule.

I fear I was quite lonely without you and Malcolm. In that loss, I allowed solitude to harm my judgment. I thought Lord H—— to be married only in the most practical sense and believed his wife kept exclusively to the country with a lover of her own.

Unfortunately, not only did I break my own rule, I did so based on an incorrect assumption.

Lord H— was a most charming and generous companion. However, in my heart I remained cool to him. In retrospect, I think perhaps his greatest appeal lay in his unavailability. I did not truly want his love, which perversely made him all the more eager to give it. How strange that my own lack of interest may have precipitated what followed.

Lady H— somehow learned of her husband's distraction and has decided to take umbrage!

She and her phalanx of titled and respectable lady cohorts have declared open war upon me, dearest Ophelia. No, it is true. I do not wax theatrical, for I find that everywhere I turn, she has influenced the world against me. Invitations have dwindled until only the lowest events request my presence. I find my home pelted with rocks and my carriage assaulted with rotten produce should I dare to venture out. All but my most loyal servants have deserted me for mysteriously high salaries, taking their knowledge of my personal dealings with them to be converted into the evilest of gossip. The newssheets are rife with innuendo and tidbits about my past lovers, making me an object of ridicule and distrust—for every man I have ever known now fears that I shall betray his secrets to the public.

So here I stand, alone but for three loyal housemaids whom I saved from terrible circumstances. They are little more than children, however. We cannot endure such bitter opinion for long. Despite my knowledge of the fickleness of London society's favor, I have given up hope that this shall soon pass. I must purchase a ticket for the Americas, simply to escape this woman's unrelenting harassment.

My anger at losing my accustomed place is great, yet I have no one to blame but myself for believing Lord H—'s assurances that our relationship would be of no concern to her ladyship. Men will say anything when moved by lust, as we both know!

I must go now to oversee the packing preparations, for my housekeeper has decided to seek a high price for my secrets and has left the household in total disarray.

I shall write you again tomorrow when my solicitor has finalized my traveling plans. I miss you, my dear friend, and my heart lifts at the thought of seeing you and your dear "Sir" again in the near future!

—S

Fitch let his hand fall to the bed, the last page fluttering to the coverlet.

How bizarre. Nothing in this letter connected the courtesan to an artist in Catalonia. In fact, the courtesan planned to go to the Americas. Possibly, Brenna had come up with her theory before she read this fax.

Which meant all that cloak-and-dagger shit had been for nothing. He still didn't know what she was up to.

Fitch leaned back on the pillows, his hands behind his head, knowing he needed to reboot. He decided to review everything that was known about The Siren paintings—*including* Brenna's theory.

1. At least fourteen portraits had been painted
2. The Siren might have once been a London courtesan who was run out of town by a jealous wife in 1827

3. The Siren was a "broken bird in a Catalan storm"
   saved by an artist who called himself a "demented
   soldier"
4. The courtesan "S" had friends named "Ophelia" and
   "Malcolm" who lived in the Americas in 1827

Fitch jumped up and slipped his laptop from its case. He did
a search for the words "Ophelia," "Malcolm," "London," and
"courtesan," and he almost choked when he saw what instantly
popped up on his screen. Apparently, there was a book titled *Un-bound*, the true account of an 1800s London courtesan who
became a Boston abolitionist. And it was written by a museum
curator with a Harvard PhD.

Now he was getting somewhere.

With a few more clicks of his laptop keyboard, Fitch filled in
a whole lot of blanks. He found an article about a museum
opening. A smiling Brenna had her arm around the curator, a
woman named Piper Chase-Pierpont, and next to them stood a
stately older woman by the name of Claudia Harrington-Howell. A later article showed an ecstatic Brenna hugging Piper
at her book launch party in Boston.

All right, then. Not only had he discovered Brenna's courtesan connection, he'd discovered that the professor could, in fact,
smile. And when she did her face blossomed. In those smiling
pictures with her friend, there was no tension around Brenna's
mouth and her pale eyes sparkled. She looked like someone who
had a robust laugh and a functioning sense of humor.

She looked like someone he'd love to get to know.

Fitch searched his laptop for a list of nearby bookstores and
when he found one that was still open, he called to make sure
they had the book in stock. Then he grabbed his jacket, ran out
the door, and caught a cab.

So he'd be spending the night in the company of a London courtesan. Who would've thought?

Brenna tightened the sash of her robe and snatched an envelope slipped under her door during the night. Was it her bill? She'd already informed the hotel she was extending her stay!

"Brenna" was written on the envelope in a rather square hand she didn't recognize. She ripped it open to find a single sheet of plain paper, and at the top was a one-stanza poem.

> *This soldat dement shall fail*
> *To capture the radiance*
> *Of his bellesa de la cala,*
> *Brighter now than ever before.*

Was this *the* poem? That was what all the fuss was about? This was Wilder's historical discovery? Like so many men she had known, Fitch Wilder had greatly exaggerated his attributes. But below it was this note:

> *This is only half of the underpainted poem. Meet*
> *me downstairs for breakfast at ten and I'll give*
> *you the rest. I know about The Swan. We need to*
> *talk.*
>
> *—F*

It took her fifteen minutes to throw on some clothes, brush her hair, and make an emergency call to Piper, who was about to leave her hotel for filming on location at a remote Bosnian cave. Brenna thanked God she caught her before her friend had lost cell service.

"But how did he find out, Bren? How much does he know about her?"

"I have no idea!" Brenna paced her hotel room. "I don't trust him, Pipes. This is some sort of trap."

"Okay, okay. Listen to me." Piper's voice was steady and solid, and it didn't escape Brenna that at some point in their friendship, the tables had turned. Brenna had always provided rational and analytic balance to Piper's spaz attacks. She'd always been the voice of worldly wisdom in contrast to Piper's state of befuddlement. But who was the befuddled spaz now?

"Your dream is within reach, Brenna." Piper began talking her off the ledge. "You finally have a shot at getting to the bottom of The Siren paintings and you might be able to complete the story of The Swan while you're at it. It's a scholarly diamond mine."

"I know."

"And this Fitch Wilder guy is an inconvenience, not a disaster. Think about it—you two aren't after the same thing. He's in it for the money and you're in it for academic discovery. But if you think you could help each other you'd better find a way to work with him."

"But he's . . . he's . . ."

Piper laughed. "I know. I saw his picture."

"What?" Brenna's jaw dropped. "I don't find him the slightest bit attractive, if that's what you're implying. I was going to tell you that he's a complete dickhead. He's crass and bossy and dishonest. All he wears are tight jeans and busted-up cowboy boots. In fact, he showed up for high tea dressed like a *cowpoke,* if you can believe it."

Brenna heard nothing but silence. "Still there, Pipes?"

"Yep."

"And?"

"You two had tea together?"

"It's a long story."

"I bet."

"Don't even."

"Fine, but could we back up for a minute?"

"If you must."

"You say you're not attracted to him."

"I did say that, yes."

"Uh huh. So just how hot are we talking, Bren? Say, on our usual scale of one to one hundred—with one hundred being hot enough to fuse sand into glass—what's Fitch Wilder in person?"

Brenna sighed. "A forty-five maybe, and that's being generous. He's in the Play-Doh-melting range."

Piper snorted with laughter. "Holy hell, Bren! This man is *really* getting under your skin!"

"Men don't get under my skin."

"Because you've never allowed them to—not until now."

Brenna scowled. "You're mistaken."

Piper sighed. "Not long ago you bluntly told me I was my own worst enemy. You helped me bust out of my little box and get what I wanted out of life, and you did it because you're my best friend in the whole world and you only wanted to see me happy."

"I did. I still do."

"Okay, so I only want you to be happy, too! And it's my turn to tell you the truth—I've never seen you like this."

Her spine straightened in offense. "I have no idea what you're talking about."

"Brenna, you're not being honest with yourself. Fitch Wilder has knocked you completely off your game—I can hear it in your voice. He threatens the hell out of you! You need to figure out why."

Chapter Eleven

London

Her stride was brisk and no-nonsense, accompanied by the familiar *click, click, click* of her don't-fuck-with-me boots. She wore a pair of perfectly fitted jeans and her hair was loose down her back. A scowl had settled upon her pretty face. When Dr. Brenna Anderson reached his table, she motioned for him to stand.

"Let's take a walk."

Fitch looked longingly at his nearly full coffee cup and fought back lusty images of the English fry-up he had planned to order—two eggs, bacon and sausage, tomato, and fried bread. He took one last gulp of coffee and left money on the table, then followed Brenna to the lobby and out the front door.

"You sure about this, Professor? It's drizzling and you don't have an umbrella."

"It's always drizzling here."

"But the hotel's breakfast is outstanding." Fitch really wanted that fry-up.

"I'm not hungry."

He turned up the collar of his jacket as he matched her stride.

She kept her eyes ahead and remained silent. Fitch figured it was up to him to hack through the ice.

"Did you know, Professor, that the late spring in Barcelona is delightful—warm and sunny and everyone's out on the street at night, glad to be set free after the chilly winter. It's my favorite season to visit."

She wheeled around so fast her damp hair swept across her lips. A thousand questions flickered in her pale blue eyes. "Barcelona?"

"The historic capital city of the Catalonia region of Spain. Ever been there?"

Her eyes squinted in resolve. "Tell me how you found out about The Swan."

"I'm an avid reader." Fitch reached into his coat pocket and pulled out the paperback version of *Unbound*. "And hot damn! This was some incendiary stuff, Professor."

She crossed her arms tightly over her chest. She did that a lot.

He smiled down at her. "I half expected each chapter to begin with, '*I never thought this would happen to me . . .*'" She wasn't entertained.

"I'm going to ask you one more time, Wilder. How do you know about The Swan? And how do you know about Catalonia?"

"How about we take that stroll?" He slipped his hand through the crook of her elbow and felt her flinch. This woman was a bundle of nerves. "I am only trying to be a gentleman."

She yanked her arm away. "Really? Because in my world, gentlemen respond truthfully when asked direct questions."

Fitch shoved his hands in his pockets and nodded silently. He'd given this a lot of thought during his sleepless night with a couple of hot courtesans, and he knew there was only one way out of the hole he'd dug for himself. He had to shore up Dr. Anderson's faith in him by sharing everything he'd discovered about The Siren Series. With any luck she'd reciprocate. Yes, he would admit to breaking into the hotel room—absolutely he would!

Eventually.

But that conversation would have to wait until he'd made headway locating the paintings.

Who knew? Maybe in a few days she would be so absorbed in her academic pursuits that it wouldn't faze her.

"How about we stop butting heads and work together, Professor?" Fitch cleared his throat and began to recite the poem in its entirety:

> *Thirteen paintings*
> *And three seasons*
> *Since you came to me,*
> *Broken bird in a Catalan storm*
>
> *This soldat dement shall fail*
> *To capture the radiance*
> *Of his bellesa de la cala,*
> *Brighter now than ever before.*

Brenna stopped in midstride. She looked up at him, tiny droplets of water clinging to her eyelashes, eyebrows, and hair. Slowly, as cars hissed in the street and the London pedestrians jostled them, her eyes widened with comprehension.

He cupped her elbow in the press of people. Fitch bent his head down to speak into her ear and was immediately hit with the smell of her skin and hair. It was the same flowery female scent that had waylaid him in her hotel room.

Stay on track.

"You heard right, Professor. There were, at one point, at least thirteen Siren paintings. We've only discovered six."

He pulled away to study her face and found the professor's lips parted in shock.

"C'mere." Fitch slipped his arm through hers again and this time she didn't resist. It started to pour just as he pulled her into a sheltered doorway.

"The painter lived in Catalonia."

"I know."

It was Fitch's turn to be surprised. *"How?"*

A smile twitched at the corner of her pretty pink lips. "The same way I know that seven portraits—not six—have been found. The same way I know at least one of them was painted in 1828."

Fitch squinted. "Where's the seventh?"

"Last time I saw it, it was hanging over a toilet in Boston. Now answer me—what else do you know about The Swan?"

"Wait. *What?*" Fitch couldn't get his brain to absorb that information, especially the part about the toilet. *"Boston?* Are you sure?"

Brenna tipped her head, enjoying his reaction. "So you read Piper's book—good for you, Wilder. And you know who The Swan is. That's great. But do you mind telling me how you made a connection between The Swan and The Siren, because *that* sure as hell was not in the book."

"I didn't." Fitch began to pull his jacket tighter against the chill when he noticed that the professor's blouse was soaked and her teeth had begun to chatter. Before she could refuse him, Fitch shrugged off the jacket and swung it around her shoulders, tugging it tight.

She drew back. "I . . . I don't need your coat."

Fitch stepped closer to her, still clutching the lapels. "Connecting a courtesan to The Siren is your theory, Professor. You mentioned it in your note to Guilford, remember?"

Her teeth still chattered. "But I didn't mention The Swan by name—"

"The book!" Fitch grinned, letting go of the lapels so he could tap the paperback inside his jacket pocket, which meant he'd just poked Brenna somewhere in the vicinity of her left breast. He hadn't meant to do that. "Look, I admit I did some research after we ran into each other. Photos of you with your author friend are all over the Internet. It didn't take a PhD to make the connection."

She pursed her lips. "Clearly."

"So your friend wrote about two courtesans, right? But only The Blackbird's story was told. That left The Swan mostly a mystery—so I guessed it was her, and you just confirmed it."

She took an unsteady step backward into the building doorway, her eyes narrowing in suspicion. "And this snooping around is supposed to make me trust you?"

"Googling is wrong. I feel so ashamed." Fitch inclined his head and tried to look remorseful. "But I had to figure out what you meant in that note to Guilford. You're brilliant, Professor, and I need a brilliant thinker on my side if I'm going to find the other eight—no, seven—paintings that may still be out there."

The professor quirked a brow. "I don't do disingenuous flattery, Wilder. And, by the way, you're not very skilled at it."

"I'm being completely genuine." Fitch couldn't recall a woman he'd ever enjoyed sparring with more than the lovely professor. "You're a world-class academic researcher who has a deep understanding of the paintings and a theory about The Siren. I have a successful track record of being able to chase down missing art and I've got a blank check to take me wherever I need to go. Together we're going to find these paintings and blow the lid off the art world."

Brenna said nothing for a long moment. He could see the wheels spinning in her head. This was good.

"If we're going to work together it has to be a one-hundred-percent businesslike endeavor."

Fitch could work with that. "Sure."

"Before we go public in any way, I get to publish my findings in an academic journal."

"Agreed. And I'm happy to give you a cut of my finder's fee."

Brenna scrunched up her nose. "I couldn't accept that even if I wanted to—Guilford's money would cast my scholarship into question."

"Have it your way, Professor."

"Oh, I intend to, Wilder."

"But it's Guilford's money that will be paying our way."

"Your way. Not mine." Brenna sighed, a furrow of worry creasing her brow. "And even after I publish, you must have my permission before you give any media interviews. Agreed?"

"Agreed. If you promise not to go medieval on my ass on Twitter."

"Fine."

When Brenna tugged his jacket tighter it overlapped by six inches around her chest. Fitch suddenly realized how delicate she was. And the hem of his coat reached halfway down her slim thighs, so she wasn't really as tall as she appeared. Her height must be an illusion created by her high-heeled D'Artagnans.

She looked up at him, a mix of curiosity and doubt in her expression. "I have more research to do before I can leave London."

"Great. We'll do it together."

Dr. Anderson closed one eye, as if she were peering through a viewfinder. He couldn't help it—Fitch laughed.

"Look, Professor. We'll build a provision into our agreement that either party can dissolve the partnership at any time. In other words, if you don't like working with me, you don't have to."

"Agreed." She stuck out her hand for a shake. Fitch had to give her credit—she did a good job of camouflaging her soft and feminine hand with that sharp grip of hers. But he knew just how female she really was.

Keep it together.

"One more thing."

Fitch nodded, figuring this was going to be good.

"When this is over, I want access to Guilford's collection. I want to study them with my own eyes. You've got to promise you'll get me in there. I don't care how you do it."

Fitch smiled. "It's a promise."

"All right, then. Let's get started."

When the professor took a step toward the sidewalk, Fitch placed a hand on her shoulder. "Aren't you forgetting something?"

She turned. "I told you about the Boston painting."

"You only mentioned it. I need the whole story. And there's something else."

She sighed. "What?"

"The phone call that bent you way out of shape—you spoke about a fax. I want to see it."

Brenna gazed upward, as if asking for divine assistance. "All right. Let's go." She marched out into the sidewalk again, the rain coming down so hard that he could barely see in front of him. Brenna pulled up his jacket to cover her head and shoulders.

As they weaved their way through the crowd and back toward the hotel, Fitch laughed at his situation. Brenna had his coat and he was soaked to the bone. It didn't escape him that this was merely a preview of his partnership with Dr. Brenna Anderson. At least he knew what he was getting into.

THE PAST

Chapter Twelve

Lost

The ghost fluttered before her open eyes. Pale and otherworldly, the phantasm surged forward powerfully, then seemed to surrender in failing strength to sink back.

From where her head lay on something scratchy and not terribly soft, she watched the ghost incuriously, as dispassionately as a stone, as it repeated the action again and again. Surge and fall. Rise and fall.

Light came drifting like fog through blue night, lighting the world enough that she saw that the ghost was nothing but a pale curtain hanging by a tall window. The weary muslin showed no life of its own, but only draped limply until stirred by the breeze.

Curtain. Window. She knew what they were and she knew that she ought to be alarmed by them somehow, but she could not recall why. All she could do was watch the light swell and fill the room, turning what had been blue and black to pink and gold. She lay in a small bedchamber, no more than a half-dozen steps across in any direction, with a square of low, timbered ceiling looming above amber-colored stone walls and thick, unadorned woodwork. She saw a single door and a single window, a thick piece of furniture topped with a pitcher and bowl, opposite the bed where she lay. As the sun rose, the simple, rustic room became glazed in rose and gilt, giving a magical shimmer to the ancient fitted stone of the walls, the plain, oaken chest of drawers, and the bare wooden planks of the floor.

Shimmering lights over my head, a hundred candles hanging above a gleaming marble ballroom . . .

She blinked. No, it was the same simple room, redeemed only by the glow that embellished every edge and plane with enchantment. The dancing confection of light made her feel something. Yearning. She was desperate to see the sky that brought such a glow. A hand lifted into her vision, reaching for the light. She looked more closely at it and it turned in response to her inspection.

The hand belonged to her, obviously. The only problem with such a notion was that the slender appendage was completely unfamiliar. Not simply because of the fading green and blue of bruising, or the scraped and scabbed fingertips, but the very shape of the fingers and the arch of the wrist were as strange to her as if they marked the flipper of a dolphin. The other hand was no better, for at least two of the fingers were swollen oddly. A strip of fabric, heavy as sailcloth, wrapped the fourth finger to the third, as if to make them one.

The oddity of that should have been frightening, to not recognize one's own hands, yet still her only emotion was the yearning to see out the tall arched window in the stucco wall, where the ghostly curtain drifted in the breeze.

She rolled to her side and pushed back the covers. Two feet, slender like the hands, also bruised and scraped, slid from beneath the coarse sheets to rest on the cool smooth boards of the floor. The sensation of touching something, the press of reality against her drifting awareness, made it easier for her to accept ownership of the unfamiliar limbs. After all, the strange, narrow feet were taking her where she wished to go.

Walk.

She stood. The feet, along with the skinned, bruised, shaking knees and weak calves and thighs, obeyed her commands. Something hot lanced upward from the appendages, increasing her appreciation of the wholeness of all the strange, new parts.

Pain. Yes, that was the word.

Pain is not real. Pain is simply a message, and like all messages, can be ignored.

She turned her head to see who spoke, but there was no one else in the rustic chamber.

At last the stumbling limbs brought her to the window and the multicolored hands gripped the thick, wooden sill. The gilt light shimmered across her vision, shattering her sight into broken glimmers. She blinked away the splintered light and stared hard until her vision adjusted to the distance of the view.

The sea.

Like the pink and gold quality of the light, the sea glowed new and strangely blue. As clear as azure glass, and as calm. Blue sky filled the rest of the view, dotted with pink-glazed clouds and pierced by a sun that seemed to burn larger and brighter than it ought to.

Sunrise.

East.

Which was somehow wrong as well, or at least, strange.

I don't know where I am.

Though painful to do so, she dropped her gaze to the battered fingers that gripped the sill. The long fingers, the fragile bones of the wrist, the way the skin folded into the elbow—whose hands? Whose arms?

She released her grip on the ledge. Balancing upon shaking

legs, she reached up to caress each arm and then a neck so slender that her long fingers fit easily around it. She released and brushed these new fingertips over features that brought no one in particular to mind—high brow, eyelids closed and trembling at the touch, slanted cheekbones, a longish nose, a pointed chin. A plain face, surely, for being so thin and sharp? Down again, to find the corners of sharpened shoulders, to trace the contours of arching collarbones, to slip down over the simple muslin shift to find admittedly petite breasts, followed by the defined outlines of rib cage, the concave dip of belly, and the jutting points of hip bones.

You're a skinny little thing, aren't you? Nothin' but a bag o' bones.

She whipped her head around to stare at the empty room. Again, a disembodied voice—but not the same one as before. She didn't know those voices. Perhaps one of them belonged to her, like the hands and the feet? She opened her mouth, but it seemed that she'd forgotten how to speak as well. It was only in her mind that she heard the soft, light voice that she thought might be her own.

I don't know who I am.

Her knees began to tremble. She grasped at the windowsill once more to steady herself, then turned back toward the bed. The early morning breeze had chilled this strange skin.

Her gaze went to the chest of drawers, which meant clothing. She was certain of this, although she did not know how. She tried to remember another chest, any other chest, that had contained clothing, but there was no such image in the vast void of her memory.

The room was very small. It was not too difficult to balance her way across it, using the rough-hewn bedposts until she could reach the chest.

There were three heavy drawers. It took a bit of effort to pull them open, for her arms were no stronger than her legs. The top one held a collection of items: a large thin book, wrapped with a strip of leather and tied shut, a comb and brush of dull and tarnished metal, a razor and a strop.

Man things.

She knew what the items were for, but found no memory of a man in her mind. No name. No face.

The next drawer held two folded shirts. Leaning one hand upon the drawer edge, she shook one out and held it up to the morning light. It was very large. It looked as if it had been well made, but now the dingy linen was spotted and streaked with some stiff substance that had dried in odd and unlikely colors.

Paint.

The word drifted into being in her mind and then she knew paint, where a moment before she'd had no notion of the substance. This was at once disconcerting and encouraging, for it meant that her mind was not empty—it was merely struggling to navigate through a heavy fog.

She held the shirt up to herself. The length covered her nearly to the knees, but somehow she knew it would not be appropriate attire. Time to keep looking.

Carefully she lowered herself to rest upon the battered knees. They hurt, but then, her ribs hurt from the simple act of breathing, so it seemed to make little difference. In the bottom drawer she found a gown. It was folded neatly, but still filled the entirety of the drawer. It shimmered slightly in the morning light. She brushed her fingertips over it and the roughness of the scabbed skin caught at the fine fabric.

Pale blue silk.

Which, her oddly randomly retrieved knowledge informed her, was made from the excretions of insects.

Unlikely, assuredly, but her mind was convinced of this knowledge. How contrary that her mind would recall such a random fact while simultaneously forgetting her own name!

She rose from where she knelt before the chest, taking the gown up with her. It was of a correct length to fit her, although it seemed a bit large otherwise. Now that it was unfolded in the light, she saw that although the fabric was rich, the dress was in very poor condition indeed. It was terribly torn, even shredded in places! And although it seemed to have been cleaned recently, it was still erratically stained with pools and streaks of brown.

Not paint.

Blood.

She backed away from the chest, stumbling a few short steps until the back of her knees encountered the bed and she sat abruptly, the gown still gripped in the battered hands.

This is mine. I died in this gown.

Which was a foolish thought, because she was obviously not dead—although she was most definitely less than whole. She clutched the gown close to her as if to warm the ice that continued to grow in her belly. Whatever had happened to the woman wearing this silk creation, the event had erased her completely. What was left was only a foggy her-ness, a nameless being.

The strange numbness she had felt upon awakening seeped away. She was aware now, aware enough to be afraid, at any rate.

Yet . . . she was safe at the moment, was she not? This room was not fine, but it was durable and sheltering. Her bed was rough, but had been kindly provided, she was sure of it. Simply look at the care the gown had received, though it could never again be worn! Someone had cleaned it as well as they could, then put it carefully away for her.

The someone who was looking after her.

The paint-spattered shirt. The razor.

The man.

Deep in her belly she felt the chill begin to spread. Shivers passed through her sore limbs and made her teeth chatter. Further weakness followed and her head ached powerfully, filling

her awareness with a great throbbing that matched the beat of the unfamiliar heart.

Retreat seemed to be in order. Leaving the gown to lie over the foot of the bed, she crawled back beneath the rough, scratchy covers—wool! From sheep!—and pulled them up to her chin.

The warmth of the bed could not penetrate the icy core of her. She became blinded by the pounding in her head, as regular as the waves that beat against the rocky shore outside her window. Now, however, the pain swelled until tears began to leak from her eyes and the room began to shimmer gray about the edges.

Raising one hand out of the covers, she reached upward to find the source of the throbbing. High upon the side of her narrow skull she found it. Heavy scabs had formed along a slash in the flesh. Even the most tender exploration sent dizzying bolts of pain through her, but by careful touch, she could detect a strange, regular pattern all along the slash.

Stitches.

The woman in the gown had had her skull smashed open.

And someone had sewn it shut again.

Nausea rode her now, as if she were a scrap of wood adrift on a stormy sea and the sickness that threatened to darken her consciousness was a passenger clinging to her for dear life. She struggled to remain awake, then realized that she was safe. This room, this bed, proved that she was protected, did it not? Safe enough to sleep, to escape the pain, and perhaps, possibly, dream of her name.

She pulled the covers high, and shivering, let the gray fog fill her vision completely as she slipped gratefully into darkness once again.

A woman entered the chamber, walking backward, pushing open the thick door with her bottom.

"*Bon dia!*" She blew a strand of silver and bronze hair from her face as she smiled at her. "*El meu nom és Beatriu, senyoreta.*"

From her nest in the bed she blinked. The language sounded familiar to one she knew, but it was not an exact match. She had the uncanny feeling that she almost knew what the woman said.

Finally, a partial translation sifted through the cracks in her thoughts. *Her name is Beatriu.*

The woman clucked and shook her head.

She now saw why Beatriu entered the way she had, for the woman carried a heavily laden tray. She saw a fresh pitcher, a plate piled with food, and a stack of folded clothing.

She tried to stand to help the burdened woman, but when Beatriu saw her grasping the bedframe, she shooed her back down.

Setting the tray upon the chest, Beatriu pressed both her hands to her generous bosom. "Beatriu." She waited expectantly.

It was her name, clearly. Beatriu wanted it repeated to her, but she could only open her lips and show her how nothing wished to fall out. That brought a flood of sympathetic-sounding words—not-quite-Spanish?—and a rueful shake of Beatriu's head.

Silkworms. Sheep. Paint. Spanish.

The woman named Beatriu seemed nothing but friendly as she fussed over the tray, and then over the woman in the bed, smoothing the covers and plumping the dingy pillows. Like everything else in the room, she was spotless yet simple. Her cotton dress was of a shapeless cut that cared not a wit for fashion, yet she was rather lovely with her open smile and large, hazel eyes. Her skin had a golden tinge to it that spoke of life in the sun and no regard for bonnets.

She could not help but smile back at Beatriu.

That arrested her new friend immediately. "Oh!" She lifted both hands as if offering up something. *"Ets bella, senyoreta!"*

Bella meant beautiful in many languages. She decided to believe she had been offered a compliment and made the same motion back to Beatriu, smiling again.

"No, no, *senyoreta!*" Beatriu rolled her eyes and patted her hair, stroking the escaping strands back into the no-nonsense bun at the back of her neck, but was obviously pleased.

In only moments, the broken woman was sitting up in bed, firmly propped by pillows plumped within an inch of their faded lives, with the covers smoothed to her waist and a plain, wooden tray placed across her lap. The plate held an assortment of meat and cheese slices, a small loaf of dark brown bread, torn in half and still steaming, and—luxury of luxuries!—a small ripe peach. She could not resist. She cradled the peach in her still-raw but healing fingertips, cherishing the velvet skin, and held it to her nose to inhale deeply of the heavenly perfume. She let out a sigh of pleasure, a smile of relief on her lips.

She recognized peaches.

Beatriu smiled. *"Bona temporada,"* she said.

She nodded, although not certain what had been said. *Fine weather,* perhaps? After the meal, the kindly Beatriu tidied the tray away and helped her lie back comfortably.

"Resta, bellesa de la cala."

The strange words transmuted into reason one by one, slowly, like falling through water.

Rest.

When next the woman awoke, it was to an odd scratching noise. It was a small, quiet sound, almost stealthy. That very furtiveness was what woke her, when a louder sound may not have.

Thief!

She was quite sure of it, although she did not know why.

She opened her eyes only slightly.

A man sat on a stool near the end of her bed, leaning back against the wall with one knee bent high and a book open upon it. A shaggy, sand-colored dog sat at his feet, gazing at her through its unruly forelock. The scratching noise continued. After a moment, she realized that he was drawing.

Then, when his gaze rose to linger on her, and he narrowed his eyes and tilted his head in an assessing manner, she realized that he was drawing her! In her sleep!

Thief indeed!

Still she did not move. She kept her breathing deep and relaxed and she stole from him while he stole from her.

He was a big, broad-shouldered fellow. Wavy brown hair fell to his shoulders. He was mussed, and his shirt was another one spattered with paint. Even his fingertips were stained about the nails with bright pigments. His clothing was rough. He wore his coarse shirt open at the neck like a field hand, and his tough canvas breeches showed wear at the knees.

Despite all this, there was something about the way he held himself that made her want to see him in a dark superfine coat and a sharply striped weskit. A cravat and high collar beneath that square chin would look most handsome—

How did she know these things?

He caught her looking. She did not shy from the directness of his warm brown gaze, for had she not caught him looking first?

At any rate, she had concluded that this was her benefactor, this dog owner, this man of paint-spattered clothing and rustic generosity.

However, a man who entered a lady's room without invitation was no gentleman—and watching her, drawing her, in her sleep? Behavior beyond the pale indeed!

So who was this roughly clad but not brutish, handsome but not well behaved, artistic but careless fellow?

He had the grace to grimace slightly at his own presumption. *"Jo sóc un mal tipus."*

She blinked. His voice was lovely, deep and slightly husky.

I could fall in love with his voice alone.

She banished that odd thought immediately, reminding herself that one cannot fall in love without knowing one's own name!

Furthermore, she did not understand what he said, except perhaps *"un mal,"* "a bad" something. The rich, rippling language did not help the way his voice plucked at strings deep within her. She swallowed, then shook her head at him.

His brow furrowed. *"Je suis un mauvais camarade."*

I am a bad fellow.

She understood him quite easily that time. She nodded. Then she raised a single brow in agreement, giving him a chiding look.

"Ah, French," he murmured to himself in yet another language. "I'm going to regret ignoring my tutor, just as he predicted."

She laughed a little at that. He smiled at her then, a sweet boyish flash of white teeth.

Oh, my.

"You are English, then?" he asked in the same language. "That is wonderful!"

She shrugged, for truly she did not know. She understood his speech. Perhaps she was English, or possibly French. She found she was reluctant to consider herself a citizen of a country where snails were a delicacy.

Why did all her most useless memories include tidbits about bugs? Her headache worsened.

"I apologize for my excitement, but my French is almost as bad as my Catalan!" He set down his pencil and closed his sketchbook without showing her the drawing. "I can scarcely buy milk in the market. If not for Beatriu I would starve." He gazed at her for a long moment, while his smile faded. "What is an English lady doing on the coast of Cataluyna? I have heard nothing of an English ship lost at sea."

She stared at him, the words *lost at sea* tossing on the waves of her memory. Pain shot through her limbs, chest, and head as she sat upright in the rough bed. She continued to stare at the handsome artist, dimly aware that her behavior was rude, but unsure where else to look, what else to do.

Within her skull the questions tumbled and throbbed. Where was she? Who was she? Who was this man? What had happened to her?

His dark eyes softened. When he spoke again, his voice had mellowed with kindness and concern. "You are in Castell de la Cala."

She shook her head. The words meant nothing to her.

"In Cataluyna."

She shook her head again. She should know what that meant. She should understand. But there was nothing there when she reached deep inside herself for clarity, nothing but a mute frustration she could not name and did not comprehend.

"Do you know how you came to be here with us?"

There was nothing. She began to weep weakly, overcome with a profound sense of emptiness. Hot tears rolled down her cheeks. In the sobs and gasps she recognized the music of her own sadness. All she could do was cup her battered face in her bruised hands and cry.

"I am sorry. I did not mean to cause you unease. There is no rush." The painter touched her forearm with a feather-light brush of his fingers. She jerked away, a reaction that she regretted immediately. He had meant only to reassure her, no doubt, and posed no threat to her.

She let her hands fall away from her face. He angled away from her, a flash of hurt in his chocolate-brown eyes. He spoke again.

"You are welcome to stay here until you are well enough to travel home. I will help you find your people."

Such a kind offer, and yet the words left her feeling nothing. Nothing but emptiness.

Chapter Thirteen

Castell de la Cala, Catalunya

The Artist was there at her sickbed with his shaggy companion the next time she awoke, and the next, and the next. Beatriu would always appear shortly after she opened her eyes, always with a tray of rustic delicacies, always with an encouraging smile.

The Artist would join her for her meal, as if he loved nothing better than soup and crusty bread smeared with melted cheese. She realized that no matter how her appetite might be lacking, he always managed to distract her with stories, spoken in English. Most of his tales were about the people of the village named Castle of the Cove. She learned that the bread came from a baker named Septua and the cheese from the convent of St. Lucia. She would nibble from sheer politeness as he spoke. As soon as he would finish his meal he would begin drawing, filling the pages even as he laughed his way through tales of village feuds so old no one recalled the origin, and tricks the children would play upon him while he pretended not to be aware. The fishing had been bad this year because of the unusual temperatures, but the crops were rich and the fruits hanging heavy.

Usually, about this point in their visit, she would glance down at her tray to be astonished at how much food she'd consumed, though she'd been so sure she wasn't hungry.

He asked her very few questions, and always obliquely, as if testing her memory. "I played in an apple orchard as a child, despite the fact that it was patrolled by a highly territorial goose whom we named Attila—" and the story would go on, always light and humorous and diverting, until he would slip a question into the stream of storytelling. "Have you ever climbed an apple tree in full bloom?"

And then she would recoil from him and shake her head because she remembered she was broken. Where others had a rich history of memories, she had a void, a hole in her soul empty of sights and sounds and stories.

At once exotic and welcoming, Castell de la Cala sat on a cliff of golden stone overlooking the wide blue sea.

Once she'd regained strength, the Artist accompanied her on an afternoon stroll through the hillside that flowed from the *castell* like a full skirt. As always, his shaggy Catalan sheepdog, Liverpool, walked at his heels.

The town center was a collection of narrow cobblestone streets lined with two-story stone homes and businesses. She shielded her eyes from the sun, looking up at rows of iron-railed window boxes overflowing with vibrant flowers and plants. It was a place of richly saturated color and warm sunshine, of simply dressed but happy people, ragged carts and farm horses.

She knew one fact with certainty—this place was not what she was accustomed to. It was not her home.

Her host greeted everyone with a warm familiarity, and she noticed that the villagers were welcoming, perhaps even reverent of the man. Although they slid many a bright glance her way, no one asked the Artist about his companion. It was clear the villagers had heard the story of the mysterious woman of the cove.

He explained that the town had been founded as a fishing village many hundreds of years ago and had grown into a farming community as well. She could see olive groves, fruit orchards, and fields of grain stretching out away from the town center.

The Artist asked her every so often if she was tired. She was, but did not dare admit it, because the walk made her feel alive. Being out in the world gave her hope that one day she would remember where and to whom she belonged.

They walked up a set of wide terraced steps that led toward the sea. She found herself standing before a crumbling stone wall. It was nearly waist high, although at other portions of its length it ranged from knee height to over her head, its top edge rising and falling like the waves of the sea framed above it.

She reached for the ragged wall, stroking the time-worn edge absently while leaning to see to the other side.

The cliff's edge was no more than a few feet in front of the wall. From there the view dropped like a fallen stone to the rocky hem of the continent.

"I found you down there," the painter said, with a tilt of his head toward the cove. "You were washed up by the storm like a mermaid who had angered Neptune."

She knew mermaids were women-fish and she knew that Neptune was the god of the sea, although she hadn't known she knew until he'd spoken of them. She hoped that if he spoke often enough, and at length, perhaps he might accidently say her name and she would know that as well.

She smiled at him and lowered her eyelids. He stopped speaking, and she felt his stare burn down upon her. Well, that was obviously the wrong tack to take. He had been speaking easily enough when she sat unsmiling and unmoving, but when she smiled he became mute. Perhaps the Artist felt more comfortable that way, like someone rambling on to a pet?

The Artist and his pet mermaid.

The constant hum of the waves was louder here . . . much louder . . . so loud it began to drown out the present moment.

My hand rested on a gilded railing as I looked down upon a varicolored mob. Men in fine black coats. Ladies in shimmering gowns so costly that a family of seven could live in satisfied plenty for more than a year upon the purchase price. Their faces are upturned, gazing back at me. I am suddenly cold with fear . . .

She pulled her hand from the warm stone and staggered backward. The Artist caught her arm.

"It is quite a drop, isn't it? No need to worry, the footing is solid. This cliff has been here through the ages of man. I quite seriously doubt it plans to go anywhere soon."

She blinked and wanted to tell him what she had seen in her mind's eye. Her lips parted, but she'd forgotten how to make the words. The mirage was already fading anyway, leaving nothing but the fear.

Somewhere, at some time, she had been rather seriously disliked. Part of her was curious to know more. Part of her flinched from the very idea of it.

The warm sun soon released the tension in her shoulders, and the Artist's congenial conversation diverted her thoughts.

"I spent rather a long time wondering where all the stones in the wall had gone. Yes, one might assume that a certain number of them fell toward the sea and may well have rolled over the edge. But surely some of them would fall on this side, no?"

The Artist had obviously noticed her moment of discomfort and, as always, tried to distract her with inconsequential conversation. She rapidly replayed his last words to herself.

. . . where have they gone?

Yes, the stones from the wall. She tilted her head at him. *Go on.*

He took her gently by the shoulders and turned her to face away from the sea, down into the valley where the village stood glowing in the late afternoon sun. And surrounding the village, the bit of lowland pasturage carved out from between the hills, green fields outlined by—

She went up on her tiptoes and pointed at the neatly stacked, if imaginatively routed, perfectly even topped stone walls surrounding the fields.

He laughed and clapped his hands once in approval. "Yes! Now, do not judge me ill when I tell you that I pondered this matter for nearly a week before I spotted what you saw in seconds."

It was a silly thought, and so plain to her now, but the thing that struck her with wonder was that he admitted to this moment of poor thinking with ease and laughing self-deprecation.

It is because you like to wonder about things, she wanted to tell him. *It is because you enjoy the questions so much that you are in no hurry for the answers.*

It was not until they walked along for several more minutes that she realized she could still feel the way his big hands had cupped her shoulders. Her skin still tingled from the heat of his palms sinking into her flesh.

Touch. It was confusing to her. She wanted to draw back, out of reach. She wanted to move closer and touch him back. Distracted by the inexplicable tangle of her reaction, she stumbled over an irregular patch of the path.

The arm that instantly snaked about her waist and kept her easily on her feet did not linger overlong. She did not have time to discover what she would do if it did.

Do I truly want to know?

Yes. No.
I don't know.

Who was she? Was she a nun, trained to shy away from even the most gentlemanly brush of hands? Was she a wife, mourning a love she could not recall? Was she a wanton, to feel such a jolt of quickening at the heat of his hands on her?

Hands. Hands coming out of the darkness. Hands grabbing her roughly, painfully, pulling her from safety into danger. Hands too strong to be fought off with her own fragile ones.

I don't like hands. No. I truly don't.

It was affirming to know her stance on something, anything, but even as she stiffened and stepped slightly to the side, away from him, there rang a note of regret and longing.

She had evidently been a rather complicated sort of person, before. That life had left its mark upon her.

It was too bad, for this man had very nice hands.

He asked to paint her. She could hardly refuse such a polite request, given his generous care of her thus far. She sat very still upon the chair where he put her. The fine gown still lay in the drawer of the chest, too ruined to function as clothing. She sat in the nightdress she'd worn during her convalescence.

He wished for her to sit on a chair. He spent some time arranging her hair, which she had left free and long according to his request.

He touched her lightly, moving her this way and that according to some reasons known only to him. She found herself growing comfortable with his gentle requests. His courtly manner toward her seemed quite right and yet entirely different. Different from what, she had no idea. She only knew that she enjoyed the feeling of his warm fingers on her chin as he lifted her face into the light.

At first she felt stiff and overly aware. What did he think of her? Did he think her odd? Plain?

He said her face was interesting. That could mean many things.

He sat upon his stool. Liverpool took his accustomed place at his master's feet.

Soon, the comfort of the chair in which she sat and the warmth of the late afternoon sun on her shoulders left her feeling calm and perhaps a little bored. She amused herself by listening to the scratching of his pencil on the paper. A long stroke meant a long line, a short stroke meant a short line, and a fast back-and-forth stroke, accompanied by much muttering on his part, led her to believe he was scratching something out.

This relieved her of any pressure to perform. If all he was doing was sketching, and badly at that, then she felt she had little responsibility to do anything but sit. Perhaps he wasn't a very good artist. She might see his sketch and think he had drawn a pumpkin or a strangely shaped fruit.

As she sat drowsing in the sun, dreamily wondering about her history, she hardly noticed the time passing. When he stood and set aside his book and pencil, she blinked in surprise, realizing the sun had set and that there was only blue-glass darkness above the sea and the light of the candle in the hallway sconce.

He stretched and flexed his fingers as he smiled at her. "That was very good. Thank you very much." He reached a hand to her and she took it. It was not until she stood up that she realized how long she had been sitting. Her body felt stiff and tired. One of her legs had fallen asleep and now felt numb when she tried to use it. It was only his grasp on her hand and his quick support of wrapping his arm around her waist that kept her from stumbling.

He seemed mortified by her discomfort. "I should not have

let you sit so long. I am such an idiot. And with you so recently out of the sickbed!"

She had to laugh at his hangdog expression. As the flash of startled delight crossed his face, she realized she had never laughed before, at least not in her memory. Not in this new life, in the flesh she now inhabited.

He laughed at her own expression of shock. In turn, she laughed again at his boyish delight. Her laugh was a new sound to her. She felt lifted by it. Lighter, somehow.

"I like the sound of that," he said softly. "You have a lovely silvery laugh. I cannot wait to hear your voice."

She swallowed. "Thank you."

He gaped at her. Although no one could've been more surprised than she was at her ability to speak, she had to laugh at him again. For someone so handsome, he could look so very silly when surprised. Or smiling a sideways grin at her, like now.

"Say something else! Say . . . *Castell de la Cala.*"

"*Castell de la Cala,*" she recited. She smiled widely at the sound of her own voice after all this time, no matter the language.

The following evening, she wandered the *castell* as she sometimes did, in the hope it would jog her memory in some small way. She marveled at the cool feel of the ancient stones beneath her fingertips, the echo of the stairwell. How many lives had been lived here? Who were they?

It struck her as amusing that she would ponder the identity of others when she still had no knowledge of her own.

She walked to the top floor of the turret and saw that light blazed from the closed door of the Artist's studio. She tapped tentatively on the warped oak, then entered at his muttered assent.

Her question was forgotten the moment she stepped inside, for her attention was riveted upon the large canvas on which he furiously worked.

Is that me?

It was a simple painting, just a woman's face framed in her hair, and though she was delicate and too thin, she was anything but ordinary. A bit of the shoulders could be seen, as the woman wore a voluminous nightdress that looked familiar—it was much like the one she'd been wearing upon her awakening.

Yet it was the woman's expression that fixed her gaze. She looked . . . new. Her eyes were wide and alert, yet as unquestioning as a young childs. There was no worldly shadow within them, no sheen of cynicism. If that woman was her, then that was how she arrived on these shores, washed clean and left empty by the sea.

She stood there but a second, though the moment seemed eternal. When she understood that this was how the Artist saw her, the pure and untainted soul revealed in those painted eyes, she found she could not bear to face him. By the time he had finished his brushstroke and turned toward the door, she was gone.

THE PRESENT

Chapter Fourteen

Somewhere Over France

This was why Brenna avoided spontaneity whenever possible.

Since Fitch had waited until the last minute to book their flight from Heathrow to Barcelona, they now found themselves in the last two available seats. He had been enough of a gentleman to give her the aisle, but that meant he was now crammed in the middle seat like a pimento in an olive, his wide shoulders claiming a portion of her assigned space.

Brenna didn't want him up against her. She didn't want to feel the heat of his solid flesh or be enveloped in his scent. She had no interest in knowing just how muscular his thigh was or feel the brush of his wool blazer. His proximity made her feel a little wobbly and unsure of herself. Briefly, Brenna wondered if Piper had been right. Had Fitch found his way under her skin? Of course not.

She adjusted the overhead air vent.

"Did you check your email?"

To avoid eye contact with him, she studied the laminated safety brochure like it was a work of literary genius. "Of course I haven't checked my email. We are still ascending with Wi-Fi restrictions in place."

Fitch remained quiet for a moment, then leaned in closer. "You could sneak a peek at your phone," he whispered.

"I won't!" She shoved the brochure in the seat pocket and glared at him. That was a mistake, because there it was again— quite close this time—that amused half-smile that made his dimples deepen and his eyes flicker.

Brenna turned away, her heart thumping so hard she worried he could hear it.

For at least the tenth time that morning, she had to remind herself why she was doing this: The Siren Series. This was about fulfilling her academic dream, and as Piper said, Fitch Wilder was a necessary inconvenience, not a disaster. As long as she remained focused on her sole objective, she knew she could get through this unscathed.

Unaffected might be too much to ask for.

The pilot soon announced that passengers were free to use electronic devices and move about the cabin. Fitch leaned in. "Check to see if Claudia has sent the next section."

Brenna closed her eyes in pursuit of patience.

"We're supposed to be working together, remember? Hey, I showed you my digital composite, right?"

He had, and it could prove to be extremely helpful when they went to look for the artist's village. Fitch had used computer software to create a composite of all the paintings, erasing the foreground image of The Siren and then matching the backgrounds to create a panoramic view of the setting.

"Yes, and I showed you the Boston portrait."

"See how well we're doing?" Fitch chuckled. "We should continue to share things as soon as they come up."

She grabbed her phone and powered it on. She turned the screen away from Fitch so she could enter her passcode in privacy. Immediately she saw a new message from Claudia with an attachment. "I'll email you a copy when I'm finished reading."

Fitch laughed. "C'mon, Dr. Anderson. Let's read it together. You can email my copy later."

Brenna pulled her lips tight. "Are you implying I can't be trusted?"

Fitch lolled his head back and stared at the overhead bin, as if his head were too heavy to hold upright. Eventually he lowered his gaze to hers once more. "Brenna? You make everything so freakin' difficult. Are you not capable of relaxing, maybe just a little bit for just a little while?"

The man in the window seat slowly turned Brenna's way, his grin an indication that he would enjoy seeing her relaxed.

But all she could think about was that Wilder had just used her given name. He'd referred to her only as "professor" or "Dr. Anderson," and the switch flustered her.

"You agreed to—"

"Fine!" She retrieved her laptop so they could see the attachment on a larger screen, even adjusting the laptop so they both had a good view. Fitch leaned his head so close to hers that she felt a single unruly curl brush against her cheek, the sensation sending a tingle down the side of her body. She told herself to ignore it, but soon Brenna was so engrossed in the elegant handwritten words that Fitch became an afterthought.

Dear O,

Much has happened and there is a great deal I must tell you. First, I most sincerely apologize for how you must have worried about me. The last you knew, I was to escape to the Americas under pressure from an angry mob—and then not a word from me for nearly ten months! It was not my intent to leave you fearing the worst, dearest friend. As I write this letter, I am healthy, whole, and happy, despite everything that has transpired.

I must share with you the events that led to my current situation, though I will do so in the briefest fashion possible. Someday you and I will sit together in comfortable camaraderie and I will burden you with every detail you can bear, and you will accuse me of telling tall tales! I assure you, I am not.

Upon orders of the unhappy wife of Lord H— I was kidnapped from my carriage after attending the opera, and then taken captive on a merchant ship called the Bodicea. *The wife had paid the captain to "dispose" of me, but I managed to convince him to drop me at a distant port and spare my life. Unfortunately, my presence among his rough crew sparked a mutiny. I escaped in a lifeboat, only to be tossed by a terrible night storm that threw me against the rocky Mediterranean coast of Catalonia. An artist living in a fishing village north of Girona found me and, with the help of his housekeeper, nursed me back to health. I lived for many months here in the sunshine by the sea, with absolutely no memory of who I was! While my mind and body slowly healed, I spent my days as no one, a woman without a past and without a single regret. It was only recently that my memory returned.*

I have no plans to come to the Americas. I plan to stay where I am, in this dear tumbledown castle in a tiny medieval village along the coast, a place where goats and sheep promenade down the streets instead of ladies in fine bonnets! In my next letter I will tell you more. For now, know that I am in love and deeply loved in return—though I haven't a penny to my name! Both are firsts for me, as you well know. Do you find it amusing that I had to lose myself to find love and ease? I assure you, the jest is not lost on me.

I write you now, my dear friend, because I have come to a most startling conclusion that I must share with you. It is thus: I have never once allowed anyone to know who I am, and now that I have been set free from the restraints of English society, I know this must change. Please indulge me as I share with you—and your dear Malcolm—my true story. I will begin at the beginning.

Newgate
I have a name, a true name bestowed upon me by my loving mother upon my christening. After all, everyone has a name, do they not?

My name has been so long unspoken that it seems unbearable to say it aloud now—as if to do so will negate all those years of careful restraint. My mother saved my life by withholding my name and I always believed it my obligation to never break that silence.

The time has come, O.

Small children can look much alike, especially as it was in our day when we were dressed much the same.

Therefore, on the day that my mother was imprisoned as a scapegoat for my father's crimes, the magistrate mistook me for a very young boy when penning the order for my mother's sentence to Newgate.

I was not the only child in that dreadful place. Some of us were born there, to women already expecting at their sentencing or to those later impregnated by the guards, willingly or otherwise.

That is what kept my mother silent on my gender. She called me Jinx, and I answered easily to the babyish nickname. It was in reference to my small stature, so it served me well in the confines of Newgate.

Children of age were regularly culled from my little circle to serve in a workhouse. Boys, even those younger than I, would put on a growth spurt and come to the attention of the greedy guards, who received compensation for such finds. They would be torn from their weeping mothers and marched away, never to return.

I lived in constant fear of discovery, once I understood the dangers I faced. If the boys' fates were sad, the girls' fates were tragic. I cannot bear to think on it, I vow.

Even so, there did at last come a day when I gained enough height, though I remained stick-thin, to attract the notice of the turnkey. He was not the worst of the guards by far. He merely meant to get his portion for delivering a likely boy to some factory or workhouse.

I was grabbed up that day with only enough time for a brief touch of my mother's hand before I was shoved indifferently through a series of locked doorways to stand in the drizzling rain in a cobbled yard with a small group of similarly unfortunate boys.

Some were crying. I was not. I kept seeing my mother's face as I was forced away from her. Her chin was high and love and pride flashed in her beautiful eyes.

My mother was a lady. No walls or bars or brutal guards could take that from her. It was all she had to give me . . . that and the furtive education, the whispered lessons as we huddled together at night for warmth, the chalky stones of the yard carried back to scratch letters and numbers onto the soot-stained prison walls.

So I stood, dressed in the coarse trousers she had

stitched for me from bartered flour sacks, surrounded by the bastard sons of Newgate prison, yet with my head high, for I, too, firmly believed I was a lady.

The children of Newgate were taken off in an uncovered cart, stuffed in to huddle together in the drizzle.

My retiring ways and my small stature had kept me from the guards' notice for an extra year or so. The boys surrounding me were no more than eleven or twelve—although no one counted birthdays in Newgate, as if part of the conspiracy to keep the children for as long as possible.

The wagon rolled on for some time through crowded, filthy streets. Like the others, I gazed wide-eyed at the city I had only heard about from the adult women. It was loud and large and there was more sky available to my vision than I ever recalled seeing. Without the high walls of Newgate around me, I felt dangerously loose and insecure, as if I might fall up into that vast sky.

At last the wheels stopped rolling and we were unloaded at the rusted gate to a large building. I didn't have the name for it at the time, but later came to understand it as a warehouse.

Some of the boys, eager to be back within four walls, rushed off the wagon to form a line as directed. I hesitated, pretending to spill my belongings from the bundle in my arms. This left me where I wished to be, at the end of the line. Whatever fate lay within those walls, I wanted a little time to assess it first.

We were led indoors to an open area between high stacks of crated goods. A group of people waited there, mostly men. Some were roughly dressed and some were cleaner. One man was attired in a good suit. His hands

*were clean and his face close-shaven. A woman stood
nearby, although I sensed her revulsion for the clean
man in her very posture.*

*This gained her my curiosity. In prison, a child
becomes very perceptive about the adults surrounding
them. One must know when a blow is coming, or when
someone is being overtaken by madness, or is
entertaining lewd thoughts.*

*The woman was richly dressed, but not elegant. My
mother was graceful even in rags. This woman was
blowsy and overblown, her mouth a red slash of
painted lips, her eyes drawn artificially dark.*

*I knew a whore when I saw one. Newgate was full
of such women. For some of the boys in front of me,
she undoubtedly reminded them of their mothers.*

Yet the whore disdained the clean, well-dressed man.

*I had only seconds to come to this assessment before
the first boy in line, the biggest of us, who had pushed
his way to enter the building first, was sold off in a
swift bidding process between two of the rougher men
looking for farm labor. I saw the guards who had
brought us to this place pocket a handful of coin and
then the rough straw boss grabbed the boy by the arm
in a vicious grip and dragged him off, ignoring his cry
of pain.*

*Hard labor would kill me quickly, I had no doubt. I
had never been physically strong, even for a girl.
Factory work might allow me to live a little longer, but
I had heard stories of the factories in Newgate, and had
no illusions of my long-term survival within one.*

*What the clean man wanted made my throat close
with terror.*

One by one, the boys were taken and the line grew

shorter. Large boys went to labor. Wiry, agile ones were taken by the factory men. The clean man, however, eyed the lads with a distinctly different criteria. He took the blond boy with the bright blue eyes, and the dark-haired one with the pretty features, and they went innocently to him when shoved in his direction. No one in the room disputed his selections.

I shuddered and kept my gaze averted from the man. I tried to distort my face with a projection of my upper teeth and twisted my shoulders to try to appear lopsided and malformed. I knew I could not keep my boyish facade in place for long, but I hoped to be taken somewhere easy for a clever girl to escape.

Even in my thirteenth year I had become wise enough to know that the man with the sickening gaze would not be easy to flee.

My turn came at last. I stood there and shivered in my damp clothes, doing my best to look poorly grown and unattractive. The straw bosses and the factory men eyed me dubiously, as if weighing the usefulness of feeding me at all.

What if none of them wanted me? Would I be turned loose to roam the streets like a stray dog? It struck me that I had no idea how to survive in the world. I had known only walls and twice-a-day porridge served from bubbling cauldrons in the prison kitchens.

I would be alone in the city. I would starve in a matter of days. I would be helpless against any who would do me harm.

Yet when the clean man stepped forward to give me another look, I longed to flee to the sure and certain doom of the London streets—for that fate seemed

*preferable to the evil emanating from the clean man's
dead, assessing gaze.*

*As he walked around me, I shot a single glance, a
plea, to the well-dressed whore. For that instant, I
allowed my face to assume its natural lines and my eyes
to fill with wit and awareness.*

*Her painted eyes widened in surprise, then
narrowed in renewed interest.*

*"Oy! I'll be having that one," she declared shrilly.
"You've 'ad your pick, then, Elden!"*

*The clean man rounded me again and I made sure to
renew my valueless mien. He looked over his shoulder
at the woman.*

*"I shall say when I am done with my selections,
Valentine," he told her coldly.*

*She flounced up to us. "And 'e's the last lad left! I've
need of a kitchen boy and this one comes cheap." She
sniffed. "Anyways, 'e ain't pretty enough for your
clientele."*

*Elden turned his icy gaze back to me. "Not all of my
clients are interested in appearances." The hollow
satisfaction in his tone sent black dread to overwhelm me.*

*I shivered numbly under his scrutiny, afraid to look
at either of them, terrified of him, not much less
frightened of what she represented, wondering if my
mother would forgive me if I flung myself from the first
high window I encountered . . .*

Brenna rapidly scrolled down the page but found only an
inserted notation: *"Severe damage for several paragraphs."*

Fitch gripped her arm. "It just stops there? Are you *kidding*
me? Did she end up with that perverted bastard, or what?"

Brenna shifted away from his warm grasp. "We'll have to wait for the next email to find out."

What he did next shocked her. Wilder rubbed his face with his palms and took a deep breath, as if steadying himself. When he met Brenna's gaze his eyes were glistening. "That poor little girl," he mumbled.

Chapter Fifteen

Barcelona

They arrived in Barcelona by late afternoon and shared a taxi to L'Example, an area north of the city's medieval quarter. The professor insisted on paying half the cab fare, and before the driver could pull away she whipped a folder from her carryall and shoved it in his direction. "This will help you manage your time while we're here."

Fitch stared at a spiral-bound document covered with a clear plastic cover. It was entitled "Research Objectives, Barcelona." He laughed, opening the folder and flipping through the dozen or so pages. Here they were, standing in the Plaça de Catalunya, one of the city's liveliest public plazas, where they were surrounded by Catalan modernist architecture, Greco-Roman statues, fountain plumes, embracing lovers, leafy trees, and reflecting pools and blue sky . . . and the professor wanted him to look at her anal-retentive to-do list.

"I didn't know you were so . . . *fastidious*."

She scowled at him. "This is my wheelhouse, Wilder. When we start rooting around in abandoned buildings I'll let you take the lead."

He felt himself smile. "Fair enough."

The document was divided into two sections, one under his name and one under hers. Topics were organized into research subcategories for each library, museum, archive, and church offices she planned to visit. There was a listing of all the curators with whom she'd made appointments and a handy, color-coded, hour-by-hour schedule for the next three days. The professor had also provided a lengthy accounting of questions about the identity and location of the artist, his background and possible military service, and any additional unattributed works. In addition, she sought any mention of an Englishwoman living in the region during that time.

Fitch tucked the folder under his arm while studying his travel companion. She stood ramrod straight in those damn boots, all sharp angles and seriousness. But the breeze played with her hair, lifting it off the side of her neck, and that hint of softness made him smile. Maybe Dr. Brenna Anderson wouldn't be immune to Spain's charms after all.

"I gotta say—the spiral binding is a nice touch."

Brenna pursed her lips. "There is nothing wrong with thorough preparation. You might want to try it sometime."

Fitch nodded. "I think I could learn a lot from you. In the meantime, the city's pretty much shut down for siesta for the next few hours, so in the spirit of advance planning, I suggest we meet back here at nine and get something to eat. My favorite tapas place in the whole world is just a short taxi drive—"

"No, thank you." She swung her shiny blond hair over her shoulder and yanked up on the adjustable handle of her rolling suitcase. "We'll meet here tomorrow morning at eight. Don't be late."

Fitch watched her click her way across the Ronda de Sant Peres, disappearing among the pedestrians as she headed for her hotel. It hadn't come as a shock that she'd refused his offer to share a friend's empty apartment—a two-bedroom, two-bath place just a few streets over, no less. She must have feared they'd run into each other by the espresso pot one morning. God forbid.

Fitch snagged his duffle bag and made his way to the flat, thinking what a damn shame it was to be in the most romantic city in Europe with the least romantic woman he'd ever known.

He laughed at himself for entertaining such a nonsensical thought. They weren't on a date. They were there to work, to find the rest of The Siren paintings and then part ways.

He was reminded of this truth the next morning, when they headed straight to the Museu d'Història de Catalunya for an appointment with a research curator. After hours of poking through a variety of handwritten tax records, property records, and wills, they found no mention of art changing hands that might be linked to Le Artiste's work. Fitch's stomach started to growl about two o'clock, but Brenna insisted they work through lunch.

"Do you want me to pass out?"

Brenna dragged her gaze up and down Fitch's frame, which surprised him, though not in a bad way. "You'll survive," was her determination.

Fitch grinned, and then gave her a similar head-to-toe once-over, noting that she seemed unnerved by the attention. "I can't say the same for you, Professor. You look famished."

She ignored him, going back to the microfiche reader in front of her.

"See, the problem is, I can't think straight without sustenance."

"Have you always been this high-maintenance, Wilder?" She scribbled down a few notes without looking at him, but he could see her wry grin.

Fitch laughed, thinking she had to be aware of the pot-and-kettle vibe of that insult. "Suit yourself, Professor, but I'm not going to deny myself lunch in the gastronomical paradise that is Barcelona, Spain." He rose from the microfiche counter and shoved his laptop into his backpack, but before he could make his exit the assistant curator appeared in the doorway. She cleared her throat politely and announced that they were shutting down for siesta.

"*What?*" Brenna swiveled around on her stool, perplexed. "I wasn't informed of any closure."

Jordina, who couldn't have been more than twenty-five, had been run ragged by the professor that morning. Through it all she had maintained a friendly demeanor, but she now looked hurt and confused. "It's . . . it's on the sign, *Professora*."

Brenna began to gather her work, mumbling to herself. "Seriously? A nap trumps my research deadline? How do people get anything done in this country?"

The young woman began to stammer, her English suffering from her embarrassment.

Brenna turned around in horror. She hadn't realized the assistant was still there, and she looked to Fitch to translate a proper apology in Catalan.

About a half hour later, Fitch returned from a nearby market with a picnic lunch. Brenna was right where he'd left her, sitting on a wide wooden bench next to the Barceloneta Harbor, her nose stuck in her notes. Behind her were rows of yachts rocking in the gentle waves, their halyards clinking like wind chimes, and at her back was the peacock blue of the Mediterranean Sea. Fitch wondered if she'd even noticed.

Brenna barely acknowledged him as he sat down and began to unwrap the fresh bread, cheese, sliced tomatoes, olives, and bottled waters.

"You offended her, you know." He broached the subject as

he set out two paper plates and plastic cutlery. She had no reaction as far as he could tell, but then again, her witness protection sunglasses hid half her face.

Brenna shoved her notes into her bag and let her shoulders droop, a decidedly unusual posture for the professor. "I was out of line and I regret it. I can be . . . well, when I'm intensely focused I can . . ."

Fitch nodded, deciding it was best not to finish that sentence for her. He concentrated on serving the picnic.

"I want to get her something, a little gift of apology. I read that there's a traditional gift-giving etiquette here. So can we find a sweets shop before we go back?"

He smiled to himself. "That sounds like a nice gesture."

Brenna sighed. "Thank you for this, Wilder. For lunch and everything, I mean."

"My pleasure." Fitch glanced up and smiled at her. "This would be better with a nice bottle of Rioja, of course, but I figured you—"

"You figured right."

That's when it happened—the corner of her mouth curled—and Fitch had his first indication that the professor might not always take herself seriously. He wished to hell she'd take off her paparazzi-proof sunglasses so he could see her eyes, just to be sure.

"So you're fluent in Catalan, I take it."

Fitch tried not to appear stunned by the professor's very first attempt at small talk. "I am. It's a strange and beautiful language. People say it sounds like a mix of Spanish and French but that's not true—it's a completely separate language that evolved directly from Latin."

Brenna nodded with interest, taking a bite of bread, cheese, and tomato.

"I'm sure you know this, but Franco's fascists did a bang-up job of trying to destroy the Catalonian culture during the civil war, but it survived as one of Spain's autonomous regions. The people are still pretty sensitive about their identity, and though nearly all Catalonians speak Spanish, they also speak Catalan. You might have wondered by all the public signs in both languages." Fitch had been busy organizing his plate while he'd talked, so when he looked up he was surprised to see Brenna's face frozen in shock.

"You're not enjoying my history lesson?"

She shook her head, closing her eyes as she finished swallowing. "That's not it. You're very well informed, actually. It's this *bread*! *Oh, my God!* It's warm and spongy inside and perfectly crusty on the outside!" She reached for another large hunk and piled it with ruby-red tomatoes. "It's probably the most delicious thing I've ever tasted, and, sorry, but I just realized I'm starving." She added some cheese. "And these olives are really good, too. I can't believe a meal this simple can be so incredible."

Fitch smiled at her outburst. It was nice to see the professor was capable of unbridled lust of some kind, even if it were directed toward a loaf of bread. "*Rural,* Dr. Anderson." He raised his water bottle in appreciation. "Rustic food. Fresh, ripe, warm, and colorful—a feast for the senses. That's Spain for you."

Brenna dabbed her lips with a napkin and nodded. "So what other languages do you speak, Wilder?"

"Italian and Spanish, French and Portuguese, with just enough Japanese and Mandarin thrown in to save my ass." He popped an olive in his mouth. "I'd be useless if I couldn't negotiate in the Asian market. But I admit—my German and Russian suck. I'm more of a romance language dude."

That made Brenna laugh, and she covered her mouth as she finished another bite. "Romance," she muttered, shaking her head, as if the word itself were preposterous. Fitch waited, but she had nothing more to say on the subject.

"You?" he asked.

She shrugged. "French, quite a bit of Spanish, and, believe it or not, Swedish."

"Were your parents second-generation?"

He watched as Brenna's spine slowly straightened, like a marionette being pulled upright by a string. Her shoulders squared. And when she spoke, her voice was flat. All the delight he'd just heard was gone. "My father was second-generation. My mother was a melting-pot American. So . . ." She turned to stare out over the harbor, slamming the door on that subject. "Barcelona is beautiful, Wilder. I want to come back sometime when I can enjoy it more."

Fitch chewed leisurely, savoring his lunch as he processed the information she'd just inadvertently revealed. First off, he'd learned that Brenna didn't want to discuss her past-tense parents. Whether they had died or she'd cut contact with them, it was clear her parents were a sensitive subject. He respected that.

The second thing he'd just learned was that Brenna Anderson was one of those people incapable of living in the present moment.

"You're here now." He gestured to the skyline, the palm trees, and the water. "Now's the time to enjoy what's right in front of you. What if you never get a chance to come back?"

Brenna didn't answer him. She continued staring out at the sea, her expression hidden by her sunglasses.

They spent the remaining hour of siesta walking along the main thoroughfare of Barceloneta. Fitch found himself talking all the while, pointing out restaurants, stonework dating all the way back to the Roman Empire, and the ultramodern structures built for the 1992 Olympics. He donated a few euros to the street musicians they passed along the way, and they stopped at a little *patisseria*, where Brenna bought the assistant a half dozen truffles.

Fitch knew better than to ask Brenna if she'd like to take a stroll on the beach. Because . . . the boots.

The professor had been quiet for most of their walk, hiding behind her dark shades, and once they'd returned to the museum she was all business. It felt to Fitch like she regretted dropping her guard, and was telling him it wouldn't happen again anytime soon.

It was early evening now. They were still at the Museu d'Història de Catalunya, now seated at a large library table poring over weather data, looking for records of storms on the coast during the spring of 1827.

Brenna sat across from Fitch, and he leaned back in his chair to watch her. He decided that if he were an artist he would paint Brenna right here, in her element, and title the portrait *A Study in Studiousness*. She sat with her laptop and four weather logbooks open in front of her, somehow managing to talk, read, and type simultaneously. She leaned forward to double-check a logbook entry and rested her cheek in her palm. A lock of golden hair slid across her forearm, and suddenly, he tried to imagine Brenna as a little girl, before she'd constructed her hard shell of professorial competency. Could it be the don't-fuck-with-me exterior was a coping mechanism? He had no idea how recent the hurt was or who'd put it there—but at some point, someone surely had.

Brenna's head snapped up. She caught him staring. Her pale blue eyes flashed with alarm before they narrowed in warning.

Whatever her story might be, she'd just told him it was none of his business.

Brenna had asked Jordina to find any record of the ship on which The Swan claimed to be held prisoner, and she entered the room smiling. "I found it!" Jordina announced. Since Brenna had apologized and handed her the little bakery box tied with a ribbon, the two of them had acted like old friends.

Brenna glanced up. "The *Bodicea*?"

"Yes!"

Jordina grabbed a chair and sat down, shoving a piece of paper toward Brenna. "The captain's name was Atticus Reynolds, born in 1792 in Lisbon to English parents. From London shipping registration records, I found that he was listed as Captain Owner of the ship from 1821 to 1830. He left the ship to his nephew upon his death that year, apparently after he was stabbed with a chair leg in a brothel in Tortuga, of all places."

"Dude knew how to party," Fitch said.

He told himself that if that part of The Swan's story could be documented, there was a good chance the rest of her claims were true as well.

They rode the underground back to the L'Example, Brenna chatting excitedly about the progress they'd made on their first day. As always with research, each new insight had led to a host of new questions.

"I'll update our schedule for tomorrow," she promised him.

Once they were back on street-level, Fitch again asked Brenna to join him for tapas. Again, she turned him down. The next day didn't go well. They struck out with church records and at the Museum of Modern Art, where they'd attempted to locate any unattributed nineteenth-century works related to The Siren Series.

Despite that, Brenna was in a particularly upbeat mood. They had an appointment with an expert in the geology and maps of historical Catalonia the next morning, and it was possible the man could use the digital composite to match the geographical location of the portraits.

"What a breakthrough that would be!" Brenna said. Fitch held the museum door for her as they exited. "We might just walk in there, show him the landscape, and *bam*! We have the name of our town!"

"That *would* be a breakthrough."

A highly unlikely one, to be sure, but he didn't want to dampen her enthusiasm. In fact, Fitch tried to capitalize on her cheerfulness and, yet again, asked Brenna to have dinner with him. Yet again, he was dismissed.

"You're giving me a complex, Professor."

Brenna smiled as she began to cross the street. "You'll bounce back, Wilder. Your type always does. See you tomorrow."

Fitch had difficulty falling asleep that night. The emptiness of the apartment pressed down on him, and eventually he gave up trying. He threw off the covers and stood before the large windows of the front room, leaning his hands against the glass. He dropped his head to peer down at the city.

Your type? He had no idea what she'd meant by that but had a feeling it wasn't a compliment. The funniest part was that all he'd ever revealed to the professor was superhuman patience, with proficiency and reliability thrown in for good measure. And that made him a *type?*

He closed his eyes as the regret hit him. If Brenna learned he broke into her London hotel room to get the fax, she would be justified in typing him in any way she wished. *Jerk. Douche-face. Thief.* He promised himself he'd find a good time to come clean, and the sooner the better.

Fitch met Brenna at their usual spot at the Plaça de Catalunya the next morning. The plaza was already surrounded by double-decker tourist buses and humming with traffic and pedestrians. "Do you mind if we sit for a minute? I got you a *cafè amb llet, sense sucre.*"

She gave him the side-eye as he placed the coffee in her hand. "Milk no sugar?"

"Exactly."

She scowled, but allowed him to escort her to a concrete bench near the fountain. "So what's up, Wilder?"

Despite the suspicion in her eyes, she looked particularly

gorgeous that morning. Not that he'd be dumb enough to say so. Her skirt was a rich caramel cotton perfectly cut to her body, the hem landing just above her swashbuckling boots. On top she wore a little white scoop-neck T-shirt and a long, crocheted sweater thing with ruffles at the collar and cuffs and fringe along the hem. She'd pulled her hair up into a messy bun. Her bug-eyed sunglasses were resting on top of her head, and the overall effect was that the professor looked chic but artsy, beautiful in a purely accidental kind of way.

Fitch pointed upward, over the fountain plumes. "Do you see that?"

She followed his gesture. "See *what*?"

"Exactly. There isn't a cloud in the sky. It's just another achingly perfect day in Barcelona and I don't want to spend it in some dingy records room of a library. I need a day off—just one day. I want to play hooky and I want to take you with me."

She shook her head. "I . . . I shouldn't do that."

Fitch leaned in, trying to catch her averted gaze. "This is your first trip to Spain, am I right?"

She nodded.

"And we're ahead of schedule—you said so yourself. And the only thing on our agenda today is the map guy, right?"

She hesitated, frowning. "As a matter of fact, he just texted me to reschedule for tomorrow."

Fitch jumped to his feet. "Seriously? So we've got no appointments today?"

"Technically, no. But I thought we could—"

"C'mon." He rose from the bench and offered her his hand, pulling her to her feet while snatching the strap of her carryall from her shoulder. She looked confused. "You can take this back to your room. We're not going to need binders and laptops where we're headed."

She glanced up at him, one eye narrowed in censure. And though she never actually said yes to playing hooky with him, her feet did. She walked shoulder to shoulder with him toward the hotel.

Chapter Sixteen

Barcelona

Brenna wasn't an idiot. She knew exactly what was happening and that she was allowing it to happen. With this fun-loving romp through Barcelona, she and Fitch had crossed another line. Only a little more than a week ago they'd been Twitter adversaries. Then, with the help of a few random encounters and some negotiation, they'd decided to become professional collaborators.

Today, they were almost friends.

By now it was clear that she'd severely underestimated Fitch Wilder. College degree or no, he possessed a fine mind, and she'd been impressed by how quickly he made connections and saw patterns in research data. He was far more knowledgeable about art than she'd assumed, and had a wide understanding of history, politics, culture, and human nature. The man could—and did—strike up a conversation with anyone.

Just moments ago, while they were sightseeing on the breezy rooftop of architect Antonin Gaudi's La Pedrera, Fitch had volunteered to take photos of a group of Italian tourists. The encounter had evolved into a vibrant conversation filled with laughter and backslapping, and now Fitch was motioning for her to join in on the fun. With a big smile, he pulled her into the circle.

"Believe it or not, we have mutual acquaintances," he told her, rattling off everyone's Italian names with ease. "And this is my colleague, Dr. Brenna Anderson. She's a professor of sociology at Harvard University." Approving nods and smiles made the rounds. Brenna greeted everyone.

The patriarch of the group reached for her hand and raised it to his mustachioed lips. "It is my extreme pleasure, Professor."

Massachusetts, this was not.

Later, she and Fitch stood at the railing along the rooftop's undulating edge, appreciating Gaudi's strange and beautiful structure. The mansion-cum-apartment building was designed in 1910 by the inventor of Catalonian Modernism. Gaudi's creation was known for an organic, wavy exterior and an interior accented by decorative ceramics and elaborately forged wrought iron. The roof was populated with stairway exits, skylights, curved archways, and rows of chimneys in vaguely humanoid—and phallic—forms.

Brenna couldn't hold in her commentary any longer. "Perhaps the Spanish are oversexed by nature. Perhaps they're simply crying out from behind the wall of religious repression. Regardless, Barcelona doesn't even try to hide its preoccupation with genitalia."

Fitch leaned his elbows on the railing and chuckled. "Please continue, Professor. I think I'm about to discover what one of your lectures is like."

Brenna glanced his way out of the corner of her eye. "All right. Let's start with the obvious. This entire building is nothing but lusty female curves and orifices, topped off by phallic structures of every conceivable size and shape. Frankly, I believe there's something on this roof for everybody."

Fitch nodded in agreement. "You've got a point."

"And look." Brenna pointed northeast to the Torre Agbar, the giant blue skyscraper with a rounded top that towered over the city center. "Just in case you haven't yet gotten your fill of phalli, there's always the giant one-eyed trouser snake in the city center."

Fitch looked where she was pointing and burst out laughing. "So is this what it's like to travel with a sexologist?"

Brenna laughed, too, startling herself at the sound. It had been a while since she'd allowed herself to laugh like that, and she suddenly felt awkward. "It's an occupational hazard, I'm afraid. I don't mean to be annoying."

Fitch shook his head and straightened, his eyes locked on hers. "To be honest, Professor, you've been less annoying today than anytime since I met you."

"Gee, thanks." She turned away with enough attitude that the fringe of her sweater went swinging around her. She didn't let Fitch see, but she was smiling.

The day continued with a leisurely walk down Las Rambla, a wide, tree-lined pedestrian thoroughfare that took them into Barcelona's historic gothic quarter, or *Barri Gòtic* in Catalan.

They wandered along medieval stone streets that seemed more like walled labyrinths, as likely to lead to a public square as a dead end. Overhead were wrought iron balconies overflowing with flowers and plants, stone Arabic arches, and archaic hand-painted shop signs. She found herself particularly drawn to the variety of rustic doorways. There were huge slabs of ancient wood held together with giant iron hinges. There were medieval stone entranceways complete with carvings of gargoyles, skulls, goddesses, and tangled vines.

Fitch remained at her side as they walked for more than two hours. "I've always thought of the Barri Gòtic's doors as a history lesson in themselves," Fitch said. "They're a reminder of every culture that has ever come through here, from the Romans and Visigoths to Muslims, Jews, and the Catholic Church."

"It's almost too much to take in," Brenna said. "I feel like I could stay here for years and never get my head around this city."

Fitch grinned at her. "I've always felt that way about Barcelona."

He gently laid a hand on her shoulder, stopping their progress. Brenna noticed she didn't flinch at his touch. In fact, her shoulder tingled with pleasant warmth long after he'd removed his hand. "Do you hear that? I think we're in for a treat."

They turned the corner and Brenna gasped. The road had opened up into a large plaza in front of a cathedral. On the church steps a brass and woodwind band blasted out a folk tune as at least forty people held hands and danced in a circle.

Fitch had to yell in her ear to be heard. "Welcome to Le Seu Cathedral! This is *la Sardana,* the traditional dance of the Catalans."

Brenna looked up—and up some more—in awe of the cathedral's gothic spires of lacy stonework that speared the blue sky. "It's stunning, Fitch."

"We'll go inside in a few. But we can't pass this up." He grabbed her hand and began to run toward the circle.

Brenna dug in her heels. "I don't know the steps!"

Fitch tipped his head back and laughed. "Brenna, you're not going to be graded, for shit's sake! Look—half the people in the circle don't know it either."

He was right. There were as many tourists as locals in the group. An Asian teenager with pierced eyebrows held hands with a little Spanish grandma in polyester. She, in turn, held hands with a large man wearing a Chicago Bears T-shirt, who was hand in hand with a woman in a fur coat and Gucci sunglasses.

Fitch didn't wait to hear her objections. A moment later she was in the circle, following Fitch's steps and laughing at her own ineptitude. The Chicago Bears dude nearly knocked her over when he went the wrong way, but all she did was laugh. She got the hang of the dance within a few minutes, and Fitch smiled at her. "Impressive!" he shouted. He looked so handsome at that instant, smiling, happy, enjoying himself . . .

Too soon, the music stopped and everyone began to clap. Still grasping her hand, Fitch led her away from the center of the plaza toward the cathedral.

"We'll do a quick walk-through and then stop to get something to eat. Are you hungry?"

Dizzy, more like it. She wasn't sure if it was because he'd mentioned lunch, or that she had a case of Sardana-induced vertigo, or if it was because her hand rested comfortably inside Fitch Wilder's.

Fitch knew he was trying to cram a month of sightseeing into a single morning, but he might not get another chance with the lovely Dr. Brenna Anderson. She could very well shut down again as soon as they stopped moving—he'd seen it happen on their first day in Barcelona. So he wanted to stretch out the day for as long as possible, even calling in a few favors so he could pull out all the stops.

They had lunch at his favorite paella place, where they shared a platter of perfectly seasoned rice piled with seafood and cooked over an open fire. Afterward they wandered through La Boquiera, Barcelona's largest open-air food market, where Brenna's eyes widened at the long rows of *jamón*, Spanish-style cured hams, that hung from the rafters. She stopped in her tracks in front of a display of chocolates, but wandered away. Fitch bought a few pieces of the toffee she'd been eyeing, and decided to surprise her later. When they exited onto the street, the sun was setting.

They walked along in easy silence for many minutes, until Brenna stopped. She turned and looked up at Fitch, the oddest combination of confusion and pleasure in those pale blue eyes.

"Thank you," she said, quickly looking away. "It's been a wonderful day."

"But it's not over, Professor."

She glanced up again, a gentle smile playing on her pretty lips. It wasn't just the warm evening light—Brenna's face had softened, the tension around her mouth and eyes smoothed away by a day of good food, laughter, and beauty. "Thanks, Fitch. Really. But . . ."

"Not yet." He reached out and stroked the side of her face. "Indulge me one more little . . . well, *extravagance*."

Brenna looked out at the evening rush-hour traffic. "We should make it an early night. We have the appointment with the map expert tomorrow."

"That's tomorrow. Right now, you need to do this. Trust me."

She laughed, shrugging. "All right, but no more Electric Slide, please."

He laughed heartily.

Brenna was quiet during the twenty-minute taxi ride. When Fitch told the driver to stop he swung around to scowl at his passengers. "The Sagrada Família closed just moments ago," he said in English.

Fitch shoved a generous tip in his hand and told the driver to have a pleasant evening. Once on the sidewalk, he reached in the taxi to assist Brenna, and the feel of her small hand in his made him just a little weak in the knees.

"Whoa." Brenna tipped her head back and stared at the massive basilica glowing in the floodlights. "It's spectacular this close up. I'm glad I got a chance to see it, if only from the outside."

"Uh oh. Then I hope you won't be disappointed."

"Wilder!"

"Casals!" Fitch spun toward the voice of his friend. He squeezed Brenna's hand and directed her toward a side gate.

"Good to see you, man!" Fitch hugged Bernardo Casals and then introduced Brenna, taking a moment to explain that Bernardo was the brother-in-law of the friend in whose apartment he was staying.

Brenna was clearly confused but appeared willing to play along.

"She has no idea why we're here," Fitch told Bernardo.

"No?" Bernardo laughed and gestured for them to follow him around a cordoned-off construction area stacked with scaffolding and machinery. He used a key card to open a steel security door. "Then allow me to explain, Dr. Anderson. I am an assistant construction supervisor here. This is my office, so to speak, and Fitch asked if you two might stop by for an after-hours visit tonight."

Brenna's mouth fell open. Her gaze darted to Fitch. "Do you have friends *everywhere*?"

"Pretty much." Fitch placed his hand on the small of Brenna's back and waited for her to start up the stairs ahead of him. Within a few moments they were on the main floor, where Bernardo led them to an entrance into one of the four smaller naves.

"You have an excellent tour guide," Bernardo said to Brenna before he patted Fitch on the back. "Here are your visitor passes, and call me when you're ready to leave. I'll be here for another couple of hours. *¡Divertir-vos!*"

"Thanks. I'm sure we will."

With that, they were left alone in the church.

He gestured for Brenna to follow him into the central nave, aware that she kept spinning on her heels every few steps, as if trying to take in everything at once.

The click of her musketeer boots on the marble floor echoed all around them. "Oh, dear God." She'd lowered her voice to a reverent whisper. "This is the most spectacular thing I've ever seen in my life. I don't even have words for what I'm seeing."

Fitch smiled. "See? I told you you'd want to come along."

There was far too much to cover in just a couple hours, but Fitch did his best to show Brenna enough so that she could appreciate the scope of Gaudi's architecture. "He started this in 1883, and he died in 1926 when it wasn't even halfway finished. Right now they estimate all construction will be done by 2026—a full hundred years after his death."

"Holy shit. Talk about a long-term project."

Fitch chuckled. "Gaudi was quoted as saying that his client—*God*—wasn't in any rush."

She stared at the ceiling arched above them. "The detail is mind-numbing—the symbolism and the reference to nature." She pointed to the massive columns in the central nave. "They're like tree roots or arteries, pumping blood to the whole organism. And the roof looks like vertebrae along a spinal column. I see stars, flowers, birds in flight . . . it's humbling to be standing here in the middle of all this genius." She took her eyes from overhead and looked at Fitch. "What do you see, Wilder?"

Oh, she'd walked right into that one, hadn't she? Fitch cleared his throat. "I see beauty in its most complicated form." If Brenna was aware he spoke of her and not the basilica, she didn't let on.

The visit seemed to spark something in her, and she chatted during the whole taxi ride back. She talked so much that she didn't notice they were in the wrong neighborhood until they'd reached their destination.

Fitch paid the driver and stood with Brenna outside the Quimet y Quimet Bar and Restaurant.

"Where are we?"

"The El Poble-sec neighborhood. Tapas?"

Brenna looked into the crowded little establishment and shook her head. "You're taking advantage of me, Fitch."

"You think?"

"Absolutely. You got me drunk on Gaudi—and on an empty stomach, no less."

Fitch felt his smile spread ear to ear. "That problem is temporary, professor."

Not counting how the waitress flirted with Fitch, the meal would go down as one of the best she'd ever had. At their tiny table surrounded by a floor-to-ceiling wine cellar, they stuffed themselves on one appetizer-sized dish after another. When she took her first bite of crispy toast topped with smoked salmon, Greek yogurt, and truffled honey, she moaned indecently. The cured beef with roasted tomatoes and red peppers was next, along with a small plate of *jamón*, seafood-stuffed olives, grilled prawns, pâté with mushrooms, and scallops with caviar. While they ate, they talked, their voices competing with the noisy and mostly local crowd, and somehow they finished off two bottles of a dusky red wine.

Way, way too much wine. But how could she resist something that tasted like smoked cherries on her tongue and felt like velvet in her mouth?

Somehow the conversation wandered to the topic of relationship status. Fitch told her he'd broken up with a longtime girlfriend the year before. "It was good until it wasn't, so we decided to go our separate ways." That was all he had to say. "You?"

Brenna told Fitch about Galen Fairchild's double-dipping problem, and even as she spoke she realized her former lover seemed pathetic to her now. She'd been out of Boston just over a week, and that life seemed as if it belonged to someone else. Compared to Fitch, Galen was a boring man-doll shoved into a pretentious custom-tailored suit.

Even with all his rough edges, Wilder had started to grow on her. She could honestly say that looking at him across this little table was no sacrifice. Brenna decided she liked his unruly hair and his five-o'clock shadow. She enjoyed that teasing half-smile of his and those deep lines at either side of his mouth. She appreciated his smokin' hot body. She was even used to his cowboy boots.

But those eyes? Those eyes knocked the wind out of her. They were alive with color and emotion. Right at that moment they were mellow, seductive in their half-lidded state. Those eyes were mesmerizing.

"Wanna get out of here?" he asked.

They decided to walk toward the Plaça de Catalunya, even though it would take at least a half hour to get there. Brenna didn't mind—she wanted to be out in the city with the warm breeze washing over them. It was early summer here. Brenna could smell it in the ocean air and see it in the lovers that seemed to be around every corner—young and old, dating and married, arm in arm and hip to hip as they laughed and kissed their way through the streets. It was a gorgeous night in Barcelona, and she was with her archenemy, Fitch Wilder, who made her feel safe and adventurous and comfortable. Imagine that.

She started to giggle.

"Something funny?" His body intentionally bumped against hers as they walked.

"Not funny, exactly. More like a shock."

Fitch shoved his hands in his pockets and nodded. "Yeah. Sometimes shit comes at you out of the blue. You don't see it and—bam!—it's right up on you."

Somewhere in her wine-soaked mind, Brenna knew that if she were sober she would call him out for such a throwaway cliché.

"That's deep," is what came out instead, which made both of them laugh.

At the Liceu metro station near the opera house, they came upon an impromptu dance, right there in the middle of Las Rambla. This time it wasn't folksy trumpets and step-dancing grandmothers, however. Sultry Latin music was provided by an ensemble of acoustic and electric guitars, drums, and a saxophone. Couples pressed close to each other as they swayed to the rhythm.

"Would you like to dance?" Fitch asked.

Brenna decided that in the future, when she would surely regret this decision, she would blame it on the wine. She slipped her hand into his. "If not now, when? Right, Wilder?"

He laughed, pulling her close without further delay and coaxing her body against his. They began to move together, Brenna instantly aware that Fitch Wilder knew how to dance.

"Bossa nova is the sexiest music God ever gave to this world," Fitch whispered.

She had no response. Hell yes, it was sexy. *He* was sexy, and she felt sexy with him. Brenna rested her cheek on his chest and let him move her however he wished. Somewhere in the back of her mind it occurred to her that this was what people meant by "letting the man lead."

What a novel concept.

Fitch eased her into the thick of the swaying crowd just as the band ended the slow number and transitioned to something a little faster. He didn't miss a beat, holding her in place with his palm pressed into the small of her back. She could feel him from her thighs to her breasts, his taut muscle against her softness.

And just like that, an image flashed in her mind—The Siren, golden and sensual and open to whatever her lover had in mind for her. Had Brenna ever been that accepting? Was she feeling that way right now?

She must have gasped aloud, because Fitch asked her, "Everything okay down there?"

She nodded. He pulled her even closer. She felt his hips sway and roll, sending her mind on a random journey that twisted and turned like the cobblestone streets of the Barri Gòtic.

In her mind's eye she saw The Siren's flesh iridescent in the Spanish sunshine . . . the feminine curves and phallic images at La Pedrera . . . she heard the music . . . remembered the taste of food so delicious it made her moan . . . and the wine! Smoky velvet on her tongue, pooling in her mouth and warming her lips . . .

Oh, God. Fitch was moving her away from the crowd, swaying and rolling his hips to the sensual rhythm.

He lowered his lips to her ear. She felt the heat of his breath. Her body burned with desire when he whispered those three little words . . .

"*Eat-pray-love,* Professor."

Oh, hell yesss.

He eased her beneath an archway and her back suddenly encountered a hard surface—a stone wall? Then something hard poked into her belly, though she had no doubt what it was. She raised her face to him and found he'd been waiting for her. That half-smile! Those eyes! Then Fitch lowered his mouth to hers. He was hot and slick, his lips tasting of wine. It seemed he kissed the way he danced—masterfully. She was finally being kissed the way she always suspected was possible.

She'd waited an awfully long time for a kiss as perfect as this one . . .

Fitch's tongue and teeth played with her lips. One of his hands went to her hair and pulled it loose from its clip while the other hand slid up into her shirt, his hot palm flat upon her belly.

The kiss continued. Brenna tried to wrap her leg around his but the tight skirt wouldn't allow it. Fitch came to the rescue, his hand slipping over her hip and down the front of her thigh, yanking on the hem and bunching it over her bottom. She moaned when his hand slid back up the front of her body, right along the center, skimming over the crotch of her silk panties. She was wet. He had to have felt it.

He grabbed the back of her thigh and curled her leg around him, and the shift allowed Brenna to feel everything Fitch had to give her. She wanted it.

Didn't she?

Don't think, don't question, don't fight. Just feel this man. Taste him. Pull him tighter. Just be here, now, even though you know the moment won't last . . . that it can't.

The balmy night closed over them. The music swirled. Fitch's kiss became deep and demanding, and any pretense she'd had about "keeping things light" had just been blown to hell and back. He pressed hard against her, and she responded by tightening her thigh against him and rolling her hips in sync with the music's Latin rhythm.

She felt weak. She was on fire. Her pulse pounded as she dug her fingers into his thick hair and moaned into his mouth. But slowly, persistently, her rational mind began to speak to her, and its voice sounded like a TV reporter with a breaking news update.

Tonight in the gothic quarter of Barcelona, Dr. Brenna Anderson was ravaged up against a stone wall by an art dealer of dubious intent. The tenured Harvard professor and self-reliant modern woman—who usually makes excellent decisions—was passionately kissed while passersby assumed there was nothing special to see, that the display was just another case of a man and a woman getting swept away by a summer night in Spain. No one had a clue that the woman's perfectly constructed world was about to crumble.

Her eyes flew open.

"Hold up," she mumbled against his lips. "No. Stop, damnit." She pushed Fitch away, her breath rapid and her chest pounding. Suddenly horrified, she scrambled to yank her skirt over her lady parts. That's when she dared look up at him. Fitch's handsome face was stricken with confusion.

"Brenna—"

She held up her pointer finger to stop him from saying anything else, then tried to collect herself. "That was a mistake." She pulled away from the wall and took a wide berth around him. "I'm hailing a taxi."

"Wait."

She kept walking, and he kept talking. He was right behind her. "This has been . . . this was one of the most extraordinary days I've ever had, anywhere, with anyone. Don't end it this way."

Uncertainty stuck in her throat. She felt a twinge of guilt, like she regretted having to hurt him. *He was a grown man. He understood how these things went.*

"Good night." Brenna quickened her stride, tugging at her top and smoothing out her hair and skirt with trembling hands. *Where was her damn hair clip?* One of her boot heels got caught in the cobblestones and she stumbled, righting herself just in time to keep from landing flat on her face.

What the actual fuck have I done?

She ran toward the major intersection to hail a taxi. Two raced by without stopping. She felt a steady hand at her elbow.

"Brenna."

She faced the street. "I'll stay here to meet with the map guy tomorrow. You go ahead to Girona without me. I'll catch up—"

"Absolutely not. We're doing this together."

She waved her arm like a crazy woman and a taxi screeched to the curb.

He tapped her on the shoulder. "Wait. These are yours. I've been carrying them around all day."

"What?" She quickly accepted a small box he handed her, then slammed the door and locked it. She caught one last glimpse of Fitch, standing at the curb with his hands in his pockets.

He looked lost.

Once back in her room, Brenna opened the little box to find six pieces of toffee, only slightly melted. He must have bought them for her at the market when she wasn't looking.

Who was this man? Why did nothing about him make sense to her?

She almost called Piper, but stopped herself when she realized it was after midnight. She would be asleep, and so would Mick and the baby. Brenna couldn't disturb everyone simply because she was having a wine-fueled existential crisis.

But back in Boston, it was early evening, and Claudia was kind enough to pick up her cell phone on the second ring.

"Brenna! How nice to hear from you, but at this hour?"

"Uh . . . it's like six-thirty in Boston."

"Oh, well, it's after eleven in London."

Brenna shook her head, confused. "What are you doing *there*?"

Claudia laughed. "You sent me on a mission, do you not remember? Our friend Mr. Guilford? Ring any bells?"

"Oh, right." Brenna plopped down on the bed and tugged

off her boots, then put a piece of toffee in her mouth. "Of course," she mumbled.

Suddenly, she felt a jolt of anxiety. "But you can't tell him anything about The Swan! You know that, right?"

"Of course, dear." Claudia's voice sounded strange for a moment, but her usual cheerful manner returned. "So what's the latest? Earlier today I forwarded something to you in an email."

"More of the letter?"

"Indeed."

"I haven't had a chance to look at it, but Claudia . . . I need to ask you a question." Brenna propped an elbow on her knee and cradled her forehead. "It's kind of personal, but I could really use some input. You know, my mom is long gone, but even if she were still around I wouldn't want her advice in this particular situation, that's for *damn* sure."

Claudia was quiet for a moment. "My dear, you sound positively *sloshed*."

Brenna laughed. "It's Spain—of course I'm sloshed! It's sex and wine and food and art around every corner."

Claudia cleared her throat. "Well, I will help you if I possibly can, Brenna, but I'm not exactly the mothering type."

"Hey, no problem, because I suck at being a daughter." Brenna popped up from the bed and took her phone to the window. She stared out at the city, wondering where Fitch was now. Had he gone back to his apartment? Was he still standing at the curb with his hands in his pockets? Had he found someone else to dance with, or had someone else found *him*?

"Brenna?"

"Right. So . . . I want to talk about Terry, your husband. Did he change the rules on you? I mean, did he show up in your life and suddenly nothing worked anymore, none of the rules you'd established about men seemed right?"

Claudia gasped, then groaned. "You're falling in love with Fitch Wilder, aren't you?"

Brenna was about to protest when she distinctly heard Claudia whisper to someone near her.

"You were right, Winston. Will you accept payment in the form of a check?"

Chapter Seventeen

Barcelona

It was nearly two in the morning when Fitch got a text. He had to blink a few times to make sure he wasn't dreaming, because it was from Brenna. "Claudia forwarded more of the letter. Emailed it to you. Sorry about earlier—timing is wrong."

Fitch rolled his eyes. Her timing had been tragic. He texted her back. "Will read now. See you in the morning. Sleep well, Professor."

He reached up for the reading light by the bed. It was one of those ultramodern metallic things that reminded him of monster tentacles, but it got the job done. Fitch opened his laptop and clicked on the email.

Hi, Brenna. Here's the last of the letter . . . the salvageable parts, anyway. Happy reading. Claudia.

Fitch opened the attachment, fluffed the pillows under his head, and settled in. At first he was puzzled by what he was reading, until he realized the letter was picking up where the last section left off.

. . . like bait on a hook hanging between the devil and the whore, and I was desperately grateful to go home with the whore.

Fitch sighed, somewhat relieved to hear she'd avoided the sex offender. But still . . . that poor kid. He kept reading.

I resided with Madame Valentine for nearly five years. I spent all of those years dressed as a male, known only as Jinx, kitchen help and general errand boy. On the London streets, I was known as a wiry, fleet-footed lad who could be depended on to carry a message or make a purchase without thievery.

Within the house, I helped the cook and kept Madame's books and her correspondence, once she'd realized the depth of my education. I learned a great deal about business from Madame. Not many fourteen-year-olds add up columns of the purchase of sheep-gut penis sheaths!

Of course, everyone there, including Madame Valentine's "girls," knew what I truly was. They also knew that Madame Valentine had something special in mind for me, so if they valued their safe harbor within those walls, they kept their peace.

As for myself, I assumed that I had never been put on the "floor" because Val, who refused to traffic in children, awaited my emergence into womanhood with the intention of holding a grand auction for my virginity. I had observed that if the cards were well played and the girl was a bit of an actress, one deflowering could net four or five clients in turn.

Regardless, I never felt a part of the femme theater. Once, when a particularly histrionic young prostitute by the name of Jewel frightened away a stout, red-faced client with her screams and wails, the women of Madame Valentine's found themselves divided.

Several of them defended Jewel's claims of inability to perform with a man sporting three testicles. The others claimed that she'd disrupted the evening and had prevented several men from properly closing negotiations.

Understandably, Val weighed in on the side of trying to

*make money. I, on the other hand, was confused by the issue.
I understood the presence of testicles in theory. They seemed
ludicrous accents to an otherwise fairly interesting anatomy.
Most of the girls thought them ugly or at least uninteresting in
themselves. Never once in all my residence in that house of
whores did I hear the words "lovely balls."*

At that point, Fitch stopped reading so he could laugh his ass
off. Eventually he got back to it.

*This observation shut even Jewel's mouth. As one, they all
turned to stare blankly at me. I realized then the gulf that separated me from the rest of the girls there.*

*It wasn't my boyish garb, or the way I ran the streets of
Cheapside as freely as a lad, or even my ladylike education,
which I did make some effort to conceal. No, the singular divide
between them and I consisted of one thing and one thing only.*

My intact hymen.

*A virgin in a whorehouse is rather like a cat in a kennel. The
other animals might accept the presence of such, and even hold
it in some affection, but it would never, could never, be a dog.*

*I believe that in that moment, Madame Valentine made her
decision. A few days later, she called me into her "morning
room" as she called her cubbyhole of an office where her desk
overflowed with accounts, to discuss my future.*

*Looking back, I think she expected me to show more grati-
tude than I did when I declared, suddenly and hotly, that I
would rather die than become a whore. Indeed, my statement
came as a surprise to us both.*

When had I decided such a thing?

*I could not say. All I knew was that in that moment, I meant
what I said. If I were to be forced to service any fellow who
showed up at the door with a farthing in his pocket and an erection right beside it, I would take myself directly to the nearest
bank of the Thames and fling myself into the filthy waters.*

All around me lived the truth of whoring. Delivering sexual favors to strangers, to man after man, night after night, took its toll on a woman's soul, even in a fairly comfortable establishment as Madame Valentine's. For although Val's house was clean and strictly run, and excessive drink and opium discouraged, and she would put the boot to any client who damaged her merchandise, it was a business. All within it were for sale to anyone with coin.

Two women chose suicide during my stay. Another went mad and bathed herself until her skin was flayed off. Yet another was murdered in an alleyway by a footpad not a block from Val's house. I witnessed more sexual acts before my fifteenth birthday than most women actually perform in a lifetime—and I thanked Madame Valentine every day for saving me from Elden and his ghastly little "private club," for the stories I heard made my head swim with horror.

I was deeply grateful for Val's generosity, and I knew it was poor repayment to the woman who had saved my life, but I could not do what she asked of me.

I was surprised when Val agreed with me.

"No, you won't do. You're naught but skin and bones, even now. Blokes don't come to this house for conversation!" She grasped her enormous breasts, one in each hand, and jiggled them in emphasis. "I could steal a man from you in a heartbeat, I could! I still got what they want!"

As I had dreaded the arrival of breasts for as long as I could remember, I could not help but nod.

"So whorin' won't do," she stated firmly, still using her breasts for punctuation. "And you're a fine hand at the numbers, and all, but you ain't truly earnin' your keep and you know it, don't you?"

I had a very clear idea just how much it cost to support every person in the house and, no, I was not particularly *valuable to Madame. Any man of business could spend an hour a week and do the same, for a very small fee. I nodded miserably.*

Madame Valentine had most fortunately laid by a second option. "I has a friend, I do. We started out in the same house, but she were special, even then. She had a pretty voice, like somethin' in a dream. A rich man come to hear her. He took her off to be his very own, and he got her fine teachers and a right smart carriage of her own. He died and left her a fortune. She took another rich lover, and then another after him. Each one left her richer than before, but she never forgot ol' Val. I did her a right thing once, a thing what kept her away from a terrible bad fellow. You met 'im once, the day I brought you home.

"So me and my friend, we keep in touch. I told her about you, how you read and write and talk when you forget to sound common. She said she might be able to do something with you, if you weren't too ugly. I told her she best be lookin' to her own mirror, for she has a nose like a drunken sailor on the mornin' after."

I recall being thoroughly confused. "I don't wish to be a whore, Val."

She shook her head and slapped the flat of her palm across my scalp, as if I really were a kitchen boy. "I be not talkin' about whorin', you twit. I be talkin about being a cor-tay-san!"

Was there a difference?

The Songbird
I had expected the notorious Songbird to be beautiful. She was not. I had expected her to be languid and jaded, a perfumed and powdered wealthy version of a whore. She was not.

Instead, Val hand-delivered me to a tiny, plain wren of a woman. Her gown was expensive, and most luxurious in make, but so severely elegant as to be very nearly unadorned . . .

The letter ended there.

"Auuuggghh!" Fitch let his head loll back on the pillows, laughing. He'd been left hanging twice in one night, two stories left unfinished.

He'd never been a fan of interruptus.

THE PAST

Chapter Eighteen

Castell de la Cala

Once she regained her voice, she peppered the Artist with questions. One afternoon while in the studio, the Artist began to arrange her hair. His fingers lingered over the crescent-shaped scar on her scalp.

"It doesn't hurt," she assured him.

"It was a frightening wound." He restlessly puttered with his brushes for a bit longer, and began again. "Of course, there is no physician in the village, but we do have Beatriu. She stitches up the fishermen and treats the children's fevers, so she saw to your head and wrapped your ribs. We did not know if you would live."

She felt quite weak all of a sudden. She did not know why she should care so much about the near death of a woman she didn't even recall, but deep within her rang a protest, like a knife tapped to a crystal glass.

If she knew nothing else about the woman whom she had been, she knew that she had clung to life on those rocks. She gazed down at the scabbed, scarred ruin of her fingertips and knew deeply and instinctively that she must continue to do so.

No matter what came her way, she must survive.

As long as you live, I shall live.

It was one of the voices—the lovely, educated one that shimmered with approval. As always, it seemed to whisper, as if imparting secrets.

She closed her eyes, trying to reach for more. Who? When? Where? But there was nothing but that brush of gentle breath across her damaged thoughts, and then it was gone.

The Artist was speaking once more, speaking with his back to her as he sorted through the painted canvases stacked against the far wall. "I shall never forget the moment when I reached to investigate some odd, silvery-gold seaweed and instead found myself with a handful of your hair." He turned to gaze at her wistfully. "I have never felt anything as soft."

She blinked and could not help but raise her hands to her cheeks. He laughed at that.

"Ah!" The Artist selected one of the canvases at last, lifting it from the vertical stack and eyeing it critically. "I never did get the sky quite right on this one."

It was another painting of sea and sky, both tumultuous and dark. She thought it quite convincing, if disturbing in its violence. The waves rose tall and pointed, like weapons daring the low and threatening sky. The usually white froth of the sea was painted in hard, ferocious slashes of bright, wrong shades, the colors of chaos and battle . . .

A wave of vertigo swept her, tossing her high until she hung weightless in the air, then flinging her heavily, harshly down. Her sore fingers gripped the arms of her chair as hard as they were able, but still the world spun. Her breath came too fast, too quick! She could not draw in enough air!

And suddenly, I remembered.

It washed over me in a great chilling wave. All my days, all my nights, every risky, outrageous, desperate act fell into order in my mind.

I was The Swan.

Large, warm hands gripped my shoulders. Brown eyes gazed into mine, locking on, holding me steady, present, fixing the horizon where it belonged once more.

The brown eyes smiled gently. "I see now that it is a much worse painting than I thought."

I have never been ashamed of doing what I had to survive, but regret . . . oh, there were great deep oceans of regret.

Not the least of which was the regret I felt for being the kind of woman I was . . . while facing the open, concerned expression of this man who held me so carefully in his strong hands.

How I wished I had a different story to tell him. How I wished I truly had been lost and stranded for him to find on his rocky beach. I wished I could be his sea nymph, his siren . . . but I would not lie to him, not him. I would never lie to him. Of all the men I had ever known, he was the one who deserved more than my carefully constructed persona.

But before I told him the truth and was promptly shown the door, I admit that I allowed myself to rest within his embrace for a single moment . . . or three. Perhaps I was marshaling my courage, or perhaps it was simply a selfish grab at a few more moments of being the woman he thought me to be, the woman I wished I were, for my own sake as well as his.

Then, swallowing hard against the tide of regret, I placed my palms upon his hard chest and pressed firmly until his arms loosened and I slipped free of his warmth and his support. I waited another moment, relishing that feeling of support, of that rare solidity of a man upon whom one could depend.

He is not for the likes of you, lovey.

Madame Valentine's voice spoke in my mind as clearly as if

she stood behind me. Sharp, astringent, but as tinged with kindness as it had always been.

I looked up into the perplexed face of my benefactor, my gentle Artist . . . my friend.

"Pardon me for a moment." I pushed gently away from his concerned embrace and left the studio. With one hand out to the stone wall at my side, I traveled down the spiral stairs to the floor below and into my bedchamber.

As if in a trance, I shut the door behind me, and with a sigh I leaned against it, tipping my head back against the heavy oak. I waited for the tension in my neck and shoulders to dissipate, but it did not. I had too much bitter sorrow wound around my soul to take my ease.

Everything I had ever done, and everyone I had ever done it to, made me into someone I no longer wanted to be. Did this mean that despite all I had taught myself, I was ashamed after all?

Who was the hypocrite now?

Closing my eyes, my back still pressed upon the door, I went over my life moment by moment. Not every moment, just the ones that changed me. Those moments in which I had made a choice, a choice that had sent me into a certain direction, a direction that had led me here.

Was I to feel shame for the things I had done to survive in the short-term and thrive in the long-term? Did it even matter now that the construct of my safety and security had been lost? I stood here a broken and penniless woman. Yet I was alive.

Perhaps the only thing I had lost was the life I no longer wished to live.

A sea breeze entered the room through the open window. It caressed my upturned face and cooled the hot sting of tears that hid behind my eyelids. I did not weep out of regret, only infinite sadness.

I missed being the girl with no past. I liked who I had become before the truth crashed down on me like cold sea waves. I suspected that the girl with no past, no fears, and no protective walls was the girl I was meant to be . . . the girl I had been at the beginning of my life.

I wept for that girl. Her sweet and open nature had stood no chance before a lifetime onslaught of the evils of the selfish and the cruel.

I wept for myself.

Then I dried my eyes, lifted my chin, and went back to the studio to face my greatest fear. What would that fine and decent man think of me if he knew the truth—all of it?

I left out nothing, sparing myself no quarter. I told him every grim and desperate detail of my childhood in Newgate prison. I described every moment of hiding in plain sight at Madame Valentine's brothel, every lesson I learned at the Songbird's knee, lovers, the Duke of Mark. I even shared the tale of Lord H— , the fee his wife paid to dispose of me, and all that had transpired with the ship and the captain.

I told him what I remembered of the storm and the rocks and of waking up without the burden of my past, of beginning to remember that I had not always been The Swan, or Jinx. That I had once been the beloved daughter of a good house, a solid family name, a girl child with nothing but the most shining life of gold and promise before her.

I did not twitch or flinch or wander the room, turning my eyes away from the Artist's fixed gaze. I stood straight before him. My confession was plain and relentless—ruthless, even. I told him as much truth as I could recall. It poured from me, that truth. I finally ran down. Silence fell in the paint-spattered studio and only the breath of the sea waves remained. I realized

then that I had never told all my truth before, never confessed
to anyone.

When the Artist finally spoke, he said the very last thing I
expected him to say.

"What became of your mother?"

There was no shock or revulsion in his voice. There was no
distaste in his expression or the sudden tension of a man who
wishes more than anything to leave the room in haste. He sat
before me, one hip cocked on his stool, one heel of his boot
hooked over a rung. His hands lay calmly on his thighs and his
beautiful brown eyes gazed at me clearly and calmly.

What of my mother?

I would have given this man anything in the world at that
moment, simply for his lack of instant rejection. I gave him all
I had to offer. More truth.

I told him how I saved every farthing Madame Valentine ever
gave me, and made regular visits to the prison. At each visit I
would hand over my letter and my coins to the turnkey named
Oliver. He was the only one I trusted, though he was not so much
better than the others. However, I had never seen him take a
prisoner against her will, nor witnessed him strike anyone who
did not require subduing, so I perhaps gave him more credit than
he was due. Though he was not actively cruel, still he took my
coins and told me that he gave my mother my messages for more
than three years.

Then one day there was another guard in Oliver's place. I
asked after my mother, and the man said he'd worked in the
prison for nearly as long as I'd been gone and he'd never seen anyone like my mother there. I doubted him, but it was a simple
matter to search the prison graveyard. The markers were plain
wood panels, most gone to rot already, but under the coating of
slick moss on one marker I found my mother's name and the

date of her death etched into the grain. She'd died mere months after I'd been taken away.

I wept furiously, and my anger was great, but Vallie reminded me that all my mother had ever wished was for me to prosper and that she was surely better off at peace than alone in Newgate. Vallie assured me it was a blessing that she had not been pining for me all those years.

"I was young and in great pain, so I chose to believe that she was right."

The Artist nodded. "Your mother clearly loved you beyond all else. Without powerful friends on the outside, how could she ever hope to leave?"

"I could have saved her." It was a statement of fact. "If I had allowed Vallie to sell my virginity to the highest bidder, I could have made enough in the brothel to free my mother."

"Perhaps . . . if she had lived long enough." The Artist looked at me with compassion free of pity. "Would she have favored such a sacrifice when you were but fourteen years of age?"

How strange. When he said it in that way, I could feel the rightness of it. Of course my mother would not have wished me to be treated so. She would have thrown herself bodily before a runaway horse before allowing me to be sold like that.

And with such simple words, such a fresh breath of sea air, the Artist's sensible explanation swept away my darkest regret.

I shook my head. "Who are you? How can you hear my tale and not fling me from your house, or . . ."

"Or try to buy you?" He laughed softly. "Pretty sea nymph, I have nothing but a palette and a brush in my vault, and nothing to take from you but what you wish to give freely."

I frowned. "I'll have you know that men the world over pine for me."

His eyes warmed and a smile tugged at the corners of his

mouth. "Oh, that I do not doubt, my siren. Even battered and near drowned, I have never seen anything as beautiful as you, lying on the beach, tangled in seaweed and your own golden hair."

Of course, I had assumed that once the Artist knew who, and what, I truly was, that he would naturally make advances upon my affections. It was, after all, what men did.

He did nothing of the sort. Instead, he began to tell a tale of his own, and I sat in stunned silence as he painted his own portrait with words. "You have told me how you came to Castell de la Cala. Much like you, I was brought here on a tide—a tide of war."

He ran one hand fondly down the stone wall at his side. "These walls have been my hiding place since the men of the village smuggled me from my makeshift traitor's prison and hid me in this pile of rocks to save my life."

I shook my head in disbelief. "Traitor? I cannot believe such a thing."

He smiled sadly. "You should believe it, for it is the truth. That word was tossed about a great deal during those days, used for everything from desertion to tupping the general's daughter, but in my case it is most accurate. I was a major in the British infantry, and my commanding officer, a young man by the name of John Babington, ordered me hanged with his last breath."

I lifted my chin. "You are an honorable gentleman in my eyes. Nothing you can tell me will change my mind."

He turned his gaze to the view outside the studio window. "I thought I was a good soldier once. A good Englishman . . . until my battalion was sent into the countryside north of Barcelona."

I joined him at the window, but leaned my back against the wall so I could see his features in the light.

"We were there to ensure the French retreated entirely over the mountains," he went on. "The French Army was in full run. I don't think it occurred to any of us that they might turn and fight. We went charging after them like a gang of boys chasing down a runaway pony, laughing and bragging all the while." He smiled slightly in memory.

"We encountered them just south of Castell de la Cala. Because they were ragged and wounded, we assumed they would be easy to manage. We didn't count on them fighting like cornered beasts. The truth was that half of them were already dying, left by their own battalion, you see, abandoned because they could not keep up. They fought like they had nothing to lose."

He shook his head. "Lieutenant Babington faltered, right in front of his own men, and fled the field. After we subdued the remaining Frenchmen, I followed him and dragged him back. No one said a word against him but he knew we had all seen it. Overcome by humiliation and fury, he turned on the prisoners."

Deep sadness entered his warm brown eyes.

"He ordered them shot on the spot," he went on. "Some of us protested. Some of us confronted the protesters. In the confusion, some of the healthiest prisoners escaped and fled north toward the village. Babington was foaming mad. He ordered us to occupy Castell de la Cala, convinced the people were hiding the French, that they were collaborators one and all."

His tone was bleak. "We did as we were ordered. We knocked on doors, searching homes and barns and shops. Babington became more frantic. It was as if he felt the escaped prisoners were at fault for his moment of cowardice, as if they were witnesses who needed to be eliminated. I knew he was not rational by that point."

I held my breath, for I had begun to fear what might come next in his tale. I had seen how war waged forever on in the hearts of those who fought it, even after peace was declared. What did this man carry from those terrible days?

He sighed. "We found nothing, of course. The escaped men had likely run right past the village that first night but Babington would not hear it. He punished the townspeople for their 'conspiracy,' ordering barns burned and shops ransacked. He even sent troops to tear down the church, which they found too well crafted to crumble. When nothing could induce the poor villagers to turn over the imaginary Frenchmen, he ordered us to pound ten-foot stakes into the village square in front of the fountain."

He stopped then. In the silence of the studio, I could imagine the ominous hammering of the soldiers placing the stakes. I knew their use. At best, whipping posts. At worst, restraints for execution.

Until this point, he'd been recounting the tale as dispassionately as if making a military report. Now, he exhaled and his body sagged, as if he hadn't the strength to stand against the burden weighing upon him. He half-sat on the edge of the worktable and spread his big hands over his face.

"I didn't believe he would go through with it, even then. None of us did. We kept waiting for the lunacy to pass, for the jest to be over, hoping that we were not witnessing a young man descending to such a horrible place."

He lifted his head and met my gaze. "We waited too long."

I swallowed against the flutter of horror in my throat. Did I want to know this thing, this truth that loomed so dark that it made my own sins easy to brush away?

Did I have the right to ask him to stop?

I drew in a breath and gave him a small nod, as if to say, *Go on.*

His rich brown eyes swam with pain. "I recall that it rained that night. The mud in the square was deep and dragged at our boots as we pulled the villagers from their homes, as if the very earth itself wished to halt the madness.

"Babington stood in the square, his face as pale as death, his oilcloth cape fluttering around him. I did not recognize the boy I'd known most of my life. I could not see the proud young commander. I could only see his insanity.

"Again, we obeyed the orders to tie twelve village men to the stakes, including the local priest. Babington commanded us to line up facing them. The guns were packed with powder and ball. The fuses were lighted, sparking like fireflies in the gloom. And still we waited for him to end it before it went too far."

I could see his hands forming into fists as they rested on his thighs. His knuckles were white. I imagined his nails digging into his palms until they might bleed. I wanted to reach for him, to take his hands in mine, to ease the tension emanating from his body. I wanted to stop his story before I heard too much.

I did nothing but wait, and listen.

"Every time it rains, I remember the smell of it, of gunpowder and wet clay earth, of sea and flowers—and beneath it all, the coppery tang of bright, fresh blood."

I gasped. "You shot them?" *It could not be. I could not bear it!*

He met my gaze. "No. I shot Babington."

In my relief, I fear I did not fully take his meaning. "Then you saved them! It is no wonder the people here consider you a hero."

He shook his head. The shadow in his eyes . . . was it shame?

"I am no hero. I am a traitor. Ask the British Army. After a shocked moment, while poor Babington fell into the mud, the rest of the company tackled me and threw me to the ground, wrested my pistol from my grasp."

I shook my head, unwilling to accept his self-denunciation. "You did the right thing. He would have killed so many innocents—"

"He was a boy!" he shouted.

I flinched from his pain.

"A stupid, proud boy! Twenty-three years old and saddled with too much responsibility, sent into battle, into command he was constitutionally unsuited for! And I failed him! I should have been willing to lay down my life for my commanding officer—but I sent him bleeding and dying into the mud like putting down a mad dog! It took him two days to die."

I moved toward him. Even in his raging self-loathing, he did not frighten me. "You did what you had to do."

He shook his head, pulling back. "I could have stopped him before it got so tangled up. I could have beaten some sense into him. I could have tied him up and sent him back to the command post, taken over the battalion myself. I would have faced charges, I'm sure, but Babington would still be alive!"

This I could not allow. I stalked him across the room. He fled me, but even in his wild grief I knew he would not harm me, so I pursued him until his back pressed against the closed door.

He turned his face away, his eyes closed, lost in his past, still punishing himself for days long over.

I took his face between my hands. "You did the best you knew," I told him softly. "You tried. You were just a stupid, proud boy too, if you recall. You too were just a young man sent into a situation you were not prepared for. You cannot punish the boy you were forever. You must forgive him someday!"

Suddenly my thoughts turned inward. *What of my Jinx?* Silly Jinx, who had believed the courtesan's life would solve all her problems, who had no idea of the tangled dangers of the demi-monde. And The Swan, who believed she had control of every detail of every aspect of her world!

At that moment, I forgave them both.

In the following days, the Artist began to ask me all about my life in London. He was curious about the oddest things, reminding me of Beatriu's interest in common village gossip: who had wed whom, how many children they had, who had inherited their title at last. He'd claimed he was just a soldier, but he seemed to know—or at least had heard of—many of my acquaintances in London. Those in society, of course, and not my dear Val or the hideous Elden. However, he had heard of the Songbird, and much enjoyed the stories I could tell of her.

I talked while he painted me. It was another simple sitting, not a formal portrait, and I sat in a chair wearing a light summer shift. If the garment had been made of translucent batiste I would have considered it underthings, but as it was a sensible chemise cut from sturdy cotton it seemed quite like clothing to me.

The Artist had requested that I sit upon an upholstered chair that had once been fine, though its velveteen had worn nearly away and one broken leg sported a makeshift splint. He said he liked the lines of it when he hauled it from heavens knew where and plunked it before the window. "It reminds me of you," he said. "All beautiful lines and fine finishes."

I raised a brow at that. In my illness I had gone far past fashionably thin into the realm of a child's stick drawing. My once polished skin had obtained a rather impressive collection of scars.

I tried to be philosophical about them, to see them as evidence of my having survived a great trauma, but sometimes in the night I ran disbelieving hands over the ridges permanently etched into my flesh and felt a loss I did not know I carried. My exterior had been a creation, I had thought. I had believed myself entirely disconnected from it, other than in the ever-careful maintenance of my greatest asset.

I had not thought myself vain at all. Yet I also would run my fingertips over my face, tiny silent tears of gratitude slipping from beneath my lids, relieved that it had been untouched by the fury of the sea.

The Artist did not appear to see the damage made obvious by sunlight streaming through the open window. I knew the thick ridge of raised tissue on my right shin was entirely visible beneath the knee-length chemise. There was no hiding the upper arm scraped raw by jagged rocks.

He was quite blind to them both, as he was to my pointed features, my too thin wrists, and the fingernails that I had lost while grappling for safety on the aforementioned rocks.

The nails, thank heaven, seemed to be growing back. I had always secretly been pleased by my delicate fingers.

The Artist posed me there in the chair with my hands on my lap and my face turned so the sun fell upon half my features. I held very still while continuing to tell my stories of the haute ton. It seemed little enough to repay him for all his kindness, so I racked my memory for any tidbit.

I even told him about the delightful Lementeur, of whom he had never heard.

"He must have arrived after my time in town." He shrugged. I realized that it was true. Lementeur had rather suddenly appeared one day, just a few years before, already a full-blown success, designing gowns for the likes of Lady Wyndham and Lady Montmorency. I smiled at the realization that my dear friend Button had mastered my own art of masquerade.

"People believe what they are told to believe," I marveled to the Artist.

His face became sad and his gaze turned down to his paint-smeared palette. "I'm afraid they really do."

I could have smacked myself for reminding him of his banishment. If I apologized, I knew I would only worsen the moment, so I blithely carried on chattering about the many stunning daughters of Lord and Lady Greenleigh and the latest antics of the infamous Lord Byron.

"I have a friend," I told him, "who actually knows Lord Liverpool, the Prime Minister."

At that moment, the drawstring of the borrowed chemise parted with a sudden and revealing drop of the neckline. Without a thought, I lifted my hands to cover myself, swiftly tugging the garment higher once more.

Then I froze, astonished. What was I doing? I had worn gowns nearly so revealing before all of society and had undressed my body before more men than I cared to count.

In my younger years of running about London in trousers and later displaying my wares—with ruthless style, of course—I had never given a thought to modesty. In the life I found myself in, modesty had been contrary to my very survival.

Yet I clutched at the broken string, and tucking my chin down, tried to pull the parted knot back together again. The damned thing had slid back up into the casing of one side. If I could only . . .

"Hold that pose!"

The Artist's voice rang with command. I froze at once, as if my spirit recognized his authority. Which was silly, for he was just a long-haired outcast on a foreign shore.

Well, I suppose I was one as well.

I dared to roll my gaze upward, for my head was bent down,

to see that he had taken up a thick brush and was painting out what he'd done before.

I had never seen him paint with such swift assurance. He almost scowled with the fury of his attention upon me. I held myself quite still, my head bent, my hands lifted to just beneath my collarbone, my fingers meeting in the center of my breast-bone, tugging the parted sections of the neckline together.

A breeze bustled in through the open window and tossed my unbound hair. A long lock of it fell in front of my shoulder, to dangle down between my almost exposed breasts. I thought that he might pause and put it back, the way he had before, but he only painted more furiously.

I recalled that he liked to allow me rest upon every hour, but this time he did not. He did not pause, himself, seeming so lost to time and even Beatriu's entrance with a pot of tea and thick slices of bread and cheese on a tray. My mouth watered and my stomach audibly protested at the scent of her fresh bak-ing, but the Artist did not even acknowledge her entry or her offering.

In the end, I went along with his obsession out of pure stub-born curiosity. How long could he paint at that speed? How long could he ignore the fading light and the calls of hunger and exhaustion?

I sat until my thighs trembled at the tension of holding so still, and my hands cramped in their stiffened position of tying a knot. My head grew unbearably heavy upon a neck now burn-ing with fire that lanced halfway down my back.

At last, as the light in the room turned a dusky blue, he stepped back from the painting and set down his brush. His gaze flickered about the room in astonishment, his hands flex-ing absently, easing the stiffness from them.

"Night falls? I . . ." Then he seemed to realize that I had held my pose for more hours than ever before, and his expression became pained. "Forgive me for my thoughtlessness. I became lost in your beauty. I nearly drowned in it."

His words brought a thrilling flutter into my belly and also a warning shiver. I had not meant to make him fall in love with me as I had all my suitors. I wanted something else from this man.

I wanted more.

Beatriu had four grown daughters, two of whom still lived in the village of La Cala. The eldest was a teacher in Girona and the next eldest had gone into the church. By Beatriu's reckoning, that meant her youngest daughters, Alba and Carme, were required to deliver twice as many grandchildren. From what I could see, they were doing their best to comply with their mother's wishes.

At random times during my stay there, I would find the *castell* swarming with children ranging from the age of barely walking to too large for Beatriu's lap, though she never stopped trying. Always, in the thick of the gang I would see a black-haired green-eyed little devil named Dìdac. I learned his name first, for it was the one most often shouted in laughing exasperation by Beatriu and the Artist.

When the children learned that I almost, but not quite, understood their language they took me in hand. For one endless spring day, I wandered through the village and surrounding farms with them as they pointed out things from their everyday lives. They seem to find me incredibly interesting and hilarious. From my baby speech to the fact that I had never actually petted a goat before seemed to supply vast amusement.

I had learned the basics of Latin and classical Greek at my mother's knee, and the Songbird had seen that I received further education. A courtesan must be an interesting woman, and a varied conversationalist, it was true. However, I had always enjoyed languages for their own sake and had found that I took them up quickly.

By the end of the day I had acquired a working vocabulary, if a somewhat childish one, and a Catalan name of my own. *Bellesa.* When I asked them what it meant, Dìdac responded with a straight face.

"*Senyora de la cabra,*" he informed me as his siblings and cousins giggled uncontrollably. *Goat lady.* I nodded seriously, hiding my smile.

I could not help but muse that being the Goat Lady might have its advantages over being The Swan.

THE PRESENT

Chapter Nineteen

Barcelona

Getting through this post-kiss morning was going to take every bit of forbearance Brenna had. Not only had she returned to the scene of the crime, but she'd returned with her accomplice. They were looking for the map shop in the winding stone pathways of the Barri Gòtic neighborhood.

Her head hurt like a son of a bitch.

"It should be on this street," Fitch said.

"Are you sure? They all look the same."

This situation could not be more awkward. Last night, not three blocks away, Fitch had nearly bossa-novaed his way into her panties, just backed her up against a wall and blew her mind. And how did she react? She ran away like some kind of ridiculous little girl afraid of her own sexual response.

Truthfully, she didn't know what she wanted—this morning or in life in general—and every time Fitch tried to make idle chitchat like nothing had happened between them, she wanted to scream.

"Am I the only one who finds it amusing that we got lost looking for a map expert?"

"Yes," she snapped. Suddenly, she stopped walking. "Wait. What's that sign say?" Brenna pulled on Fitch's shirtsleeve, pointing to a deeply recessed doorway, and an engraved brass nameplate lost in the shadows.

Fitch read it out loud. "*'Aleix Serra,* Mapes Antics in Contemporanis.' That's our guy."

A little bell tinkled when Fitch opened the door for her. "Watch your step."

She descended down two stone stairs into the shop, noting how centuries of footfalls had worn depressions in the steps. It made her smile to think that they were quite literally walking in the footsteps of history.

Fitch tried to take her elbow. "I'm fine," she said, easing away from him. Even that gentlemanly touch was enough to remind her of how he'd yanked up her skirt, gripped her thigh, and pressed against her . . .

She had to focus.

Brenna took a quick look around, deciding the establishment had a distinct *Harry Potter* wand shop feel to it, with two narrow horizontal windows providing the only natural light. Every inch of the walls was covered, either by cubbyhole cabinets stuffed with rolled-up maps or by framed atlases of the towns and provinces of Catalonia. She wouldn't be the slightest bit surprised if a wizened little wizard popped up from behind the cluttered desk.

Instead, a rather regal looking middle-aged man ducked his head as he passed beneath the doorway to a back room. He immediately broke into a smile.

"Dr. Anderson? Mr. Wilder?" Aleix Serra shook their hands and welcomed them. He gestured for them to sit at a wooden worktable pitted with age that took up most of the shop's floor space. He offered them *café,* but Brenna politely declined.

"Thank you for seeing us," she said.

"It is an honor, *Professora,* and I'm sorry we had to reschedule."

"No problem at all."

"I must admit I don't get many visits from esteemed members of the Harvard faculty."

Brenna knew that Serra was being self-deprecating. He retired from the Universitat de Barcelona's history department, where he'd been considered the region's foremost scholar on the historical geography of Catalonia.

Serra turned to Fitch. "I saw your interview on BBC recently—how extraordinary to find such a treasure trove of artwork in one apartment!"

"Absolutely," Fitch agreed.

Brenna changed the subject before they got sidetracked discussing Wilder's charismatic media appearances. "As I mentioned, we're conducting research on the history of The Siren Series portraits, which we believe were painted somewhere in this area of Spain. Ultimately, we're looking for any additional unattributed paintings that might remain here in Catalonia."

Serra nodded.

"We've brought something. Could you take a look at it?"

Fitch had already opened his backpack and unrolled the digitized composite of all known portrait backgrounds. He spread it out on the table in front of Serra.

"This is an overlay of the setting for six individual oil portraits," he explained. "We've erased The Siren from the foreground to better reveal the other details."

"An interesting technology," Serra said, tracing his finger from left to right across the wide printout. "The year?"

"Between 1827 and 1828."

"And what makes you think this is Spain?"

"Two things," Brenna said. "We have discovered correspondence from a woman who claims to have washed up on the Catalan shore in 1827. She says she was rescued by an artist living in one of the fishing villages north of Girona."

"Hmm."

"And then there's this." Brenna got out her laptop and pulled up an image of the underpainted poem. "This was beneath the paint of the most recently discovered portrait. I would just like to remind you not to mention this to anyone."

"Of course."

Brenna was so nervous she began tapping her boot heel against the stone floor. Without looking her way, Fitch reached under the table and pressed his hand to her knee, urging her to stop. The historian began to read aloud.

> *"Thirteen paintings*
> *And three seasons*
> *Since you came to me,*
> *Broken bird in a Catalan storm*
>
> *This soldat dement shall surely fail*
> *To capture the radiance*
> *Of his bellesa de la cala,*
> *Brighter now than ever before."*

He looked up, a hint of a smile at his lips. "The poem is in perfect English and yet the artist refers to himself as a demented soldier—in Catalan. Quite curious."

Brenna and Fitch nodded in unison.

"So the letter, the reference to the storm, the use of the language, and the seaside setting have you looking in Catalunya?"

"Yes."

Serra scowled as he continued to study the composite. "And you want to know precisely where these portraits were painted?"

"Please."

"Here's the problem with that." Serra looked at them both. "There are about 112 kilometers of coastline from Girona to France."

"That's seventy miles," Fitch mumbled to himself.

"Yes, and most of it looks much like this, with rocky volcanic outcroppings, jagged coves, and windblown junipers that hold the cliffs together with their roots."

"Ugh," Brenna said.

"Even more unfortunate, this particular combination of geological elements can be found in many east-facing Mediterranean locations on the European continent, including Italy, Sicily, Greece, France . . ." He shrugged.

"However . . ." The retired professor raised both palms to put a halt to their disappointment. "I must go back to the poem. Only the elite in Catalunya were educated in another language in those days, but if the artist were of elite birth, why did he paint only in this rustic setting?"

"The woman was English," Brenna said.

"Ah, well that might account for it, but that still leaves the *soldat dement* reference, and that is a puzzle."

"It is," Brenna said. "It seems the only self-identifying 'soldiers' of that time would have been those who fought in the Peninsular War over a decade before."

Serra nodded slowly. "Correct. Catalunya was a piece of beef fought over by the rabid dogs of France and England during that time. We suffered terribly. It took decades for towns and churches to rebuild."

The historian suddenly popped from his chair and disappeared into a far corner of the room, where he bent to peer into a row of cubbyholes. He returned with what was obviously a tied-up map. He removed the string and turned it toward them, smoothing it on the tabletop as he unrolled it.

"This is a reproduction of a historic 1814 map showing Cataluyna immediately following the Penninsular War. It shows the location of battles and skirmishes in relation to the villages, monasteries, shipyards, castles, and churches of the time."

Fitch and Brenna leaned forward to better see where he pointed.

"If your artist lived on the coast north of Girona, he would have been in one of these towns."

"That's a lot of towns," Fitch said.

"Approximately thirty in 1828." Serra smiled apologetically. "How do you intend to narrow down your search?"

That was when Brenna found herself looking at Fitch, who gave her a shrug. "Well, there's the castle," she said, perking up. "On the upper left corner of three of the paintings the artist included a segment of a castle."

"That will narrow it some." Serra snagged the panorama from beneath the map and examined it again. "Perhaps only a third of the villages would have had standing cliffside castle structures at that time."

Brenna nodded.

"But there are no identifying characteristics, I'm afraid."

Fitch sighed. "Seems like you can't swing a dead *gat* around here without hitting an old castle."

Serra laughed. "True."

"What about the trees and other vegetation visible in the paintings?" Brenna asked. "The wildflowers? The color of the soil?"

Serra shook his head. "Again, these are common features of the region. But there is something else I should mention." Serra pointed to the overlay and the two twisted trees reaching toward each other on the cliff, a background image that was included in four of the six paintings. Brenna straightened.

"These are *genebre* . . . juniper trees, and they can live for hundreds and sometimes thousands of years under the right conditions. Here, on a cliff exposed to the elements like this, their life span would be shortened somewhat, but you could get lucky. These trees may still be there."

"That's fabulous!"

"But Dr. Anderson, you must know that almost two hundred years have passed, and in that time erosion from wind and seawater, along with the changing sea levels, will have altered the landscape. If you do happen to find the town, do not expect the geography to look exactly as it does in the portraits."

A few moments later, Brenna and Fitch gathered their things and thanked Aleix Serra for his time. He rolled up the map of Catalonia and handed it to Fitch. "This is my gift to you both. I wish you *bona sort* in your search."

Brenna hugged him. Fitch shook his hand. And just as she started to climb up the steps leading to street level, Serra cleared his throat behind her.

"I don't wish to tell a Harvard professor how to do her job, but have you thought about looking in the *musue* of the Santa Maria de Monsserrat abbey?"

They both spun around in their tracks.

"The Benedictine abbey?" Fitch asked.

"Yes." Serra took a few steps toward the door, rubbing his chin. "They have a significant collection of art there, much of it from lesser-known Catalonian artists from the nineteenth century, and I know for a fact that they display only a small fraction of what they own."

"Oh." Brenna blinked.

"They usually don't allow the lay public into the museum library, so you would have to have an introduction. Do you know anyone who might be able to get you—?"

"Yes." Fitch said. "I know a guy . . ."

"Of course you do," Brenna whispered.

When they were back on the main street a few moments later, Fitch looked sideways at her. "How long do you plan to avoid talking to me? I ask this only because I think the monks on Montsserat Mountain have taken vows of silence, so you'll fit right in up there."

Brenna took a deep breath. "I need some time to think things through."

Fitch gave her a quick nod.

"Should I even bother asking how you know someone who can get us into a Benedictine abbey?"

He smiled. "It's complicated, but one of my regular employers, Jean-Louis Rasmussen at the Michel-Blanc in Paris, introduced me to a patron whose father donated his entire collection to the monastery a few years back."

Brenna stopped listening. Her headache was back. All she could think of was getting something to eat and taking a nap—a siesta, of all things. The last time she recalled ever wanting a nap was in preschool. *What was happening to her?*

During the walk back, Brenna's mind raced through the next research steps. After the abbey they would have to drive up and down the coast to attempt to locate the artist's village. How long would that take? Would they ever find it? How was she going to decide what to do with Wilder in the interim?

She liked him. A lot. But it felt different than with other men—*she* felt different. Gone was her usual sense of control. Gone was her ability to maintain a safe distance. She wasn't even sure she wanted distance. She wanted to know more about him, spend more time in his company, experience more things with him at her side. The bottom line was that Fitch was fun.

But if she slept with him, the arrangement eventually would end in disenchantment, the way it always did. And then what? Their rift could jeopardize her work.

When they neared the Plaça de Catalunya, Brenna sensed that Fitch was about to mention lunch, so she blurted out that she needed to pack. He seemed fine with that, and promised to text her when he'd heard back from the abbey.

Fitch went his way. She went hers.

As Brenna folded and organized her clothes, she decided to

call Piper. She needed to tell Piper what was going on with Fitch. She felt like she would explode if she didn't say it out loud. Piper was the only person in the world who knew her well enough to understand this had never happened to her before—she'd never felt like she was being swept down a raging river without any way to steer the boat.

Piper didn't answer, and that meant Brenna would have to deal with this on her own.

She could do it. She was smart as hell. Unfortunately, this wasn't something that could be resolved by intellect alone, no matter how hard she might try.

She spent that evening researching the history of the Santa Maria de Montserrat Abbey. She wanted to be prepared for what lay ahead.

Fitch chose the sexiest Audi convertible on the car hire lot, never once questioning the extravagance. H. Winston Guilford wouldn't give a rat's ass how much this trip cost him—as long as Fitch came back with another painting. Their phone conversation last evening only served to remind him of that.

Fitch had called Winston with an update on what they knew, what they still needed to find out, and how they planned to do so. After a long silence, Winston finally spoke.

"She *was* a courtesan? You're absolutely certain?"

Fitch heard disappointment in his voice, and truly felt for the guy. Winston's bubble had just been popped. He'd learned that his dream girl wasn't exactly as fantasized, and Fitch knew from personal experience how much that could hurt. But he wanted to end the conversation on a positive note.

"I am certain we're headed in the right direction, both figuratively and literally," he had told Winston. "I have no doubt we're going to find the artist's ghost in some little coastal town, and when we know who he was and what he was doing here, we'll know where to start digging for more of his paintings."

"Don't fail me, Fitch."

"I don't intend to, Winston."

He pulled up in front of Brenna's hotel a few minutes before nine. Brenna was outside with her luggage, wearing her uniform of boots and sunglasses, though Fitch had to admit that the white skinny jeans she'd chosen really made her d'Artagnans pop. He chuckled to himself as he opened the trunk and wedged her belongings inside.

They hadn't even made it to the B-10 before it became obvious that Brenna wasn't in a talking mood. Fitch decided not to let it bother him, since he had other things on his mind. His senses were buzzing in anticipation. He had a hunch the day would bring something unexpectedly wonderful, and these hunches were never wrong. In fact, the last time he felt this was the morning he walked up those Paris apartment building steps and into the arms of a long-lost *Siren*.

"Do you mind if I turn on the radio?" he asked.

"I'd enjoy that."

Fitch selected a station of classical Spanish guitar, deciding that this might be one of those moments worthy of a soundtrack. After all, he was driving a convertible sports car up a spectacular, twisting mountain road with a beautiful woman at his side.

Once out of the city, they headed into the jagged Monsterrat Mountain, the views of shining Barcelona and shockingly blue sea becoming better with each hairpin turn. More than once he saw Brenna point and heard her gasp.

In all his visits to Barcelona, he'd never made it up to the abbey, though he'd certainly heard of it. There had been a Benedictine presence on the mountain since the eleventh century. During the civil war, when Franco outlawed the Catalan language and culture, the abbey defied the ban, conducting Mass in the native tongue and serving as safe haven for the resistance. The most celebrated element of the abbey—and its original reason for being—was their worship of *La Moreneta*, the Black Madonna. The wooden statue was alleged to have been carved in Jerusalem in the early days of the Church, and the Madonna was now the patroness of Catalonia.

"I can't believe how gorgeous this is," Brenna said. She was turned away from Fitch, leaning out the car to see over the guardrail. "Red tile roofs, the sea, vineyards, and olive groves everywhere you look. It's like a fairy tale. Maybe that's why the artist—whoever he was—wanted to live here."

Fitch smiled. The truth was, traveling to a place like this was always better if you had someone to share it with. It was a luxury he'd seldom experienced.

The higher they climbed, the closer they got to the rocky outcroppings. They looked like sandcastles against an endless blue sky. Then they spotted the abbey tucked into a ridge between mountain peaks. "Look!"

He was about to comment when Brenna suddenly turned to him. "Wilder," she said. "We got carried away last night, but we are both intelligent adults. We shouldn't let it mar our working relationship. So I believe we should clear the air."

"Oookay," he said, keeping his eyes on the narrow road, not sure what had prompted her to begin a conversation she claimed she didn't want to have.

"What happened is understandable if you know the social science behind it."

God, she was cute. "The science of wine, women, and song?"

"Exactly!" She seemed pleased with his insight. "It was the end of a long day. We'd enjoyed a variety of shared experiential novelties, a construct known to spark sexual attraction between strangers."

Fitch took a turn a little too fast, and the Audi's tires squealed. "Experiential novelties? Is that anything like latex novelties?"

Brenna chuckled. "No. It's all about neurotransmitters. I'm sure you've heard of—or even utilized—the maxim about danger and sexual attraction."

"Please refresh my memory."

Brenna absently pushed her windblown hair from her face. "Studies have shown that if you throw real or imagined danger into a first date, the girl may perceive you as being a far better mating choice than you actually are. For example, if you take her to a Halloween haunted house or go bungee jumping, and you both survive the experience, you're more likely to get laid afterward."

Fitch sighed. "Ah, yes . . . sweet mystery of love."

Brenna narrowed her eyes. "Mock me if you must, but multiple studies show that having an adventure—trying new foods, visiting new places, and being swept away by novel forms of art and music—can release dopamine and norepinephrine in the brain at levels as high as those produced in times of danger. To the human brain, the result is the same: an elevated drive to procreate."

"Stop. Please. You're turning me on."

Brenna crossed her arms over her chest and gazed out at the view, which had become even more breathtaking during the course of her lecture. "I'm simply trying to provide some perspective."

"Okay. I have some perspective, too. Want to hear it?" He screeched around another sharp twist in the road.

She turned toward him again, pulling down on the bridge of her sunglasses so she could glare. "Sure."

"I like you, Brenna."

It got awfully quiet in that car, even though the wind whipped over their heads.

"You're brilliant and funny. You never give up. You're a hot mess of complexity with a dab of crazy and that intrigues me. You're attractive, especially when you smile. But when you laugh—God! You turn into the most beautiful thing I've ever seen. I wish I got to see you laugh more."

She nudged her sunglasses back into position and turned straight ahead. He saw her swallow hard.

"Anyway, my perspective on the other night is that it was wonderful and perfect. So what's the big deal if we happen to enjoy each other's company while we track down The Siren's story?"

Brenna said nothing.

"It's not like I'm asking you to move to Santa Fe and bear my children."

That got a snort out of her, which made him smile.

"You said it yourself," he continued. "We're both intelligent adults. And I think we have a choice here. We can choose to see if this might turn into something or we can choose to let it die on the vine. But either way, we've got to work together. We've got a mystery to solve."

Brenna sat quietly for a moment, but when she eventually responded it was in a voice soft enough to vanish in the wind. "I agree, Fitch. With everything."

Chapter Twenty

Montserrat Mountain

They parked in a visitor spot and walked past the stunning, pink-brick basilica and across the plaza toward the museum. Suddenly, the church bells rang out, and Brenna jumped. Their deep clanging was deafening, shaking the air, and vibrating up through her feet and into her bones.

"Now *that's* a doorbell," Fitch said.

They continued toward the museum, a modern structure built mostly underground. Brenna saw a smallish man in a black robe waiting for them on the front steps.

"Don Josep Soler?" Brenna had to shout over the bells. She wasn't completely sure of the etiquette of greeting a monk, so she hesitated to hold out her hand, but Don Josep reached out to take hers with both of his, smiling. He did the same with Fitch.

The museum director welcomed them inside, and while escorting them through a maze of hallways and into an elevator, he gave them a brief introduction to monastic life on the side of the mountain.

"There are seventy monks in residence," he said, "and their primary purpose is creating a peaceful place of worship and reflection, while also running a publishing company, a museum, and a variety of other commercial enterprises that help pay to maintain the abbey."

He pushed the button for the basement floor.

"You should really stop by the gift shop," he said. "We sell a variety of liquors here, and I hear the *crema Catalana* has a sweet and nutty flavor."

"This is my kind of monastery," Fitch said, which made Don Josep chuckle.

He had served as the director of the museum collection for seven years, he said, and explained that the monks had kept art and antiquities at the abbey for safekeeping since the early days of the monastery.

"During the Peninsular War, all the treasures were stolen or destroyed by the French and English, so the abbey had to rebuild its collection from scratch. We have grown through generous gifts and estate donations to what we are today—a place for El Greco, Picasso, Monet, Gaudi . . ."

He opened the doorway to the museum's archive offices and ushered them into a conference room. In the middle of the table sat a coffee service and a small platter of sweets.

"Please tell me how I can help you."

Brenna and Fitch explained that they hoped the museum might know of unattributed works by Le Artiste, and shared with him the discoveries that had led to their visit. He listened patiently and poured himself a *café*.

"You know, of course, that secular nudes would not be in our collection. A few cherubs, certainly, but I am familiar with The Siren Series and I can tell you we have no such portraits here."

Brenna explained to Don Josep Soler that they were most interested in works by unknown Catalonian artists, in the hope they might stumble across something done in a similar style to Le Artiste's known work.

"We are particularly interested in the time period from about 1820 to 1850, paintings that straddle the romantic and impressionist styles," she told him.

Don Josep nodded, obviously thinking. "Please come with me. We have dozens of unattributed paintings of that period, but most are landscapes, I'm afraid."

They followed him to a large work area and storage facility, where two monks behind desks seemed startled to see visitors. In Catalan, Don Josep asked one of the monks to assist them with finding the paintings in question.

For half an hour, Fitch and Brenna wandered through the narrow aisles of the storage area with Don Josep and his assistant, waiting as each canvas was pulled from a storage bin and presented. There were seascapes, mountains, depictions of peasants in the fields and fishermen with nets. There were paintings of winemaking, plowing, and baking. And castle ruins—a lot of castle ruins.

When the assistant pulled gently upon the edge of one tattered canvas, Brenna and Fitch instantly gasped.

"Can we get a closer look at that one, please?" Fitch's words were as calm as if he'd asked for a gas station receipt. Brenna's knees began trembling, and she gripped his arm. She just needed to know he was there.

The style wasn't identical to The Siren Series. It was obvious his skill and sensibilities had matured over the years, especially his use of light and interest in movement. But there they were— the exact same junipers, reaching up as if to hold hands over the rocky cove below. And to the left, in the corner, was a peek at the old castle turret.

"It's him." Brenna's gaze flew to the bottom right corner and to the "L. A." painted in a bold hand. "Fitch, it's really him."

"I can't even . . ." He shook his head in disbelief. "Uh, may we please see the back?"

The assistant nodded eagerly and turned the canvas around. Oddly enough, on the bottom olivewood strainer were the words *Didac Vilaro, 1819.*

Brenna gulped and she looked to Don Josep in wonder. "Is that the artist's name?" Her mind was spinning—if this was indeed painted in 1819, it was when The Swan and The Blackbird were the toast of London, gliding across marble ballrooms and amassing their collections of jewels, property, and men. Astounding. By the time Brenna returned to the here and now, Fitch was in mid-question.

". . . anything similar? Are there other paintings like this one?"

Don Josep's head was cocked to the side, a quizzical smile in his eyes. He said something to his assistant in Catalan and motioned for them to follow him.

"Are we being kicked out?" Brenna muttered to Fitch.

"No. They're bringing it to us in the conference room."

Within ten minutes, three paintings had been delivered to the room and placed on display easels. Brenna stood near Fitch as they stared, open-mouthed, at the canvases. Brenna must have reached for Fitch's hand at some point—or he'd reached for hers—because their fingers had become tightly intertwined.

In addition to the familiar junipers and cove, there were portraits of a child and a woman, obviously peasants. The subject of one painting was a dark-haired boy of no more than three, who stood in an overgrown lane, leading a goat by a threadbare rope. The child's face was smeared with berry juice and his mischievous green eyes sparkled. The other painting featured a sturdy woman, perhaps in her fifties, one hand shooing the painter away while she hung laundry to dry. The artist had captured the woman's feigned aggravation, but her soft smile indicated she was flattered to be found worthy of a portrait.

"The back of the portrait of the boy is labeled 1821, the woman 1825," Don Josep said.

Brenna had no idea how long they had stood there, staring in silence, but Don Josep's comment caused them to turn around.

The Benedictine monk was seated at the table, grinning. "These paintings have a story I think you will want to hear. Please join me."

As soon as they sat, Don Josep opened a file and placed it before them. He handed them each a pair of white cotton gloves and gave them permission to touch the original documents inside. They leaned their heads together and read the Catalan as Don Josep summarized in English.

"To answer your question, no, Dìdac Vilaro was not Le Artiste. We knew him as Don Diego. He contributed greatly to our monastery's recovery, arriving here in 1844 to help rebuild the community and the abbey. He grew up in a little town about fifty miles from here, on the coast, and when he moved here he brought these paintings with him. They were his personal treasures, you see, and they became the first three oil paintings in the abbey's new collection."

"'Castell de la Cala,'" Brenna read aloud. "It says that's where he was born. Is this his biography we're reading?"

"Yes, but a personnel file, as well. Every brother who has ever served our community has one like it. I can provide copies if you wish."

"Yes!" Brenna and Fitch blurted out in unison. Don Josep laughed.

"The painting of the little boy is Don Diego himself, who was born Dìdac Vilaro in 1820. The woman is his grandmother, Beatriu Mata. And, if you keep reading, you will discover that the painter was very special to Don Diego. Not only was the artist considered a hero for saving Castell de la Cala from destruction in the Peninsular War, he saved little Dìdac's life many years later."

Brenna and Fitch simultaneously raised their heads.

"The artist rescued him from drowning when he was eight. Don Diego was quoted as saying. 'The moment I was snatched from the sea, I knew I must spend my life in the service of others, and in the service of my God.'"

"Oh, my God, oh, my God, oh, my God!"

Brenna must have shouted those apropos words into the wind ten times before they'd made it down the mountain, and Fitch couldn't blame her. Suddenly, there were three more paintings. They had a backstory. They had a destination—Castell de la Cala—and they were on their way.

"There's so much to do." That was the mantra she'd been using in between the "oh-my-Gods."

"And we'll do it all—every single thing on your list." Fitch reached over and brushed strands of windblown hair from her face. A bold move, maybe, but he wanted nothing more in that instant than to touch her. She didn't flinch, which made him smile.

"But we have so much to do!"

Fitch laughed. "We can't do a damn thing in a car, in the middle of nowhere, without an internet connection, so why don't you take a deep breath and appreciate what's around you?"

They had descended the opposite side of the mountain to where the narrow road met a larger regional highway. Fitch turned right at the traffic circle, knowing he would remain on that road all the way to the ancient city of Girona. Sixteen miles beyond there they'd find the village that was once the artist's home—Castle on the Cove, as it would be known in English.

Brenna cranked the radio station and the Spanish guitar chords swirled into the wind. She lifted her face toward the afternoon sun and threw her arms into the air, her hair whipping in a wild curtain behind her.

As they drove on through the rolling hills, peaks of the Pyrenees came into view on their left, the border between France and Spain. The afternoon light was starting to change, transitioning into that golden hour in Catalonia, the time of day Le Artiste often chose for his paintings. It made sense, since this light gilded everything it touched. It even made Fitch a little homesick.

"This place reminds me of Santa Fe."

Brenna brought her arms down from the wind and smiled at him. It was an effortless smile. Spontaneous. So lovely it made his heart leap in his chest.

"Is it the light?"

Fitch nodded. "And the Spanish architecture, most definitely, but also the sky and the mountains. This is one of those places on earth that's just plain good for the soul."

Brenna's smile mellowed and he heard her sigh. "It's kind of unearthly, really, like a Hobbit film or the set of a chick flick."

"Eat-pray-love, baby."

Brenna laughed, then reached out to rest her hand on his headrest. "So tell me, Wilder. What made you so interested in The Siren Series to begin with? Is it just about the money?"

The question surprised him, but he figured it was legitimate. "Nope."

"Just wondered."

"I grew up with The Siren paintings because of my father's work for Guilford. I even got to see them in person several times."

"Okay, now you're just rubbing it in." She sounded hurt but she smiled as she said it.

He smiled back. "I remember I thought her so beautiful that she had to be magic. I mean literally, I thought she was from another world. But the art itself mesmerized me, too, even then.

I loved how Le Artiste captured an instant of color, light, and energy—like he had superpowers that allowed him to freeze time."

Brenna inclined her head as she listened. "And now?"

"I need to finish this puzzle, Brenna." Fitch saw the upcoming tunnel and turned on the headlights. "I want to know everything about The Siren and her painter. How did they meet? Who were they and what was their story? Why did they love each other so intensely? And now—with your help—we're close to figuring it out."

"We are, aren't we?"

"Hell, yeah, we are." He paused. "And what drives you? Because I've noticed you're just slightly driven."

Brenna told him about Lowell Snowden, her mentor and department head, and the faculty politics that jeopardized his position and her own. She told him of the pressure from complaining donors, which he thought was the most ridiculous thing he'd ever heard.

"Poor old guy. But you have tenure, Brenna. Surely they can't—"

"They're trying to push me out, and they want to hear by July if I plan to come back. Instead, I want to hand them enough data to propose a groundbreaking academic paper on The Siren Series. It might even be enough for a museum exhibit. Either way, it would give me the power I need to tell them to kiss my ass."

Fitch nodded soberly. "Then that's what you'll do."

When they exited the tunnel a few moments later, the vista had changed and they now looked down onto a fertile valley. The light deepened. Brown brick farmhouses were now burnished in orange. Long, tall cyprus trees cast their shadows on the land.

"Brenna?"

"Hmm?"

Fitch knew that if they weren't in the car he'd take her in his arms and kiss her. He was dying to feel her lips on his again, her soft body against him. He was dying to tell her the truth.

He was falling for her.

But there was a problem. He couldn't do or say anything until he'd come clean about his foray into breaking and entering. Anything less would be unfair. He would confess, and soon, because it was the right thing to do. He had no illusions that she would forgive easily.

A sweet little smile turned up her lips. She was waiting for him to continue.

"I . . . I just wanted you to know that whatever happens—wherever this treasure hunt takes us and whatever happens between us down the road—that this has been a remarkable couple of weeks. I've had so much fun with you, and I'll never forget it."

Her hand had remained on his headrest, and he now felt fingertips brush through his hair. The caress sent a rush of heat through him. He turned to her. She'd taken off her sunglasses and was gazing at him with a mix of tenderness and doubt.

"Thanks for saying that," she said. "I feel the same."

They drove on, taking the time to catch up on all the little things they hadn't yet told each other—houses, friends, family, coworkers. Fitch told her about the small *casita* he kept near the gallery in town and his ranch twenty miles outside Santa Fe.

"Horses and everything?" she asked. "You really are a shit-kicking cowboy."

Brenna was an only child. Fitch had two older sisters and a whole mess of nieces and nephews. Brenna's mother and father were both gone. Fitch's mom was alive and well and lived with his sister in Albuquerque.

"Maybe you can come visit me after this is all over," he said. "I'll take you on a whirlwind tour of New Mexico."

"I'll do the same for you in Boston." When Brenna glanced at him, he noticed that her face had turned a soft, golden brown—despite her addiction to SPF 70 sunblock—and that freckles had spread across the bridge of her nose to her cheeks. She looked more beautiful than he'd ever seen her.

He wanted more. A lot more. He wanted *her*.

Exiting another tunnel moments later, Fitch glanced to the north and noticed a wall of dark clouds coming down from the Pyrenees. Since the sun was still warm and the feel of the air was glorious, he wanted to stretch out the moment as long as possible. Soon enough, he'd have to tell her about stealing the fax. And that could change everything.

She might hate him.

Or she might forgive him, which was the outcome he would prefer.

God, I hope I haven't fucked this up.

"Looks like we're going to get rain," Brenna said. "Should we pull over and put up the top?"

"In a few minutes." He reached across and placed his hand on her knee. "There's something I want to tell you. It's a confession, really, and I don't think it can wait any longer."

THE PAST

Chapter Twenty-One

Castell de la Cala

One cool early morning, I strode along the path to the village, my steps light but firm. No ladylike mincing, for I had marketing to do before the afternoon struck. The sun promised to be hotter than most Englishwomen would enjoy, but for the moment the air was chilled by the breeze from the sea and the lane was shaded by the twisted olive trees on either side.

My feet were bare of shoes or stockings. The sandy path held a few sharp rocks but I happily traded the risk for the freedom of my plain muslin skirt and petticoat fluttering against the skin of my legs. A more pleasurable dance I have never known.

As I walked with my basket swinging from my arm, I tilted my head back, to squint against the dappled effect of the morning sun through the narrow leaves of the olives. Shade and light took their turns upon the skin of my face and upper chest. Warm, then cool, then warm again. In all my hedonistic days, I don't think I ever felt anything so outrageously free and sensual as simply lifting my face to the light of day.

My hair was only loosely tied in the back with a bit of blue silk torn from my old gown. I'd felt too lazy to braid it neatly, and I'd thought only of being out of doors, so now the constant pull of the sea breeze had tugged the shortest strands free. I let them dance across my vision without bothering to brush them back, for it would do no good. They would only rebel again and again.

Tonight I would have to sit and work out the tangles by the fire in the studio, letting the easy crackle of the burning wood accompany the strokes of the old wooden comb in my hand. I pictured the Artist in his chair nearby. He might watch the light dance in my hair, now even fairer than ever for its time in the sun. Or he might pull his sketchbook close. The scratching of his pencil would accompany the crackle of the fire while through the great arched window of the *castell*, the sea would roll against the rocks encircling the cove. Such was the quiet music of my life now.

No string quartet had ever pleased my ears more.

I had run into the morning without stopping to break my fast. Now, as I passed a small grove of fruit trees, I lifted my skirts to step lightly to the top of the low, ancient stone wall that lined the path. Ripe peaches beckoned. I stretched up high, my toes gripping the time-smoothed stone. I stole one, then hopped back down to the path with a small laugh, feeling like a naughty child.

The juice from the overripe peach ran down my chin and over my fingers as I relished its explosive sweetness. A small brook ran along the other side of the path. I knelt there to swish my sticky fingers in the clear water. After I leaned out over the water to rinse the juice from my face, I dreamily watched the ripples of my actions smooth away. My reflection jumped and wavered in the moving water, but soon the surface was clear enough for me to gaze at myself in wonder.

The polished, calculated perfection of The Swan was gone and so, too, were the pale and bony androgynous features of Jinx. Instead, in the clear light of this Catalan morning, I saw a countrywoman, flushed from the sun, her eyes bright with health and amusement, whose lips curved at the corners from a naturally ready smile.

She was not stunning. She was not sleek or fashionable. Her narrow features had filled in from her indulgence in hearty country fare. Her hair blew free, lights of summer shimmering among the careless mane.

I leaned closer, waiting for my reflection to still for a moment, as the brook flowed.

There they were. There, in a spray across the bridge of my nose.

Freckles.

I had freckles on my nose, like a rustic!

I sat back upon my heels in surprise. Idly, I dried my damp fingers on my handkerchief as I contemplated the true and final fate of The Swan.

The Swan was dead.

I felt as though I ought to hold some sort of memorial for her, to observe a hard-won life lived to the fullest. I pictured an exquisitely staged funeral, complete with all the right flowers and all the right mourners.

Yet, did I mourn her? Did I miss being that creature of poise and grace, of flawless mystery and ruthless fashion? I had done it so well for so long. Did that not mean something to me?

The Swan had been alive. She had been a real woman of taste and energy. She had made waves, incited gossip, and ignited mad fashions.

Then she died, somewhere off the coast of Catalunya. Lost at sea. Lost to time.

It was then that I realized The Swan had never been me at all. Or rather, she had only been a piece of me, just like Jinx. A skin I had worn for a time, an armor of protection perfectly sculpted to deflect the wounds that could be delivered by a careless world, a tool of survival.

Losing The Swan was not an amputation at all, but merely the act of taking off a mask. Like Jinx, she had served her purpose. She had protected me and kept me safe from destitution and danger—for the most part.

"I want to paint you, all of you, everything you are."

I did not jump at the sound behind me. Perhaps I had become accustomed to the melodic tone of his voice over the months, or perhaps my new life had released me from all underlying anxiety. Regardless, his words—and the fact that he had been watching me without my knowledge—only made me smile.

As I turned to gaze up at him, I knew full well what he had just asked of me—he wanted me to pose for him, nude. Since I had only been nude in the interest of commerce, I knew it would be a novel experience. I decided to comply with his request. I trusted him. He had saved my life, kept me safe, and asked nothing of me but to stay and heal. In addition to all that, I no longer feared to see myself through his eyes. I knew who I was now, and I understood that without the masks and the armor I was woman enough for him, for his colors and brushes.

"Yes," I said.

He tossed back his head and laughed. "All right, then." The Artist reached down to where I sat in a patch of wildflowers and pulled me to a stand, his brown eyes sparkling in the sunlight.

"But not *quite* yet." I slipped my arm through his and nudged him back toward the sandy path. "Beatriu has sent me to the market for honey and I dare not return without it."

He smiled down at me. "You are as wise as you are beautiful."

We spent the rest of the morning in easy companionship. I laughed at his ridiculous stories and attempted to sing for him, melodies from my days in the demimonde. A true gentleman, he somehow managed not to plug his ears. We wandered through the market at our leisure, purchasing the honey straightaway but both wanting to linger. At the stall of a village seamstress, my Artist pulled a coin from his pocket and presented me with a silk hair ribbon of the palest blue, an inch wide and hemmed with a fine hand.

"Storm-cloud blue," he said, pulling my hair free from the tattered dress scrap and shoving it in his pocket. "An exact match of your eyes."

I stood still, there in the middle of the busy village market, as my Artist tied the silk ribbon around my hair.

With the most elegant of manners, he then stood before me, bent at a sharp angle at the waist, and bowed.

"M'lady."

I laughed at the absurdity, him with his wild sun-streaked hair and me in my peasant muslin and dirty feet. I curtsied in return. "Major."

We walked arm in arm back to the ruins of the *castell*, our faces uplifted to the warm sun, our hearts fluttering in the breeze.

"Are you quite sure about this?"

Again in the studio with the Artist, I smiled at the concern in his expression. Surely he realized that in my life as a courtesan, I'd spent more time in the nude than clothed. I kept my thought to myself, however, unwilling to bring the past into this newly made present.

I was no longer a courtesan, or a bereft girl. I was now simply a woman. He was not a soldier, a traitor, or even a hero. He was simply a man.

For a moment, I tugged the borrowed dressing gown closer, not because I was shy or chilled, but because it was his. It held the soothing masculine scents of turpentine and pipe tobacco and the radiating heat that seemed perpetually emanating from his skin.

Then, without any further hesitation, I opened the amber

silk wrapper wide and let it slip off my shoulders. As it pooled around my feet, I watched his face.

His handsome features showed both artistic and manly appreciation in equal parts. I'm sure I saw intense desire spark in his gaze, but he banked it quickly and allowed the painter to take the fore. I found myself fondly expecting the strange half-distant, half-focused expression that overcame him when he painted.

I was not to be disappointed. He tilted his head as he gazed at my unclothed, unmasked, scarred self.

"You are ivory and gilt," he murmured.

These were not words of seduction, I assure you, for his next words were, "and the fabric of that chair is horrible behind you. It won't do at all."

For the next few minutes, he bustled around me as I stood there. He'd built the fire up so that I was not cold and I found myself most relaxed by his professional fervor, so different from lust yet as pure a desire as I've ever seen.

He wanted me. Simply me, naked, unadorned, practically uncombed! His need at the moment was to capture me on canvas. His other needs he kept to himself. It was very gentlemanly.

And entirely frustrating.

Finally, he'd arranged the chair to his satisfaction. He'd used his own dressing gown to hide the distracting upholstery, and had piled cushions about it until it more resembled a chaise lounge than an upright wingback.

With a wave of his hand, he guided me into it.

"I want to pose you as I first encountered you, on the beach. You looked . . ." His hands opened as he tried and failed to describe me.

I smiled. "Like a piece of broken driftwood?" I asked helpfully. "Pray, do not say like a beached whale."

He shook his head without laughing, so entirely was he lost

in his artistic vision. "You looked like a fallen angel, like a banished sea siren." He blinked at me somberly. "I was so struck by your abandoned perfection that I fear it took me nearly a full minute before I realized that you were injured."

"Do not distress yourself." I reached for him then, laying my hand over his. "I dare say anyone would have been startled, and you've taken such beautiful care of me since."

That spark flared again in the warm depths of his brown eyes. Then he slowly drew his hand from beneath mine. "If you will lie back and fling this arm out so—"

As he explained, I began to see what he wished. The amber silk of the dressing gown was the sand. The folds of an old green shawl were the waves tugging at my bare feet, the back and arm of the chair were the rocks against which I'd been tossed by the sea.

Although I had no memory of my arrival on the Artist's beloved beach, strange thoughts began to occupy my mind as I lay upon the makeshift landscape as if I'd been flung there.

What if someone else had found me? What if no one had found me at all? Might I have been abused in my lost and vacant state? Might I have died?

I reassured myself that people of Beatriu's quality would likely care for anyone so unfortunate, but the notion was chilling. I put it firmly from my mind. The Artist had saved my life. For all my mad misadventures, I had in the end been flung into the finest of hands.

While I'd been distracted by dire imaginings, he had begun to work. By this time, I knew the stages. First, he madly stroked the paint down on the canvas, creating shapes and shadows, curves and blocks and points of solid color, light and dark.

Then his brush slowed. Before, he would glance back and forth quickly, from me to the canvas and back. Now he began to truly look at me as his painting hand outlined curves and hips and breasts. I watched from lowered lids as he lost himself in the paint, the canvas, and me.

I loved it. I loved how he looked at me, as if he saw through me like clear salt water, through me and into me, as if I stood in a hall of mirrors where each reflected the other, mirrors within mirrors, into infinity. He saw where I began. He saw where I would go. He saw me now, just as I was, freckled and scarred and unpolished, as plain as I had been as a brothel kitchen boy . . .

And found me beautiful.

For the first time in my life, I believed it. Perhaps I would not have been adored by the risqué portion of the haute ton, nor sought after by cold, hard men of wealth, but that had never been my true self. The life of The Swan was a finely wrought gilded cage, and I had never allowed any man to see beyond the bars, even if one had ever tried.

No, the beauty I felt was that of a woman at peace with herself and her decisions, at rest with her past, in hope of a finer future, and rather delightfully satisfied with the present.

Except for one thing.

"May I rise?"

The Artist blinked at me, as if refocusing his vision from the painterly to the human. "Oh? Yes, of course. You must be stiff by now . . ."

I did not smile at his words. It would not be fair to tease him in his intensely involved state. It would be best for me to be decisive and direct.

I flowed up onto my feet, my inflamed arousal having kept me from stiffening up whatsoever. The heat that rolled over my bare skin had nothing to do with the roaring fire on the hearth and everything to do with the sun-bright curls of his hair and the beard-shadowed line of his jaw and the streak of cerulean blue he wore on his cheek. How I loved him at that moment.

I loved him.

It was not something I'd truly been aware of, but neither was I startled by the realization. This man, this solitary, banished man with his paint-stained fingertips and his faded clothing, this aching soldier, this reluctant hero, this gifted creator—

This man was the only man I had ever loved. The only man I would ever love. And the more he withheld his desire from me, the more he guarded his speech, the more he tried not to touch me, the more I needed to touch him.

The poor fellow never stood a chance.

I gathered the boldness of The Swan, the iron will of Jinx, and even the vulnerability of that lost, new soul and focused all of them—all of me!—on the poor, unsuspecting Artist.

His dark eyes widened as I approached him.

"Do you wish your wrap?"

"No."

He swallowed and backed away a step. "Do you wish some refreshment? I think Beatriu left some—"

"No. I do not want to be clothed, or fed, or looked after any longer." I wondered if he realized that he held his palette like a shield before him and his brush like a sword. Was he fending off my wishes, or his own?

"I am not an invalid, dear man. I am not broken, or failing, or lost—not any longer. I am a grown woman, conscious of my own desires."

He looked down, away, anywhere but at me. Nevertheless, I saw the flush of arousal rising up his throat. I saw the thickening of his cock within his canvas trousers.

I gently took the palette and brush from him before I found myself requiring turpentine in my bathwater, and set it aside on the worktable.

When his hands were empty, he flexed them, as if he was not sure what to do with them.

How long had it been for him? He was a healthy male, a

handsome man. The village women were decidedly grateful for his presence.

At that moment, I realized that he had not taken advantage of anything they may have offered him. Like the gentleman he was, he had viewed the women of la Cala as his dependents. He had saved them, he continued to look after them, and he would never, ever press his advantage.

I admired him for it. In addition, I was very grateful that I was not a gentlewoman, and that he was not my dependent. Else I would never have had the courage to do what I did next.

Without his shield and sword, he was defenseless before me. I took pity on him and moved in very slowly.

The Swan rolled her hips with every step. Jinx looked him frankly in the eyes. The lost girl allowed her hopes to rise as his gaze darkened and his breath quickened with undeniable desire.

I reached out to him again and pressed my palms to his chest. I felt his heart thud against my touch.

"Are you sure . . ."

His question died beneath my heartfelt kiss.

Thankfully, although the man had taken some convincing, he then responded wholeheartedly! A deep moan escaped him, one that made me ache with aroused sympathy.

"Yes," I whispered into his mouth. "Yes, I'm sure, I'm so very s—"

He dove upon me then. His long arms wrapped tightly around me. His hot mouth devoured mine. I felt the thick hardness of his cock against my lower belly and I pressed myself closer still.

The taste of him, the feel of him, the heat—oh, my God, the blistering blaze of him! I hungered, I ached, I longed.

Never. The word rang in my tumbling thoughts. *Never.*

Never had I felt this way.

This was no practiced play of love. This was no calculated affair.

This was utter truth.

With that thought, all sense of the past or future left me. I became a being of Now, and Need, and sweet, hot Longing. I wrapped my fingers into his curling hair and pulled his mouth hard onto mine.

He dug his hands into the flesh of my bottom and lifted me, sliding me up his hard body to better ravage my mouth with his kiss. The wary loner had fled and the man that remained was a famished huntsman who had finally found his prey. I wrapped my thighs around his hips and captured him right back.

He carried me to the chaise lounge he'd created and fell with me to the cushions. I tightened my fists in his hair and never stopped kissing him.

At last. Oh, sweet heaven, at last!

He tore off his clothing and lay his long body between my thighs. I reveled in the weight of him on me. His hands swept up my body and wrapped around my breasts.

I slid my fingers around his waist and up the rippling muscles of his back. His apparent leanness had belied the strength of him. He exhaled against the base of my neck and shivers ran up my body from my toes to my hair.

How could I have known that my body could take me over in this way? How could I have known that a man, the right man, could sweep me away one sense at a time. The sight of him, the scent of him, the feel of him, the sound of his voice . . . Dear God, I could not wait to taste him!

I pushed his shoulders and, as if he could read my mind, he rolled with me until I straddled him. My breath caught as I gazed down at him. For a moment, I stroked my fingertips over his brow, and temples, and down over his unshaven cheeks to cup his jaw in my palms.

"I love you," I said simply. Protestations of never-ending devotion were words I'd heard so many times. Every time they had left me wondering about their true meaning. I wanted him to have no doubt.

"I cannot breathe when you look at me that way," he said humbly. "If I tell you that I love you, will you believe that I have known it for weeks, yet been afraid to say it aloud?"

I smiled down at him and slid my flattened palms from his shoulders down over his chest. "I'll believe anything you say, for it is you who say it."

He looked alarmed at this. "You should not have such faith in me," he warned.

"It is far too late for that, my dear Artist. You have won my trust entirely."

"I——"

"Dear man, you have a naked woman on top of you," I pointed out with teasing exasperation. "I would not squander this moment, if I were you." I bent close enough to him that my hair fell around our faces. In this intimate seclusion, I gazed into his eyes . . . and bit him gently on the tip of his nose.

This nip shocked him from his wary hesitation. His eyes narrowed at my playfulness. I grinned down at him, one eyebrow raised in challenge. "Is it not rude to keep a lady waiting?"

His hands had slipped to rest upon my thighs. Now his fingers tightened, testing the resilience of my flesh. I rolled my hips to press myself against him. He moaned and his hands hardened upon me. That was good. I found I did not want him to hesitate, to be gentle, to hold back.

"I withstood the fury of the sea," I reminded him softly. "Do not treat me like glass."

His brown eyes darkened nearly to black. I wondered what manner of man I had unleashed.

I could not wait to find out.

He lifted his head and sucked my nipple into his mouth.

Hot sensation lanced through me. I arched my back as I

gasped in a breath, pressing more of my soft flesh into his seek-ing mouth.

My breathless sigh unleashed him. He grabbed me with large, urgent hands and dragged me to him. He drew hard at my nipple, making me whine and squirm at the mingled plea-sure and pain. I relished every sensation. Then he wrapped one hot hand around that breast and moved his mouth to the other. Then he lifted my body, pulling me up, kissing my skin softly all the way.

At last, he drove his tongue between the deepest folds of me. He rolled his tongue over the rigid little button that was the center of my pleasure.

"Oh *yesss*." I rolled my head back as I knelt over his chest, dizzy with the pleasure rippling through me, until he changed his motion to drive his tongue deeply into me. I cried out and my balance failed me, lost as I was in the waves of sensation. I fell against the back of the chair, clinging as if to a piece of driftwood in a tossing sea. I lost my way, lost my voice, rotat-ing my hips, moving against his mouth, abandoning myself en-tirely to the pleasure rippling through my body.

When my breathing had calmed and my shivering had eased somewhat, I released the back of the chair and slid down, fall-ing limply across his chest and torso.

" 'Twas not fair," I panted. "I wanted to taste *you*."

He laughed, a brief rumble in his chest. "Fear not, the world has not yet ended. There is time."

I caught my breath and then mimicked his action, sliding down his body, kissing all the way. I grasped his erection with one hand. Pulling myself closer, I welcomed the tip with wet open lips.

A deep groan ripped through him. His big hand came to rest upon my head, a caress and a tentative objection. "I would not ask you—"

I lifted my head and tossed back my sweat-dampened hair. "I cannot understand you, for your Catalan is abysmal."

He dropped his head back onto the pillow with a gasping laugh. "Then I am entirely without options."

I opened my mouth and sucked his enlarged head deeply between my lips. I had done this for other men. This time, I did it for myself. I needed the sound of his pleasure in my ears, the taste of his orgasm in my mouth.

"Damnit!" He reached for me, raising me up so that he could roll upon me, between my thighs. He was groaning as he pushed my hair back to gaze pleadingly at me, his brown eyes gone dark with desire. "Now—I need you so—"

I opened my thighs and wrapped my hands about his muscled buttocks. "Now."

He drove himself hard into me.

After this first desperate entry, he was careful, allowing me to set the pace. I moved tentatively at first, pulling him closer with my legs wrapped about his waist until he began to pant from the struggle to restrain himself. When I was fully impaled upon him, I went up on my elbows to kiss him as he followed my lead. We meshed our rhythms easily, as if we had been making love for years, yet each touch and taste and slide of him within me felt like nothing I had ever known.

I knew this man. I loved this man. I was his and he was mine.

The kiss and the sweet, tormenting pleasure continued, stretching time. I lost myself to it, to the taste of him, to the feel of his mouth on mine.

My softness wrapped around his hardness, his callused hands on my breasts, my nipples hardening in his palms. The ache grew and time turned strange amid the slow, mind-stealing pace.

I orgasmed, quite without effort. I cried out in surprise and fisted my hands in the covers, holding him into me as hard as I could with my knees gripping his hips.

My head fell back as I keened, falling into the swirling, sparkling depths of pleasure.

I didn't know. Never had I been released from my mind and thoughts this way. Never had I trusted enough to abandon calculation and performance. In this moment I was no one but his lover. He was no one but mine. And nothing mattered but this.

He growled deeply as he thrust, pouring himself into me, as lost as I was in the rippling surprise of our mutual pleasure.

The bliss shivered on and on, each moment folding into the next as I fought for breath, impaled upon him as I was, forced to feel every throbbing inch of him deep within me.

When at last we both stilled, we fell back upon the cushions, breathless. Our chaise construction had slithered apart beneath us without our notice. He lay with his head upon my bosom and his strong arms curled around me. I closed my eyes and floated free as my fingers toyed with his curling hair.

"You are—" he began.

I flinched and pressed a finger to his lips. He was about to tell me how wonderful I was, how perfect, how splendid a lover I was. I wanted no review of my performance, no compliments.

We were together, and we were enough.

He wrapped his hand around my shushing finger and moved it away from his smiling lips. "You are lying in paint."

I threw back my head and laughed like a child, a belly laugh that drew him in. Our laughter filled the crumbling *castell* like light fills a room.

Chapter Twenty-Two

Castell de la Cala

We spent the next several weeks in a blur of lovemaking. And yes, painting.

I never tired of posing for him. He painted me on the beach. We made love in the sand. He painted me in the garden. We made love against the rock wall. He painted me in my chamber window, facing the sea, with my wrapper dropped halfway down my back. We made love in an actual bed, for the first time.

On a brilliant morning in late May, when the strawberries had ripened and we fed each other upon their plumpness until the juices ran down our chins, he kissed me deeply. Then he pulled away from my eager embrace and stood.

"We must dress."

I wrinkled my nose at the notion. "Why? It is yet early morning. Beatriu knows not to disturb us until noon at least." I gave him a playful leer. "Don't you want to paint me on the bed again?"

His dark eyes blazed briefly, but he suppressed it. "We have somewhere to be today. There is a festival in the village and you are the guest of honor."

I blinked at that. I adored everyone I had met in the small village of La Cala, but I had assumed that I was viewed with the suspicion of being foreign, not to mention my untoward arrival upon their shores. Now, realizing it was not so, I felt cowed by the honor.

"I have only the one gown," I told him, biting my lip with worry. "I love Beatriu for making it, but it is an everyday sort of dress."

He only smiled and dropped a kiss upon my furrowed brow. "I will fetch you hot water. You should wash and wear whatever you like."

The pitcher of steaming water he brought me was a luxury after all the chilly baths we had taken in the sea. I bathed well and brushed my hair until it shone. Then I reached into the chest for my single gown.

It was not there. In its stead was a shimmering fold of blue and amber.

"Oh!" I gently removed it from the drawer and let its length drop from my hands as I held them high.

It was a simple but elegant concoction of sky blue silk and rich shimmering golden brown. Then I realized that the bodice had been cleverly pieced together from remnants of my opera gown that had held their beading.

How distant that night seemed now! As if a thousand years had passed, in memory if not in time.

The silk of the skirt seemed familiar somehow. I looked up to see the Artist leaning in the doorway with a smug grin upon his face.

"You sacrificed your dressing gown!"

He smirked and tilted his head. "It looked better on you anyway."

I twirled around with the dress pressed to me, letting the skirt swirl wide. "A gown of sand and sky," I said.

Suddenly happy about our outing, I threw him out of the room and put my energies into dressing my best, suggesting he do the same.

The gown fit nearly perfectly. I realized that Beatriu well knew my measurements from the first gown she'd crafted for me. It was only a tiny bit snug in the bust. I smiled, wondering if that had been at the Artist's request. Men did love a snug bodice!

I twisted my long hair high and wound it about my head, fixing it with two sticks I'd made from old paintbrush handles and wrapping it with my pretty new hair ribbon. I gazed into the small, speckled looking glass that hung over the chest and decided that I looked quite fetching, if I did say so myself!

With a smile, I left the chamber to seek out my escort for the day.

When I saw the Artist's transformation, my breath left me entirely. He had dressed in the studio, leaving the chamber to me. I pushed open the door to see a tall and handsome soldier.

He turned and gazed somberly at me, as if he feared what I might think of him. "It is the only good coat that I have."

Upon second glance, I realized that it was merely the cutaway coat of the British Army, without the striped trousers or highly polished black boots. Instead, he had donned his least paint stained canvas trousers, although there was a faint but betraying handprint in burnt sienna upon his left buttock. I ignored it, even though the size of the handprint matched my own.

In addition, the coat was minus the customary gold buttons. I wondered if he'd sold them at some point, perhaps for paints.

"You look very handsome," I assured him. He did, too. The fitted coat showed the width of his shoulders and narrowness of his trim waist, even more than a dozen years later. He'd bound back his hair as well, in a neat queue behind his neck in the fashion of military men. I squinted at him, picturing the

customary tricorn hat and showy ostrich plume, and then decided they were not required. He looked just like himself. Part
soldier, part painter.

All mine.

For now, a voice whispered in my mind. I had lost my belief
in permanence at a very young age. *Forever* was a meaningless
word to someone who had lived and lost as I had.

I lifted my chin. All the more reason to savor each second I
had with him.

"I'm ready to meet my adoring public," I said haughtily.
Then, dropping the theatrics, I looked down at myself. "Do you
think they will know that my gown is made of rags?"

He laughed aloud. "Yes. Half the women in the village had
a hand in sewing it."

"They did?" I was awed by the gift.

I grabbed for his hand and we ran from the *castell* like
naughty pupils escaping the schoolroom. On the lane to the village, he kept my hand in his, as naturally as if our ten fingers
had been designed to interlock.

As we wound through the cobbled streets, passing the first
few stone buildings of the village, we could hear the celebration
taking place in the central plaza. Brass horns and flutes played
a lively folk tune. I heard children screeching with glee and male
and females voices laughing and shouting. I tugged at the Artist's hand like a child, eager to join in on the fun.

La Cala's town plaza was filled with flowers. Garlands of
braided blooms spilled from every window and poured down
the ancient stone walls like fountains. The beaming faces of
villagers turned toward us, and their smiles widened further in
welcome. I found myself quite overcome by the beauty and joy
around me.

I knew not the occasion—as the Artist had insisted it was a surprise—or even why I had been chosen the guest of honor. I realized it did not matter.

With great shouts of laughter, the youngest men and women swarmed toward us. I nearly pulled back, but the Artist would not release my hand.

"They adore their 'beauty of the cove,'" he murmured in my ear before the mass of boys and girls overwhelmed us.

The girls swarmed about me. The boys playfully bullied the Artist into releasing my hand. He was swept away from me, carried off in the tide of their youthful antics. The giggling girls chivvied me closer to the fountain, where I spotted a flower-bedecked litter awaiting. Pushed from behind, I tumbled into the seat with a laughing shriek, then yelped in earnest when the litter was hefted before I found my balance.

Hanging on for dear life, I was lifted high above the shoulders of four burly farmers. Laughing people crowded around the litter as I was taken for a promenade around the square. Upturned faces threw smiles at me while more flower petals were flung in a rain that clung to my hair and filled my lap.

From my new vantage point I searched the crowd for the Artist. I saw him hoisted upon the shoulders of two very large fellows as Liverpool barked excitedly at their heels. The horde carried the Artist around the fountain in the opposite direction from me, the men clapping and stamping to the musicians' folk song. My own circle was colorful with full peasant skirts and bright shawls as the women danced and sang the Catalan song. As we passed each other, we reached our hands in laughing pleas for succor, only to have our escorts playfully swoop us away from each other.

This simple country dance was more joyous than all the balls I'd attended in all of London's finest halls—combined.

Once my escorts brought me halfway around the fountain

again, they deposited my vehicle at the bottom step of the village *parròquia*, the parish church rebuilt after Babington's vandalism.

I was urged into releasing my deathly grasp on the sides of the litter by two laughing women I recognized as Beatriu's youngest daughters, Alba and Carme. I pretended to resist them, much to the appalled shrieks of the other women, who helped to detach me from my blooming shelter. They crowded about me, chattering as they straightened my tumbled appearance with quick hands. A crown of pink rockrose and yellow broom was rested upon my brow as my cheeks were pinched to encourage a becoming glow.

It all took less than a minute. Then I was giddily expelled from my attendants and led to the first step of the church stair.

Before me stood the Artist, apparently none the worse for his adventure but for the crown of yellow broom and red poppies that sat lopsided upon his head. I laughed at the sight of shaggy Liverpool sitting at his feet. The dog panted happily at me from beneath a matching headdress.

Then something caught my attention. A man stepped forward from behind the Artist and my heart began to thud at the sight of him. He wore robes and a surplice.

The priest had arrived from Girona.

The dress. The flowers. The shouted folk song that I'd barely understood, except for the words *beautiful* and *handsome* and *babies*.

I swallowed hard against the sudden lump in my throat. This man was like no other man I had ever known. I trusted this man with more than my life. I trusted him with my very heart. I smiled shyly at him then, for although I believed I knew what was to come, it would indeed be a first for me.

His eyes brightened to the happiest glow I had yet seen in them. And then, before the entire cheering and clapping village, the Artist went to one knee on the wide step and held out his hands to me.

I gazed down at him and placed both my hands within his. *"Sempre,"* I replied. *Forever.*

He stood, and with a whoop that set Liverpool to barking, he swept me into a deep, public kiss! In front of a priest!

Fortunately, the clergyman remained cheerful during this display.

At that point, we were bustled inside to stand before the altar. The church filled and then overflowed. It seemed that no one wanted to miss the wedding of the *soldat dement* and the *bellesa de la cala*!

I recall little of the ceremony, though I remember that it was formal and beautiful and that I managed to give shaky but coherent replies. My foremost recollection is that my knees shook the entire time and that I had difficulty catching my breath at the look of profound joy I beheld in my beloved's eyes.

At the end of our vows, the Artist took my hand and slipped a ring upon my finger. It was a heavy gold circle, a man's signet ring. He leaned close.

"With this ring, I wed thee," he murmured in English.

"Sempre," I whispered back, in Catalan.

He smiled then, a carefree, boyish grin that I had not yet seen upon his face, that I suspected had not rested there since his battalion had marched into the village of la Cala so many years ago.

A great cheer went up from the audience and we turned, blushing, to be presented to them by the priest. His words were inaudible beneath the great roar of clapping and shouting.

When I put a hand to my cheek I found that it was wet with tears. I do not know that I have ever been so afloat in emotion in my life.

We were dragged across the square by our enthusiastic

attendants, where a fine house with colorful shutters stood, gnarled wisteria branches growing high upon its walls. It was Beatriu's family home. Although she had appeared to be the Artist's simple housekeeper when I had first encountered her, she was from a prosperous family, which underscored the depth of her loyalty to the man who had sacrificed everything to save her husband from Babington's firing squad.

We were escorted upstairs to a chamber of dreams. I could not see much of it in truth, for it was filled to bursting with flowers. Someone had clearly become carried away. Garlands hung over double-glassed doors that looked over the square. The wide bed was heaped in loose blossoms. Trailing bouquets were fastened everywhere one could imagine fastening something: on the bedposts, on the drawer pulls of the chest, on the dress hooks on the wall! The polished wooden floor was strewn with petals of many colors. The perfume of the flowers was intoxicating.

We were both rushed toward the double doors, which were open to reveal the crowd gathering below our balcony.

"*Dement!*" they shouted. "*Bellesa!*"

Some stout ladies in the front, Beatriu among them, began a chant. "*Nadons! Nens!*" Babies, children!

We responded by laughing and running back into the bedchamber, where we scooped up the loose blooms mounded upon the bed. The Artist began to fire them from the balcony with military precision. I think he bounced one off every man who had chivvied him in the square!

I preferred to toss mine gently into the hands of the young girls who clamored for my *benedicció,* my blessing. When our flowers were spent, we were pulled back into the room by our attendants, who laughingly pushed us toward the bed.

"Enough!" the Artist shouted at them in mock temper. "*¡Ja n'hi ha prou!*"

After much giggling the door was shut and we were left alone at last.

The Artist glanced at me, blushing.

I laughed aloud. "I wouldn't mind a few *nadons* and *nens* running about underfoot."

He grinned sheepishly. "Perhaps we could start with one *nadon* at a time."

We reached for each other then. I stepped close and he lowered his head to touch his brow to mine.

"Did you mind the ruse?" he asked. "Beatriu assured me that women love surprises, but I thought you might dislike the lie—"

I put my fingers over his lips, feather light. "There is more truth in your every breath than I have ever known from any man." I smiled softly at my husband. "I trust you with my heart, with my life."

THE PRESENT

Chapter Twenty-Three

Near Girona, Spain

Brenna stared at him in disbelief, her mouth open.

"I'm sorry for not telling you the whole truth."

"*What . . . the . . . actual . . . fuck?* You broke into my hotel room? While I was in the *bathtub*?"

"Absolutely not. You were out getting a pizza. But then you came back . . ."

"So this whole thing's been a setup—a lie."

"No! Absolutely not." Fitch had known this would be bad. He just hoped they could find a way to get past it. "My only lie was how I found out about The Swan. I read Claudia's fax and *then* I googled some of the names in it and found the book and—"

"Stop the car."

"We're in the middle of an olive grove."

"Stop. Now."

"Don't, Brenna. I'm not going to leave you here by the side of the road to—"

"*Me?* Oh, hell no! *You're* getting out and I'm driving off into the freakin' sunset! Now stop the damn car!"

"We're only about twenty minutes from Girona."

"Good! Then it will only take you all night to walk there! Just . . . pull over. Oh, my God." Brenna shook her head and looked away, laughing bitterly. "How? How is this even *possible*?" She turned toward him again with eyes wild with anger. "I *know* better! How can I still be surprised when a man turns out to be a giant asshat-doucheface-lying-sack-of-balls?"

Big, fat raindrops plopped on the windshield. And on their heads.

"Oh, this is fucking perfect." Brenna palmed her forehead. "Just put up the top, would you?"

That was exactly what he'd been trying to do. The Audi Cabriolet had a dash-mounted button that controlled the automatic roof. It had worked just fine in the abbey parking lot, but now it was dead. In the meantime, the raindrops were no longer individual drops, just a steady downpour.

"What are you *doing*?"

"It's not working."

"What? Pull over!"

"Uh . . ." Fitch looked to the side of the road, seeing nowhere to go. They had just gone up a hill and were on a ridge. The guardrail was inches from the pavement and the two-lane road had no median. He continued to pound on the button—useless.

"What the hell, Fitch?"

He spoke calmly but loud enough to be heard over the rain. "Open the glove compartment. Get out the operator's guide. Find the instructions for how to manually close the top."

Brenna scrambled, pulling a thick packet from the glove compartment. As the rain poured down she flipped through the pages, cursing like a drunken dockworker.

"There's a panel on the left edge by your door. You have to pry it off."

"Great." Prying while steering wasn't an option, so he turned the windshield wipers to maximum and floored the engine, trying to get over the ridge to a place they could pull over. In the meantime—which was probably twenty seconds though it felt like an eternity—Brenna had gone into full meltdown mode.

"Oh, holy shit! My laptop! My research!" She flung off her seatbelt and spun around to hang over the front seat. She threw Fitch's jacket over her carryall. "Hurry!"

"Cover mine, too!"

She suddenly plopped back down. Out of the corner of his nearly blind eye he saw her power the seat to its maximum recline position. It took a second for him to realize she was creating a roof for their electronics. Now she was curled into a fetal position, soaking wet, clutching the manual.

What a fucking disaster.

The first chance he got, Fitch slammed on the brakes and pulled into what looked like a farm lane. It was hard to tell in the blinding rain.

Brenna began barking out a series of commands. "Get out. We have to pull up the top by hand. From the back."

They both jumped out of the car and ran to the rear of the Audi, the rain beating down on them. Fitch watched helplessly as Brenna slipped in the mud, her high-heeled boots finally getting the best of her. She windmilled and twisted, then went down face-first. He ran over to help her, but she smacked his hand away, instead using the tire to pull herself from the muck. Fitch stared at her in disbelief—her face and hair were dripping with slimy farm mud. Her white jeans were now a solid reddish brown.

"Go! Get back to your side of the car!"

They worked together to pull the nylon top up and over the interior, only to find that the roof would not close all the way. Brenna hadn't even gotten in the car when she began telling him what to do next. "Take the key out of the ignition."

He did.

"Use it to pop open this little thing." Brenna pointed to a small indentation in the windshield casing while simultaneously reading the mud-smeared manual. He used the key to pop open the cutout.

"Look at the far left end of the dash. Stick the key in a tiny hole at the bottom and pry off the cover." He did exactly as she said, his hair dripping in his eyes, and the endpiece went flying into the mud. He saw a panel of electrical components.

She walked him through each step as he dislodged the Allen key, shoved it into the windshield cutout, and manually turned it to lock the top in place.

They sat there for a second, saying nothing, listening to their own rapid breathing and watching the windshield fog.

Brenna suddenly gasped. "My phone!" She'd left it in the center console of the car, and it was now floating in a puddle of water. She grabbed it but it squirted out of her slimy hand, out her open window, and into the mud.

"Goddammit to hell!" She stumbled out of the car and made a lunge for her phone. Fitch jumped out to help her.

"Back off, Wilder. You've done enough." She snagged the phone from the sludge and began pounding on a variety of buttons and toggles, none of which powered it on. With a scream of frustration she hurled it into a ditch, where it landed in a patch of yellow and pink wildflowers. When her eyes flashed at him he expected to see rage. He saw anguish and grief, instead.

"I'm a Harvard professor!" The raindrops began to wash the mud from her hair and face, leaving long streaks of clean skin down her cheeks.

"What am I doing here? With *you*? I hate men like you. I hate my life. I wish I'd never come to this ridiculously romantic country!" She took a shuddering breath and began to look around her. "I told myself it was fun to have a 'spontaneous adventure' and dance in the street and get the hell kissed out of me up against a stone wall! And now look! I don't have a phone! I don't know who you are. It looks like you're just a liar and a sneak! And . . . and I . . . don't even know who *I* am anymore!"

Her flat belly heaved beneath her soaked shirt and pants. Fitch could see every curve and valley in her slim body. He could see she was about to cry.

"What can I do, Brenna? How can I make this right?"

Her only reply was an exhausted shake of her head. He felt like a real tool.

They got in the car again. Fitch started the engine, only to find the wheels were stuck. In angry silence, Brenna operated the steering wheel while he pushed, but they got nowhere. He decided to pop the trunk to look for a mat or piece of carpet to provide traction to the back wheels, but gazed down into a flooded compartment.

Brenna called out from inside the car. "Any luck?"

"Not exactly."

She joined him by the trunk and they both stared. Their bags were swimming in several inches of water. Brenna's colorful suitcase had gone a long way toward disintegration, its blue dye swirling in the rainwater.

"This can't be happening. No. Just, no." She reached in to unzip her bag. Her clothes were soaked through and tie-dyed several shades of blue.

"Okay, that's it. I'm done." She slammed the trunk closed and extended her arms from her sides. "We're getting out of this shitty-ass mud, and you're going to drive me somewhere I can take a hot shower and cry myself to sleep."

"That sounds like an excellent plan."

She let go with a barking laugh. "It's not *your* plan, Wilder. *We* don't have any plans anymore. I just want you to drop me off and go away. I never want to see you again."

"Brenna, I know—"

"You don't know a single thing about me!" She closed her eyes and shoved her dirty fingers into her muddy hair. When she looked at him again, the pain in her eyes made his stomach drop. "I wish I'd never met you."

Eventually they made it out of the mud, and after an utterly silent five-minute drive, Fitch pulled off toward the nearest reasonably sized town. Santa Coloma de Farners had always been just a spot on the map to Fitch, so he had no idea what to expect. The rain had stopped. At the town square he asked an older man if he knew of a place to stay without a reservation. He pointed off to the south and offered some convoluted directions, which Fitch followed to the best of his ability.

He pulled up to a charming old stone house on a narrow cobblestone street. The door opened, and a woman in her forties appeared on the stoop, waving her hands in despair at the car's condition. When Brenna appeared in all her muddy glory, the woman made a series of *tsk, tsk* sounds and began chattering rapidly, leading Brenna by the arm.

"What . . . ?" Brenna shot Fitch a helpless look, not quite following what the woman was saying.

"She's going to make sure you have a nice comfortable room." Brenna nodded and let the woman take her inside. Fitch chuckled and shook his head, well aware what the guesthouse owner had really said: that her father-in-law called to tell her tourists were on their way and that the man was a terrible driver. Then she'd added: "What have you done to this poor woman?"

That was the question, wasn't it?

THE PAST

Chapter Twenty-Four

Castell de la Cala

The first months of summer flew by in a haze of joy. It seemed as though each day lasted only a moment, yet was rife with an eternity of emotion.

We were as free as children in our laughter and as wild as animals in our lovemaking. We feasted on the fruits of summer and upon each other. I do not know of any song or poem that could capture those dreamy, sensuous hours we spent in each other's arms.

It may seem that we ignored our pasts and denied our former pain—yet it was not that way at all. We spoke at length about our experiences, as if we could not reveal ourselves to each other quickly enough. In that sharing, an acceptance that neither of us had ever dreamed could exist with another soul, we freed ourselves and each other from the burdens of guilt and regret.

We ate, we laughed, we played, we loved. My dearest lover, my beloved artist, my *soldat dement* . . . my husband.

One morning, we were awakened from the profound sleep of the deeply satisfied by the tumbling waterfall of children running down the stone stairs below our bedchamber. Beatriu's horde of grandchildren had performed one of their instinctive migrations to the *castell*.

"Something tells me that Beatriu is baking today," my husband murmured in my ear.

I slipped my arm about his lean waist and pressed closer, for the sea breeze held an early chill and he was warm. And because the sound of his heartbeat against my ear calmed the world and soothed my sleep-fogged mind.

"I'll wager it will be honey-cakes," he continued sleepily. "They would not be here in force for anything less."

It was true. For a taste of honey-cakes, they would even carry the littlest ones on their backs along the lane that switched back and forth up the *castell* hill.

I poked my husband gently. "I would rise early for Beatriu's cakes, but you know I cannot keep anything down until noon. Therefore, you must brave the rioting horde to save one for me to have later with my tea."

He chuckled and slid his palm lovingly down between my breasts to soothe the sweet rise of my belly. We were both most proud of this strange and lovely swelling of life. I daresay we were rather sickening about it, like most expectant parents.

The little stranger fluttered against my husband's palm, eliciting our instant admiration and pride. Beatriu claimed that a son grew within me, for boys showed themselves earlier than girls, she said.

I merely smiled at her decisiveness and said not a word about my own suspicion that our child had already been making his presence known at our wedding. After all, Beatriu was an excellent seamstress. I do not think she would have made the mistake of sewing the bodice of my wedding dress too tight. My breasts were already beginning to increase on that wonderful day.

Son or daughter, we cared not at all. I would cherish a

brown-eyed girl child of my own, and my husband would be putty in the hands of either gender.

We dawdled in bed a bit longer while I sipped at some tepid water and nibbled a bit of dry bread that Beatriu had left in our chamber the evening before. When I knew I could keep down a bit more, we threw on our simple country clothing and pattered down the stairs just like the children had done.

Beatriu paused in her baking of wondrous things to prepare a coddled egg for me, which she served with her great-grandmother's special tea. The entire village swore by the effectiveness of this blend of herbs to relieve the waves of *nàusea matutina*. I inured myself to the grassy tang of it because it truly seemed to help soothe my discomfort.

She soon shooed us all from her domain like the annoying brats we were. My husband and I joined hands and followed the herd of *nens* to the cove. I knew the water would be warm and clear and the sun would freckle my skin even as it brightened my husband's hair. I did not mind a bit. What place had the vanities and fashions of English society in this blooming paradise?

The children played tirelessly in the mild surf and chased the receding tide toward El Sentinelles, the rocks that perched like jagged palace guards around the cove. The half-circle of stones no longer set me back with recollections of my painful arrival. In the blue and gold summer day, they seemed nothing but benevolent.

In my thick linen chemise, I paddled out with Beatriu's energetic grandson Dìdac, and together we poked at crabs and anemone in the tide pools. Back on the beach, in the shade of the cliff, I cooed at his fat little sister, Mara, until she fell asleep in my lap. Her wisping curls and round cheeks made me ache with longing to meet my own child. As she slept, I watched my handsome husband play sea monster for the appreciatively screeching gang of older children.

Finally, we climbed back up the path to the *castell*, our appetites whetted by our swim and the comfortable surety of honeycakes in our near future. My husband and I returned to our proper adult status just in time to carry the littlest ones uphill.

After cakes and milk and an hour of siesta sprawled on faded quilts spread beneath the rose arbor, the children again assembled their swarm and buzzed on back to the village. Beatriu set out a cold supper for us in the larder and marched home on their heels.

Alone at last, we sipped chilled cava and nibbled on fruit while we contemplated the coming hours of the afternoon. Picking berries seemed too strenuous. I protested the notion of fishing on the grounds that the fish would then have to be cleaned.

As I lounged upon my chaise and let my hair down to dry, I saw my loving husband turn once more into the Artist. His gaze traveled down my body with that strange hungry intensity. His fingers began to twitch. I knew he needed to sketch. I smiled my assent.

"But I will not move from this spot," I warned. "Bring your paints outside if you will, but if you try to make me shift my weary self to the studio, I shall dig my very nails into the patio stones."

He did not laugh but only hurried off to collect his brushes and paints and canvas.

When he returned, he took some time posing me. I found it most thoughtful that even in the heat of his creative madness, he wished me to rest in comfort. He finally decided upon a simple pose, seated nude upon the edge of the chaise as if just awakening in bed. When he asked me to lean back upon my hands, I realized that it was the gentle swell of my belly that inspired him.

"Your first portrait," I whispered to our child. "Papa wants you to hold very still."

He painted until the sun set. Then he put down his brush and palette and came to me. We made love slowly, at great peace with the end of another perfect day.

Even now I think on that day and know I would not change a single moment of it.

The next morning dawned cloudy and blustery, the complete opposite of the balmy day before. Rain was on the way, my husband informed me. We denied the loss of our perfect summer weather by remaining in bed long past our habit.

He touched his forehead to mine. "How could I have known such a thing as this existed? How could I have known to blend two souls together, like pigments, to make an entirely new color?"

I closed my eyes against the sweet tide of joy that swept over me. "I love it when you talk about paint."

He chuckled and kissed my eyelids with exquisite gentleness as he rolled between my welcoming thighs. We came together in slow, easy movements that were as natural and unforced as the waves rippling over the beach below us. The precious communion of him inside me, of our limbs entangling, of our breath mingling, was a gift.

I forgot myself, as I always did beneath his touch. Without thought or reason, I let the waves of tender passion sweep me away from myself. How could I have known that heat could warm as well as burn? How could I have known that the ultimate vulnerability would bring me my greatest reward?

I arched against him. His movements became mine. My sighs became his. We lost ourselves in the tangle of sheets and mingling of moans and deep, tender thrusts that drove us higher together. We clung to each other, hot skin, damp hair, needful hands. He kissed me when I orgasmed, as he always did. I held his dear handsome face between my hands and touched my lips to his as he came deep inside me.

We fell asleep again, still joined, with his arms wrapped around me and my hands in his hair. Tucked into each other, we spoke softly of raising our little one among the kind hearts of la Cala, and how happy we were not to be confined in chilly, sooty London. Why the entire world did not wish to live upon the coast of Catalunya, I could not fathom, although I rejoiced that they remained ignorant of the perfection of the place.

We talked of improving the *castell* somewhat, just enough to house all of our many future children. I would learn to bake, I declared, for it seemed a shame not to acquire at least a little of Beatriu's vast knowledge of sweets.

My husband admitted to an interest in farming. He knew a bit about it from his boyhood in England, he said. That was the first time he spoke of his past without pain, but I did not wish to call attention to it by exclaiming my curiosity. We had time enough to learn everything—about our adopted home, about becoming parents, about each other.

All the time in the world, I remember telling myself as I cuddled close to him. Our long happy lives stretched out before us. Surely after all we had endured, the fates would look kindly on us now.

Then a wailing arose below our bedchamber window. Beatriu, calm, unflappable Beatriu, screamed for *"¡Dement! DEMENT!"* I scrambled off the bed to grab for my gown as my husband dove across the room to the window. Opening the shutters, he leaned out.

"¡Beatriu! Què és el que tem?" What fears you?

"¡Els nens! ¡La marea entrant!"

He leaned out farther, despite his nudity. "The children—what?"

I gasped. "The tide!"

"Oh, God," he whispered in horror, pulling on his trousers. "Oh, God, no."

We ran from the chamber, down the stairs, and out across the patio. The path to the sea was meant to be taken slowly, at leisure, but we raced down it with scarcely a thought to our bare feet. Beatriu was halfway back to the beach when we passed her.

"*¡Dónát pressa!*" For the first time, her round face showed every one of her fifty-four years. "*¡El Sentinelles!*"

My heart pounded. The children were trapped on the encircling rocks of the cove . . . and the tide was coming in.

My husband grabbed her by the shoulders. "*Nens? Cuants?*" She shook in terror in his grasp. "*¡Vuit!*"

Eight children! All but the babies, then. My husband paled. "So many . . ." The agony in his gaze as he turned to me told me everything. He would never be able to save them all.

My gut went cold, for I knew that he would try anyway.

"*¡Beatriu! ¡Cerqueu el seu marit i el seu vaixell!*" I barked the command to fetch her husband and his boat with the remembered authority of the mistress of the house.

She nodded and obeyed, turning to scramble back up the trail. I followed my beloved down, for he had raced ahead. Even as I attained the beach, he had thrown himself into the choppy water and had begun stroking powerfully through the incoming waves.

I could see the small shapes cowering upon the great rocks. If only the sea were calm, it would be nothing but an adventure. But the morning's clouds had promised a storm and the sea was already ill at ease.

I stalked restlessly up and down the beach, never taking my eyes off the children and the head and shoulders of my husband swiftly making his way toward them. There was naught else I could do. My city upbringing did not make me a strong swimmer and I could not risk the life I carried within me. My helplessness drove me to a frenzy of worry.

The clouds were darkening by the moment. The first spurt of raindrops fell as my husband returned to the beach with one child clinging to his back and another tucked into one arm. I ran into the surf to pull the children from him, carrying the smallest up to dry land.

The girl was none the worse for wear, just frightened for the others. They boy was unharmed. I sent them both to wait high above the tidemark.

I returned to my place at the edge of the waves, though the incoming tide was driving me closer to the cliff behind me. Then, a sand-colored blur sped past me and dove into the waves. I had not seen Liverpool thus far that day, for he sometimes occupied himself on long rambles about the farms. Now he paddled earnestly out to aid his master, though I called him back until my voice failed me.

When my beloved returned, it was more slowly. He had two of the smallest children in his arms and could only kick his way to the shore. Liverpool passed him by, towing one of Alba's daughters. When the dog reached the beach, he left his charge in my care and turned right back to help his master.

I took the three children into my arms. They were half-drowned and shaking. The waves had begun to beat at the rocks. Their fingers were raw and scraped from their effort to hang on against the battering of the sea.

I took them to the others and spared a moment to rub them down and comfort them before returning to my vigil at the sea's edge. Superstitious fear gripped me. I held a dark belief that if I lost sight of my beloved, I would never see him again.

THE PRESENT

Chapter Twenty-Five

Santa Coloma de Farners

An hour after arriving at the guesthouse, Fitch had showered and enjoyed two servings of Senyora Andreu's seafood casserole and now sat at the small dining table downstairs, a cup of espresso cradled in his hands. He'd already contacted the car hire office in Girona, which would deliver a replacement vehicle in the morning. The young man on the phone asked Fitch if he required another convertible, which had made him laugh dryly.

Senyora Andreu had softened quite a bit once Fitch thanked her for making sure Brenna was comfortable—in perfect Catalan—then told her about their car trouble. So now, when she returned to ask about dessert, her face was open and kind. Fitch politely declined and said he would be going to his room.

"You've upset your young lady terribly." She gathered the dishes. "I know a lovers' quarrel can feel like the end of the world, but it will blow over. It is obvious she cares for you, though she might not admit how much."

Fitch was amused at the busybody matchmaking but didn't have the heart to tell Mrs. Andreu just how spectacularly wrong she was.

"We're professional colleagues. We're headed to Castell de la Cala to do historical research."

She looked at him, puzzled. "You are researching the festival?"

"What festival?"

Senyora Andreu laughed, and within a minute she'd returned with a tourism brochure for something called the *Flor de la Vida* festival, which appeared to be a mishmash of folk traditions in honor of summer and flowers. She placed her hands on the tabletop and bent down to give him a stern look. "You picked a bad time to try to be studious in la Cala. It's a tourist place this weekend—you'll be lucky to even find a spot to park."

Fitch shook his head. "Rotten timing all around," he mumbled in English. He thanked Senyora Andreu for the delicious meal and the brochure and headed upstairs to one of the guesthouse's two rooms. His was on the left of the hallway. Brenna's was on the right.

Brenna had been perched on the terrace outside her room for at least an hour, her feet propped up on the wisteria-covered wall, watching the sun go down. The storm had been short and violent, and the sun had reappeared almost the moment they'd arrived at the guesthouse. She'd been gazing at a small castle about a quarter-mile down the road. It was a simple medieval design made of fieldstone, with two round turrets on either side of the central structure.

Someone had lovingly restored it. A patio out front was landscaped with flowers, shrubs, and cypress trees. The castle was surrounded by gently rolling vineyards that, at the moment, were soaking up the last splash of evening light.

And she'd been thinking . . . what was the point of living in such a charming place unless the people within its walls were good to each other and truly loved each other? She thought of Le Artiste and The Siren. Piper and Mick. Claudia and her beloved Terry. She knew those couples would have been happy in a castle or a camper-trailer.

But such contentment was rare, she knew, and Brenna never imagined it was available for someone like her.

She'd grown up in an outwardly charming place. The tidy gingerbread Victorian outside Minneapolis was accessorized by trimmed bushes and wraparound porches with hanging flower pots. A pretty wife and her handsome husband lived there with their cute little blond-haired daughter, an only child.

At seventeen, Brenna had sued to become an emancipated minor, and she'd won. The judge had been a gentle older woman who said Brenna was one of the strongest and most capable young women she'd ever had in her courtroom. "I am sure you'll find success and happiness."

One out of two wasn't bad, right?

Brenna heard a soft knock on her door and called for Senyora Andreu to come in. The owner of the guesthouse had mentioned she'd be back with tea.

Brenna turned to her—and a small sound escaped her throat. It was Fitch. He looked as lost as the night she'd left him standing on a Barcelona curb.

He had cleaned up and changed clothes, and was wearing a white button-down shirt that made him look even more handsome than usual. His hair had been combed back, and he wore jeans and running shoes. In his hands he carried a bottle of wine and two glasses.

She gestured for him to take the nearby seat on the terrace. He did, setting the wine on the stone floor at his side. They tentatively caught each other's eye. Brenna had no idea how to start the conversation. She only knew it had to begin somewhere.

"Brenna, I just wanted to say—"

"Stop."

Fitch rested his elbows on his knees and dropped his head, and the regret she saw in his rounded shoulders nearly choked her. She placed a hand on his back and held it there, the heat of his skin seeping through the fabric. He turned his head and looked up at her, his eyes wide with confusion.

"I am the one who needs to apologize."

Slowly, he straightened. She saw him swallow. She wondered if he were the kind of man who ever cried. Fitch seemed to feel things deeply. Brenna kept her feelings on lockdown. Always had.

She removed her touch from his back and reached for his hand. He gave it willingly. "Look, Fitch. I've been thinking about this and I get why you broke into my hotel room. I do."

One of his eyebrows rose in interest.

"I was the woman who had a Twitter tantrum, saying recklessly untrue things that could have damaged your livelihood and reputation. I feel terrible about that."

He nodded silently.

"And I'm the woman who was condescending and bitchy when we spoke on the phone. I'm truly sorry for that, too. But . . ." She took a deep breath. "Breaking into my room was wrong, and I mean all-over-the-place wrong."

"I am so sorry, Brenna. I deeply regret it—I regretted it immediately."

"I accept your apology. I realize I issued you a challenge. You were playing the game. But here's the thing you need to understand—you can *never* do anything like that to me again. It's deceit. I can't handle deceit, no matter how small. It completely crushes me. Do you hear what I'm saying?"

"Yes. I won't. *Ever.*"

Brenna sighed, knowing she had to continue. She closed her

eyes so she didn't have to look at him. "I'm falling in love with you, Fitch, and that's a first for me. But there's something you need to know. I'm going to give you the CliffsNotes version because there's no point in dwelling on it. This all happened a long time ago and I never talk about it, but it will explain some things, I think."

She felt his fingers brush down the side of her cheek. His touch was so tender and sweet that it gave her the courage to open her eyes. She found his face twisted with worry.

"I guess you could say this is a Minnesotan tragedy of Shakespearean proportions."

He gave her a sad smile and nodded for her to continue.

"My dad was a con man, an actual grifter, Fitch, who stole millions from his business partners and customers. He controlled my mother to the point that she was nothing but dust inside—empty. She became a shell of a person with no thoughts or voice of her own."

Fitch blinked.

"I watched her give everything to that man, and I despised her for her weakness. I resented her almost as much as I hated my father for his lies and cruelty. He went to prison when I was sixteen. Six months later my mother died of cancer. Apparently she'd been ill for a while but didn't want to bother me or my father with it."

"Oh, God, Brenna."

"So I became an emancipated minor at seventeen and lived on my own until graduation, when I moved to Boston for school. I never went back to Minnesota—*ever*. My dad's been out of prison for a decade and I've never communicated with him."

"Wait." Fitch straightened. "You said both your parents were gone."

"Yes, I did. It's true. My mother is dead and my father is dead to me."

He fell back against the chair.

"I made myself hard inside, Fitch. I love Piper like a sister and I have a lot of friendly acquaintances, but I've always kept men at arm's length so there'd never be a chance of . . ." She shrugged.

"Becoming your mother."

Brenna nodded. "So the result is here I am, a thirty-four-year-old woman who lives for her work. That's all I have."

"I understand," Fitch said.

"The problem is I love sex."

"That's a problem?"

She chuckled and went on. "And I'm endlessly fascinated with how the human sex drive impacts every conceivable social institution—which is probably why I decided to study it as an academic. So where does that leave me? I couldn't just write men out of my life. So I chose men who wouldn't require much of me, men I wouldn't mind losing. I always establish an exit strategy before anything starts."

Fitch frowned. "So you've never been in love before?"

"Oh, God, no."

"Your father was the only man to break your heart. You wanted to keep it that way."

Brenna felt her throat tighten. She nodded. "Yes. And since I'm being painfully honest here, I think when I lost my mind today and called you all those names, I was really talking to him, not you. On some level you threaten me. My tried-and-true system doesn't work with you. That's where all the 'I don't know myself anymore' drama came from."

Fitch pulled her hand to his lips and left a soft kiss on her fingers. "I thank you for telling me this, Brenna."

She nodded.

"But that 'sack of balls' thing . . . can't say I've ever heard that one before."

They both laughed. That's when Brenna knew that if Fitch had a superpower, it was his ability to make her laugh at herself.

"Would you like a glass of wine?" He'd already started unwrapping the stopper of a bottle of sparkling cava. How could she refuse?

They sat together for a long moment, though it was anything but silent. The sound of an ancient fountain below rippled endlessly, providing a gentle backdrop for the boisterous chorus of crickets and tree frogs. Eventually, Fitch spoke.

"I love your outfit, by the way."

Brenna glanced down. She'd totally forgotten that she was wearing something Senyora Andreu had provided. It was a floaty cotton peasant skirt and a white bandeau top. And she was barefoot, with no makeup, sans bra and panties. "Not exactly my style. I've got to go shopping as soon as possible. Everything in my suitcase was ruined except for a pair of sandals."

In the faint light from her room, she could see Fitch boldly check her out, from head to toe. "You're more gorgeous than I've ever seen you, Brenna. You look relaxed and comfortable in your own skin. 'Spontaneous adventure' looks good on you."

She was speechless.

"C'mere." Fitch took her wineglass, pulled her from her chair and into his lap. Slowly, she allowed herself to relax. She curled up against him and he wrapped his strong arms around her. He smelled so good. He felt so solid and real and strong. He cradled her tightly and kissed the top of her head. When he spoke, his voice was deep and gentle.

"I want you to know I can work with this. There's nothing about you that scares me away—quite the opposite. You were brave enough to tell me who you are, and that's all I could ever ask for."

"Thanks." Her voice sounded small and shaky.

"So where do we go from here?"

When Brenna smiled her cheek pressed against his chest. "I thought maybe Castell de la Cala."

Fitch's laughter vibrated through her.

"I mean it. Let's stay on track with The Siren Series and see how things develop with us. I'm open to it, Fitch. I'm falling for you, which is something I've never said to a man before in my life."

He kissed her hair again. "Then can I make one last confession?"

Brenna pulled away so she could see his face. He was giving her the half-smile that had managed to melt her resistance from day one.

"I'm not falling for you," he said. "I fell at first kiss. I'm already down for the count."

Brenna lowered her mouth to his, and she groaned with relief at the touch of his warm, welcoming lips. Finally—another kiss from Fitch Wilder—and somewhere in her heart, hope sparked. Maybe she'd been wrong. Maybe there was something out there wonderful for her after all, and she'd found it when she'd found him.

They woke to melodrama. As Brenna and Fitch made their way down the narrow stairwell they heard Senyora Andreu in the middle of a heated telephone conversation in the kitchen. "No!" she yelled. "I won't lie to guests like that! Besides, they were too young to get married and you know it. *What?* I realize you have a problem, but it's not *my* problem!"

"Maybe this is a bad time," Brenna whispered as they took their seats at the table.

Fitch shrugged. "She told us to be down here at eight."

He couldn't stop staring at Brenna. He couldn't stop smiling. Last night was magical. They'd talked on the terrace until it got chilly, then went into her room, where they curled up on her bed and slept in each other's arms.

He never knew that not having sex could be so satisfying.

Now Brenna sat next to him, her hair falling soft and wavy across her shoulders and a gentle smile on her face. Her eyes were a striking pale blue in the morning light, and those adorable freckles seemed more prominent across her nose. He couldn't resist—he leaned over, cupped her face, and placed his lips on hers.

A loud *bang!* broke the mood. Senyora Andreu had smacked five breakfast plates down on the tablecloth, walked away, then made several return trips, throwing down plates of soft-boiled eggs, toast, fruit, and an assortment of meats, tomatoes, and cheeses. She came back a moment later with coffee.

She poured from the decanter, then slammed it onto the table with a sigh. "All right," she said to her guests. "Where are you staying in la Cala?"

Fitch and Brenna shared a sideways glance. "We don't have plans yet," he said.

Senyora Andreu folded her arms and nodded. "Good. Then I have a favor to ask of you."

The replacement car was delivered at noon, a full three hours late. The delay gave Brenna enough time to check her email at an internet café. The owner allowed her to print out the latest attachment from Claudia, which contained the last letter. Then she managed to do a little shopping in town, though she learned she'd have to wait until they got to a larger city to replace her phone. There wasn't much of a clothing selection, either, but Fitch cast his vote for more cottony skirts and funky tops. As a present he bought her a pair of dangly earrings of silver, opal, and topaz. She left the shop with her new outfit and an appreciative Fitch at her side.

"How long have you had this gypsy fetish?" she teased him.

"About an hour."

After a friendly goodbye and last-minute instructions from Senyora Andreu, Fitch and Brenna made their way to Castell de la Cala. They had an address, a name, and a general idea what was expected of them that day, but they were still a bit stunned by the turn of events.

"This is a little bizarre if you ask me." Brenna glanced at Fitch behind the wheel of the Volkswagen. It was another gloriously sunny Catalonian day and they were circumventing Girona, headed for the coast. "There's almost something . . . I don't know . . . *inevitable* about it all."

"Downright preordained, really."

She frowned at him. "I'm not sure I'd go *that* far, but it has been odd—almost like The Siren left a trail of bread crumbs for us."

Senyora Andreu's favor was an odd one. Her brother, who lived in Castell de la Cala, was one of the organizers of the *Flora de la Vida* festival, held every year at this time. He'd called her in a panic that morning because the most essential element of the Flower of Life celebration was a bust. The couple scheduled to marry that morning and play the role of festival newlyweds had called off the wedding at the last minute because of an argument, and he needed to find a replacement in a matter of hours.

Once Senyora Andreu explained what would be required of them, they'd happily agreed. It turned out they'd need to spend the night—alone—in a historic house called Casa Mata, home to that family since the Middle Ages.

They had stared at each other in silence, recognizing the name. Could it be the family of Beatriu Mata and her grandson Dìdac Vilaro? If there were unattributed paintings by Le Artiste to be found anywhere in la Cala, the home of the future Don Diego would be a great place to start looking for them.

"Can I tell you something weird?" When Fitch cast a sideways glance Brenna's way, she could see he was quite serious. "You promise not to make fun of me?"

"Sure."

He cleared his throat. "That morning in the Paris apartment when I found the painting . . . it felt as if The Siren gave me a mission, like she trusted me to tell her story. I know it sounds woo-woo. I didn't hear any actual voices or anything if that's what you're wondering."

"The absence of auditory hallucinations is always good news."

Fitch laughed. "But really, Brenna. She told me that if I wanted the job, it was mine."

On their way to Castell de la Cala, Brenna began to read aloud the latest letter. Fitch allowed himself to be transported to another time and place by Brenna's voice and The Swan's words . . .

> "*The notorious Songbird eyed me with interest. 'So, you are Val's kitchen boy. You are as flat as one, to be sure. Still, I expect that when we wash that face it will not be entirely without promise.'*
>
> *The Songbird had a speaking voice like honey and cream, like a warm fire on a chill day, like silk sheets on naked skin. Her words, though mildly cutting, did not register in my mind for a long moment.*
>
> *Val put her palm into the middle of my back and gave me a little push. I stepped forward and curtseyed.*
>
> *I saw The Songbird's eyes narrowed in speculation*

when I arose to tower over her. It seemed that I had overturned a few of her assumptions as well.

She flicked her fingers at Val, indicating that her old friend should remove herself and leave us alone. Val did so with surprising respect, although I saw a smirk of satisfaction on her face when she glanced back at the two of us as she departed.

Then the little woman before me walked around me, tapping a fingertip to her lips. I used the time to examine her as well. I could see her clearly in the mirror before me, even as she circled behind me. I decided that she had a rather pretty mouth, and her hands were fine and dainty, though constantly in fluttering motion. Her plainness was a lack of any defining beauty in her features.

'What is your name, child?'

'Jinx.'

'What? Joanna? Jane? Surely not Jinx, not truly.'

I shook my head. 'No, not truly. But it must do, I fear.'

She stopped before me, her arms folded across a small but still pert bosom. 'I cannot call you that. With that ridiculously long neck of yours, I should be better off calling you Swan.'

And so she did. Often. 'Swan, a courtesan knows the difference between a cigar and a cigarillo!' And, 'Swan, pray, shorten your stride. You may no longer lope about like a colt!'

And finally, 'Swan, have you decided upon your first lover?'

I had not . . ."

Brenna squinted at the printout. "It seems there are a lot of damaged sections here. There are snippets about her first few years as a courtesan, the men, the balls, the dresses, the barons and earls. But . . . oh, wow."

Fitch glanced over. Brenna was frowning at the paper. "What is it?"

"She says that she got to the point where she felt she didn't have to rely on anyone, that she could follow a path of her own creation. But then she writes this: *'I swore to myself that thereafter I would always put my own safety first. But for once. That was when I met the Duke of Mark, and as you know, dear Ophelia, I would pay dearly for making an exception.'*" Brenna went quiet.

Fitch couldn't believe it. "I hate it when these letters leave me hanging like that!" He looked over to see that Brenna was merely taking a sip from her water bottle. "Oh. Sorry."

She laughed, nearly choking on her water. "Don't get your panties in a twist, Wilder. There's more."

"He was an astonishing fellow, handsome, wealthy, and titled, but with a dangerous edge to him that intrigued me. He behaved beautifully for the most part, with only the rarest bouts of temper in evidence at first. Those explosions of passion seemed to me to be only expressions of his natural possessiveness toward me. It was because he adored me so, I told myself.

I became obsessed with him. I did not know at the time, you see, that I did not truly have a courtesan's heart. I had the training, the wardrobe, and the reputation—but my heart was that of a lonely child, longing for someone strong to lean on, longing to be held tightly and protected.

Three years passed as if in a dream. Yet still he belonged to me, and I to him. I did not tell The Songbird or Val of my growing compulsion. They were very

*pleased with my placement, and of course with their
percentage of the Duke's staggering allowance.*

*Val turned boutique with her house, keeping only
the most lovely and talented of her girls, catering to a
much more wealthy and powerful clientele. With these
new conduits into the worlds of politics and
government, she began to trade in information, and
grew wealthier still.*

*The Songbird began to age at last. She was still
vibrant and fascinating, still a source of joy for all who
heard her sing, but as the drink stole her energies, she
ventured forth less and less, preferring the company of
close friends who shared her craving.*

*Without realizing it, I became more and more reliant
upon the Duke. I did not see how he carefully carved
away at all outside attachments, how he detached me
from my society, even from my own entertainments.
Although the world may have seen a woman of means
and independence, in truth I was a slave to my
obsession with the Duke.*

*You may ask how I could not know this of myself. I
have no answer, but that it does not do to
underestimate the impact childhood yearnings have
upon the adult.*

*Then he went away for a time on business. It was in
the absence of his powerful presence that I became
aware of my own isolation.*

This alarmed me deeply. I turned to my mentor.

*The Songbird was sympathetic, but her advice was
harsh. 'End it. End it at once. Would you throw aside
everything you've gained to pant after some man who
will never make you his own?'*

So I ended it. I kept the most valuable gifts, for they

*were part of my payment. I took over the rent of my
house from the Duke's solicitor, and canceled the new
gowns I had ordered on the Duke's credit.*

*Then I wrote a succinctly polite letter of parting and
personally put it into the hand of his butler.*

*Then, though my heart beat with a strange fear, I
put on my most screamingly fashionable gown and
took myself off to the most magnificent gathering to
which I could wrangle an invitation. Alone.*

*I knew the gossips were watching. This would be the
most convincing communication to the Duke that I was
truly finished with his company.*

*Was I cruel? I only meant to be purposeful, to
convince the Duke—but more importantly, myself—that
I was a separate and complete being, that I was free.*

*The Duke did not take the rejection well. The night
that he returned to England, he pounded on my door
with his big fists. The noise made me afraid, but I told
myself that he would shout and carry on, but that he
would not hurt me. I opened the door.*

*The Duke beat me senseless on the marble floor of
my own foyer. I had known that there was a darkness
in him, but in the black hours of that night he revealed
his true brutality.*

*My maid, Posy, found me and helped me into a
warm bath to soak the bruises away. 'Bastard marked
ye black and blue, miss, but he didn't lay a hand on yer
face.'*

*I shook my head. 'I don't even recall opening the
door.'*

*'Aye, well . . . there's a knot on yer skull like a plum,
there is! You must've hit that marble floor like a sack o'
potatoes.'*

I did not ever fully recall that night, although I had many disturbing dreams that fled my mind as soon as I awoke, but left me shaking and crying even as I opened my eyes.

Posy set some of Val's peacekeepers at my door and that knowledge helped ease the nightmares. In a week I was up and about. In another week, Val appeared with a man, one of the most recognizable men in London. He was a small, spry fellow, dressed in the very latest cut, with his thinning hair swept back into a tidy queue and a smile that managed to be both gentle and mischievous at the same time.

I stood to greet him. 'But of course, I know you! You are Lementeur!'

He bowed deeply. 'I am. And you are the incomparable, The Swan herself.'

'That is what I am told,' I said as I smiled back. I could not help myself, though my smiles had been hard-won of late. 'Please, come and sit.'

He settled himself with a graceful flick of his tails, perching upon my sofa like an imp, poised to spring up, bound for tomfoolery.

I settled myself carefully next to him. My body was mostly recovered, but I still flinched at certain movements. 'How may I be of service, sir?'

He reached out to take my hand. His touch was butterfly-gentle, so I did not pull away. 'Dear child. I am here to be of service to you.'

I blinked at him. Lementeur was the greatest dressmaker in all of London. Royalty fought for a place upon his appointment list. He could make any woman look like a queen, no matter her size or features. His reputation was as that of a magician, spoken in low

tones of wonder, carried from woman to woman,
whispered about the edges of every ballroom where one
of his gowns floated majestically on some fortunate
lady.

'I mean to make you the most desirable woman in
all of Britain.'

I blinked at him, but could not resist answering his
playful smile with one of my own. 'Sir, are you
implying that I am not already?'

He laughed and his blue eyes twinkled. 'That's the
stuff, my dear!' He leaned forward conspiratorially.
'You are known to be lovely. You are known to be
fashionable. But how would it suit you to be the most
lovely, the most fashionable?'

My recent social downfall would be forgotten. Any
rumor of the Duke's disfavor would be met with a raised
and disbelieving brow. I would own the ballrooms of
London, gowned in styles that would make countesses
curse and princes pine!

I smiled at the little magician before me. 'You mean
to make a bushel of crowns from me, don't you?'

He pursed his lips. 'Three or four at least.' He gave
me a little nudge with one elbow. 'Come, dear. You
know it will be fun.'

It came about precisely as Lementeur predicted. In a
Lementeur gown that had the tiniest bodice I had ever
seen, that frankly could only be worn by a woman with
the bust of a boy, and a skirt made of the sheerest silk
I've ever dared wear outside a bedchamber, I made my
first appearance at a ball thrown by the Countess of
Maitland.

The Prince Regent danced with me until I feared for
his heart. Every ranking man present elbowed for a

place at my side, although I only spoke to the few most powerful and engaging.

It became my practice to arrive late and leave early, feigning boredom. This only compounded my reputation for being exclusive and discerning. I was elevated to some outrageous level of connoisseurship. If The Swan remained at a ball for more than an hour, it was labeled a screaming success! It surprises me still, how swiftly such people fall into mad fads and enthusiasms.

Lementeur's mission gave me distraction and purpose, and I was not required to take a new lover for some time, for the gifts and jewels—bribes for my 'consideration'—kept me nicely for the time being.

Then the day came that something completely unexpected happened. A mad young girl accosted me in Lementeur's dress establishment and practically dared me to turn her into a courtesan.

Her name was Ophelia."

THE PRESENT

Chapter Twenty-Six

On the Road to Castell de la Cala

Brenna bounced in her seat, her excitement overflowing. "Oh my God, she's talking about Ophelia Harrington! I can't wait to show this to Piper!"

Fitch grinned at her. "Maybe we can finish it first?"

Brenna bent over the pages again.

"I trust you remember that day. I had no intention of doing any such thing, of course. The notion, in the beginning, was to seemingly give in to your willfulness but to frighten you away from attempting to flee the match you so disdained.

How could I know that it was an existence you were meant for, perhaps more than I myself? You reveled in your freedom. It brought you to life. Our profession, was to me, an option to survive. For you, it allowed you to thrive.

How I loved you. How I envied you.

I accepted my life. You devoured yours. You made me long for some of your hunger for experience. You made me look at myself and wonder if perhaps I was not yet still in hiding. I had been taught too well. I could not be my true self because I had no notion of who that woman might be. I had never met her, I'm sure.

However, with your entry into my existence, I became happier than I ever remember being. You made me brave. Even when the Duke of Mark finally found a way to publicly humiliate me, you were there, as was your dear Sir, to rescue me from my own devastation at being having such a personal matter revealed.

I don't know how the Duke learned of my early life in Madame Valentine's establishment. However it came to pass, at least the Duke did not learn my true name. Should he have, I doubt even your brash plan would have restored me to consequence among the demi-monde.

Being the daughter of a prisoner was one thing. Being the daughter of a famous thief and his murdering wife would be quite another.

Yet here I speak it. Through either incompetence or avarice, my father cleared the accounts of all his friends and clients. He then set his own death scene in our parlor with copious amounts of blood and a smeared letter opener that belonged to my mother.

Then he disappeared with the funds and allowed her to be blamed for his murder. If it had not been for the lack of an actual body, she would have certainly been hanged. What my parents did or did not do—and I shall ever maintain my gentle mother's innocence—I have nothing to be ashamed of.

You taught me this and more, Ophelia. Your gleeful crunching of the London life between your teeth made me wonder if I could ever find that self in me. It was

*your friendship that allowed me to see that Jinx was a
mask, and The Swan, however shimmering, was a mask
as well.*

Yet who was I without a mask?

*It would take many years and a catastrophe for me
to find out.*

*I shall write more later, my dearest friend. Until
then, I remain yours most truly . . ."*

Fitch took his eyes off the road and peered over at the letter
in Brenna's hands. "Is it signed? What's her name?"

Brenna pushed him back. "It says 'this portion of the document was beyond restoration.'"

Fitch shook his head. "Man, this is pure torture. I want to
know her real name. Let's hope there's another way to find out."

The instant the medieval stones of Castell de la Cala came into
view, Brenna's imagination shifted to overdrive.

The village appeared at the end of a winding road rising
from the valley, its ancient stone walls winding upward toward
the tumbled-down castle like flowers swirling around a wedding cake.

The modern world hadn't changed the area much, and if it
weren't for the bumper-to-bumper traffic heading into the festival and a few telephone wires, Brenna thought the entire landscape could be plunked down into a historical on-screen epic.

When she told Fitch as much, he laughed at her enthusiasm.

She dismissed him with a theatrical wave of her hand. "As
an academic, there's nothing more thrilling to me than finding
a piece of untouched history."

"I understand, believe me. If I weren't steering the car, I'd be
clapping my hands like a little girl."

Brenna snorted. "I can't see you doing anything like a little girl, Wilder."

He laughed, too, and when the traffic paused for a moment, Fitch leaned over for a real kiss and Brenna obliged. By the time the driver behind them lost patience and laid on the horn, she was breathless and a little giddy.

Traffic finally started moving again. They drove into the narrow winding streets of the village until they could progress no farther. Brenna took the handwritten instructions from her bag and told Fitch where they would find a parking lot known only to the locals.

Picking up the small overnight bags that held their fresh things, they made their way through a happy, expectant crowd. The closer they got to the square, the more flowers they saw. Arrangements of local blooms were everywhere, some lush and overblown, some spare and modern. There were words spelled out in blossoms and sculptural arrangements built on chicken-wire frames. Fitch pointed out a giant colorful watering can made entirely out of carnations.

Brenna grabbed his arm. "We look like open-mouthed tourists. Come on. We're supposed to be on the central square."

They followed the crowd through narrow cobbled streets and under ancient archways until they found themselves standing at the base of a wide stairway. It had been filled with flowers of blue and white that mimicked floodwaters pouring down the steps. Dozens of fish made of bright gold chrysanthemums leaped in the floral current.

Brenna blinked at the display. "Wonder how many hours went into this. *Dayum*."

Fitch nudged her. "Watch your language, Miss Bag o' Balls. You're standing in front of a church."

She clapped her hands over her mouth and looked up, past

the distracting decorations. "Oops." Then, "Senyora Andreu told us to look for the church, didn't she?"

Fitch nodded. "She said Casa Mata was just opposite, and that it had a lot of wisteria—"

They scanned the area in unison. Fitch grabbed her hand. "I see it!"

Ducking through the families with strollers and the hawkers selling fresh-flower head wreaths, they ran to the blue-painted door. Ancient wisteria grew up along either side of the entry, the gnarled trunks as big around as Fitch's waist. The purple bunches dangled in glorious profusion, twining so thickly over the facade that they could have been entered in the festival's decorating contest.

They looked past the shield of purple blooms to see a middle-aged man sitting on the steps of the house, puffing with nervous intensity on a cigarette. He looked up as they approached, hope easing the stress etched on his fleshy features. He stood quickly, grinding out his cigarette on the step while using his other hand to smooth down his thinning hair.

"*Hola!* You are the Wilders, *si?*"

Brenna bit her lip. "Umm . . ."

Fitch stuck out his hand. "I'm Fitch Wilder, yes. And you are Juame Mata?"

The man clapped his hands together in dramatic relief. "*Si, si!* The happy couple! You are just in time! Please, come in."

Brenna held back. She wanted to enter what might be Beatriu Mata's house in the worst way, but she wouldn't lie to do so. "Mr. Mata. There's something—"

"It is good that you are here." Juame cut her off. "The other couple, so sad, no? Cracking up on their wedding day—and over something so silly!"

"Breaking up," Brenna corrected the man absently. She was

looking at Fitch, who nodded in agreement that they needed
to come clean about the ruse. As Senyora Andreu had explained to them, only the chosen newlyweds were allowed in the
historical landmark on festival day, as they would become central
to the reenactment of the "flower of life" celebration, whatever
that meant.

"Juame, just a moment, please." Fitch stopped him before
he turned toward the front door. "You should know that
we're not . . . well, we're not newlyweds. We're not even married."

Juame didn't look all that shocked. "My sister tells me this,
but there is no time to, how do you say—?"

"Quibble?" Fitch offered.

"Yes. So let me ask you—since it is the heart that matters
here today, is there any chance that you two will marry in the
future? Someday? Maybe?"

"Abso-freakin'-lutely," Fitch said.

"Fitch!"

Juame clapped his hands together. "Good! It's settled!"

Before Brenna could protest, Fitch leaned down to whisper
in her ear. "No worries. I speak only the truth." He left a quick
kiss on her cheek.

Fitch placed a gentle hand on Juame's shoulder before he
opened the door. "Senyor, do you know if this was the home of
a woman named Beatriu Mata and her grandson Dìdac during
and after the Penninsular War?"

Juame turned around and blinked at them with expressive
sea-green eyes. Then his face broke into a surprisingly boyish
grin. "Don Diego of Santa Maria de Montserrat?"

"Yes! Him!" Brenna felt a buzz of excitement.

"Oh, *si, si*. Don Diego is very well known here, and the Mata
family has always lived in this house, since the *castell* was built
in 1534. We own it still, though it's a tourist rental now."

Brenna found herself comparing Juame's face with the portrait of little Dìdac they'd seen the day before.

Fitch grinned at her, his eyes crinkling at the corners in the way that made her toes curl in pleasure. "See?" he whispered. "Preordained, baby."

"If you believe that sort of thing." They crossed the threshold into the nearly five-hundred-year-old stone home, and Brenna noticed she didn't sound so sure any more, even to herself.

Juame pronounced Brenna's white peasant skirt and turquoise silk shell to be *perfecte* for the festival. Then he expressed deep admiration for Fitch's *autèntic* Western boots. Fitch immediately wrote down Juame's shoe size and email address, promising to buy him an identical pair from Santa Fe's Boots and Boogie custom bootmaker.

Juame excused himself for a moment and Brenna narrowed her eyes at Fitch. "I think I'm catching on."

He grinned. "Just making friends."

"Uh huh. And now you know yet another guy, who probably knows a few other guys . . ." She shook her head. "You're . . . you're viral!"

Fitch threw back his head and laughed. "My secret is out!" Then he pulled her close for a quick kiss before Juame returned from making *aranjaments* for their mysterious part in the festival.

"Ah-ah!" Juame reentered the front hall, where they waited. He showed them their lovely upstairs room with French doors that opened onto the balcony overlooking the square, then took their bags, dropping them to the floor of the newlywed suite. "Save your kisses! You will need all of them for the *Flor de la Vita* festival!"

Brenna looked alarmed. "We will?"

Their host wiggled his eyebrows. "Just wait!" Juame waved them downstairs, out the front door, and into the square. He shoved a business card in Fitch's hand. "Call if you need anything. Anything at all. Now, come! Come! It's time to start!"

Brenna found herself with Juame and Fitch one moment, then surrounded by laughing women the next. She tried to circumvent the large group, looking over the crowd for Fitch's much taller head. The women seized her arms and pulled her back, giggling all the while.

"*¡Núvia bonica!*" they exclaimed. When one of them noticed Brenna's confusion, she spoke in English. "Pretty bride." Then she told the rest of the women to do the same. "*¡Parla Anglès!*"

"Welcome to the festival! Happy honeymoon!"

Brenna reminded herself that she'd been given a role to play. "Thank you."

"Smile!" The women giggled as they ordered her around. "*¡Somriu!*"

She couldn't help but grin shyly back at them. From teens to women in their thirties, they were luminous in their colorful sundresses, with their hair tied up with fresh flowers. They spun her around, examining her from every angle.

Some sort of whispered judgment was made, then a wreath of brilliant blue flowers was placed upon her hair.

"Oh!" Brenna lifted a hand to lightly touch the fresh blossoms. "Should I put up my hair?"

They shook their heads as one. "Your hair is like sunlight, *bonica,*" her translator informed her.

Brenna found herself moved by their open admiration. She'd spent so long in competitive circles, she'd forgotten what it was like when people simply were kind. She resolved to be nicer herself, and gathered her translator close for a quick hug.

Then, in a swirl of pretty skirts and laughter, she was swept across the cobblestones to where a flower-covered throne awaited her. When she sat, she found herself being lifted into the air by a team of four shirtless hotties. One cast an admiring glance over his shoulder and smiled at her. *"¡Bellesa!"*

The experience seemed surreal, but then again, when was the last time she'd been carried on a flowered throne through a medieval square by four shirtless bodybuilders? She could almost hear Piper's voice: *At times like these, it's probably best to just go with it.* The thought made her laugh, and once she began, she found herself unable to stop giggling. With a sudden rush of happiness, she held on tight and decided that "go with it" would be her new mantra.

Then she saw Fitch and her giddy laughter turned to belly-deep guffaws. He was being carried on the shoulders of two thick-armed guys even bigger than her own minions. Upon his head he wore a huge wreath of poppies and some kind of yellow wildflower, which got jostled and slipped down over one eye. His grin was just as wide as hers as he raised his arms in the air to encourage the festival crowd further.

He was soaking it up, of course. Fitch's deep appreciation for the moment made him a sucker for a community party.

I love that about you, she thought, stunned at the truth in that private observation.

His gaze caught hers at that moment and his grin softened. They passed each other as the procession wound around the square. She reached out to him with one hand. He did the same. Their fingertips brushed for just a second, and when Brenna pulled her hand back to catch her balance, she felt the heat of his touch tingle her skin.

Once more around the square and then Brenna's litter-bearers came to a halt and lowered her to the cobblestones at the base of the church steps. Fitch was delivered next to her.

Brenna's girl-gang returned, along with an identical male

ensemble responsible for Fitch. The crowd urged them up the stairs, along a narrow pathway through the floral waterfall. At the top step, a priest awaited them.

Brenna's eyes widened. Around his neck he wore a garland of purple blooms over his traditional surplice.

"Um . . . Fitch?"

He followed her worried gaze. "Huh. Didn't see that coming."

"But is he . . . are we . . . is this . . . ?"

The priest winked at them.

Hours later, Fitch and Brenna were thrust laughing into the Casa Mata honeymoon suite by their enthusiastic festival minders. The door was shut on them amid shouts of encouragement and giggles. Fitch was about to tell Brenna he was thrilled to be alone with her, when he began to sneeze.

Flowers—everywhere. While he and Brenna had been making their debut appearance as a faux married couple, the room had been stuffed with blooms. All colors and all varieties were piled high on every surface. He sneezed again. And again.

"Are you all right?" Brenna stared at him.

He wanted to reassure her, but he couldn't catch his breath! He could only shake his head and wipe at his streaming eyes as he sneezed another time, and then another.

When he felt Brenna shoving him, he went blindly, trusting her.

Fresh air rushed past his face. He leaned his hands on the wrought iron railing of the balcony and breathed the clear evening air into his lungs. He felt Brenna gently patting him on the back as the burning in his nostrils began to subside.

"Are you allergic?" she asked.

"I wasn't when we were outside." He caught his breath,

straightened, and brushed his eyes with his sleeve. Wild cheers startled him. He blinked down at the crowd now assembled directly under the balcony.

Everyone stared expectantly.

Brenna cleared her throat. "I guess Juame forgot to tell us about this part, too."

"Juame can buy his own damn boots," Fitch muttered.

A woman called out, *"¡Besa-la, besa-la!"* The crowd went wild.

"They want us to kiss," Fitch said, grinning. "We can't let them down, can we?"

He slipped an arm behind Brenna's waist and dipped her, bringing his lips to hers. Though the kiss was supposed to be for festival purposes only, Fitch couldn't seem to stop. He moved his mouth on hers, tasting her sweetness and feeling her surrender beneath him.

They both came up for breath to appreciative cheering.

Suddenly, a new chant began. *"¡Les flors! ¡Tireu-nos les flors!"*

Brenna cast a glance at Fitch, then tentatively reached up to remove her flower wreath. Fitch stopped her with a mischievous smile. "If they want flowers, then let's give them flowers."

Laughing, they threw every single flower out of the bedroom, tossing them into the waiting hands below. The crowd loved it. Kids went chasing blossoms across the square, and adults put toddlers on their shoulders to snag some of their own. Finally, the room cleared of all things allergenic, Fitch and Brenna waved good night to the festival-goers and shut the balcony door on their honeymoon act.

"Whew!" Brenna leaned back against the doors. "This town loves them some *flors!*"

Fitch sniffed the air and was reassured it no longer burned his nose. He turned to Brenna. "So." He tried his best not to stare at the only bed in the room. It was going to be a challenge keeping his mind on the task at hand. "What should we do first? Supper or snooping?" He was fairly certain he knew the answer to that question.

"We've got supper?"

He'd guessed wrong. Brenna had chosen pleasure over work. With a smile of satisfaction, Fitch pointed out the brimming picnic basket supplied by Casa Mata for the happy couple. Brenna gazed reverently into the piled goodies within. *"Jamón!"* She held up a large slice of smoked ham. She dug farther. "And there's fresh bread, cheese, olives, and pâté! Oh, wow! We've got chocolate bonbons and cakes! And wine!"

Maybe the professor was coming around. "Supper it is."

Chapter Twenty-Seven

Castell de la Cala

Stuffed and slightly tipsy was no way to start a treasure hunt, but Brenna knew this was their one opportunity to roam Casa Mata without an audience. Never in her life had she poked around a private home taking stock of the owners' art collection. She wouldn't count on finding The Siren portrait, as she had in Claudia's powder room, because that was just a happy accident.

"So this is your wheelhouse, Wilder. How do we go about casing the joint?"

Fitch laughed. "We're not here to steal—we're here to *investigate*. There's a difference."

"All right. So what are we looking for? Secret passageways? Creaking floorboards? Hidden wall safes?"

He cradled his half-empty wineglass pensively. "How about we walk around and look at the paintings on the walls?"

Brenna blinked in mock boredom. "And I was hoping to have another adventure."

Fitch grabbed her hand. "The night is young, my bride."

They laughed their way down to the first floor and toured its three rooms. It wasn't a large home, just a sitting room, dining room, half-bath and kitchen downstairs and two bedrooms and a full bath upstairs. The house had been tastefully modernized while leaving its medieval bones intact—there was a wide cooking hearth in the otherwise gleaming kitchen, and gothic stone arches in every room.

It took just minutes to walk through the first floor, and they saw nothing but a few framed photographs and posters along with some lovely antique botanical prints. No hint of Le Artiste. The only two oil paintings were abstract color field works by a known twentieth-century Spanish painter, and though Fitch paused to admire them he soon shrugged and walked away.

"I wonder if Juame knows these are fakes," he said.

Next, they found the cellar, which had been turned into a wine tasting room, complete with a big-screen TV, cocktail tables, and recessed lighting. The only art on the walls were vineyard posters.

"Huh," Fitch said, puzzled. He nosed around behind the bar and found a door that led to a storage room filled with glassware and paper supplies. Though he looked behind shelving and glanced up at the ceiling, he saw nothing of interest. "That's kind of disappointing—I sometimes get lucky in cellars."

"I'm not sure that's anything to brag about," Brenna said.

As they headed back upstairs, Brenna asked, "So what happens if we actually find something?"

"The first step will be determining provenance and ownership, and that might be a nightmare. But we'll cross that bridge when we come to it."

The second upstairs bedroom featured a display of antique photographs but no paintings. However, Fitch seemed quite interested in a built-in bookcase and cupboard unit that took up an entire wall. He asked Brenna to hold his wineglass while he tapped and knocked on the wood in a half-dozen places. Next, he opened all the cupboard doors and pulled out the contents so he could rap his knuckles on the back of the unit. When he was done, the floor was piled with videotapes, magazines, and plastic storage containers of knickknacks.

"Anything?" Brenna finished off the rest of her red wine and then Fitch's.

"Aside from Juame's original Star Wars VHS collection, I'd have to say no." He returned all the items and stood. "Let's head up to the attic." Fitch went to retrieve his wineglass and feigned shock. "What happened here?"

Brenna shrugged. "Maybe the ghosts got to it."

After stopping in the honeymoon suite for a refill, they found the attic entrance in the bathroom ceiling, of all places. It was a dusty proposition to get the trapdoor open and the foldaway stairs extended, but eventually Fitch began to climb up. Brenna shamelessly took advantage of her viewpoint, sipping her wine as she admired Fitch's compelling masculine assets.

A light flashed on and Brenna shielded her eyes.

"Oh, boy." Fitch glanced down at Brenna. "If you're coming up you'll have to be very careful where you step. It's a good thing you're wearing your cute sandals instead of your d'Artagnans."

Brenna had already set the wineglasses on the sink and began her ascent. She stopped. "My *what?*"

Fitch grinned down at her, his slightly long hair falling across one eye. If he weren't so devastatingly adorable, Brenna might have managed to summon some indignation, but she was already laughing.

"You know, your musketeer boots."

She shook her head. "Funny. Well, they're ruined now, so that's one less thing you can tease me about."

He chuckled. "I can always get your shoe size and—"

"Just go up, Wilder."

The attic was smaller than she'd expected, with severely sloped eaves supported by ancient timbers and one small window at each end. But it was crammed with enough crap that she knew it would be a while before they could rule it out as a hiding place.

"Whatever you touch, put it back exactly as you found it, okay?"

"Okay," she said.

"Your white skirt's going to get dirty."

"I'm willing to sacrifice in the name of research."

Nearly two hours later, she and Fitch had taken turns showering off the grime on their skin and hair and changed into clean clothes, which, for Brenna, meant another Spanish peasant skirt and scoop-neck T. It was fully dark now, and the stars were out. They sat on the balcony overlooking the plaza, sipping more wine and finishing off the bonbons while they enjoyed the sound of the bronze fountain in the center of the square. In the festival commotion Brenna hadn't even noticed it, and now, in the dim light of the plaza, she couldn't make out its form.

"We gave it our best shot," she said. "Where should we look next?"

Fitch was seated with his elbows resting on his knees, a wine-glass dangling from his fingers. But he wasn't looking at her. He was looking directly over her head, to the outside wall of the house behind her. He was frowning.

"What is it?" The hairs on her forearms stood up.

"There's something off about the roofline on this side. Do you see it? The angle is gentler on the exterior than it is inside the attic."

Brenna looked over her shoulder and felt her eyes widen. She turned back to Fitch. "Does that mean—"

"We're going back up."

* * *

Fitch couldn't believe he missed this the first time. Now that he and Brenna had managed to move the stacks of junk furniture away from the attic wall, it was obvious.

At some point in the past—probably a long time ago—someone had decided to erect lathe and cover it with plaster, much of which had started to crumble. At the bottom toward the center, the crumbling had revealed what looked like a low door. A gentle touch of his fingers sent the whole section of plaster crashing to the floor.

"Whoops," he said. "Didn't mean for that to happen."

"What do we do?" Brenna looked horrified. "We can't just bust into a wall, can we? Shouldn't we get Juame's permission?"

Fitch pulled out his cell phone, noticing that he had two bars—maybe enough to get through—and dialed the number Juame had given him. He picked up after five rings.

After a brief explanation of the situation, Fitch asked him in Catalan if they could open the already exposed door. Juame was clearly hammered, likely the result of a full day of festival partying, but managed to do a bit of yelling and cursing.

"Juame," Fitch said, his voice calm. "We saved your ass today and I know a guy who can repair this in ten minutes. We will get everything back exactly as we found it, you have my word."

After a few more minutes of wrangling—and a reminder that Juame would be getting a pair of hand-tooled custom-made leather boots from Santa Fe—they had permission.

Brenna stared at him, her jaw unhinged. "I've never seen anything like you," she mumbled.

It took little effort to pry away the remaining chunks of plaster. The doorway was only about four feet by three feet, enough for him crouch his way inside. "If I find anything, I'll pass it through the opening, okay?"

Brenna nodded.

"It's pitch black in here, so I'm just going to be feeling my way around with my flashlight app."

He felt a tingle travel up his spine. The space was dark and sealed off, just like the apartment in Paris. That meant whatever they found would likely not be faded by light. And the air was dry, which meant no mold. When his fingers bumped into canvases he gasped in surprise.

He located a total of five canvases stacked against the real attic wall, and he passed them through the opening one at a time to Brenna's outstretched hands. He found a large leather folder, too, and then crawled around the periphery to make sure he'd left nothing behind. When he finally made his way back into the open attic, he found Brenna sitting cross-legged, holding one of the canvases. Her eyes were glistening with tears.

It was a time-consuming process, but they managed to bring everything to their suite and carefully dust off what they could. When Fitch returned from showering off the dust, Brenna was propped on the bed with dozens of pencil sketches spread out around her.

"Got room for me?" He crawled on the bed with her. Fitch didn't know what to think or feel at this point, because what they'd discovered was more than historical treasure, it was a love story, told in its entirety through the paintbrush and the pen, an overwhelmingly beautiful and sensual story intended to remain utterly, completely private.

There were five additional unframed oil paintings, each one of The Siren in an erotic pose, her lush sensuality on display to the artist who adored her. Inside a large leather portfolio they'd found a total of twenty-five pencil sketches on loose paper. Some were unfinished but all of them brought to life not only The Siren but the artist as well.

He'd drawn their lovemaking, their limbs tangled in passion

and their faces on the brink of ecstasy. They were the most achingly beautiful things Fitch had ever seen.

But there was also a diary. Tucked into the portfolio was a stack of loose pages filled with the handwriting so familiar to them now. The Swan—The Siren—had written down the entire tale of her abduction, injuries, recovery, and finding the love of her life.

It took hours to read everything, but they read it together. He read much of it to Brenna as she lay in his arms, but some of it Brenna read to him while his head lay in her lap. The intimacy of that shared moment was something Fitch knew he would never forget.

They reached the last few pages, only to find that the tone had changed. Gone was the day-to-day account of The Siren's serene life in the castle by the cove. The sentences were clipped. The joy was gone.

It was Fitch's turn to read aloud, and he told Brenna how a sudden storm had swooped in while several of the village children were swimming in the cove. The artist swam out to save them.

"Dìdac," Brenna whispered.

Fitch kept reading.

"In that moment, I hated the water. Cruel, capricious sea! How dare it wield such power over our lives? Rage and dread choked me.

Then I saw my beloved coming back to me. I waded as deeply as I could maintain my footing to meet him. His handsome face was haggard and exhausted. He placed little Dìdac into my arms. The boy's face was bluish with cold and his small hands and feet had abraded to raw flesh in his fight to cling to the rocks—but he breathed.

I looked at my drained husband and nearly begged him to

leave the rest of the children to die. I feared for him. I feared for myself and my child in a world without him. I looked my beautiful soldat dement *in the eye and nearly implored him to be a coward, just this once.*

I said nothing. His agonized gaze told me everything I needed to know. He loved me. He did not want to die. Nor could he back away from the task before him. As long as there was the slimmest chance, the tiniest hope, that the last two children could be saved, he meant to go back into that pitiless, deadly sea.

Without a word, with weariness in every movement, he turned away from me to fight the tide once more.

I swallowed my cries of protest and carried poor Dìdac up the beach to where the other children waited, weeping and shivering.

A cry rang out above me. I looked up to see Beatriu's husband and three other men bounding down the path as quickly as they could with a small wooden boat held above their heads. Relief swept me.

Saved. We were all saved now.

The boat only took three, so two men whom I only vaguely recalled from my wedding day remained behind. I gave them the task of carrying the rescued children up to the castell *where Beatriu could better tend them. I refused to leave the beach.*

The other two men took up the oars and stroked hard out into the surf. I do not think I had grasped the size and force of the waves until I saw the boat tossed upon them like a bit of driftwood.

I turned my desperate gaze out onto the cove waters, searching for my beloved. I saw his dark head for the merest second, his upraised arm as he swam and the single small person who rode upon his back. Upon the rocks I saw no one at all.

Did Liverpool have the last of Beatriu's grandchildren? I realized I had not seen the shepherd dog for quite some time.

I pressed a hand to my mouth. One child was already lost. I knew my love would never forgive himself.

A wave crashed over the two dark heads in the water, sweeping them out of sight.

I did not see them come up again.

Hours later, I stood wrapped in a quilt, still on the beach. Someone had built a fire and forced me away from the waterline to warm myself before it. That was as far as I was willing to go.

The tide had come in. The rain had stopped. The sea had calmed. The men had taken shifts in the boat, had made pass after pass inside and outside El Sentinelles. I had seen them stop once and pull the limp, sopping body of Liverpool into the skiff. There had been no other sign of the last two children, or of my husband.

The waves rolled in gently now, as if in placation. I was frozen inside. If the sea wished forgiveness now, I had none to give. The heartless waters had brought me to this place, had saved my life, only to take away my very heart.

It was not an even exchange."

Brenna shot up to a sitting position, her eyes huge with disbelief. "*What?*"

"He didn't make it."

She went rigid. "Wait. He died saving the children?"

Fitch nodded slowly. "I'm afraid so."

"No! Oh, nooooo! He wasn't supposed to die!"

With a trembling hand, Brenna reached for the loose sheet of paper Fitch held carefully by the edges. She read over it for herself—not that she didn't believe him. She just couldn't comprehend the cruelty of the world. She looked up at Fitch and found his chin trembling. He was just as upset as she was.

"He died saving Don Diego! Fitch, he *drowned*. They'd just gotten married! And then he *died!*"

She felt his arms go around her shoulders, but it offered little comfort. She could barely breathe. It felt as if a stone were caught in her throat and jagged glass had wedged in her lungs. The sadness was sharp and ugly and she felt as if it would rip her apart if she didn't . . . if she couldn't . . .

A strange sound escaped her mouth, a moan of desperate grief. It was followed by another and another and suddenly she felt herself crack open inside. The next instant she was doubled over in silent agony, trying to breathe, on the edge of something horrifying.

"It's so incredibly sad. I know. But it happened a long time ago, sweetheart."

Fitch's soft whisper was the tipping point. She collapsed into him. Everything that she'd shoved deep down inside her—for as long as she could remember—exploded from her. Her crying was loud and messy and full of rage and it went on and on. Brenna found her cheek pressed against Fitch's thigh, the fabric of his jeans soaked with her tears.

"It's not fair." Her whole body shook. "This is why . . . this is why I've never wanted to love someone, why I tried not to love *you*. It's too risky."

More sobs rocked her. She felt Fitch lean over her, stroke her back, and cover her body with his. "It's all right, Brenna."

She sat up, pushing him away, suddenly more pissed off than she'd ever been in her life. "No, it's not all right! Don't you see? Nothing lasts! Nothing matters—their love was wonderful and important and it *didn't even fucking matter*! He . . . he just . . ." Her body sagged. "People fall in love and what happens? They either end up killing each other a little bit every day or one of them up and dies!"

"Oh, Brenna."

She cried and cried and cried. At one point, she sensed Fitch get up from the bed and return. She eventually looked up at him.

"Here, sweetheart." Fitch held a damp washcloth in his hand, and it was only then she realized she was a snotty, wet, hysterical, gasping mess, and likely covered in red blotches. She pressed the cool cloth to her face and tried to breathe evenly.

"There's another way to look at this, you know."

Brenna peeked over the edge of the cloth. "Yeah?"

He nodded gently. "Instead of concluding that nothing matters and nothing lasts, you could say that *everything* mattered and *everything* lasted for them, that their love shaped the future." Fitch gestured to the sketches scattered all over the bed and the paintings propped against the wall.

Brenna sniffed, but she was listening.

"Think about just how much their lives mattered. These paintings, these sketches, this diary—it lives on." He stroked her hair and bent toward her, catching her eye. "And that's just the start, baby. They had a child together. Who knows, maybe that child went on to have children, too. And this town—and everyone in it—survived because of what he did. If it weren't for him Senyora Andreu might not exist, or Juame. And think about Dìdac. He survived because of the artist, and that boy became Don Diego, who helped bring the Montserrat abbey back to life."

Brenna knew everything he said was true, but she couldn't let go of the most important fact. "But The Swan—The Siren— all she ended up with was pain."

Fitch leaned in and kissed her lips with the utmost care. He cradled her face in his hands and said, "She found happiness with the artist. She opened herself up to love and experienced joy for the first time in her life. If ever a woman deserved to be happy, it was her."

Brenna said nothing. She lowered her chin. Fitch tipped it up again.

"And you, my sweet professor. You deserve love and joy, too. It's here if you want it—*I'm* here."

She gave him a single nod. Maybe it was the crying. Or the wine. Or the chocolate. Or the thrill of finding the true story of The Swan. Regardless, she felt completely hollowed out inside, and this time she decided to try filling the void with something other than work and achievement and control. She decided to try love and connection.

"I want you, Fitch. No more arm's length."

THE PAST

Chapter Twenty-Eight

Castell de la Cala

"Senyora, the man will not go away."

I looked up from my letter, blinking at the kind face of my dear guardian and benefactress, who stood in the doorway of my little study. "What man, Beatriu?"

"He is a little Englishman, he is *groller*. Rude!" Beatriu's English had improved much over the past four years, as had my Catalan. She continued, "And he says he wants to see the Lord Anns Wo—Wid—"

"Aynesworth, you peasant cow!"

Beatriu's solid form shifted slightly. I realized that she had planted herself firmly between me and the rude little Englishman. In a flash, I stood before her, staring over her stout shoulder at the man physically trying to push her aside.

"You will refrain from assaulting Senyora Mata this minute, sir!" It seemed that I could still play a convincing mistress of the house, for although he met my furious gaze with a sneer lifting his lip, he desisted his attack on Beatriu's unyielding person. I carried on my righteous indignation while taking Beatriu's hand to lead her from the doorway.

"What is the meaning of this intrusion? I do not appreciate this invasion into my home, Mr—?"

"Mr. Sands." He stiffened and lifted his chin. I saw a slight figure and a travel-stained suit. I also saw superiority and contempt in his gaze, along with the light of moral affront.

Oh, bother. One of those.

"My lady, I came all this way to—"

"To be mistaken in your destination, sir. I am not 'your lady.'" I folded my hands before me. "Now you may feel free to continue your search, but I can assure you that there is no lord within a dozen miles of this village."

He all but rolled his eyes at me. "I am the solicitor for the estate of Lord Matthew Aynesworth, late Earl of Swindon."

I gave him an impatient nod. "I see my error, but this is still not a name that I am familiar with in this area."

He blinked at me. "You're not serious."

I gave up on him and turned to gaze out the window at the late afternoon. I wanted the unkind little man to leave me alone. I wanted to walk down to the cove as I had every evening for the past four years and sit with my husband as dusk fell over the sea.

He approached my side, digging into the case he carried in one hand. "Ah! Here it is!" He removed something and held it out to me. "Do you recognize this man?"

I looked down and caught my breath. In his hand he held out a small oval portrait, a miniature painted upon a slice of ivory and framed in silver. Familiar brown eyes gazed out at me from the image.

"Well?"

I took the miniature from the annoying fellow's fingers and moved closer to the window, holding the precious thing in the last of the afternoon light. How I had wished I had the talent to preserve the image of my beloved! My sketching ability was poor and my painting gifts nonexistent. I had thought I would have nothing but memory to serve me, bright and gleaming now, but faded over time.

I stroked a fingertip over the features held in my palm. He was young, perhaps sixteen or seventeen years of age. His face still held a bit of youthful roundness in the cheek and his brow had yet to be lined with the worries of war. The painter had captured the light of laughter in his eyes, but they had been much brighter then, before the shadows rose within them.

I saw the solicitor's hand reaching from the edge of my vision. I wrapped greedy fingers around the miniature and held it behind my back as I turned.

"I know nothing of the Aynesworth name, but this is my husband's image. Why do you seek him?"

His reaching fingers twitched in protest, but he could hardly pin me down and yank the painting from my hand.

"If he truly is your husband!"

I was not afraid of him, or of his scorn. The attitudes of judgmental people felt about as important to me as the opinions of seabirds on the rocks—noisy but easy to ignore.

"I insist upon speaking to this man directly. I've been sent to deliver the news of his eldest brother's, the earl's, recent demise."

I stared at him for a moment as I realized that he did not know. Yet, how could he?

"My husband is dead, Mr. Sands. He drowned a little more than four years ago."

The puffed-up little man deflated before my eyes. "Oh. Oh, my. Then there are no heirs left at all—"

The door opened in a burst and a small body hurtled through with Beatriu in hot pursuit. "Senyor Lucas!" she cried. "*Noi dolent!*"

My four-year-old son turned upon Beatriu with outrage in

his large brown eyes. "I am not a *noi dolent*! I am a good boy! Right, Mama?"

Mr. Sands turned hopeful eyes my way. "My lady, is this the son of Lord Lucas Aynesworth?"

I narrowed my eyes at his somewhat insulting question. "You have been gazing at that miniature for your entire journey. Why do you not tell me?"

It was true that every feature of the small painting was repeated in our son, but for his flaxen baby curls. I still did not know if his hair would turn dark with age or remain as pale as my own. Even so, the skeptical little man before me could not deny the exact resemblance.

I bent to give my little Lucas a quick hug and sent him back to Beatriu. "Mama has business just now, sweetie. I shall come and get you soon for our walk to the cove."

Beatriu shut the door behind them, after giving me a significant look that told me that any number of large men were available to escort Mr. Sands from the premises should I so require.

The little man did not miss a thing. "Your servant is most loyal to you."

"She is not my servant, but a dear friend. She cares for us out of gratitude and her own good heart." I gazed at him for a long moment. Men such as this came at times of change and disruption. I steeled myself to learn what the former earl's death meant to me and my son.

It seemed that my husband had been the third son of a fairly wealthy earl. Third sons did not have much chance of inheriting, usually, which explained why he may have sought a career in the military.

"After your husband's notorious actions during the war, his family allowed his disappearance to go unremarked, as far as the public knew. Secretly, the family kept an eye on him for some time. Nobility does not like its lambs to stray far from the flock, you see, even those in exile."

Considering that I had likely encountered more members of the nobility in my former profession than this minor fellow ever would, I could imagine.

"He did the honorable thing," I said curtly. "His family ought to have been proud of him."

Mr. Sands shrugged. "They may have been. I know that his portrait still hangs in the hall in Aynesworth Manor. I saw it there myself when I attended the earl's deathbed."

That detail made me feel somewhat more kindly to Mr. Sands.

"At any rate, the middle son passed without heir about ten years ago in a hunting accident. The late earl had remained in mourning for his wife, who died delivering him a stillborn baby. He was still in his early forties when his heart began to weaken earlier this year. That is when I was called . . ."

He went on at some length about articles of title, estates, and accounts, but I barely listened. My thoughts were of my beloved and his simple life in the *castell*. I did not believe for a moment that he had found it a punishment or an exile. He had loved the old stones, his paints, and the people of la Cala and they had loved him. I had loved him, just as he was.

I realized that this new knowledge changed nothing of our time together. His past had not been a secret between us. It had merely been a story he had not yet told me.

Because we had believed we had all the time in the world.

By that time, Mr. Sands's lecture had begun to wind down and he gazed at me expectantly. I thanked him gravely for his time and told him that I must think matters over. I invited him to return on the morrow for my answer.

He gaped. "Your answer? I did not bring you a question, my lady! Your son's rank is a fact! He has an obligation to—"

I raised a brow. "Lucas has an obligation to be a four-year-old boy and nothing more. Now, please go. Return tomorrow."

"But—but where shall I stay? There is nothing here but this pile of rocks and a pathetic excuse for a village nearby!"

I folded my hands before me, rather than shove him bodily from the room. "Good evening, Mr. Sands."

After he left, I stared out the window for some time. I missed my beloved. I wished I could ask him his wishes. Should I keep Lucas here, to grow up with Beatriu's grandchildren in the sunlight and sea air? Should I take our son to England, the land that had spit his parents out like unwanted seeds?

Needing to feel closer to my husband, I went to a room I seldom visited—his studio.

I shut the warped wooden door behind me and inhaled the faded scents of spirits and oils. Those, plus the tiniest tang of pipe tobacco, brought him back to me as little else could. I closed my eyes. "What should I do?"

He did not answer, yet I felt comforted nonetheless. It occurred to me that he might have some information about his past in his papers. I had never searched through them, for I knew everything I needed to know.

Now, I wished to know one thing. Had he loved his home and his family? Had he wished to return to them someday, or had he been content to leave them behind forever?

There was a shelf high upon the wall where a few piles of paper lay stacked. I went up on tiptoes and pulled them down, placing them upon his worktable.

I saw scrawled notes about the proportions of colors used to make other colors of paint. I found some dusty coins and slipped them absently into my pocket for Beatriu's household budget. In the center of the stack I found a simple leather folio, not much more than a crude leather envelope sewn with twine. I undid the tie that held it closed.

I gasped at what I found within. I knew that my husband had sketched me many times, but I had never seen a single one of these. Now I gazed upon drawing after drawing of me . . . with him.

The two of us, kissing, sleeping, laughing. My head thrown back in passion as he moved above me. My sleepy smile upon first awakening.

I had wished I had an image to remember him by. Now I had dozens.

The pain struck me in a violent wave. Oh, my beloved Artist, my noble Lucas . . . I shoved the drawings away from me lest they suffer from my falling tears.

"Lucas . . . oh, my Lucas . . ." I whispered, over and over again as I emptied my heart, sobbing.

"What is it, Mama?"

I wiped my eyes quickly with one hand as I flipped the erotic drawings over on the table. Then I turned to my son with a shaky smile.

I knew what I must do. My husband had sacrificed his world for the people of la Cala, and then he had died for them. But if he were still here to be called, he would have gone home to do the same for his people in England.

He would want his son to do no less.

I gazed proudly at our beautiful boy. "We are going to take a long trip, sweetie. To a land far away."

THE PRESENT

Chapter Twenty-Nine

Castell de la Cala, Present Day

Fitch jumped from the bed and began clearing everything out of the way. Unfortunately, because of the fragile state of all the papers and sketches, his progress was comically slow.

"Hold that thought," he said to Brenna. He carried a sketch by its edges and placed it upon the bureau. "Just keep thinking about how much you want me. I'll be right there. This shouldn't take more than an hour—two, tops."

Brenna smiled, rising from the bed to help him. Fitch was right, of course. The artifacts they'd spread all over the bed would have to be moved if they wanted to roll around and ravish each other, which she surely hoped was on the agenda.

She began moving single diary pages and laying them out on the floor along the wall. "I've wanted you since I first saw you in that pub in London," she said, working as fast as she could.

"Tell me more."

"I nearly jumped your bones in that tea room. You had me at 'oolong.'"

"Ha!" Fitch shook his head, grinning while he worked. "I imagined smearing clotted cream all over your naked body and going to town."

She snorted. "I fell in love with you when we danced in the street. I've never danced in the street in my life."

"There's plenty more where that came from."

That was it—the bed was clear—and before Brenna could say anything more, Fitch had pressed up against her back and slipped his arms around her waist. He nuzzled her neck, his lips hot and slick against her skin.

She moaned with the relief of his touch. He took her breath away when he slid his large hands down her hips, around her thighs, and back up to cup her breasts.

"I want you out of these clothes," Fitch whispered.

Brenna felt his fingers hook into the waistband of her skirt and panties. She trembled as he pulled both away from her body at once and they pooled on the floor. The bra and top were history soon after.

She turned to face him, and found his face wide with wonder and disbelief. "You are so beautiful it hurts," he said.

Smiling, she slid her palms up his chest and began to unbutton his shirt. She let her fingertips linger on his skin as she peeled it away from his muscled torso. Saying nothing, Brenna spread her hands across the bulging front of his jeans, noting how his breath hitched at the touch. Slowly, teasingly, she dragged the zipper downward, unbuckled the belt, and unbuttoned the waistband.

She gazed up to see he'd thrown his head back in ecstasy. Slowly, sensuously, he lowered his gaze and locked it on hers. He began to back her up toward the bed.

Brenna knew that for the first time ever, she was about to truly give herself to a man. She was willing to take the risk in order to find joy. If The Swan was brave enough to do so, she could as well.

The back of her knees nudged the bed. Fitch gently settled her on her back. She watched with great interest as he lowered his jeans and kicked them across the room. He leaned in, his face just inches from hers. She saw so much desire in those exquisite eyes.

Suddenly she felt a twinge of self-consciousness. She'd just cried her guts out in his arms. "I must be a wet mess, Fitch."

A sexy chuckle escaped his lips. "I can work with that. But I do have a special request."

"Already?"

He laughed. "I just want you to let go with me, Brenna. Loosen your grip. I'll catch you if you fall." He gave her one of his half-smiles, and it was *on*.

Finally, she was skin-to-skin with Fitch Wilder, all of him muscled and hard against her. Their mouths met, ravenous for connection. They grasped for each other like it was a matter of life and death. Hands demanding. Their bodies in a dance of desperate need. Part of Brenna became lost in a wordless state, where her senses ruled and her mind stilled in complete concentration.

Another part jumped for giddy joy—*this*! This was what she'd never dared reach for. *She was in love.*

Fitch rolled with her, grasping at her ass as he lifted her, easing himself into her body in one long, slow stroke. Brenna gasped at the sensation of being filled—body and soul—and let her head fall back in bliss. She felt the tears roll across her temples as he moved his hips, going deeper.

"Brenna. I want to see you."

She brought her head upright and smiled down at him. There he was—her lover—a man who was chiseled and strong and good-hearted and beautiful. And his eyes glistened. Just like hers.

"I love you, Brenna."

"I love you, too, Fitch."

"It's an honor to be your first."

She lowered her lips to kiss his damp eyelashes, then moved her salty mouth to his. It was odd, this tender openness she felt, this melding of affection and sex.

This romance.

Fitch felt the light strike his closed eyelids and forced himself to take a peek at reality. A part of him feared it had all been a dream.

"Good morning, you wild man. Or Wilder-man. Maybe wildest man."

Brenna sat next to him in the bed, her naked skin golden in the early morning Mediterranean light, her pale hair luminous on her shoulders. She was propped against the pillows, the leather portfolio in her lap.

"We never finished reading last night," she said.

"Yeah. I think we got distracted."

Brenna giggled, resting a hand on his bare chest. "We got distracted at least five times."

"That explains why I can't seem to feel my legs."

"There's something I need to read to you."

Fitch closed his eyes again, reveling in the touch of her hand on his chest. "Sure."

"You can stay right where you are if you want."

"Good." He smiled.

"It's another letter in The Siren's handwriting."

"I'm all ears."

"My love,
The time has come to make a number of painful
decisions. I trust you would approve, for I am making
them with you in mind.
The paintings are my dearest possessions, these

*markers of our sweet, short time together. I cannot bear
to show them to the world nor can I destroy them, so I
have chosen to leave them in the care of Beatriu for
safekeeping—all but one. I have shipped the smallest
portrait to my friend Ophelia, for I wish for her to see
me as I truly am. The rest will remain here in Castell de
la Cala, where they were created. Perhaps one faraway
day, after I am long gone, they will find their way back
to the world, bringing joy and beauty to unknown eyes,
a testament to the brave soldier who became a painter,
the English gentleman who became a peasant. Perhaps
one day the world will get a glimpse of the kind heart
and passionate skill of Lord Lucas Aynesworth, Earl of
Swindon. I can only hope this will come to pass.*

*I must soon board a ship, but for now I stand on
our balcony. I can feel your caress in the warm Catalan
breeze. I can see the golden warmth of your eyes in the
sparkle of the coastal sunlight. Your eyes taught me so
much, my love. Seeing myself through the lens of your
gaze is the only reason I have the strength to go on
without you.*

*You were not my first lover, nor my only friend, but
you will always be my only heart. No one will ever
breathe such life and truth into me the way you did.*

*Crashing onto your shore saved me. I would do it
again and again, if only to hold you close to me for a
single moment more. The scars I bear are sweet
reminders of waking up empty, waiting only for you to
fill me with myself. I had to lose myself to find myself.*

*How can I bear to go back to cold, inhospitable
England? You will not be there, except in the child you
gave me. His eyes can see more than most, just as yours
did. His heart is as wide open as the sky above the sea.*

*I will spend my life making sure that England does not
chew him up and spit him out as it did you and I, my
dear.*

I must leave you behind.

*But because you lived, I live. Because you loved, I
love. Because you mended my spirit, yours will live on
in our son. And within me.*

*I was born a lady, only to become a prisoner, a boy,
a courtesan, a prisoner once more, a helpless child, and
at last, because of you, my truest self.*

I lovingly remain,

> Angelica Whittaker, Lady Aynesworth
> Countess of Swindon"

Fitch popped up in bed, his heart hammering. "That's her name?" He saw Brenna's satisfied smile. "The Swan. The Siren. Jinx. Her true name is *Angelica? The artist was an earl?*"

She nodded. "And just think . . . a few years after she's chased out of London society and marked for 'disposal,' she returns as Lady Angelica, Countess of Swindon."

Fitch shook his head slowly and whistled long and low. "Look out, Lady H—."

Though it was only about 7:00 A.M., they exited the front door of Casa Mata and walked together to the center of the *placa*. A few early risers strolled by and greeted them cheerfully.

"*Bon dia,*" they said in return.

Fitch and Brenna stood before the fountain. It rose about ten feet into the air, a cast bronze figure of a man with two children. A little girl rode on the man's shoulders, his hand securing her chubby knee. The man's other hand rested protectively on the head of a little boy who clung to his leg. A bronze plaque had been set into the cobblestones of the *plaça*. Written were these words, in Catalan:

> *For the soldier who saved our village*
> *from heartless men and rescued our children*
> *from a merciless sea. You will have our gratitude*
> *forever.*

Fitch reached for Brenna's hand. "You know, after all we've seen and done and uncovered, this morning feels more like the beginning to me than an end."

Brenna sniffed and nodded in agreement. "I have a feeling there's a lot more to discover on this journey, Fitch."

He wrapped his arms around her and kissed the top of her head.

"I'm sorry about the crying. Now that I've started I can't seem to stop."

He chuckled. "Face it, Professor—you're a hopeless romantic."

Epilogue

Barcelona, One Year Later

"Are you sure the title isn't too sensational?"

Fitch moved to Brenna's side. Together they tilted their heads back to study the banner hanging over the entrance to the Museu Nacional d'Art de Catalunya. He draped an arm around her shoulder and read it aloud.

" 'LE ARTISTE IN EXILE: The Secret World of Lord Lucas Aynesworth's Siren Series.' Nope. It still sounds perfect to me—after all, it's true."

Brenna tried to calm herself by taking a deep breath. "I guess it's a little late to change it anyway." The exhibit would open in less than ten minutes, and a year of painstaking research, planning, design, and plain old begging and pleading would be over. The doors would open this evening to the much-anticipated exhibit of fourteen oil paintings and twenty-five sketches accompanied by diary entries, underpaintings, and letters.

The collection would tell the story of an exiled British soldier and a stranded courtesan who created a timeless tribute to love and art.

"Have I told you how exquisite you look tonight, *Professora*?" Fitch nuzzled her neck and laid his palm against the exposed skin of her plunging backline. The pleasure of his touch made her quiver.

"*Gràcies,* Senyor Wilder. You clean up pretty good yourself." That was an understatement. When Fitch stepped from the hotel bathroom in his slim-fitted black tuxedo she'd almost fainted. There was something smokin' hot about a longhaired, unshaven cowboy in formal wear. *Her* cowboy, specifically.

She turned and whispered into Fitch's ear, "I should probably tell you—my brain is positively flooded with dopamine and norepinephrine right now."

He chuckled. "You keep that up and we won't make it to our own opening."

Voices echoed behind them, and Fitch and Brenna turned to see the crowd begin to file inside. It was a well heeled and sparkling group, many of whom were invited because of their generous contributions to Barcelona's premiere art museum.

Fitch whispered in her ear, "Here comes our favorite power couple."

H. Winston Guilford and Claudia Harrington-Howell arrived arm in arm, a study in old money and new love. Fitch and Brenna owed them immense gratitude. Not only had Claudia convinced Winston to loan his Siren collection to the museum indefinitely, he finally agreed to let Fitch test each painting. Though no additional poems were discovered, they'd found several underpainted landscapes, leading to a more complete understanding of the artist's scope of work.

Brenna greeted them enthusiastically, and when the cheek kisses and handshakes ended, she escorted them into the great hall.

"Are you ever going to make an honest woman out of Claudia?" Fitch asked.

Winston didn't have a chance to answer the question, because Claudia jumped in. "Oh, heavens no!" she said, slipping her arm in Winston's. "We quite like shacking up, as it turns out. But the same could be asked of you, Mr. Wilder."

Brenna and Fitch shared a sideways glance. They had often joked that they'd been married since the priest blessed them at *Flor de la Vida* festival, and had the wedding video to prove it. In their more serious conversations, Brenna had told Fitch she loved him with all her heart—but wasn't convinced she was the marrying type. His response was always the same: he was committed to her, not an institution. Still, she could see it in his eyes tonight—he really wanted the whole enchilada.

"Maybe someday," she told Winston.

Once Claudia and Winston had their champagnes and were wandering toward the exhibit, the noise of the crowd increased. Brenna and Fitch saw many friendly faces and a few wild cards, but her primary attention was on the beautiful little family that had just entered.

Piper and Mick's formal attire was accessorized with children. Piper carried their kicking four-month-old son, Cullen, in a front carrier. Mick had Ophelia in a contraption on his back. And though Brenna and Fitch had spent much of the last two weeks with their friends, it meant the world to Brenna that they'd come to share this special night.

"You look stunning, Bren," Piper said.

"You do, too!"

Her best friend rolled her eyes. "Right. Spit-up goes great with sequins."

The women laughed but then Piper gripped Brenna's hand. "I'm so proud of you guys. I mean it. This is such a spectacular achievement."

Brenna smiled with wonder. "These last few years have been awfully eventful for us, haven't they?" She leaned down and kissed Cullen on his baby-powdered head. "Thank you for sharing this with me, Pipes. It wouldn't mean nearly as much without you."

They hugged, promising to catch up later in the evening.

"Earl is here," Fitch said.

Brenna laughed. "Stop torturing me. You know it's *the* earl. Not just 'Earl.'"

The modern-day Lord Robert Aynesworth, Earl of Swindon, made his entrance. Not for the first time, Brenna was struck with his similarity to Lucas, his fourth great-uncle. They shared the same rich brown eyes and unassuming smile, though the new Lord Aynesworth's interests lay more with polo and clubbing than fine art—at least until recently.

Finding the unknown portraits and sketches in Casa Mata's attic had led to a lengthy legal ordeal to determine ownership. Because Lady Aynesworth's diary entries said the paintings were left to Beatriu Mata for safekeeping—but did not will them to her as property—the rightful owner was determined to be any surviving heir of Lord Aynesworth himself. That led to Robert.

The current Lord Aynesworth was thrilled to learn of his ancestor's fame, and not only agreed to loan the newly discovered paintings to the museum but provided them with the large oil portrait of the young artist that still hung in the manor house in England.

"Yo, Earl! How's it hanging?"

Brenna pinched Fitch on his tuxedo-clad butt.

"Dr. Anderson! Wilder! This is damned thrilling!" He kissed Brenna's cheeks and shook Fitch's hand all while scanning the crowd.

"Looking for someone in particular?"

"Yes, quite. I'm looking for Guilford as a matter of fact. Has the old boy arrived? I wanted to chat him up about something."

Fitch pointed Robert in the correct direction, then spoke to Brenna from the side of his mouth. "Earl's still trying to get ahold of the first five paintings. He's got Siren fever, just like Winston used to have. It must be contagious."

"Oh, no." Brenna groaned, ducking behind him.

"What?"

"That Hollywood producer is here! Seriously, Fitch—how am I supposed to discuss a possible movie when I haven't even finished writing the book? There's still so much to do."

In addition to writing articles for academic journals, Brenna's first draft of *Breathless: A True Story of Love and Art* was due to her publisher in just three months. Unfortunately, writing had taken a backseat while they'd prepared for the exhibit.

Fitch stood directly in front of her. He placed his hands on her shoulders and locked his eyes on hers, a reminder to keep her feet planted firmly in the here and now. "Sweetheart, just revel in it. Isn't it nice to be wanted?"

She raised an eyebrow. "Depends on who's doing the wanting."

Fitch gave her one of his mischievous half-smiles. Even after a year together, Brenna still melted when he did that, and since he was well aware of the effect it had on her he exploited it at every opportunity. The funny thing was, Brenna didn't care if he had her number—because she had his, too. And so far it was all adding up quite nicely.

She noticed Lowell Snowden at the entrance and waved to get his attention. The now-retired sociology department chair had decided to leave Harvard about six months ago, just before Brenna turned in her resignation. "I'm too tired to keep fighting and I can't go in the direction they're pushing me," he'd told Brenna. "I don't regret it at all—turns out there's an entire world outside the ivory tower."

Soon after, Brenna had asked if he would be available to

work as editor for her academic writing and consult with her on the book. The offer had made him quite happy and for Brenna it had been a joy to work with him again.

The decision to leave Harvard had been a difficult one for her, but she realized her passion was leading her elsewhere. Gone was the drive to prove something to the world of academia—or to herself. Her achievements there could never be taken from her; it was time to move on.

"Top-shelf crowd tonight." Lowell greeted them with a smile, looking dapper in his tuxedo and bow tie, and after a brief chat he wandered deeper into the museum. As gentle strains of the string quartet floated through the great hall and voices and laughter echoed around them, they visited with one guest after another.

Many of the research assistants who had helped them along the way arrived, and they thanked each and every one of them for their contributions. Montserrat Museum Director Don Josep Soler came to represent the abbey, and Brenna and Fitch once again thanked him for loaning Don Diego's three paintings to the museum.

"You've done a remarkable amount of work here, and all of Catalonia is grateful." Don Josep gave them a gentle smile. "Because of you two, we have a new understanding of our history."

If he hadn't been a monk, Brenna would have kissed him.

Fitch's occasional employer Jean-Louis Rasmussen arrived with several members of the Musee de Michel-Blanc's board of directors. As always, Brenna enjoyed watching Fitch network in impeccable French. It never failed to amaze her how wide he had cast his relationship net—both personally and professionally. The people in Fitch's life seemed to cross every artificial boundary that separated people, and she loved him for that.

Next came the map expert Aleix Serra, followed by Senyora

Andreu and her brother, Juame Mata. Brenna and Fitch laughed when they saw that Juame had paired his rented tuxedo with his custom-made cowboy boots.

"Lookin' good," Fitch told him.

His sister rolled her eyes. "I think he sleeps in them."

A steady stream of guests continued to arrive, and as they greeted them all, Brenna knew her heart was full. Somehow, this journey had given her a sense of community, place, and belonging she'd never had before. As strange as it seemed, a half-Swedish girl from Minnesota had reached the conclusion that she was at home in the Catalonia region of Spain.

That decision came after an exhausting year of travel. In addition to Fitch's work trips, they'd logged a lot of frequent flier miles traveling back and forth from Europe to the States. Brenna was ready to be in one place for a while, a place where she could write and appreciate the unfolding of every day. She looked forward to a new chapter in her own story, including life as an author, Fitch's business partner, and maybe one day a mother.

Before they headed into the exhibit hall, she and Fitch turned to look up at the banner one last time.

"Pinch me," he said.

"I already did."

"Then pinch me again."

Brenna laughed. "It's been a wild ride, Fitch. The Siren changed our lives forever. She changed us."

Fitch's hand cradled hers. "If we ever have a daughter we'll have to name her Angelica."

"If we have a boy we'll name him Lucas."

Fitch's head snapped around in surprise, and the look in his gray-green-gold eyes was priceless. "What are you saying? You'll come to Santa Fe and bear my children?"

Brenna produced a half-smile of her own. "I was thinking we could do all that here, in Catalonia."

"Yes!" Fitch pumped his fist into the air, his outburst more suited to a football match. "You've just made me so happy, Brenna, and I know a guy who knows a realtor who—"

She grabbed him and pulled him into a kiss, just to shut him up.